HIS NAME WAS WREN

ROB WINTERS

Black
Cube
Press

Contact the author rawinters@me.com

Follow the author on twitter @robwinters

Sign up to the mailing list at https://www.robwinters.co.uk/books/wren

---

Copyright © 2020 by Rob Winters
Cover design and map by the author

Stars photo by Graham Holtshausen
unsplash.com/@freedomstudios

For Sarah, Thomas, and Harrison.

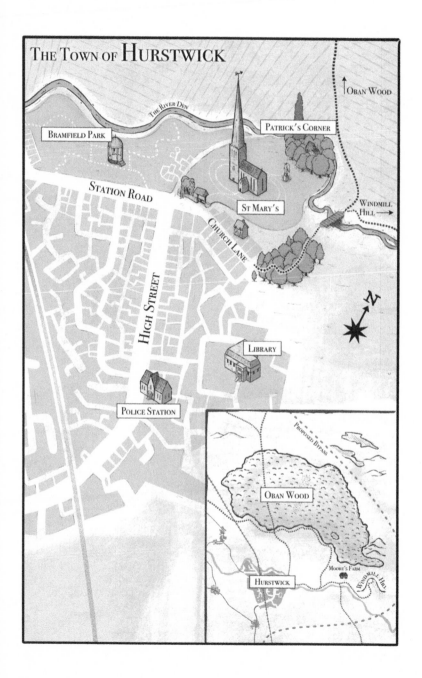

1

THE HURSTWICK INCIDENT

September 1944

A loud thudding on the door broke Henry Crinklaw's concentration. He slammed down his pencil and left his small dimly lit room in a huff, his gangly legs carrying him down the narrow wooden stairs to the front door. "I made it clear I'm not to be disturbed," he said, wrenching it open and spilling light onto the dark street.

"Henry!" roared a rotund man standing on the pavement. Behind him sat an elegant black car, its headlights dimmed, its driver leaning against the long bonnet rolling a cigarette. A woman in the back seat, her face caught in the glow from the hallway, glanced at Henry then turned away.

"Mr Haywood?" Henry said, recognising his superior. "What are you doing here? I mean...sorry, sir. This is an unexpected surprise."

"Surprises generally are unexpected, Henry. Are you going to invite me in?" The man's jolly demeanour was evaporating as he waited for his invite.

"Yes...of course. Come in, sir." Henry Crinklaw stood

aside, and Malcolm Haywood entered, bringing with him a strong odour of cigar smoke.

"And you should really turn that light out," he complained as he climbed the stairs.

Henry followed.

"Well, this *is* cosy," Malcolm said, stepping into the modest accommodation. He walked over to the fire, which threw a jittery glow around the room. The only other source of light came from a lamp angled down upon a messy desk.

"Drink, sir?" asked Henry, opening a small cabinet.

"This isn't a social visit, old boy," he said, "but you go ahead. If I were stuck in this little town, I'd be drinking non-stop."

Henry poured himself a drink and watched as Malcolm Haywood studied the wall. It displayed everything they knew of the crash. Every inch was covered. Mostly photos: upturned trees, rocks split in two, the decapitated church, and the half-destroyed stone shack, with the church bell protruding from its side. There were several images of footprints, wooden rulers next to them for scale. Most appeared to be the boot prints of a child accompanied by a small dog; other prints were larger, sleeker and possibly barefoot. Lines of string linked each image to a pin in a large aerial photo, which showed the town and the long black scar in the woods to the north.

To the side of the aerial shot was a map of Europe. It was criss-crossed with lines representing flight paths of known German and Allied planes from the night of the incident. None came close to the lonely red pin marking the small market town of Hurstwick.

The wall was impressive, but even with the vast amount of data collected, they had no idea what had come down in the woods that night. Henry suspected he was about to get a dressing down for the lack of progress. Malcolm would no doubt want to hear about all the breakthroughs he hadn't made, all the leads he hadn't followed up (because there were none), and all the clues he had yet to uncover. They'd given him an impossible task.

Henry took a deep breath, turned his drink into a double, then joined Malcolm at the wall.

"Over two months, Henry," said Malcolm, removing his gloves and hat and dropping them on Henry's desk along with a brown file retrieved from inside his coat. He angled the lamp to throw more light to the wall. "And what have you to show for it?"

It was a question that didn't need an answer, but Henry answered anyway. "Nothing new, I'm afraid, sir." He took another deep breath, disguising it well, he thought, with a simultaneous swig from his glass. His eyes flicked to the brown folder, then back to the face of his superior. He took another large gulp of his quickly disappearing drink.

"So it's a mystery?" Malcolm said after a pause, rolling on the balls of his feet.

"Well, sir, I suppose it—"

"I don't like mysteries, Henry. I get concerned. Mysteries cause confusion, and I don't like confusion either. I like things neatly labelled and filed away. Dealt with. Done. We are trying to win a war, Henry, and right now, things are looking good. Brookie thinks so, anyway. But he's not thinking about this, is he?" He gestured to the wall. "Whereas I *am* thinking about this. I think about this a lot. And I'll say it again — I'm concerned."

"Sir, I must—"

Mr Haywood cut him off with a wave of his chubby hand. "However, we are where we are, and we seem to have found ourselves a little mystery that refuses to be dealt with, haven't we?"

"Yes, sir. I suppose—"

"*So*," he said, cutting him off again, "I brought something for your little wall of irregularity." He nodded to the folder on the desk.

Henry put down his now almost empty glass, picked up the folder and opened it. Inside was a grainy photo of a rocket, mid-launch. Henry shot Malcolm a confused look. *Why was he showing him a picture of a rocket?*

Malcolm Haywood nodded. It was a nod that said *carry on, there's more.*

Further photos showed pieces of wreckage lying in fields. People bent over damaged fragments of pumps, valves, tubes and motors. Finally, he came to a short transcript describing a test launch of a rocket.

Henry looked up, still confused. "Sir, is this relevant? We ruled out rockets and flying bombs on day one. We would have found the wreckage; there would have been a crater."

"That, Henry, is a V-2 rocket, as I'm sure you are aware. On its own, not very interesting with regard to your investigation. But if you look at the transcript, it's *frightfully* interesting. It comes from one of *ours* on the other side. She took the photo; according to her, it was a test launch — not meant for us. They shot it straight up just to see how high it would go."

Henry scratched his head. "With all due respect, sir," he swallowed, "I don't see a connection here."

"It was a historic moment," continued Malcolm, as if Henry hadn't spoken. "At any other time, we would have celebrated this event. Because, that thing," — he jabbed his finger at the photo — "that marvellous and terrible thing, became the first object to leave the Earth's atmosphere. That thing, Henry, went into space."

Henry looked down at the photo again. It was indeed an impressive achievement, he thought. Then his look of confusion returned.

"Look at the date, man," said Malcolm, impatiently. "It's from the night in question."

"But surely a coincidence, sir. Like I said, rockets leave wreckage and craters; they explode. None of those things happened. It can't have been this rocket that landed in those woods."

"Of course it wasn't, you fool."

"Then, sir, I just don't understand..." Henry Crinklaw was now desperate.

Malcolm smiled. He was clearly enjoying being a step ahead. "That rocket," he said, "had a trajectory that would have seen it land in the Baltic Sea. *Not* in the woods outside Hurstwick—"

Henry's face had given up looking confused. He stared blankly as Malcolm Haywood continued to talk.

"—But we know it didn't land in the Baltic Sea." He took the folder from Henry's hand and placed it on the desk, spreading out the photos of the wreckage. He stabbed a stumpy finger at each image. "*That* was found in Kent. *That*, just south of Paris. And *that* was recovered from Blizna in Poland, as part of Operation Wildhorn. *All* are believed to be pieces of that same rocket." Malcolm's smile was widening as he realised Henry was starting to get it.

Henry grabbed a pencil and rushed to the map. He drew a small cross next to Kent, another south of Paris, and a third next to Blizna in Poland. He then stepped back and placed his hands on his hips. "Well. I'll be.... That is some spread."

"Indeed," replied Malcolm, retrieving his gloves and hat from the desk. "The boffins estimate the rocket came apart violently at an altitude of sixty miles. As it wasn't carrying explosives, we can only assume that it—"

"Hit something," Henry interrupted.

"Bingo."

5

"But what? What is there to *hit* sixty miles up? Nothing is sixty miles up."

"Looks like you'll be staying here a little longer, Henry."

Henry didn't reply; he just stared at the map.

Malcolm scanned the wall, putting on his gloves. His eyes moved from item to item. "I don't see the drawing," he said.

Henry frowned, trying to remember where he'd put it, then hurried to the desk and rifled through a box of files. Eventually, he removed a piece of paper and pinned it to the wall.

It was a child's drawing of a man in black with very long black hair.

"Did you find the boy?"

Henry Crinklaw shook his head, not taking his eyes from the drawing. "The officer doesn't remember much about him. Just a small boy with messy hair. It's all I have to go on."

"Well. You better get to it, don't you think?"

"Yes, sir. I suppose I should."

THREE MONTHS EARLIER

George Moss was under his bed. Just moments before, he'd been sound asleep on top of it. Now he was under it, hands clapped over his ears, waiting for the house to collapse. But it didn't.

Instead, bits of plaster and dust settled on the wooden floorboards and the threadbare soft toy that had fallen off his bed during his escape from it.

George was expecting more — more sounds, more shaking, and maybe some rubble. But all that followed was silence.

Why had nobody come to wake him? He hadn't heard

the siren. Had it even gone off? He removed his hands from his ears to make sure. No, nothing.

Voices came from outside. He couldn't make out the words, but some were panicked while others tried to calm. George scrambled from under the bed and rushed to the window. He drew back the blackout curtain and peered out into the darkness. From the churchyard, directly beyond the wall of his back garden, a huge cloud of dust, illuminated by the moon, billowed into the air. He watched it slowly grow, until it consumed his garden, and he could see no more.

Then came closer voices. These were from his hosts' bedroom across the hall. Mr Furlong was telling Mrs Furlong to stay put.

"Should we get to shelter?" she called after him.

"Don't think it's a raid, my love," he called back. "It's as quiet as anything out there. But if you hear that siren, you get down there with George, OK?"

George's bedroom door opened, and Mr Furlong poked his head in. "You OK, lad?"

"Yes, sir. What was—"

"Nothing to worry about. You stay in here." He hurriedly closed the door and was gone.

George pulled on his dressing gown and ran to the top of the stairs in time to see Mr Furlong limp out the front door. Quickly, George returned to his room, grabbed his lamp and the box containing his gas mask, then crept down the stairs.

Chip, the Furlongs' small scruffy dog, joined him by the front door and followed him outside. They were greeted by a world of dust that caught George at the back of his throat. Undeterred, he continued down the short garden path and onto the lane. He should have been fearful, but wasn't; the stillness and dust-filled air amplified his curiosity. It felt dreamlike, magical.

Church Lane was narrow and cobbled and lined with

cottages on both sides. The thick dust hid those cottages from George. All he could see was the soft glow of Mr Furlong's lamp ahead. He followed at a distance, keeping his lamp switched off while Chip walked beside him.

As he neared the end of the lane, the dust grew thicker and poured over the stone wall of the churchyard.

There was a small gathering of people by the wall, huddled around a man sitting on the floor. As George neared, he recognised the sitting man as Patrick, the groundskeeper. He lived in a small shack in the far corner of the churchyard. The poor man was covered, head to toe, in white dust. Contrasting the white was a single dark streak of blood that ran from his temple to his neck. Father Elliot, the parish priest, dressed in a long nightgown, examined the wound. He didn't look worried by it, and Patrick seemed more bothered by the attention he was getting.

Mr Furlong reached the wall. He stood peering over it into the impenetrable cloud of dust, his weak blackout lamp only able to illuminate a few feet ahead.

As more people arrived, George realised he was the only child present. Not wanting to be seen and told to go home, he moved into the shadows.

"You OK, Patrick?" said an unfamiliar voice from the growing crowd.

"Little bit shaken, but I'll live," he answered, his voice croaky and dry.

"He's just fine," added Father Elliot, who stood aside as the town doctor arrived with his medical kit.

"What was it?" said another.

"Damned if I know," said Patrick.

"Nazis dumping their bombs before heading back, I s'pect," said another voice in the dark.

"Here, take this," said the doctor, handing Patrick a lit cigarette. "That'll sort you out."

"Good heavens!" a woman shrieked. She stood at the edge of the group in her dressing gown, her hands to her mouth, her head darting, searching the sky. More desperate cries erupted from the crowd as they followed her gaze.

George looked too but was confused by what he saw. The dust, still thick at ground level, had started to clear higher up. He saw nothing to cause distress: just the moon and a clear sky.

Then he understood.

The church spire, the pride of the town and one of the tallest in England, was gone.

Father Elliot swayed on his feet. Before he could fall, he was caught by the doctor, who sat him down next to Patrick and lit another cigarette.

The cries died down. Eventually there was silence, interrupted only by the occasional sound of masonry falling unseen in the darkness beyond the wall.

A murmur of excitement then grew as three ghostly figures, caked in dust, emerged from the churchyard and joined the group. George overheard as they talked of large boulders littering the place, breaking many of the graves. Patrick's shack had been partly crushed by a bell from the tower. They said he was lucky to be alive.

Mr Furlong approached Patrick and crouched beside him. "What did this?" he asked.

"A bomb, obviously," boomed the voice of a large man standing behind them. George recognised him as Mr Fuller, the butcher and head of the Hurstwick Home Guard.

"No," Patrick replied. "Not a bomb. I was awake at the time, and I didn't hear no plane. No explosion either. I don't know what it was, Don. But whatever it was, it came down in the fields, maybe even the woods," he gestured north past the church. "I 'eard it. Never 'eard anything like it before in my life, like the earth being torn apart. It was deep. I felt it through me feet."

"Right then," said Mr Fuller, addressing the crowd, "arm yourselves with whatever you can get your hands on and meet by the bridge at the top of Church Lane. Bring your medical kit, doc. Just in case it's one of ours." George thought the man seemed to be enjoying the situation as he herded people back to their homes. "Bring dogs!" he shouted as an afterthought. He marched off with self-importance, swallowed by the dust.

As the crowd dispersed, Mr Furlong spotted George and limped towards him, a worried expression across his brow. "Back to the house, lad."

"What's happening, sir?" he said, running to meet him with Chip.

"They've hit the church," he said, placing a hand on George's shoulder, steering him back the way he'd come, "but it's nothing for you to worry about. No one's hurt; just a few scrapes is all. Let's get you back inside, and *please* stay inside this time."

"Was it a bomb?"

"Don't know what it was," he said, looking up to the clear expanse of sky once occupied by the spire. "Probably a plane. Might even be one of ours. We're gonna take a look." He quickly added: "But not you, George. I need you to look after Mrs Furlong, OK?"

George didn't answer. He was looking up too.

"Are you hearing me, George?"

"Erm, yes, sir. I won't go with you. Promise."

The moon, ignoring the nationwide blackout, shone down upon the men marching along Church Lane with their dogs and lamps. The younger men of the town were overseas fighting, but these men, some very old, walked with a haste and boyish enthusiasm that belied their age.

At the end of Church Lane, they took the narrow dirt track through a dense thicket of trees. They stopped before the small wooden bridge spanning the river Den, which formed a natural border between town and countryside. While their owners waited for reinforcements, the dogs, feeling sociable and excited to be out at such an hour, went down to the dark murmuring water for a drink and a sniff. When the search party had grown to a capable size, the men took their dogs and lights across to the fields, leaving the bridge, and the stream flowing under it, in complete darkness.

Then in the dark, after a moment of stillness, another light appeared as George emerged from the bushes. Chip was by his side. Annoyed to have missed the largest canine social event of recent times, the little dog sniffed around for any messages left behind, while George waited for the gap between them and the search party to widen. Once satisfied, they set off over the creaky bridge and onto the moonlit fields. Chip led the way.

Nothing seemed out of place on the fields, so the party ahead advanced towards Oban Wood, a dark silhouette against the night sky. As George neared, he saw a dent in the tree line. The men had seen it too. They changed course and moved towards it with urgency. George, feeling a rush of excitement, quickened his pace as he followed.

When the party reached the edge of the wood, the dogs' behaviour turned erratic. Some ran in circles, barking, while others cowered behind their masters. A lurcher darted back towards the bridge, bolting past George and Chip with its lead flapping wildly behind it. George quickly grabbed Chip by the collar as he made a move to follow. Unable to give chase, he sat, tilting his head, looking to the dark wood. Could he hear something George could not?

After a moment of madness, the dogs settled. And with slightly less haste than before, the party entered the woods, the yellow glow of their lamps lighting the trees as they went.

"We'll wait," said George, "then follow in a bit, aye, boy?" He patted Chip for comfort; his *own* comfort. "Or," he added, glancing back to the bridge, "we could just, maybe, go home?"

Chip didn't answer. Instead, he found an interesting spot on the ground and had a sniff. At the same time, the last of the lamps disappeared into the wood, leaving George vulnerable and alone on the field. When a cloud then crossed the moon, dropping a blanket of blackness around them, he felt his determination begin to unravel. Chip whined, then growled.

"Ok, Chip. I agree, we should go home. Mrs Furlong might need us."

On the way back to the bridge, the moon reappeared from behind its cloud. Chip stopped and looked behind them. George was about to hurry him along when movement caught his eye. In the distance, a single shadowy figure was drifting slowly across the field towards them.

"They're coming back," he said, turning off his lamp. "We need to go now."

George stepped up his pace. As the bridge came into view, he glanced back to see if the gap between the figure and himself had widened. But there was no one there. Something wasn't right. He sprinted to the bridge, and on the other side, he left the dirt track immediately and hid in the nearby undergrowth. He held Chip close, staring at the path while trying to steady his breathing.

He waited.

Several minutes passed, and George was getting uncomfortable. Branches were digging into his back, and the trickling stream was talking to his bladder. "OK, Chip," he whispered. "Whoever it was must have gone back or taken another way. Let's go."

But Chip didn't move.

"Come on, boy." George pulled his collar, but still the little dog refused to budge.

Just then, there was a creak from the bridge. Then another. Someone was crossing.

George sat back down and peered through the gaps in the undergrowth at the moonlit path. A shadow grew along it, followed seconds later by a dark figure, darker than the surrounding darkness; a shadow within a shadow. He was dressed entirely in black. Long, black, damp hair obscured his face. He carried something over his back — a pack of some kind. He was tall, thin, and bent, walking slowly with sharp movements, as if every step was painful. He was injured, but George had no desire to help him.

The figure crouched suddenly as if sensing he was being watched. His head spun back to the bridge, and the field beyond. After a pause, he slowly turned away from the bridge to look straight towards George.

George tried to sink further into the bushes, but they were too dense. He thought about running but found he could no longer move. Chip was shaking next to him. George pulled him closer.

The man couldn't *possibly* see him; it was too dark, and he held no lamp. But that belief faded as the man, slowly and with purpose, moved closer to the bushes, to where George and Chip sat trembling. At this distance he could now see a hint of the man's face. His dark eyes were set against the palest of skin. The rest of his features seemed missing — a blur of a face. George blinked hard to clear his vision, trying to bring the rest of him into focus.

The figure stretched out a pale hand, reaching into their hiding place. George recoiled as the hand, with long, pale fingers, drew nearer to his face. He tried to scream, but couldn't. There was nothing he could do; nowhere he could go. He closed his eyes and waited for the hand to clasp him.

There was a sharp rustle of bush as the hand quickly withdrew. He opened his eyes. The man was now back on the path, looking towards the bridge. And George heard the *crunch* of footsteps and voices as men from the search party returned.

Quick. Quick. Be here quick, prayed George.

He tried to spot them, but his view was blocked. When he looked back to the dark figure — he was gone.

Not realising he'd been holding it, George let out a huge breath as he exploded onto the path. With his lamp back on, its beam darting in all directions, he looked for the stranger. *Impossible,* he thought; how could he disappear so quickly? He was injured. Where could he have gone?

"George? Is that you?" Mr Furlong, supported by another man, was crossing the bridge, his limp worse than ever. "What in god's name are you doing out here?"

"Where did he go?" George said, ignoring the question and shielding his eyes from the lights now dazzling him. "He was here. Did you see him?"

"What are you talking about? I told you to stay—"

"He disappeared! He was here. I think he was hurt. And then he wasn't here. He couldn't have gone far." George was struggling for breath.

Donald Furlong let go of the man at his side and hobbled over to George. "Calm down, lad," he said softly, grasping his shoulders "I'll take you home. You shouldn't be out here, not tonight."

"But sir," he said, still far from calm. "I saw him. He must be from the crash. Did you find the plane?"

Mr Furlong frowned and looked to his companion, who shifted uncomfortably and gazed back towards the woods.

"No plane, son," said Mr Furlong.

"But the church? The crash? The—"

"No plane, George," he said, more firmly this time.

Mr Furlong turned George around, and together they walked back to Church Lane where the dust had now mostly settled.

Several women were still out, talking over the low walls that separated the small front gardens of the lane. They were wearing their nightclothes. Some looked worried as they waited for their husbands.

When the men returned, they would talk of a giant scar in the woods and damage of unimaginable scale. But they wouldn't come back for many hours yet; the sound of excited dogs and puzzled men filled Oban Wood for the entire night. Then the mists of dawn would come and cover the dark earthy scar like a cool, soothing bandage.

That night in his room, by the dim light of his lamp, George drew a picture of the stranger while the image was still fresh in his mind. After, he cleared his bed covers of the dust and bits of plaster then climbed into bed and kissed the photo of his mum and dad he kept on the bedside table. He drifted off to sleep, thinking about the stranger, wondering who he was, where he was from, and where he was now.

2

GEORGE INVESTIGATES

"Morning, sir," said George as he sat down at the kitchen table for breakfast.

Mr Furlong had been drying a plate at the sink while gazing out the window. He flicked the tea towel over his shoulder and smiled at George. "Morning, lad. Just heard school's closed today. Everyone's helping with the clean-up at St Mary's, including your teachers."

"Oh," said George, happy that school was closed, sad for the reason.

Donald Furlong was a short, friendly-looking man in his late forties. George had liked him the moment he'd met him. His face was full of kindness and had immediately put George at ease after his nervous journey from London. Donald's wife, Jenny, was just as nice. She was kind, funny, and had made him feel at home from the very first day.

Mary, the Furlong's only child, had lived there too, before leaving for her new job in London. They'd seen her off from the station only three months before.

On the platform, George asked her what she'd be doing in her new job. She covertly tapped her nose, and said: "If I told you, I'd have to kill you." She had then laughed and swept him up in a squeezing hug. He loved Mary like an older sister, and he missed her like one. It would be Christmas when she would see them again. He couldn't wait.

George was an evacuee. Evacuated just after the war started, he'd been living with the Furlongs for almost four years. His mother was a nurse at the Royal London Hospital, while his father was overseas fighting the Nazis.

His mother wrote to him regularly, but he'd heard less from his father as the war dragged on. He was proud of his parents and what they were doing for the war effort. In comparison, George often felt useless; just a child to be protected and cared for. He wished he could do more.

"You sleep alright, boy?" asked Mr Furlong, placing a plate into a cupboard, then removing another from the draining rack.

"Yes, I think."

"Good." He smiled. "Late night last night; thought you'd sleep till the afternoon. Eggs for breakfast?"

"I *did* see someone last night, sir," George blurted out. "He crossed the bridge, just before you came back. I wasn't making it up."

Mr Furlong didn't respond straight away. Instead, he looked out the window briefly, then down to the plate he was drying. He put it away, then walked to the table and lowered himself into the chair opposite George. "I believe you saw someone, I do," he said. "It's just...I suspect you saw someone from the search party, that's all. I came back because my leg was playing up. Maybe someone came back before me."

"No, sir. He looked different. Very different." George removed the drawing from his pocket, then slid it across the table. Mr Furlong looked down at the picture, raised an eyebrow, then made a *huh* sound.

"Look," he said with a sigh, "the damage was bad, and we don't know what caused it, but I don't think there was *anyone* involved—"

"What do you mean, sir?" said George, confused.

"Well," he paused, then let out another sigh. "There was no wreckage. No parachute. No fire damage, nothing. Just a load of upturned trees, a trench as long as the high street, and the half-destroyed church."

"But *something* did it," insisted George.

"That's for sure. Something *did*. But as for *what?* Well, that's for sharper minds than mine." He pushed himself up and walked to the cooker. "Nice drawing. Looks a bit like a woman though, with all that hair."

After breakfast, Mr Furlong left to help with the clean-up at the church, while George and Mrs Furlong cleaned the dust from the chicken run and allotment, where the cabbages now looked like giant snowballs.

When his work was done, George returned to his room. He retrieved a notebook from the drawer of his desk, one his mother had given him for Christmas — she sent one every year. The book from the previous year still had plenty of untouched pages left, and paper and notebooks were in short supply because of the war, but he thought this deserved a fresh book. On the front, in his neatest handwriting, he wrote: *The Hurstwick Incident. An investigation by George Moss. Age 12.* He folded his drawing of the stranger and placed it inside.

George decided to take his drawing to the police station. If Mr Furlong wasn't interested in odd-looking mysterious strangers, maybe the police *would* be.

The station was a large redbrick building halfway down

High Street. It was a hive of activity. As he entered through its wide front doors, George was buffeted by people coming and going. Being small, even for his age, he was easy to overlook. The crowd seemed to swallow him up and sweep him along, until eventually, he got washed up against the tall wood-panelled front desk, where everyone around him seemed to be talking at the same time.

Next to him stood an old lady in a woollen hat. She was telling a young, disinterested, desk sergeant about her cats, and how they'd abandoned her in the middle of the night and failed to return—all seven of them.

"So sorry to hear that, Mrs Taylor. But—"

"—Baker, and it's *Miss*," she replied.

"Apologies, *Miss* Baker," he continued. "But as you can see," he waved a hand loosely at the chaos behind her, "we are *very* busy right now. So, if you could be a dear and write down a full description of your lovely dogs—"

"—Cats!"

"Sorry, *cats*. Write a description, and I'll pin it on the board outside, how's that sound?"

Just then, George was shoved aside by an officer in uniform, who lifted a hinged portion of the front desk and entered the office beyond. The old lady was now fighting her way back through the crowd with a clipboard and pen in hand.

George, who had somehow found himself next in the queue, stood on tiptoes and peered over the desk. "Excuse me, sir?" he said to the desk sergeant.

The man looked down and raised an eyebrow. "All ages today," he muttered to himself. Then to George: "Lost a dog, have we?"

"Erm...no."

"Cat, then? Hamster? No, don't tell me...chimpanzee?"

"No, sir. I—"

"Well, what animal *have* you lost, young man?"

"I haven't lost an animal, sir," George answered, confused.

"Well, you're the first today. How can I help?"

He was about to answer when a tall, thin man in a grey pinstripe suit approached the desk. He turned, then cleared his throat to address the crowd. "If you are *not* here to report a missing animal, then please remain and form an orderly queue. *If* however, you *do* have a missing animal, we are very sorry to hear about it, but I'm *sure* you can all understand, after the events of last night we are far busier than usual. So please, if you will, return home and come back on a quieter day. I'm sure Patch, Fluffy, Buster, or Mr Tiddles will return to you in time."

A disappointed groan rolled around the room. Unhappy to have their missing furry companions treated in such an offhand manner, they departed, discussing how odd it was that so many pets had fled on the same night. George didn't think it was odd. He remembered the behaviour of the dogs on the field.

The crowd thinned, leaving only a few, but George had lost his spot at the front to Mrs Moore from Moore's Farm. A powerful-looking lady, she wore dungarees and a headscarf. She thumped the desk with her fist as she spoke, describing her husband's clothes that had been stolen from her washing line. When she was done, she was asked, very politely, to fill out a form and take a seat.

The thin man who had addressed the crowd returned, cutting in before George to speak to the desk sergeant. "Nigel, we have a few gentlemen from the War Office arriving on the ten thirty-two," he said. "I'd like you to meet them and take them straight to Oban. They'll want to see the site as soon as they get here."

"Yes, sir."

"And if they intend to stay, which I'm sure they will, I'd like *you* to be their chaperone, OK?"

"Yes, sir," the sergeant replied again, without enthusiasm.

"Good man." The thin man reached behind the desk to collect his coat and hat from the hooks on the wall, then briskly left by the main entrance.

"Baby-sitting duties," the officer grumbled under his breath, before turning his attention to George. "You again. So if it's not a missing animal, what is it?"

"I saw a man—"

"Amazing," he replied, in a dry tone that George tried to ignore.

"I saw him leave the woods last night after the crash that destroyed the church." George produced his sketch and placed it in front of the now slightly more interested-looking sergeant.

"You sure this is a man?" he questioned, peering over his thick-rimmed spectacles. "Looks like a woman to me."

"Definitely a man."

"Very long hair for a man."

"It's a man with very long hair."

"If you say so," he said, placing it down and waiting for George to continue.

"He came out of the woods after the search party went in. I saw him crossing the field, and again down by the bridge at the end of Church Lane."

"Then what?"

"Well," George hesitated. "He disappeared."

The sergeant sighed and dragged his hand down his face, dislodging his glasses. "It's gonna be a long day," he said.

George felt like he was losing him again. "He's definitely from...whatever crashed in the woods. I know it." He tried to remain calm, but his cheeks were getting hotter. It was clear this policeman, like Mr Furlong, was not taking him seriously.

"Look, young man," said the officer, leaning forward and lowering his voice. "I was up there this morning. I saw the..." he struggled to find the right words and settled on "*crash site*, and I can tell you one thing: no one could have walked away from that. No one." He sighed again, then looked at the lengthening queue behind George. "You run along now, OK? People are stacking up behind you again, desperate to bother me, and I'd really like a cup of tea at some point today. So off you pop."

He waved George away. The next person, a short man with curly grey hair, approached the desk, nudging George aside.

"I'd like to report a family member gone missing," said the man.

"Oh," said the sergeant, straightening up. "What's this family member's name?"

"Shep," said the man.

George slid his drawing across the desk, closer to the sergeant. He had now removed his glasses and was pinching the bridge of his nose, looking very much like a man in need of a cup of tea.

It was a cold morning despite the bright June sunshine, but George didn't notice as he left the police station and powered back up High Street, determination denting his brow. Neither Mr Furlong nor Nigel, the desk sergeant, had taken him seriously, but he knew the man on the bridge was important, and he was going to prove it.

At the end of the street, he turned right, into Church

Lane, where normally he would have been greeted by the imposing spire of St Mary's. Instead, George gazed up, squinting at an empty expanse of blue, birds circling, searching in vain for their recently obliterated perching spot. He wondered if it would ever be rebuilt.

The lane was busy. Men with wheelbarrows passed each other at the churchyard gate. Empty going in, full of rubble coming out. They skilfully pushed the heavy barrows up the narrow wooden ramps of awaiting coal lorries and horse-drawn carts. By the wall next to the weeping willow, a long table had been set up. It was covered in Union Jack flags and laden with tea urns and plates of biscuits. Spirits were high, considering the circumstances, and nobody seemed to mind George grabbing a cheeky biscuit as he passed.

The usually colourful cottages and gardens were covered in a layer of white dust; if not for the blue sky, the scene would have looked like a black-and-white photo. As George turned into the short garden path of the Furlongs' cottage, he playfully slapped a white rose. It exploded in a cloud of dust, revealing a brilliant yellow underneath. He coughed and waved the dust away, pushed open the front door, and called to Chip. Seconds later, there were scratches of paws on wood, and the small obedient dog skidded into view. George reached for the lead hanging by the door. "Come on, boy. I need that nose of yours."

They took the same route as the night before, over the bridge and across the field. Chip ran ahead, chasing off a pair of woodpigeons taking a stroll in the sugar beet.

Soon they were at the edge of Oban, where they entered just below the dent in the tree line.

Broken branches littered the ground, still covered in their bright green leaves. These amputated branches became larger the further in they went, allowing more light to enter the diminished canopy. Eventually, they found trees that seemed to have exploded entirely, sending yellow and white shards of wood far and wide, filling the air with the smell of damp sawdust. Trees became trunks, and trunks became splintered stumps. Until even those ceased to be.

George stopped and his mouth fell open. He stared in amazement at what lay before him. Stretching into the distance was a deep trench lined by hundreds of uprooted trees. It was as if a giant axe had swung from the heavens and cut Oban Wood in two.

Mr Furlong was right. Nobody could have survived this. But someone had. And George had seen him.

Far off in the distance, marking where the trench ended abruptly, George saw people gathered around a large mound of earth. Determined to get a closer look, he clipped the lead onto Chip's collar and travelled north, alongside the scar.

As he came to the end of the destruction, George heard voices and climbed the bank of soft earth to peer into the trench.

Two men were sat on a fallen tree with their backs to him. They surveyed the damage while drinking tea from flasks. Other men busily searched the area, picking up objects, studying objects, throwing said objects back to the ground, before removing caps to scratch befuddled heads.

George had lived in Hurstwick long enough to recognise some of the men. The two who sat before him were Clive Myatt, the town crier, and Mr Hatton from the bank.

Mr Hatton said something to Clive in a hushed tone, but George didn't catch it.

"Secret weapon?" boomed Clive, who didn't do hushed tones.

"Must be," said Mr Hatton, giving up being discreet. "What else could cause this much damage, and not leave a trace of wreckage?"

Clive looked around, picking crumbs from his beard as he thought. "Could be...a space rock?" he suggested, looking back at the banker.

"A meteorite?"

"Is that a space rock?"

"Yes. But no. This," the banker gestured to the surrounding destruction, "has to be a secret weapon, no doubt about it. Some kind of ray or something. This place will be crawling with army and government types by the end of the day, mark my words."

Clive continued to suggest alternative theories, including flying bombs, bouncing bombs, earthquakes, and even Martians.

George hoped the men would give up and leave, allowing him to have a nose around. Instead, more arrived. Finally, when it looked as though the whole town might turn up, George decided to move on.

"Let's go, Chip" he whispered. "Not much we can do here." He pulled on Chip's lead, but Chip wasn't ready to go. He was sniffing the ground. "What is it, boy?"

Chip had found a footprint. A long, thin footprint. Not a boot print like the kind left by the men in the trench, but a *foot*print. He could see the ball of a foot and a heel — no toes, though.

Suddenly Chip pulled away, then stopped again. George followed the little dog's nose and found another print. Chip pulled George again with surprising force, and he tripped and fell, letting go of the lead. Chip was off.

Unrestrained, Chip moved faster through the woods, with George scrambling behind, pleading with him to stay.

But wait, shouldn't he call the men and tell them about the footprints? They would help, wouldn't they? He decided against it. So far, grown-ups had refused to take him seriously. Anyway, he couldn't lose sight of Chip.

After several attempts, he caught up with Chip and successfully grabbed his lead. The little dog was still on the scent. He would sometimes lose it, but then double-back to find it again before heading in a new direction. He wagged his tail as he snaked his way through the woods, moving further from the trench until they emerged back onto the field just east of the spot they had entered.

Across the field, George could still see the small clump of trees and the wooden bridge. The de-spired church and the town were behind it. To the south-east he saw Windmill Hill topped with trees. Nestled among the smaller nameless hills around it was Moore's Farm.

Chip was no longer pulling at the lead. He was still sniffing the ground, but in a more general *just having a bit of sniff around* kind of way.

"Come on, boy. Where next?"

Chip just looked up at him, tail still wagging. The ground out on the field was dry and cracked with no footprints to follow. And, according to Chip, no scent.

"Oh, Chip!" cried George, stamping with frustration. Chip whined in response, and his tail dropped. George sighed, then scratched Chip behind the ear — his favourite place to be scratched. "Sorry, boy. You tried your best, didn't you?"

With no plan of what to do next, George trudged across the field, back towards town, throwing a stick for Chip as he went. When they reached the bridge, Chip ran across and down the bank to drink the cold, clear water, while George sat on the bridge, dangling his legs over the side.

From his jacket pocket, he removed the notebook and pencil. He left the first few pages blank, saving them for a recap of last night. On the following pages drew a picture of the vast trench from the woods. Then he sketched a footprint next to it and wrote a description of the scene. When he finished, he placed the book and pencil away again, and thought about what to do next. He noticed Chip patiently sitting below him on the bank, looking up. Next to his paws, in the mud, was a single narrow footprint.

They were back in the game.

Chip was on the scent once more. It took them east, following the stream. On a few occasions, nettles blocked their progress and George had to remove his shoes and wade into the water to avoid them. After about half an hour, Chip left the stream to follow the scent up a steep dry bank, which took them to a footpath running alongside a wooden fence. On the other side was a cluster of buildings: Moore's Farm.

Chip ran up and down the path, nose to the ground, tail in the air, in search of the scent. But he stopped and looked at George apologetically, he'd lost it.

George sighed and approached the fence, looking beyond it for another footprint, but the ground there was dry and revealed nothing. He gazed at the buildings in the distance.

Farmer Moore had a reputation for being a fearsome fellow who was tough on trespassers. The local children saw it as a challenge to make it across his land unseen, but those who got caught never tried again. George had never fancied it himself. The idea filled him with dread.

It was probably for the best that the hunt was over, he thought. He should have told the men in the woods about the footprints. What did he hope to achieve by tracking this person down alone? Was he going to capture him, take him to the police single-handed? He'd been foolish—

Before George could complete his sensible train of thought, Chip had squeezed under the fence and cantered off toward the farm buildings. The little dog had evidently rediscovered the scent and was almost out of sight.

George cursed as he scrambled over the fence to follow.

When he reached a gap in the old stone wall surrounding the deserted yard, his legs were shaking. He wasn't sure who he feared the most — the stranger from last night or Farmer Moore.

Contained within the old stone wall were buildings of red brick and black wood. He could hear pigs, and smell them, but couldn't see them. There were sounds of chickens and horses, also unseen. But the loudest noise was the constant buzz of flies.

On the far side of the yard was an open gate, with a wide track leading to the farmhouse on the hill, where clothes hung outside, gently swaying in the breeze.

One building dominated the yard: a black wooden barn. Under the deep eaves of its roof were two openings into its loft. They felt like eyes bearing down on George and sat over the mouth of a large, slightly open, double door. Next to the barn was a yellow van that was either being rebuilt or dismantled; George couldn't decide. Next to this, he found Chip. He was panting, his head low and his tail motionless, staring at the barn with nervous eyes. The little dog dared go no further.

3

WREN

Rahiir opened his eyes.

But it was bright, so he closed them again. Instead, he listened to the sounds around him.

Animals were nearby, in another building. He heard their snorts and squeals and escaping gases from across the yard. He listened to the birdsong outside and the buzzing of insects. At the edge of hearing he heard wheat sway lazily in the breeze.

He began to breathe deeply. With each deliberate, and painful, breath he increased his area of awareness, expanding beyond the barn and the yard to the house on the hill. He heard the clank of dishes and soft music over a dusty crackle. He went further, and heard the squeaking of a bicycle wheel. Further still brought sounds of laughter and voices and metal cutting into dry earth; in another direction came the trickle of a stream and the splash of a fish turning sharply to avoid a small excited animal running through the shallows.

He opened his eyes. These sounds were far away. He was alone — for now.

It had been dark when he entered the barn. Now,

sunlight shone through the open door and the ill-fitting boards of the walls. A million particles of dust churned and swirled in the shards of light above him. He thought of stars.

As he lay in shadow against sacks of grain, he looked upon a tractor that sat before him. It brightened. It wasn't glowing. Light was passing through it from the other side until soon the tractor appeared glass-like, revealing the partly open door beyond, where flying insects buzzed in tight circles over a small muddy puddle. The puddle was a footprint — his footprint. He had been careless.

He tried to recall how he got there. He remembered the crash, the bridge, the stream, and the young boy hiding in the bush. He remembered the sleeping house with the clothes hanging outside. The same clothes now lay next to him, pegs still attached.

A sharp pain shot from his shin to his hip as he attempted to move. He screamed silently through gritted teeth and pulled his bag closer. From inside he retrieved a small white disc. Holding it between thumb and forefinger, he placed it on his leg and moved it slowly over the hidden injury. The disc glowed bright as it passed over damaged bone and tissue. As the pain eased, tiredness quickly replaced it, and he sunk back against the sacks of grain.

Sleep was about to take over, but was delayed by a light flutter of wings. A tiny, fragile-looking bird was hopping along the workbench by the open door. It jumped onto a rusty toolbox, then flew into the rafters high above. Perched on a beam, it looked down to him. Then, wanting a closer look, it descended to settle on the wheel arch of the tractor. It was almost close enough to touch.

The small bird considered him. Its tiny head made darting movements as it took in the peculiarities of this new type of creature. Rahiir closed his eyes, but he was not resting or sleeping — he was searching. When he found what he was looking for, a smile played at the edge of his mouth. "Wren," he said, in a deep soft tone, his eyes still closed. "Wren," he repeated, even softer. Then his head rolled back, and he fell into a deep sleep. The bird moved on to see if it could find anything else as interesting as the stranger in the barn.

It probably wouldn't.

"What is it, boy?" asked George, crouching next to Chip.

Chip ignored him and continued to stare ahead.

The yard had recently been washed down. And in a patch of mud, in the shade of the barn, was a single footprint next to the open door.

"He's in there," George whispered, as he stood and crept forwards. "You stay here." Chip didn't need to be told; he wasn't going anywhere.

As George approached, the thought of someone inside, lying in wait, caused him to stop and rethink his plan. Then he remembered he didn't have a plan; he was just doing one thoughtless thing after another. He glanced over to the farmhouse in the distance. He should run there now and tell them someone was in their barn. But if he was wrong, and there was nobody in there, he'd look foolish and would probably get in to trouble. Farmer Moore wouldn't go easy on him.

No. First he would have to be sure that the stranger was in there, before running for help.

George looked around the back for another way in. He didn't find one, but he did find a long wooden ladder, which he carried around to the front and placed under one of the loft openings. He glanced again over to the farmhouse, hoping that nobody was looking from the windows, then began to climb.

When he reached the top, he found himself short of the hatch by a few feet, so he placed one foot on the top rung and stretched up with his hand. Once he had a firm grip on the edge of the hatch, he reached with his other hand, then pulled himself up and into the opening, while pushing off from the ladder.

It didn't go well.

He got in, but the ladder fell back to the ground, sending a loud crack echoing around the yard.

George shot a look towards the house while listening for movement below, but the only sound, over the flies, was his heart thumping in his ears.

Chip walked to the fallen ladder, his tail between his legs. He sniffed it, then looked up to George and whined. It was a *you're on your own now, kid* kind of whine.

No going back now, thought George, as he turned to face the gloom of the hayloft.

He crept between bales of hay stacked three high and three deep, then came to a narrow gantry. It spanned the open space below, passing through a network of rafters to join an identical loft on the far side. It looked too exposed to cross, so George crawled to the edge of the loft and peered down into the barn.

There was a grey tractor below, illuminated by a slice of sunlight. Beyond it, beneath the loft opposite, sat smaller pieces of machinery barely visible in the darkness. There was no sign of the stranger. If he was here, he would be in the loft opposite or somewhere underneath George.

He eased himself further over the edge. More of the tractor came into view, then something else. First came the feet, then the shins, followed by knees and thighs; stark and still against the straw-covered floor were the long black legs of the stranger. George knew it was him.

He pushed himself back, his heart now drumming even louder in his ears.

He's here. Go get help, he thought. Then he remembered the ladder now lying across the floor of the yard. He shouldn't have come in here. He was stupid. And now he was trapped. Trapped and stupid.

He tried to remain calm and crept back to the loft hatch. Maybe if he could see someone at the house, he could attract their attention.

He watched and waited, but there was nobody there. He considered dropping into the yard, but it was too high. He would break a leg. If he threw a bale of hay out first, would that break his fall?

He tried moving one, but it was too heavy.

There was only one way down, but he was too scared to take it. He had seen the ladder attached to the walkway joining the two lofts. It would take him down to the ground, but he would be uncomfortably close to the owner of those black legs.

Much quieter than before, he crawled back to the edge of the loft and eyed the ladder. If he was going to climb down, he would need to know if the stranger was awake or asleep, or better still — and he hated himself for thinking it — dead.

Holding on to a beam that crossed behind him, he leaned out over the edge. Once again he saw the legs; as he leaned out further, a black bag and a pile of clothes came into view too. Desperate to see more, he leant further out, stretching his neck as far as he could. The man in black was tall and thin but strong-looking. One long-fingered pale hand was resting across his chest. His face was paper-white.

His eyes, the largest and blackest George had ever seen, were open — and staring right at him.

CRACK. The beam came away in George's hand, and he fell forward. He reached out, finding another beam, which he gripped onto with all his might. He was now hanging above the stranger, who hadn't moved, but whose eyes were still fixed on him. George's flailing legs desperately tried to find footing, but there was nothing. He tried to pull himself up onto the beam, but he didn't have the strength. Eventually, his legs gave up their crazy dance, and he hung there, staring at those big black eyes.

The intensity of the stranger's stare soon faded. The eyes blinked, then looked away from George.

No longer able to hold on, George dropped to the ground. He landed in a squat, just feet from the stranger, and got his first close-up view of the man he'd been tracking. If he *was* indeed a man.

It was those eyes.

They opened and closed slowly, as if tired or weak, and were like black pools of oil, the whites barely visible at the very edges. The rest of his face was just as strange. The reason George couldn't remember the man's *other* features when drawing him the night before was now clear: he *had* no other features. Where his nose should be were two small slits for nostrils and a slightly raised ridge. When the man opened his mouth to take in a breath, George noticed a sharp set of teeth behind his thin grey lips. His jawline went from his pointed chin and rose to meet his ear, which was small and positioned unusually high on his head. His other ear was hidden under long, jet-black hair, which fell over his broad, sloping shoulders.

His clothes were as featureless as his face. A single piece of black material covered his entire body from his neck to his long, slim feet. It bore an intricate pattern that looked like the veins of a leaf, but there were no seams, buttons or buckles. The bag, by his side, was made of the same stuff; it reminded George of the cocoon of a moth or a butterfly, or a fish egg sack you might find washed up on the beach. It had a long strap, and again, no buckle or seam. What was inside or how it opened, he had no idea.

The stranger seemed satisfied that George was not a threat, and he soon closed his eyes, turning his head to rest on the sacks behind him.

George relaxed a little, too. He sat cross-legged, and continued to stare at the stranger. Then he shook his head in disbelief. "Well," he whispered, "you're definitely not a German."

George's observations were interrupted by a truck thundering through the yard, briefly blocking the light as it passed the door. He spun to face the sound and listened as the truck came to a halt. Its engine was still running when he heard its door open and a man grumble about a ladder blocking the way. Then came the sound of the ladder being pushed aside, followed by the truck door slamming shut. The truck drove off; when the sound of its engine faded, the yard outside was peaceful once more.

George sighed, then turned back, only to find himself staring into the black eyes of the stranger, his pale face an inch from his.

He grabbed George's wrist. George tried to scream but couldn't. The man pulled over his bag with his free hand and started removing items from it, his eyes never leaving George's.

George was terrified. He should have called to the driver — it was too late now.

"Will...you...help...me?" the man asked slowly, his mouth forming the words carefully as if saying them for the first time. George's wrist hurt. The stranger seemed to sense his pain, and loosened his grip, but not enough for George to escape. "Will you help me?" he asked again.

George wanted to scream for help, but nodded out of fear.

The stranger tilted his head. "Is that...yes?"

"Yes," George said, nodding again. "Yes."

The man found what he was looking for: a small white object the size of a pen.

"What...what's that?" George asked, not sure he wanted to know.

The man held his gaze, and George thought he was having second thoughts about whatever it was he was about to do. But then, the stranger took a deep breath and gripped one end of the object between his sharp teeth while twisting the other with his hand. There was click and then a hum. With a small quick movement, he jammed the object into the back of George's hand. George felt a sharp pain that quickly passed. The stranger released him, then scuttled back to the sacks of grain, kicking up dust and straw.

George backed up too, slamming into the large rear wheel of the tractor. Still feeling the sting, he checked his hand and saw a bead of blood. He wiped it away with his thumb to reveal a pinprick, then massaged his aching wrist.

The stranger was studying the pen-like object as it started to glow brightly from within. The brightness increased until it lit up the dark barn with a cold blue light, casting shadows of the stranger's long fingers against the walls.

George had never seen light like it.

When it faded, the man stabbed the device into the

palm of *his own* hand. It emitted a short sharp *hiss*. Then he withdrew the object and cast it aside.

With difficulty, the stranger moved to a kneeling position, placing both hands on his thighs. He closed his eyes and attempted to control his erratic breathing; his jaw grinding, his brow creasing. To George, he looked like a man readying himself for pain.

Sweat poured from his paper-like skin as the muscles in his face began to spasm. His nostrils flared as he breathed deeper and faster. He exposed his teeth and grimaced. Blood poured from his grey gums as several of his razor-sharp teeth fell to the ground. The man bent over in pain, holding the sides of his head as he twisted and squirmed.

George began to cry; not with fear, but with sympathy. He could almost sense the suffering, and he quickly realised what he was witnessing. The man's face was changing. His nose, once almost non-existent, now had a definite ridge and was still growing. His nostrils grew wider, his jaw squarer. His hands went to his stomach as he doubled over in agony. Until this point, the man had suffered in silence, but now, no longer able to bear it, he roared in pain.

Chip finally found his courage and raced into the barn, barking at the man now writhing on the floor. George grabbed his collar and pulled him close. "No, Chip! No."

The cries suddenly lessened and eventually stopped altogether. The man's quick, heavy breaths slowed as he collapsed into a foetal position, whimpering in the darkness.

George stared at the man's back and remained silent against the wheel of the tractor, one arm clutching his knees to his chest, the other holding Chip tightly at his side. He wanted to approach the man to comfort him, but he was afraid.

Twenty minutes, maybe more, passed in silence. George

was about to speak when the man started to move again. He rolled on to his knees and, with great effort, pushed himself upright. He brought up a shaking hand and pulled his matted, straw-covered hair away from his bloody face, then spat a mouthful of teeth to the ground. His hand moved to his nose, to his jaw, and then to his ear. His eyes were dark but no longer black.

George was now looking at a very different face; no longer strange. Not strange at all. In fact, it was very familiar.

George's ability to move had returned, but he didn't feel like running anymore. He couldn't shake the sense of familiarity he got when looking at the stranger. He had seen him before. Then he realised: the stranger looked just like his Uncle Frank – if Uncle Frank had long black hair and had just been hit by a bus. And Uncle Frank looked a lot like George's father.

George looked again at the pinprick in the back of his hand, and to the pen-like device on the ground, and then to the stranger opposite.

He looked weak, as though he might not last the night. With his new, more familiar, face, it was easier for George to read the man's emotions. His eyes were full of sorrow and shame. George wondered if he felt guilty for hurting him, so he held up his hand and pointed to the pinprick on the back. "Look, it's OK," he said. "I'm not hurt. It's fine."

The man said nothing. Instead, he glanced down to his possessions strewn across the ground.

Under his watchful gaze, George returned all the items to the bag. Each one was fascinating and unusual: objects that looked light but felt weighty; some that looked heavy but held no weight at all. The most familiar was a rope, but even that was strange. It remained curled in a loop with no knot to hold it together and was silver. There were textures and materials he had never seen before. Suddenly, every object he had ever touched seemed crude and clunky in comparison.

After returning them all, George was amazed to see the bag seal itself. As he took the bag over to the man and placed it by his side, he wondered if he'd be able to open it again; he doubted it.

George stepped away from the man and kicked straw and dust around the ground to hide the blood, then grabbed a bucket and filled it with water from a hose in the yard. He placed it beside the stranger, then dunked the least greasy rag he could find into the water and wrung it out.

"To clean yourself," he said, handing the rag to him. Blood, mixed with dust and straw, covered most of his visible skin, but George could see no open wounds.

The man dabbed at his face with the cloth. Then he stopped and sucked the water from it instead.

"Ew, disgusting," said George, taking the cloth from him. "Hold on." He ran off to the workbench where he'd seen a mug. The mug was filthy; whatever had been in there had festered for a long time. But there was a tin on the shelf containing a few pencils and a screwdriver. He emptied it and looked inside. It wasn't spotless but was far cleaner than the mug.

"Here," George said, filling it with water. "Drink this."

He drank in small sips, his face twitching in pain with every swallow.

"Can you climb?" asked George. He pointed to the ladder and then to the loft. "I need to hide you up there," he said.

The stranger closed his eyes, and George noticed rapid

eye movement behind the lids. When he opened them again, he looked up, then nodded slowly to George.

It took a lot of effort, but he helped the man to his feet and guided him to the ladder. He climbed surprisingly well for a man in his state. George followed, then led him into the hayloft and to a dark and concealed corner. It was just in time: the slow, rhythmic sound of heavy hooves came from outside. George ran to the hatch and poked his head out to see Farmer Moore leading a great black shire horse across the yard, heading to the stable, just across from the barn.

George hurried back down to retrieve the stolen clothes and the stranger's bag, and made it back to the loft just as the barn below filled with light. Mr Moore — a giant thick-set man, forearms like thighs — had entered.

Chip, forgotten by George, was unbothered by the new arrival. He wagged his tail and approached the big man.

"Oh, my," said Mr Moore, kneeling to pet the friendly dog. "You been spooked too, boy?" he said, checking the dog's collar for a name. "Chip of 12 Church Lane. Well, Chip of 12 Church Lane, you not the only one. Ivan, too, and he's a great big 'orse. Took me ages to find and calm the daft beast." He stood and glanced around the barn. Not seeing anything unusual, he grabbed the toolbox from the work-bench and turned to leave. "I'll get you back home once I've fixed the van," he said as Chip followed him outside.

George collapsed against a bale of hay, listening to Mr Moore clunking around under the bonnet of the van outside, while the stranger slept in the darkest corner of the hayloft.

"It'll be alright," he whispered. "I'm going to help you. I'm George, by the way."

The man stirred, and a small sound escaped his lips.

George couldn't hear, so moved closer. "Are you trying to say something? Your name?"

The man spoke again, barely a whisper. "Wren," he said.

"Wren," repeated George. "Where you from, Wren?"

But the man didn't talk again, so George returned to his hay bale and waited for Farmer Moore to leave.

It was lunchtime when Mrs Moore came down from the house carrying a plate of sandwiches. George listened as they talked. When she left, Mr Moore continued to clatter about below. But now, as George poked his head out to take a look, he was under the van, only his muddy boots visible.

It was his chance to escape.

George turned and took one last look at the sleeping stranger. "I'll be back tonight," he whispered, "and I'll bring food."

He took a few handfuls of hay from the floor and sprinkled them over the man, then stood back to admire his camouflage skills. Not the best, he thought, but there wasn't time to do better.

George hurriedly climbed down the ladder, then crept from the now wide-open doors and crossed the yard. Chip, who had been licking pickle from the empty plate next to the feet of the farmer, spotted George and followed. In no time, they were following the hedgerow back to the boundary fence, which George climbed over and Chip squeezed under. Together they marched off along the dusty, tree-covered path back to town.

"Penny for them," said Mrs Furlong as George pushed the last of his peas around his plate.

George smiled. "Just thinking about school," he lied. "Hope it's open tomorrow." An even bigger lie.

"We'll see," she said, placing her knife and fork together. She stood and took her empty plate along with Mr Furlong's into the kitchen. "I want you to have a bath when you've finished," she shouted over the noise of the running taps. "You look filthy."

"OK," he replied.

After the final pea had disappeared and after a long soak in the tin bath, he sat in an armchair waiting for Mrs Furlong to leave the kitchen so he could raid the larder.

Mr Furlong had already retired to the living room with his newspaper, where he would no doubt have his usual post-meal nap. When Mrs Furlong eventually joined them, she gave George a sweet smile, ruffled his still-damp hair, and clicked on the radio.

"Anything you'd like to say to Mary, dear?" she said to Mr Furlong as she sat at the bureau in the corner.

George knew the answer; it was always the same.

"Just send her my love," he said.

The scratching of Mrs Furlong's pen, the music from the radio, and a full stomach meant Mr Furlong's head was now lolloping back and forth as he fought with consciousness. It was a battle he would inevitably lose.

George glanced at the clock on the mantlepiece. It was almost eight thirty, but it wouldn't get dark until gone ten. If he left now on his bicycle, he could get to the farm, drop off the food, and be back in time for bed.

By eight forty, Mrs Furlong was engrossed in writing another letter, probably to her sister in Canada, while Mr Furlong snored quietly in the armchair, his newspaper resting on his lap.

Silently, George sloped off to the kitchen, watched only by Chip from his basket next to the unlit fireplace. Once there, he placed a tea towel flat on the side and opened the larder. He took a slice of bread, a small piece of cheese and a thin slice of ham. He was careful to only take a little. Ham

42

and cheese were rationed. If he took too much, Mrs Furlong would notice.

He wrapped the food in the tea towel and stuffed it inside his gas mask, which he'd hung by the back door in preparation. He returned the gas mask to its box, looped its string strap over his shoulder, then stepped outside.

It was a perfect midsummer evening. As he pushed his bicycle up the garden path towards the gate, he listened to the pleasant tick-tick-tick of the well-oiled chain. There was another sound; this one distant and growing louder. It was the deep rumble of aircraft and was quickly followed by the slow wail of the town's air-raid siren. *No, no, no. Not now!*

"George? Where are you going?" Mr Furlong was in the doorway, putting on his boots. "He's out here, Jenny," he called back inside. "Come on, young man. In that shelter!"

Across the gardens, George saw his neighbours exiting their homes. With newspapers tucked under arms and teddy bears clutched tightly, they descended into their bunkers. Mrs Barlow from next door, who didn't have a bunker of her own and shared theirs, entered through the back gate. George moved aside to let her through.

"No time for dilly-dallying, George," she said as she hurried past him, gripping a bag of knitting to her chest.

Reluctantly, George dropped his bike to the ground and followed the Furlongs, Chip, and Mrs Barlow down the brick steps, into the dim and humid shelter.

It wasn't long before tiredness started to scratch behind his eyes, but he refused to lie down in case sleep took him. So, he sat bolt upright on the bed, thinking about the stranger in the barn, while watching the Furlongs play cards under the flickering, naked lightbulb. Hopefully, the all-clear would soon sound, and he could complete his food drop. But sneaking away after this would be difficult. If he couldn't think of a convincing story to tell the Furlongs, they would send him straight to bed.

The rhythmic sounds of Mrs Barlow's knitting needles filled the shelter. Each clickety-click added weight to his eyelids. And when the all-clear did eventually sound, George wasn't awake to hear it. Instead, he woke the next morning in his bedroom with no idea how he got there.

George was annoyed at himself for falling asleep, but was relieved to learn school was once again closed while everyone continued to help at the church. After breakfast, he left the house in a hurry and rode his bike to Moore's Farm. When he arrived at the fence, he hid his bike under the bushes by the pathway and climbed over. He jogged along the narrow track by the hedgerow towards the yard, the box containing his gas mask and food bouncing off his back as he went.

As he slowed to walk alongside the stone wall, he heard voices on the other side. At the gap in the wall, he stopped and listened, then slowly poked his head around. The tractor was now parked outside the barn with a long trailer attached. It was just below the loft hatch, where Farmer Moore was throwing down bales of hay. Below, two women wearing dungarees were on the trailer, moving the bales into neat stacks. Another woman, pushing a wheelbarrow containing a sack of grain, emerged from the barn's wide-open double doors. George didn't like what he was seeing, and he kicked himself again for falling asleep in the shelter.

Any minute, he expected to hear the call from Farmer Moore to fetch the police. Wren would be taken away, arrested, interrogated — maybe even executed for being a spy. But the call didn't come. And when the trailer could take no more hay, Farmer Moore left the barn, wiping his brow with the back of his meaty forearm. He climbed onto the tractor, fired up the engine, and rolled out of the yard. The women sat among the hay bales, laughing as the trailer bounced along the track, hitting every pothole as it went.

As soon as they were no longer in sight, George sprinted to the barn, pausing in the doorway. There was silence. Fragments of hay hung in the thick air as sunlight travelled, unhindered, through the now empty loft, illuminating the rafters above him.

The ladder had been moved. Instead of leading to the walkway, it now led straight to the section of loft where he'd hidden Wren. George climbed it, the handrails still wet with sweat.

At the top, he slowly lifted his head and peered into the loft. There, in the middle of the now *empty* space, surrounded by dust-filled light, stood the tall, dark figure of Wren.

"Hello, George," he said.

And so it was that George fell from the loft for the second time in two days. This time, he failed to grab anything to save himself. He didn't need to. He braced himself for an impact that never came. On opening his eyes, he saw the roof above him then turned his head to see the ground below him. He was weightless, his body slowly turning until his feet found the ground. When they did, he felt his weight return.

A creak of floorboards and soft footsteps came from above, and Wren's face appeared over the edge of the loft, wearing a subtle smile. George looked down at his feet and then at the floor where he should have been laid out cold. He looked up and returned the smile; only his was less subtle, more of a dumbstruck grin.

4

NEW TOWN

July 2018 (Week one of the summer holidays)

Max Cannon stepped out onto his balcony for the last time. He looked across at the city just starting its day, then to the three tower blocks, identical to his own, that made up the Manor Fields Estate.

It was a view he knew better than any other, having looked upon it since he was tall enough to see over the balcony wall. Every curtain, washing line, window box, and budgie cage was familiar to him. This was the only home he'd known for fourteen years.

He looked down over the edge, trying to soak up every sight so as not to forget. Directly below was the playground. It was already starting to fill with small children, its swings, seesaws, and roundabouts moving rhythmically like mechanical watch parts. On a warm day like today, they wouldn't stop moving until nightfall.

He watched the old woman from the ground floor as she made her regular visit to the shop on the corner. She pushed her trolley, stopping only to feed the pigeons and to stroke one of the many cats that preyed on them.

Max then looked towards the bollards next to the phone box, where any moment now a woman in bright yellow Lycra would enter and jog through the estate. She would stop to stretch on the waist-high wall surrounding the playground, then continue through the car park before disappearing behind Milton Tower. He waited. And sure enough, there she was — right on time.

Next, his gaze drifted to the benches that circled a clump of trees in the centre of the estate. They were empty now, but in a few hours, kids his age and older would populate them. Kids that he knew, but didn't know him.

Something smashed behind him, inside the flat, and broke his trance. It was followed by a gruff apology.

Remembering why he was outside, Max walked to the end of the balcony to retrieve his binoculars. Just then a pair of thick hairy arms reached past him and snatched away the table they sat on. Max lunged forwards and rescued them before they hit the ground.

"Good save," said the voice of either Ron or Reg from Ron & Reg Removals Ltd.

Max sighed and held them close to his chest. They had once belonged to his father.

All that now remained on this once jam-packed balcony was himself and one large plant in a ceramic pot. Ron — or Reg — squeezed past to take it. Then it was gone. Max smiled, behind the pot, lost for many years, was another pair of binoculars. These were much smaller than the ones now secure around his neck, and made of bright orange plastic and covered in green algae. He picked them up and placed them on the window sill, then took one last lingering look at the London skyline before turning away and disappearing into the flat.

An hour later, Max's mother was hugging him excitedly in the lift. They were wedged between Ron and Reg. One of them — Max was not sure which — was holding a plant; the other held a lamp. Max was holding his breath. The smell of lift piss and removal-man BO was not his favourite. Once outside, they crossed the car park towards the large van containing all their worldly goods.

"You want to say goodbye to your friends?" said his mother, looking to a group of kids gathered by the park.

"Not really, Mum."

"Go on, you won't be seeing them again. That's Brian, isn't it?"

It *was* Brian.

Max could count the number of friends he had on one hand, and that hand was a fist. He had no friends, and he was alright with that. Brian had come the closest to being a friend, but only because Brian's mother was friends with his mother. They had a few "play dates" when they were smaller, but when Max tried to continue the friendship at school, Brian, like everyone else, ignored him.

"Go on," insisted his mum. "We're not going anywhere until you say goodbye. You'll regret it if you don't." Max sighed and his mother nudged him away towards the group. "Go on. I'll be in the van," she said, turning away.

He approached the group of boys. They were huddled around a tall skinny boy watching a video on his phone. It must have been a good one, because all of them were sniggering.

Brian, one of the smallest in the group, straddled his BMX while standing on tiptoes trying to see the video. He had short blond hair and wore a West Ham football shirt.

"Hey, Brian," said Max.

Brian, and a few of the others, looked up and stared at Max.

"Oh," Brian said, his smile fading as he searched for Max's name. "Erm...hi, Mark."

Max didn't correct him. "We're moving away today." He nodded to the van and noticed his mother looking from the window, with a smile that was both proud and sympathetic.

"Oh," Brian said again, glancing to his friends and raising a single eyebrow. One of the group suppressed a laugh.

"So," said Max, "bye then."

"Yeah, bye, I suppose." Brian smiled, but the smile failed to reach his uninterested-looking eyes.

Brian's friends were now looking back at the phone, ignoring Max.

"Bye," repeated Max awkwardly. He turned to walk back to the van, his cheeks glowing red. Then Brian said something to his friends that Max didn't catch, and the group erupted into laughter.

"Stay in touch!" yelled a boy who wasn't Brian.

"Yeah, don't forget us, will you?" called another.

The laughter continued as Max climbed into the van and sat next to his mother.

"See," she said. "Sounds like they're going to miss you."

"Yeah, Mum."

They didn't have a car. Instead, they would be making the hundred-mile journey to the new house in the removal van. Its single row of seats could comfortably seat four, but Ron and Reg were larger than most. Max spent the entire trip squeezed up against the passenger door, fully expecting to be ejected onto the motorway at any moment. His mum read a book, while Ron and Reg spent much of the journey arguing over which celebrity voice to choose for the sat-nav. They settled on Elvis.

Max spent his time staring out of the window, watching as the city turned into suburbia and suburbia into country-side. As the cab of the van got hotter and hotter, Max's mum gave up reading and fanned herself with her book. Then, after two hours of driving, Elvis told them to exit the motor-way. So they did, and ended up on a dual carriageway. Running alongside it, beyond a line of countless orange traffic cones, was a road under construction. This unfin-ished road went from tarmac, to stone, and then to sand, before it veered away and was lost behind rolling green hills.

Soon, the van made a turn onto a minor road, with high bushes and trees on either side, and wound its way through small picturesque villages. Max was just starting to nod off when they bounced over a level crossing. He was startled, but then relieved when he heard the sat-nav deliver its final instructions. "At the end of High Street, turn left onto Church Lane, *baby*," shortly followed by: "You have reached your destination. *Thank you very much*."

"Well? What do you think?"

Max looked to his mother to see which house she was referring to. Without the usual *sold* sign outside, he needed a clue.

He followed her gaze, then said, "It's a house." He was hot and uncomfortable and finding it hard to be keen.

"No. It's a *home*. *Our* home," she replied. She released the seatbelt and returned it over her shoulder. "Isn't it lovely?"

There was no point denying it; the small terraced cottage was lovely. It had a lovely green wooden door under a lovely pointy porch. Lovely lush green ivy climbed the walls, framing the lovely white wooden frames of the windows. Lovely. Max would love to stay in such a place for a long weekend or even a week. But lovely or not — it wasn't home.

Despite his misgivings, he smiled at his mother. He hadn't seen her this happy for...well...ever. "Yeah, Mum.

It's...lovely." He climbed out of the van, stepped onto the cobbled road and pushed his shoulders back in a stretch.

"You're going to love this place, Max. This move will be perfect for us. I know it will." She climbed out after him and stood with her arm over his shoulder. "Get a load of that fresh air." She inhaled deeply. "You don't get that in London. Did I tell you, Hurstwick has the highest number of centenarians — that's people living to a hundred — of any other town in England?"

"Once or twice, Mum."

Ron and Reg climbed out the other side and had a stretch and a scratch. One of them spectacularly broke wind, ruining the fresh air, and resulting in an approving nod from the other.

Max's mum eyed them with disgust then smiled at Max, beckoning him to follow her across the road, where she opened the waist-high white picket gate and walked up the short path to the door.

"Want to look inside?" she said, unlocking and pushing it wide open.

"Have to eventually, I suppose." He smiled at her and stepped over the threshold.

"Get in." She pretended to smack the back of his head as he passed.

The house was dimly lit and smelt dusty. Their footsteps echoed as they walked down the narrow hallway and peered into the empty rooms. A sitting room, a kitchen, a dining room. His mother had seen the place before, but Max hadn't. He looked around while she watched him with a smile on her face.

Upstairs were two bedrooms for Max to choose from, one at the front of the house, one at the back. Max went straight to the window of each to see which had the best view, hardly considering the attributes of the rooms themselves. The view from the front was disappointing: he could see the cottages on the opposite side of the lane but not much else. So Max chose the room at the rear. It looked out over the garden, which backed on to a churchyard. A green wall of trees blocked the view of the churchyard itself, springing from them was the tallest church spire Max had ever seen. Anyone else would have loved the view. Max wanted to be higher.

"Right," said his mum once Max had decided. "I'll go find the kettle." And she left him in his new room.

Standing at the window, he looked down at their new garden. It was long and narrow and looked like a jungle compared to the neat gardens on either side. At the bottom of the garden was a small neglected-looking shed, surrounded by a tangle of bushes and weeds. Set into the stone back wall behind it was a gate leading to an alley running between the gardens and the churchyard wall.

Directly below his window was the flat roof of the ground-floor extension, dotted with moss and bird droppings. Max wondered if he could climb down to it. Something to try later, he thought, if he was feeling brave.

He suddenly became aware of a girl sitting in a deckchair in the garden next door. She was looking up at Max and saying something Max couldn't hear.

His look of confusion caused her to make an *open the window* gesture with her arms. It was one of those old windows that you pulled from the bottom. He tried to lift it, but it didn't move. He pulled harder, but no luck. He looked down at the girl and shrugged. She made another gesture this time, as if flicking a latch. He found one on top of the lower panel and slid it across. The window then slid up with ease.

"Don't have windows in London?" the girl said with a grin.

"Not like this one," he replied, his cheeks flushing for the second time that day. Well, they do, he thought, just not in his flat.

"Were you having a good look?"

"Sorry...what?"

"You were staring at me. It's not polite to stare."

"No...I wasn't. I was staring at...nothing."

"Oh, I'm nothing now, am I—"

"No, I mean, I wasn't staring at anything, I was just...." His cheeks were glowing now.

"It's OK," she smiled. "Just messing with you."

Max took a deep breath. "Er...how'd you know I'm from London?" he asked.

"Easy. You have London hair," she said, still smiling.

Max raised his hand to his hair. He didn't think his hair was very...anything, really. Certainly not *London* hair, whatever that was. He'd never had it styled. He just let it grow, until he could no longer see, then his mother would send him to get it cut. She often called it a mop.

The girl laughed. "Kidding," she said. "It's a small town. People talk."

"Oh," Max said, feeling daft.

Her hair was shoulder-length, black with a single stripe of red down one side. She wore black jean shorts, Converse trainers with no socks, and a black and white striped T-shirt. Max guessed she was older than him, maybe fifteen.

She rose from the deckchair, tossing her magazine to the lawn, and walked to a bench against the wall separating the two gardens. She stood on the bench and rested her arms across the top of the wall. "What's your name?" she asked.

"You mean...you don't know?" He smiled and felt a little triumphant.

"Well. You look like a Max to me."

His smile disappeared.

"Small town," she said, laughing again. "I'm Ellie."

Max gave an awkward nod that was supposed to say *nice to meet you,* but looked more like a nervous tic.

Ellie ducked her head to glance into the lower windows of both houses. Satisfied no one was watching, she lifted herself onto the wall. And in an excellent impersonation of a tightrope walker, she moved along it before effortlessly climbing onto the roof of the ground-floor extension, which she crossed and came to a stop outside Max's window.

"Not unpacked yet?" she said, looking into the empty room.

"Not yet," said Max as the girl gracefully entered and sat on the window sill.

Max backed away. He wasn't sure he liked having this strange girl in his room. She seemed nice enough, but a bit too forward for his liking. More than ever, Max wished to be back in the high-rise where people didn't climb up to say hello.

He leaned awkwardly against the door, his hands behind his back, while an uncomfortable silence filled the room.

Keen to break it, Max said, "What school do you go to?"

"Highwood Park," Ellie replied. "Why did you move from London?"

Max shrugged. "Do you like it? The school?" It would be his school soon.

She narrowed her eyes, noticing the evaded question. "Love it," she said flatly. "Anyway, we're only in week *one* of the summer holidays, so I'd rather not think about school." She stood and walked around the room.

Something smashed downstairs, followed by the usual gruff apology. His mother replied, saying it was fine, but

Max heard the frustration in her voice; frustration at herself for not going with the slightly more expensive removal company.

"What does your mum do?"

"Librarian."

"She'll be working for Mr Hall, then. He's an odd one."

"Odd?" replied Max.

"Well, more of a creepy git really. He freaks me out. Anyway, I try and stay away from libraries if I can help it. Your dad?"

"Died before I was born."

"Oh. Sorry."

Max shrugged.

There was another long silence, and Max couldn't think of anything else to say. He watched her as she looked around the room. She seemed completely comfortable with the silence, and for a second Max envied her.

"I better start unpacking, I suppose," he said.

"S'pose," she nodded.

Another silence.

"So..." Max said, moving away from the door and nodding to the window with his most polite smile. "It was nice meeting you, Ellie."

"Oh yeah. Of course," she said, suddenly aware of the hint. She sat back down on the window sill. "Nice meeting you too, Max," she said. She swung her legs around and lowered herself down to the roof of the extension. "See you around," she said, not looking back.

He watched her skilfully navigate her way back to her garden and resume her position in the deckchair.

Max closed the window, vowing to never open it again.

55

Max's mother raced from room to room like a plate spinner, trying to keep Ron and Reg from destroying all of their stuff. Max offered his help, but she suggested he explore the town instead, and maybe buy some more milk on the way back.

He stepped outside into the bright warm sunshine and was immediately knocked into a bush. Ron-or-Reg barged past holding a large box marked *FRAGILE!* and *THIS WAY UP* in large, upside down, red letters.

Once the coast seemed clear, Max pushed himself from the bush, opened the gate, and turned right onto the lane.

He walked past the small two-storey cottages with their colourful flower-filled gardens. Some cottages had names instead of numbers. The Farthings, Willow Lodge, Elm Garth. He didn't think theirs had a name, but made a mental note to check when he got back. The cottages on his side of the lane came to an end, and he passed the low stone wall of the churchyard and its wooden gate, topped with a neat thatched roof. He carried on and ducked under a large weeping willow. It grew on the other side of the wall but draped its branches over, across the narrow pavement, and gently swept the lane.

He stopped where the cobbles met the tarmac of High Street and Station Road.

Station Road lay ahead, one side lined with shops, pubs, and restaurants, the other side open to a large green park. The busy High Street, to his left, was lined on both sides with shops and looked a more likely choice for finding milk.

He felt self-conscious as he walked down the street. He imagined everyone staring at *the new kid in town*. But when he'd built up the courage to lift his head and look around, he realised not one of them had given him even a *first* look.

After a few minutes of walking, he followed a small brown sign, pointing down a narrow side street to the library. The shops on this street — mostly art galleries, jewellers, and hairdressers — were smaller, huddled together, and leaned in over the road. They had crooked roofs and tall, thin, fragile-looking chimneys. A strong gust of wind, and they'd probably topple, thought Max.

At the end of the street, he emerged into a busy market square that smelled of fried onions. Stalls surrounded an ornate clock tower in the centre. At the edges of the market, Max saw a collection of small fairground attractions for children much younger than him: a bouncy slide, a helter-skelter and a mini carousel.

Avoiding the crowds, he kept to the fringes and made his way to the library, nestled between the town hall and a grand-looking bank. He didn't go in. Instead, he studied the noticeboard outside. There were fliers for fitness classes, music events, craft fairs, and 'missing cat' posters. There was an official-looking notice titled *Hurstwick Bypass Plans*. It was weather-worn and dated from the year before. It showed a map with the new bypass, highlighted in green, passing the town and the woods to the north. Next to it was a "Stop the bypass" poster. This one looked less official and was printed on bright green paper, decorated with clip art, mostly of rainbows, butterflies, and frogs.

Max walked around on the edges of the market for a while, then, beginning to feel worn out by the heat and the bustling crowds, he decided to explore the large park he'd seen earlier.

Once there, he instantly felt better. There were still lots of people, but not so tightly packed; he felt he had room to breathe. A large glossy board next to him, listing the park's flora and fauna, told him he was standing in Bramfield Park. He walked along its pathways, shaded by large trees that hissed in a breeze he couldn't feel, past people sitting on benches reading books or looking at their phones. Away from the paths, on the well-trimmed grass, footballs were kicked and frisbees thrown. Less active people lay out under the broad oak trees dotted about the green, while others relaxed in the shade of a grand-looking bandstand.

With the sun beating down on him and all the good shady spots taken, Max decided to head back to the cottage to check on progress. From the entrance to Church Lane, he could see Ron and Reg trying to squeeze the sofa through the tiny doorway — it wasn't happening. So, desperately needing shade and peace and quiet, he entered the churchyard.

The churchyards he had seen before, from the tops of buses in London, were run-down, dark and creepy. But this place was bright and pleasant and full of birdsong. There were two circular pathways. The inner path hugged the church tightly while the outer path ran between the gravestones and the boundary wall. Max took the latter and felt his skin cool as he moved from bright sunlight into the shadow of the church tower. He looked up to admire it, silhouetted against a bright blue cloudless sky. As he did, a strange feeling passed over him; a sense he was being watched, that he wasn't alone.

A loud noise from behind startled Max, and he turned to see two woodpigeons striking each other fiercely with their wings. He quickly forgot the odd feeling of being watched and turned his attention to the statue upon which the feuding birds were doing battle.

It was an angel with one arm. Barely visible beneath a cloak of vine and ivy, its cold stone eyes looked down over a track disappearing into a neglected tree-filled corner of the churchyard. The gravestones in the corner were weather-worn, their inscriptions unreadable. They looked old; Max imagined them belonging to a small ancient church long gone — one replaced by the grand structure behind him.

The trees there were large and mature. One in particular, some kind of pine tree, towered above all others to climb almost as high as the church spire itself — but not quite.

Max felt strangely drawn to this forgotten corner, and found himself walking towards it. He didn't consider himself brave at all, but as he moved along the narrow track, probably worn by deer or foxes, he felt no fear.

The pigeons fled as Max passed under the gaze of the angel. He came to a tangle of nettles and weeds that choked the trail, but he pushed on through. Gradually the undergrowth died away as it became starved of light, and he soon found he could move more freely.

Now deep within the corner, he breathed in its cool air, and in the dim light wandered between the thick trunks of old trees. As he rounded the base of the giant pine he had seen from outside, a small stone shack came into view. It was consumed by nature, half-collapsed, with a large bush growing from within. There were strange boulders dotted around it. Some were the size of footballs, others the size of microwave ovens; one was the size of a small car. All were the same sandy-grey colour and freckled with lichen. On some, the edges were too straight to be natural, making the place feel like an ancient ruin, with Max its discoverer.

Behind the shack was a steep bank, on top of which ran a low mossy wall in a state of disrepair. A trickle of a stream came from beyond the bank, but all other sounds were now absent. He could no longer hear the people from the park that neighboured the churchyard, or the birdsong; there was only the soft crunch of his footsteps over the springy ground.

As he approached the shack, he began to feel cold. He crossed his arms over his chest and raised his shoulders.

Just then, a twig snapped under his foot, causing roosting birds to flee the collapsed portion of the shack in panic. Max let out a high-pitched squeak in fright, then laughed nervously at how jumpy he seemed to be.

He placed a hand on the wooden door barely clinging to its hinges, and pushed. Paint crumbled under his fingertips, but it opened without argument. Max peered into the gloom, expecting graffiti, beer cans, and the smell of urine, but there were none of those things. Only dead leaves covered the flagstone floor of the main room, and a green hand of ivy clawed at the back wall, consuming a rusty wood burner. Daylight entered from two adjoining rooms at the crushed end of the building, rooms that were home to tall weeds and fallen rafters covered in bird droppings. Only nature had dared enter the place since being half-destroyed by...well...what had destroyed it?

As he stood in the doorway, a loud snap of a branch came from up in the trees, quickly followed by a rustle from somewhere behind the shack.

"Hello!" Max called, turning to look.

Another sound, this time from behind him — *inside* the shack. He spun and stepped back in time to see movement from within. The door slammed shut, ejecting flecks of dried paint into the air. He froze. Through the small, cracked window next to the door, he saw another movement.

Max turned and raced towards the mass of undergrowth that stood between him and the safety of the churchyard outside. He didn't look back. With his arms raised to protect himself from the brambles, he ploughed through the thorns snagging at his clothes, trying to stop his escape. Driven by adrenaline, he burst through, past the angel, down the path, and into the light.

When he felt he was at a safe distance, he stopped and

turned to the corner, expecting to see something; a face perhaps, staring through the trees. There was nothing.

Not used to running, he bent over and placed his hands on his thighs and breathed heavily. Still shaking from the adrenaline rush, he straightened up, brushed himself down, and examined the scratches on his forearms.

A breeze circled the churchyard, moving from tree to tree. Max relaxed; *it must have been the wind*, he thought. *Wind closed the door, and I saw a pigeon move in the shack. That's all it was.*

"You're new," said a voice from behind.

Max spun to see a boy sitting against a headstone a few metres away in the shade of a tree, his bike on the ground next to him. He'd been reading a comic, but now he was looking at Max.

"I can tell you're new," he continued. "No one from around *here* would be crazy enough to go in *there*." He nodded in the direction of the angel.

Max glanced towards the corner and then back to the boy. He looked about the same age as Max. He was black, tall and thin, and wore a white cap with NASA across the front. The cap pushed his afro hair out to the sides and his thick-framed glasses magnified his eyes. He looked at Max, waiting for a reply.

Max, who was still trying to regain his breath, wasn't sure he wanted another conversation today; two in one day would be a record for him.

"Yeah," he said finally, "I'm new." Max nodded politely and started to walk away, in a manner he hoped communicated that the conversation was over.

"Just visiting? Or do you live here?" asked the boy, not receiving Max's subtle *end of conversation* signal.

"Moved here today," replied Max.

"Wow. *Really* new, then." The boy stood, rolled up the

comic and stuffed it in his back pocket, then mounted his bike. He leaned down to read the name on the headstone. "See ya...Philip...Butterworth." Then he turned back to Max. "So what do you think of it so far?"

"Well," said Max, tentatively eyeing the headstone, "It seems...nice."

"Does it?" said the boy, surprised.

"Well. It's only been a couple of hours. Do you like it?" Max asked.

"Never really thought about it," said the boy. Then after a long pause, "Yeah, I do. Can be dull, though. But, yeah, it's alright."

The second uncomfortable silence of the day arrived as Max walked along the path and the boy rode slowly beside him.

A small, waist-high information board caught Max's eye as they rounded the corner. He would have ignored it, but he was looking for something to help break the silence.

Large type across the top of the board read *The Hurstwick Incident.* But it was the illustration that captured Max's attention. It showed a plane cutting through the church tower, sending boulders in all directions; the ones he'd seen around the shack.

"Ah, the Hurstwick Mystery," said the boy, circling the board on his bike.

"Mystery?" Max said, eyeing the board.

The boy nodded, and Max read the description to himself.

On the night of June 20th, 1944, this church spire, the third tallest in England, was destroyed after a German Messerschmitt BF 109 collided with the great tower, and came to rest in Oban Wood to the north of Hurstwick.

The spire was restored to its current state in 1957 after the Hurstwick Festival Fundraiser.

Wreckage from the downed plane can be found on display at the Hurstwick Public Library.

Old black and white photos accompanied the text. There was one of the church without its spire, with people standing around among the piles of rubble. Another showed a familiar-looking shack, with a large cracked bell jutting from its side. Another photo taken during the restoration showed a group of smiling men holding their tools aloft, the rebuilt tower encased in scaffolding behind them. Last, there was a photo of some wreckage in a display case, presumably in the library.

"Interesting," said Max as he stepped back and looked up at the church spire. "But you said *mystery*?"

"I did," said the boy, looking up at the spire with Max. "Some oldies say it was a big cover-up. But most believe what's written on the board there."

"What would they cover up?"

"Loads of theories," the boy said with a shrug, "but secret weapon is a local favourite. Some say a German weapon, others say something built by us. Anyway, it was a long time ago. Not relevant now."

Max looked at the board again, placing his hands either side of it, like a president about to give a speech. "What do you think?"

"Aliens." The boy laughed. "Anyway, I've got to go. I'll see you around," he said, and started to cycle off.

"Yeah, bye," replied Max. He raised his hand in an awkward half-wave.

"What's your name?" called the boy.

"Max."

"I'm Isaac!" shouted the boy in return, giving a far less awkward gesture, part wave, part salute.

Max watched him disappear around the corner, then returned his focus to the board. The sun caught a few letters of a word scratched into the Perspex surface. Max tilted his head slightly until the whole word came into view.

LIES!

5

THE LIBRARY

Max sat cross-legged on his living room sofa, watching TV as the sun outlined the edges of the drawn curtains.

He was bored.

Well, he thought he was bored. He couldn't be *entirely* sure, having never really been bored before. Back in London, he would spend hours, sitting by himself, watching the world from his balcony. It might have looked like boredom to those around him, but it wasn't. He was content; he was happy.

But with his new diminished elevation and no real view to speak of, plus a constant fear of being spotted by the girl next door, his binoculars remained unused and packed away in a box marked 'Max's stuff'.

He would have to find other things to occupy his time.

It was Monday, week two of the holidays, and his mother's first day of working at the library. Week one had flown by; he'd been too busy unpacking to be bored. But now, with most of the unpacking done, he found himself watching the fourth wildlife documentary in a row. Yes — he was definitely bored.

He yawned and clicked off the TV, just as a gazelle

grazed its way towards a leopard, hidden in the long grass. Max climbed from the sofa, feeling like he'd somehow saved the poor animal, and threw open the curtains. Outside, a group of girls were standing in the lane. They glanced at him, then looked away as Ellie joined them. As she turned to close her gate, she noticed Max, and waved.

Max waved back, feeling embarrassed to be caught at a window yet again.

"New boyfriend, El?" said a tall, thin, blonde girl.

Ellie punched her hard in the arm, and the others laughed as they made their way down the lane towards the high street.

Max watched them go. Then he put on his trainers, picked up his key and his phone, and left the house. Fifteen minutes later, he was passing through the automatic sliding doors of the library. It was bigger and busier than he'd imagined and, to his relief, air-conditioned. A low and long semi-circle of a reception desk greeted him as he entered. His mum was standing behind it, placing books on a trolley, while a tall thin man, presumably Mr Hall, spoke to her in hushed librarian tones. Her face lit up when she saw Max. And when Mr Hall wasn't looking, she blew him a kiss and winked. Max smiled in return but didn't go over.

Ellie was right; there was something odd about Mr Hall. He was a very tall man who seemed to love wearing black. He wore a smart black suit over a black shirt, and although Max couldn't see his shoes behind the desk, he would bet good money they were black, too. His long hair, pulled back into a ponytail, was also black, with grey appearing at his temples. But his love of black was not what made him odd — it was his face. It was a pale, pointy face that somehow managed to look old despite the lack of wrinkles. It looked like a face that had gone unused for most of its life, apart from the odd scowl and frown here and there.

66

Another man sat behind the desk. He was sitting at a computer, assisting an elderly member of the library. Younger than Mr Hall, and not at all odd-looking, he noticed Max and gave a friendly nod, before returning his attention to the computer screen.

Behind the reception, in what looked like a storeroom, was an old grey gentleman with a large bunch of keys hanging from his belt. He was removing books from a cardboard box and placing them on metal storage shelves.

Max walked past the reception, into the bright open space of the main hall, with its high ceiling and its maze of packed bookshelves. He chose to go down the least busy aisle, passing a small hunched old lady, reading the back of a thick novel plucked from the crime section. Further on, the bookshelves made way for a long wooden study desk, where people sat reading and working on laptops. Behind this desk, along the back wall, three archways led to smaller rooms. The signs above read Children's Literature; News and Local History; and Audiobooks, Films and Video Games.

He liked the idea of looking at the video games. He didn't own a games console, but a small part of him hoped there was one set up in the room. There wasn't. But he looked at the games anyway, just to kill time.

"It's Max, right?" said a familiar voice.

He turned to see Isaac entering the room. "Hi," he replied. It was the first time he'd seen him since the churchyard.

"Getting that one?" asked Isaac, nodding to the game in Max's hand.

"Just looking," Max placed it back on the shelf.

"Good. It's not a great one." Isaac walked to a revolving stand full of games and picked one out. "Now, *this*," he said, passing it to Max, "*is* great."

The game was *Alien Fodder 3*; the cover showed a burly soldier firing a gun the size of a small horse at an alien bug thing the size of a small house. "Looks good. But I don't have a console."

"Wait...what?" said Isaac, genuinely shocked. "Really?

"Really," said Max. Isaac didn't say anything for a while. He looked as though he was trying to imagine life without video games. Max added, "Never needed one before."

"Get one," replied Isaac, almost pleading.

Max shrugged and smiled. "Maybe," he said. "Well, I *am* kind of bored. But anyway, it's a while until my birthday."

"Come over and play mine," Isaac said, smiling back.

Max didn't know what to say. No one had ever asked him over to their house before. "Thanks," he said, looking back to the game in his hand. "I'd like that."

"No problem. Where do you live by the way?"

"On Church Lane," said Max, "next to the—"

"Church?" interrupted Isaac. He laughed and shook his head and picked up another game and inspected the back. "Fancy part of town. You must be loaded."

"Hah, no," replied Max, also picking up another game.

They talked for a while about which games to play and which ones to avoid. After he advised Max on what console to get, Isaac went quiet while trying to decide on which game to take out. It would be Max's first video game, which Isaac still couldn't quite believe, so it was an important decision and one that couldn't be rushed.

"I'll catch you in a bit," said Max, leaving him to it. There was no reply. "I'm going to have a look around," he said louder, backing out of the room.

"Oh yeah, sure." replied Isaac, not looking up. He'd laid out four games on the floor and was staring at them intently.

Max remembered that the wreckage from the plane crash was supposed to be on display somewhere in the

68

library, so he made his way to the News and Local History room; it seemed like a sensible place to look.

The room was full of books — unsurprisingly for a library — and had a long rack of newspapers and magazines down one side. A large, dark wooden table dominated the centre of the room, where a very beige-looking man with a bushy white beard sat alone, reading a local newspaper. He wore a beige short-sleeved shirt and beige shorts with brown sandals over his beige socks. The man glanced up as Max walked in. Max smiled politely then looked away, searching for the display.

He found it in the far corner of the room; a dusty case containing several pieces of twisted metal. Each fragment had a number, corresponding to a faded diagram of an aircraft posted on the wall. Next to the display was a map. It was curled at the edges, and showed the town and the woods to the north. Hanging above all of this was a wooden hand-painted sign: The Hurstwick Incident of 1944.

Max was surprised by how low-key the display was, as if it had been hidden away, forgotten.

He leaned in and read the small plaque next to the cabinet.

"On the night of the 20th of June 1944, the tower of St Mary's Church was struck and destroyed by a Messerschmitt BF 109. These are the only surviving fragments of the aircraft, which were recovered from its final resting place in Oban Wood..."

Before Max could read any more, he noticed Isaac's reflection in the glass cabinet.

"You like this history stuff, don't you?" said Isaac, moving his face close to the glass for a better look at the twisted wreckage.

Max nodded. "Well, it's pretty cool. A plane slicing off a

church spire, then exploding in the woods — doesn't happen every day."

"Hah!" The laugh was loud and sarcastic and came from the beige man sitting at the table. "Don't believe everything you read, boy." He lowered his newspaper and stared at them. "That," he said, pointing to the wreckage, "is nothing but lies. They didn't find those trinkets in the woods. They didn't find anything in those woods." The old man glared at them, waiting for a response. When none came, he returned behind his newspaper with a huff.

Isaac nodded sideways to the door, indicating that they should leave and *definitely* not start a conversation with the man.

"So what *did* land in the woods?" asked Max.

Isaac sighed, hung his head, and stared at his trainers as the man lowered his newspaper to the table.

"'Twas not a plane, that's for sure," said the man. "You really think a small aircraft could completely obliterate a church tower, and then still have the energy to travel all that way, destroying a huge section of wood? No way is what I say. It would've been travelling at supersonic speeds and made of something stronger than...well...whatever those things are made of." He waved his hand vaguely at the display case.

Isaac raised his head. "The man *actually* has a point," he said, looking surprised.

"Of course I have a point, cheeky bugger. Anyway, by the summer of forty-four they were only sending over doodle-bugs, flying bombs, not Messerschmitts. Anyone with half a brain can see through that lie. My old man did. He was there and knew more than most, being a police officer an' all. But still, there it sits in its stupid little glass case with its ridiculous shiny little plaque pretending to be the truth. It's a load of old bull—"

"You're a bright ray of sunshine this morning, Mr Bartley." The young man from the front desk entered, pushing a trolley full of magazines and newspapers.

"Hey, Ben," said Isaac, "how's it going?"

"Couldn't be better. Sun is shining, birds are singing, and I'm stuck here with you lot." A broad grin grew across his face. "Nowhere I'd rather be, of course."

The old man made a grumbling sound as he removed his reading glasses and returned them to their case with a loud snap. He picked up his hat from the table, then gave the younger man a disapproving stare as he got up to leave.

Ben responded with a warm, genuine smile. "Same time tomorrow, Mr Bartley?"

Mr Bartley grunted something unpleasant under his breath, then left.

Ben watched him leave, then picked up the paper from the table. His bright mood faltered as he read its headline: "Bypass Halted Due to Rare Newt Find". Then, aware the boys were staring, he lightened up and placed it onto the rack. "What game today?" he asked Isaac, as he unloaded magazines onto the shelves.

"*Alien Hunter 6*, one of Old Man Bartley's favourites." Isaac smiled.

"Poor aliens," laughed Ben. "And that's *Mr* Bartley to you," he said, in a not too serious tone.

"Max," said Isaac, "meet Ben. He's the reason we have video games in the library."

"This is true," said Ben. "But if you could just borrow a book or two when you take out a game, I would appreciate—"

"Yeah, yeah," said Isaac, "I know." He looked to Max. "You see, Max, Mr Hall hates having games and movies in here. But Ben sold him on the idea, saying kids would come in for the games and leave with a book. Education by stealth."

"You make it sound so dubious, Isaac." Ben smiled as he placed the last of the magazines onto the rack. "Well, Max, it was nice meeting you."

"You too," said Max, as Ben left the room.

They headed to the front desk to collect the game, Isaac grabbing a random book on the way.

Max's mum was at the counter. Max made awkward introductions, then let her know he was going to Isaac's house for the afternoon. She made an awkward moment even more uncomfortable, by being *way* too happy that he'd "*found a new friend*". Isaac thought it was funny. "Mums," he said, rolling his eyes as they left the library.

Max spent the rest of the day at Isaac's house blasting aliens in a room dedicated to fun. It had a battered old sofa, a large TV screen, several games consoles — at least one from each decade since the 80s — and walls covered with movie posters. It was also a mess. Isaac called it the den and shared it with his older brother, Jacob.

When they tired of playing video games, Isaac showed Max his room. It was just as messy as the den and smelled of glue and paint. An unfinished model rocket sat on a desk under a light with a magnifying glass attached. Over the back of a chair was a dressing gown adorned with NASA and SpaceX badges. Posters of rockets and planets filled the walls. Above the bed, a long shelf displayed more rockets, each intricately painted and labelled with their names and launch dates.

"Let me guess," said Max, "you like space?"

"Well done, Sherlock," replied Isaac with a grin. "Want to see something cool?"

"Well, I thought these were cool," he nodded towards the rockets. "But if you have something cooler..."

"Oh, I do. Follow me."

Isaac left the room and disappeared down the hallway. Max followed and found him with his ear pressed against a door. As Max approached, Isaac opened it, peered into the gloom, then entered. Seconds later, sunlight filled the world's tidiest bedroom as Issac drew back the curtains, revealing himself as the messy one of the family. He then opened a set of double doors built into the wall, stepped back, grinned, and gestured for Max to enter.

"Wow," said Max, now standing next to Isaac.

"I know, right?"

Mounted inside, looking like a giant mean insect, was the slickest-looking drone Max had ever seen.

"I present to you...DragonFly," he said, in his most dramatic voice. "My brother's pride and joy."

"That is..." Max couldn't find a suitable word. "Wow," he said again.

"Yup. It sure is," replied Isaac. "A top speed of fifty miles per hour, thirty-two minutes' flight time, operating range of one and half miles, omnidirectional obstacle avoidance, 4K video, three-axis gimbal image stabilisation, low-noise carbon composite propellers, and — cool little flashy lights."

"Does he let you fly it?"

"Hah! He saved up *two* years for this beast. He'd kill me if he knew I was *looking* at it. You see, I tend to break his stuff. Sometimes."

"So *have* you flown it?"

Isaac looked sideways at Max — then smiled.

Over the next two weeks, Max spent most of his time hanging out with Isaac. They spent long days playing video games in the den, riding their bikes around town, and taking shelter from the intense summer heat under the broad trees of Bramfield Park. Isaac would talk about rockets, movies, and video games while Max, not having much to add to the conversation, was happy just to listen. But when Isaac left for his family holiday to Saint Lucia, Max was once again alone.

In an attempt to stave off boredom and keep his mother happy, he joined the library. And he now spent most of his time there, sitting at the long study desk, reading. He felt comfortable there. People could just sit alone in the library, without feeling the need to interact with each other. After a few days, Max realised why he *really* felt so comfortable; he had reverted to high-rise Max. He was people-watching again. Only this time, not from above. By the end of the week, he knew all the staff by name and was familiar with their habits and routines.

Mr Hall was the most interesting. Max had noticed a strong bond between other members of staff, with lots of friendly banter. But their easy-going attitudes would evaporate in the presence of Mr Hall. Like a shadow, he would glide around the building, extinguishing light and laughter wherever he went. But like most people, he ignored Max, and Max was fine with that.

Max was used to people ignoring him. When he was younger, he'd found it frustrating and upsetting, but eventually, he'd accepted it as a thing, a curse even, and moved on. Ellie and Isaac noticed him, though. He wasn't sure why, but he was glad of it. Maybe it was hard to ignore the new kid who moves in next door. Or the kid who bursts from the trees in a quiet churchyard and hurtles towards you in a mad panic. Or maybe his curse was gradually, finally, lifting.

Ben was also immune to the curse. He always greeted Max warmly as he entered through the library doors of a morning. But maybe that was a part of his job.

Max had seen Ben a few times outside of library life. Once, he had seen him entering the churchyard, pushing an elderly gentleman in a wheelchair. A few days later, on a misty morning, he'd seen him again with the same old man, this time sitting with a group of silver-haired men and women by the bowling green.

One of them was Mr Walsh, the caretaker at the library. Max enjoyed watching him the most. He was always busy doing something, fixing something or going somewhere. He could hear him coming a mile off. It wasn't his huge collection of jingling keys that gave him away, but the jolly tune he seemed to whistle at all times — except in the library when Mr Hall was nearby, of course.

Despite looking older than most trees, Mr Walsh was mobile, fit and strong, and his eyes were sharp. He lived in a small cottage next to the vicarage between Bramfield Park and the churchyard. As well as being caretaker at the library, he was handyman at the church and groundskeeper at the bowls club. Max had seen him serenely pushing a large, old lawnmower up and down the green, creating a perfect pattern of diagonal lines, a metre wide. He was quite possibly the most content person Max had ever met.

Finally, there was Old Man Bartley. He didn't work at the library, but was there almost as much as the staff. He was the opposite of Mr Walsh. Constantly frowning, he looked as though he might scream at any moment. He reminded Max of an angry garden gnome.

Every morning, Mr Bartley would be one of the first through the doors. In the News and Local History room he would sit in the same chair and read the paper. Once the paper had been devoured up to the sports pages, he would flick through a book — a different one each day — while making notes in a small journal. At around one in the afternoon, he would stand, don his Panama hat, glance angrily towards the dusty display case of lies, then head to the exit, eyeing everyone with suspicion as he went. Suspicion of what, Max had no idea.

It was a Saturday morning. The sounds of the busy market square descended through the library's open windows, set high in the ceiling, and found Max sitting at his regular spot at the long study desk, flicking through a book on British wildlife.

Life in the library was anything but wild, but that morning, an interesting change had occurred. Mr Bartley was late. He was never late. Even stranger, when he did finally arrive around eleven, he was smiling. Max had never seen him smile.

Even that wasn't as strange as the thing that occurred fifteen minutes later, when Mr Bartley gestured to Max to join him.

Max, certain that the old man was trying to draw the attention of another person, perhaps behind him, turned around. But there was nobody there.

Max got up slowly and entered the News and Local History room, where Old Man Bartley was eyeing a map on the noticeboard. It was an updated version of the bypass map Max had seen outside on his first day.

"They changed the route of the bypass," Mr Bartley said with a grin, followed by a little awkward old man dance.

Max had heard something on the radio that morning. Apparently, to avoid destroying the habitat of a population of rare newts, the bypass was being redirected. Residents of

Hurstwick had hoped the change would see the bypass curve north through the fields. Instead, it had been decided, it would curve south, cutting through the centre of Oban Wood. Apparently, the wood held no special status other than being quite nice to look at.

Max was confused. It was good news for the newts, for sure, but it didn't explain Mr Bartley's joyous mood. "Why's that a good thing?" he asked, hesitantly.

"It's not a *good* thing, it's a *great* thing," he replied, clasping his hands together in celebration. He walked over to the large old map next to the display. "It means they have to dig a huge trench right through that wood. And when they do," he said stabbing a finger on the map, "they're going to find something. Something to put an end to this lie."

"And...what's that?" said Max.

"Ha! Well...you know." He swallowed and placed his hands on his hips, his eyes darting between Max and the map. "The thing." He nodded to the map. "The whatever it was...that came down in those woods. Might not be the whole thing, I grant you, but a part of it...perhaps."

There was a glint of madness in the man's eyes. He wasn't making much sense, and Max struggled to find a response. "Right. OK," said Max, hoping it didn't sound as if he thought the guy was mad.

"You think I'm mad, don't you?"

"No, of course not. I—"

"Don't worry," he whispered. "They all do." His smile returned, and he picked up his hat from the table. "But they won't for long. The rate they're going, they'll be at the edge of the woods in a few more days, as long as those protesters leave well alone."

Max watched him march from the room towards the

reception, where he tilted his hat towards Mr Hall and disappeared through the sliding doors.

Later that morning, Max found Mr Hall looking at the bypass notice, a sour expression on his pale, sharp face. Max couldn't be sure if it was more sour than usual. He decided it was.

6

THE DIARY

It was closing time at the library. Max sat in a comfy chair next to the front desk and flicked through a comic while watching the staff close up for the night.

Mr Walsh opened the normally automatic doors with one of his many keys and waved off the last few stragglers into the warm summer evening. There was a mechanical whirl as the outer shutters started to fall. Max watched them slowly descend, then hit the ground with a metallic clang.

"Hey, Max," said Ben, pushing a trolley piled high with books. "Waiting for your mum?"

"Yeah," replied Max with a smile.

Ben spied the comic Max was reading. "Any good?" he asked.

Max nodded, and Ben gave an approving thumbs up and continued down the ramp into the main hall. According to Isaac, after the success of the video games initiative, it had been Ben's idea to stock up on comics, too.

Mr Walsh was now over by a bank of switches on the wall behind the front desk. One by one, he flicked them; with each flick, a section of library disappeared into shadow, until the only light remaining came from the open door of the backroom; it illuminated the reception, but didn't quite reach Max. Mr Walsh entered the room, leaving Max alone and unable to read in the dim light. So, he placed the comic aside and waited for his mother.

The library was noisier when closed than it was when open and full of people; the staff stopped talking in whispers, and the sound of shutters and cupboards echoed throughout the building. He could hear his mum talking to Mr Walsh over the clank and clink of a dishwasher being filled.

He yawned. Then, for the second time in four weeks, he had the feeling he was being watched. He tried to brush it aside. It was absurd. You can't *feel* when you are being watched, he told himself; that's just something people say in movies and books to build tension. But the feeling wouldn't go. He shifted uncomfortably in his chair and stared into the darkness of the main hall.

Only the first few metres were visible: the ramp and the bottom half of the closest bookshelves. As he tried — and failed — to force his eyes to adjust to the darkness, he imagined someone hidden, watching him. Then something moved in the darkness. At first Max thought it was just his imagination. But as he continued to stare, he became certain of it. A vague shape was forming at the far end of the hall. It was darker than the darkness around it and seemed to be growing. No. Not growing. Moving. Moving towards him. For a moment, he thought his eyes were playing tricks. But still it approached. Max's heart hammered in his chest as he looked around; he was still alone. When he looked back, there was a pale face suspended in the darkness.

It was Mr Hall.

Max breathed a sigh of relief as the rest of Mr Hall emerged from shadow. He sailed past Max, paying him no attention, and entered the backroom to join the others.

"Hey, darling." Max's mother appeared. She was smiling while looping her handbag over her shoulder. "Are you OK?" Her smile faded and was replaced by a look of concern. "You look like you've seen a ghost."

Max stood and walked to her. "More of a vampire, really," he said.

"Shh, don't," she whispered, suppressing a laugh. She darted a look towards the room she'd just left. "He might hear you." She then performed her best Dracula impression and leaned in for the kill.

Max laughed, pushing her away. She pulled him in for a hug. "Come on, honey. Let's grab a takeaway. Payday today."

They left by a side door and wandered off across Market Square, heading to the Jade Garden, the best — and only — Chinese takeaway in Hurstwick.

That night, feeling full and content, Max returned to his room. After almost four weeks it now looked like a proper bedroom, everything unpacked and in its place.

The room was warm and stuffy, so he opened the window. But the air outside was just as warm and provided no relief. He gazed across to the church, illuminated by a yellow spotlight. Above its clock was a section of tower that looked as if it might house the church bells. It had three tall arches on each side, each one closed off with slats, like Venetian blinds made of stone.

As he stared at the tower, he tried to imagine a plane smashing through it. Max had a good imagination, but even he couldn't see an aeroplane slicing through it, then continuing on to the woods. He suspected Mr Bartley was right about that part.

Max didn't have a theory about what had happened all

those years ago, but he was intrigued by the idea that there could be another explanation, that the official story could be a lie.

A soft knock on the door interrupted his thoughts, and his mum popped her head in. She looked tired and ready for bed. "Goodnight, sweetheart," she said.

"Goodnight," he replied with a sleepy smile.

She tilted her head and frowned. "Missing Isaac?"

"No," Max snorted. He left the window then sat on his bed.

"Oh, OK," she said. "He's back tomorrow, right?"

Max nodded as his mother walked over and planted a kiss on his forehead and sat on the bed next to him. "I know you weren't keen on moving here," she said. "And I know it's a big change, but you'll get used to it." He nodded again, and she patted his leg and ruffled his mop of hair. "You never know. You might even grow to love it here."

"You love it already, don't you?"

"I do," she said, excitedly bouncing her feet up and down on the floorboards. She then stopped as if realising something.

"What is it?" asked Max.

Her smile slowly broadened, and Max saw a mad glint in her eyes. "No downstairs neighbours to worry about," she said. She then stamped her feet repeatedly. This time even louder. "I keep forgetting."

In the flat, she continually worried about making too much noise for the neighbours downstairs, mostly because they themselves could hear everything upstairs — *everything*.

She stood, gave him another kiss on the forehead, then danced a silly stamping dance out of the room, noisily slamming the door behind her.

"Goodnight, sweetheart!" she shouted as she stomped down the hallway.

"Goodnight, nutter," Max said, but she was already gone.

He turned on his bedside lamp, walked to the main light switch by the door and flicked it off.

On his way back to the bed, he stubbed his toe. The pain was instant. He hopped around the room, holding his foot and biting his lip. Then he fell onto the bed, massaging his toe, glaring angrily at the raised floorboard probably dislodged by his mother's crazy dance.

The pain soon passed, and he dressed for bed. Too warm to get under the covers, he lay on top, his mind drifting, thinking about his first few weeks in his new home. They'd gone better than expected. He'd made a friend in Isaac, and Ellie next door seemed nice, and he enjoyed spending time at the library. Then he thought of Mr Bartley again, and the church tower....

KNOCK KNOCK!

Max was pulled back from the brink of sleep. "Yeah," he said and turned to face the door.

There was no answer — just another knock.

"Come in, Mum."

Silence.

With a sigh, he clicked on his lamp, and with heavy limbs heaved himself off the bed and across to the door. When he opened it, he found himself staring at an empty hallway, nothing but his shadow on the wall opposite. He looked up towards his mother's bedroom and saw a warm sliver of light under her door.

"Brilliant," he said to himself. "A haunted house." He closed the door and turned to face the bed.

KNOCK!

From his new position, he realised it wasn't coming from

the door. The knock was low and muffled and was coming from under the floor.

He stepped closer to the loose floorboard and waited for the knock again. He didn't have to wait long.

This time it was preceded by a slight rolling sound. Max dropped to his knees and prised the floorboard up with the tips of his fingers. It came out easily, and he placed it to one side.

The dark void below gave no clue to the origin of the noise. Max went to the bedside table, rummaged around in its small cupboard, found his torch, then rushed back and knelt by the opening.

The cavity under the floorboard was about a foot deep and filled with cobwebs. White spiders with long thin legs ambled away from the unwelcome light, giving him a clear view of a wooden box. It was about the size of a shoebox and covered in dust. Max guessed it had been there for a very long time. As he stared at it, fear and curiosity wrestled in his mind. Curiosity eventually won, and he reached in to retrieve it, annoying the spiders further.

As he lifted it, something heavy rolled freely inside, making the same knocking sound he'd just heard.

Not fancying a room full of spiders, he placed the floorboard back to its original, flush, position. Then he placed the box on the floor and flipped its small bronze latch with his thumb. The lid opened with a squeak. Inside, he found a solid metal ball and a pocket-sized notebook, curled at the edges. Written in black ink on the cover were the words, *The Hurstwick Incident. An investigation by George Moss. Age 12.*

Max picked up the metal ball. About the size of a snooker ball, it was heavy and smooth, and its milky-white surface reflected the room around him. He placed it back into the box and removed the notebook. The thin spine of the book cracked in defiance as it opened. Inside, notes and drawings filled every inch. The first page had a sketch of the church, its spire missing. The page opposite showed a plane crashing in the woods, a thickly drawn question mark next to it. Max's heart began to race.

Attached with a paper clip to the inside cover was a folded piece of paper. Max opened it. It was a sketch of a man in black with long dark hair, the word "Wren" written next to him.

He placed the drawing on the floor, then turned the page.

June 22nd, 1944.

No one believed me about the stranger down by the bridge. So two days ago I decided to start my own investigation. I was hoping to find a German pilot or a spy. Instead, I found a man called Wren. He is not a spy or a pilot, and he is definitely not German. He is different from us...

Max stopped and looked at the picture of the man once again. No longer sleepy, he continued to read.

7

A POCKET FULL OF MEAT

1944

Wren could disappear. George had suspected this was the case. He suspected he'd disappeared that first night by the bridge, and again days later when Farmer Moore was emptying the hayloft.

The first time George witnessed it, was When Mrs Moore came to the barn to collect cups that had piled up on the workbench. George had crawled to hide behind a wooden barrel. He was about to instruct Wren to do the same when he just popped out of existence, causing George to think he was now one of those kids with an imaginary friend. Minutes later, when Mrs Moore left, and Wren reappeared looking exhausted, he poked him in the shoulder several times to make sure he was real.

George didn't know how he did it. But as the farm got busier, Wren was relying on the ability more often; it was becoming a drain on his energy. So, after a month of hiding out in the barn, it was time to find a new place to stay.

In the dead of night, under a full moon, George and

86

Chip crept from the Furlongs' cottage and made their way to the farm. Wren was waiting for them by the gap in the stone wall, wearing his ill-fitting stolen clothes and his bag across his back. Together, they set off over the moonlit countryside, heading towards a steep hill in the distance. They passed through the small wood at the foot of the hill, then climbed to the top, where they could see for many miles in all directions. Below them, black hedgerows divided the endless fields, while ahead Oban Wood stretched to the horizon, like a large splash of ink on dark blue blotting paper.

As Wren stood silent, taking in the view, George looked to the east watching a line of bombers climbing into the air until he could see them no more. A few minutes later, Wren was on the move again, descending the hill. George and Chip followed.

They crossed more fields, George talking quietly as they went. Wren listened. He didn't talk much, but George knew he understood. He smiled and nodded in all the right places. They walked until the sky to the east turned indigo, then left the fields, entering Oban Wood — Wren's new home for the summer.

He spent the long summer hidden there, in a den they built together. George, impressed by Wren's ability to disguise the den, would often have trouble finding it, so resorted to tying a small red ribbon to a nearby branch as a clue to its whereabouts.

They built the den as far from the crash site as possible, as that was still a place of interest to the locals. The ageing band of bankers, bakers, and blacksmiths that made up the Home Guard had increased their patrols around the back lanes. George had spotted them more than once marching through the woods, rifles at the ready.

But it wasn't just the locals they had to worry about.

After the crash, the War Office sent investigators to the town. A few days later, a small company of soldiers arrived and set up camp outside Oban. On one of his visits to the crash site, George saw a line of them searching the area inch by inch. Every day, he lived with the fear that they would discover Wren and take him away.

Eventually, the military moved out, but not before making the controversial claim that wreckage of a German plane, and the remains of its pilot, had been found. The locals didn't buy it for a second. After all, many of them had spent days searching the woods themselves and found nothing. It was a clear attempt to quash rumours of a new Nazi secret weapon — the popular theory in town. Dutifully, the local newspaper reported "the find", never hinting at the real mystery or controversy.

George relaxed once the army had left, but not completely. One investigator remained: a tall, wiry man by the name of Crinklaw. Nobody knew his title or the position he held at the War Office, but he stayed behind, renting a room above the barbershop on the high street. He would often see Mr Crinklaw being chauffeured around by his personal police driver, a man George recognised as the desk sergeant he'd spoken to the morning after what the papers — and everyone including George — now called "The Hurstwick Incident". George did his best to steer clear of both of them.

As the hot summer passed and autumn neared, the woods were no longer the best place for Wren. He seemed to suffer from the cold, and would shiver in temperatures that George found quite comfortable. Wren possessed what George called a "glow stone". It glowed brighter than a hot coal, was cool to the touch, but somehow warmed the air like a hot stove. But as magical and strange as it was, it was not enough to keep Wren warm on the coldest of nights. He needed somewhere else to stay. After days of searching, George found Patrick's Corner.

Patrick, the groundskeeper, had abandoned his remote corner of the churchyard the day after the flying church bell had crushed half of his tiny home. He moved in with his sister above the Beehive Inn on Station Road. Being a regular at the inn, it couldn't have worked out better for Patrick. He would still tend the grounds, but now he kept his tools in a small shed at the opposite end of the churchyard.

No one had reason to visit Patrick's Corner anymore. The mess from the incident had been mostly cleared, apart from a few boulders dotted around the shack. And there was no money or labour to make repairs. So the churchyard should remain quiet, at least for the winter.

The shack was small, with only one room left undamaged, but it was warm, sheltered, and well hidden by the surrounding trees. And because it was so close to Church Lane, George could visit every day.

George was getting good at stealing. He hated doing it but could think of no alternative — Wren needed food. Apart from the odd fish George caught, and the berries and nuts foraged from the woods, stealing was his only option. Luckily, Wren could go without food for many days before feeling hungry. But he was hungry now.

It was early on Friday morning, and High Street was starting to come alive. George watched from a darkened alley across the street as Mr Fuller the butcher opened up for the day. He pulled down the canvas awning, placed his chalkboards by the door, then checked his pocket watch. He glanced up the road while stroking his fat moustache, then disappeared back into his shop.

A few minutes later, at the end of the road, Mrs Waldron rounded the corner. A tall and elegant woman in her 30s, she owned the small antique shop next door to the butcher. She glided down the street in her long, slightly faded, green coat and yellow hat and gloves, her right arm hooked up, holding a bright yellow handbag in the crook of her elbow.

Mr Fuller watched her; his chubby face pressed against the inside of his shop window between chains of hanging sausages. When she got closer, he flattened his hair with the palm of his hand, dusted down his striped apron and re-emerged with a broom, ready to sweep an already clean pavement.

"Morning, Mrs Waldron. And a fine one it is, too," he said in his cheerful way, bowing slightly in her direction.

She returned the pleasantries in her more reserved manner, rummaging in her bag for the key, while Mr Fuller continued to describe the fine morning they were having.

This was George's moment. Thumbs firmly hooked behind the straps of his school satchel, he crossed the street and slipped down the narrow alley leading to the back of the shops. He had five minutes before the delivery boy arrived. Plenty of time, he told himself.

He parted the beaded curtain of the open back door and stepped inside, where he was greeted by a headless pig lying across a large wooden table. The first time he'd seen such a sight, he'd stumbled backwards into the alley in terror. Now he was prepared and avoided looking directly at it. He also avoided looking at the two other pigs hanging from the ceiling, along with rabbits and a couple of pheasants.

Next to a large mincing machine stood a delivery bicycle on its stand. Its detached basket was placed on a table next to a pile of neatly wrapped packets of meat and an open book, containing the orders for the day.

It was a reminder to hurry.

He rushed to another table, home to a larger pile of meat, yet to be wrapped and organised. George grabbed two sausages and two slices of ham, then wrapped them in paper and stuffed them into his pockets. As he hurried to the back door, he heard a car approaching. He stopped and held his breath, hoping it would pass.

It was slowing down.

Quickly, George fell to his knees and scrambled behind the large mincing machine. He watched the alleyway intently, then felt a twist in his stomach as a small white van stopped outside. He pushed himself further back behind the mincer. He heard a door slam, then the rear doors of the van opening. He considered making a run for it, but he couldn't move. He could almost see the disappointment on Mr Furlong's face, and it froze him to the spot.

Moments later, a large man in a long white coat and black boots entered. He brought with him two buckets and an offensive smell that hit George instantly. He slapped a hand over his mouth and nose, trying not to gag.

The man placed the buckets down near the door with a horrible slopping sound, then walked through to the front of the shop, where he greeted his colleague cheerily.

With the way clear, George scrambled from behind the mincer, his feet slipping on the sawdust-covered floor. He then jumped over the buckets and burst through the beaded curtain into the alleyway, feeling a mixture of guilt and triumph. Fresh September air filled his lungs as he ran as fast as he could. *That was close — too close.*

As he sped along the back alley, his satchel bouncing and bobbing on his back, he spotted a delivery bicycle outside the bakery a few doors down. It was a three-wheeler with a large box at the front. And it was unattended, its lid was up, inviting George to slow and peer inside. He pulled out a small loaf of bread, then continued his mad dash, not believing his luck.

"Oi!" came a yell from behind, but George daren't look back. He rounded the bend, ducked down a tight alley and emerged, once again, onto High Street. There he slowed to a walk, which he hoped looked casual. His lungs burned and his legs shook like jelly, but he felt happy as he headed to Patrick's Corner with a small loaf up his jumper and a pocket full of meat.

As George crossed Bramfield Park, under the hissing leaves of beech, oak, and ash, his heart rate settled, and his breathing returned to normal.

The north end of the park had recently been transformed into allotments. He walked the path between them, seeing what else he could grab. But an old man sat on a stool outside a small shed watched him with suspicion. Perhaps later, he thought.

Past the allotments, the ground dropped to meet a small lively river that he followed east towards the church.

The river path was empty, with no early-morning dog walkers or fishermen to avoid. George walked along it, watching the last of the damselflies darting above the water's surface, then came to the place where the ground beside the path climbed to a steep bank.

After a quick glance up and down the path, he scrambled up the bank, using exposed tree roots as steps. At the top, he climbed over the low mossy stone wall that ran along its peak and slid down the other side. It wasn't the quickest or most graceful way into Patrick's Corner, but it was the most discreet.

George would always feel a strange, warm prickly sensation when entering the corner. To him, it felt like passing into a bubble of kindness. It was a subtle feeling which he'd also felt around the den in the woods. But he never asked Wren about it, he was never really sure if it was real or in his head.

He brushed himself down and approached the stone shack. From his angle it looked uninhabitable. Masonry and wooden beams spilt from the corner crushed by the bell, which now lay, with its damaged siblings, under a sheet against the side of the church. But as he rounded the shack, it looked less damaged; its wooden door and small square window were unharmed. George pushed open the door and called into the darkness quietly. "Hello," he said. "It's me."

There was no reply as he stepped inside.

He removed the food parcel from his pocket and the loaf of bread from his jumper, then placed them on the small table underneath the window and peered into the gloom.

Wren was sitting in his regular spot in the darkest corner. His legs were crossed, his eyes were closed, and his bag was by his side.

George slid off his satchel and took a seat at the table, waiting for his friend to join him. While he waited, he idly picked at an old scab on his knee, pulled up his socks, and looked around the sparse shack. Most of Patrick's belongings were gone; he'd left only the table, with its two creaky chairs, and a battered old armchair, next to which was a small wood-burning stove, cold and unused.

A few minutes passed in silence, then Wren opened his eyes and smiled at George. He then spied the parcel of food on the table. "Thank you," he said in his soft, low voice.

"No problem. Easy one today," lied George with a casual shrug. "Any luck last night?"

Wren shook his head and stood, then put the food inside his bag, and took it to an empty corner of the room. As he placed the bag into the corner, there was a barely audible fizzing sound as the bag vanished. As always, George was amazed; it was one of his favourite tricks.

Wren then settled into the battered armchair, his fingers steepled against his chin as he stared at the flagstone floor.

"Do you think someone else found it?" asked George.

"Maybe," he replied, "but they would not know what is it."

George thought about correcting his English but decided against it. He was doing remarkably well for someone who had only been speaking the language for a few months. With every passing week, Wren sounded more and more like an Englishman.

"Are you stuck here without it?" asked George.

"Kelha is," he replied. "I have another way." He pulled back his sleeve, revealing a silver-white bracelet on his wrist. George had seen it before but assumed it was just a piece of jewellery.

"What is it?" George asked.

Wren didn't answer straight away, and George wondered if he would answer at all.

"I sometimes feel I tell you too much, George," Wren said with a grave look.

"No," said George hastily. "No. You can tell me anything. *Everything*. I won't tell." He leaned forward in his chair, eager for him to continue.

There was a long silence, then Wren sighed. "If Kelha heals," he said, "she will send a message to my home. And when they come, they find this." He tapped the bracelet again, then rolled his sleeve back over it.

"And they'll take you home?" George asked.

Wren nodded slowly, then looked away.

Kelha was the ship that had brought Wren to Hurstwick in such spectacular fashion. After Wren's hasty departure from the crash site, her final act was to bury herself deep beneath Oban Wood, where she could heal without being disturbed.

George had once asked Wren to draw her. He drew a perfect cube — not what George had imagined at all. He'd pictured something sleek and strange-looking and was secretly disappointed by the simple drawing. Even so, he desperately wanted to see Kelha up close. Wren talked about her as if she were intelligent — as if she were alive. But without the key, George would never get to see her, and neither would Wren.

The key was the only way to recover Kelha from her hiding place, and at some point, between the crash and Moore's Farm, Wren had lost it. Every night, Wren left Patrick's Corner and re-traced his steps in search of it. On weekends, George would look too, but with such a large area to cover, the task seemed hopeless.

George sat silently, watching Wren, now deep in thought. Looking at him, he found it hard to believe he was the same man he'd discovered in the barn almost four months earlier. No longer did he wear the strange clothes he'd arrived in; instead, he wore the brown trousers and white collarless shirt he'd taken from Mrs Moore's washing line. Mr Moore was broader than Wren, but shorter, so the fit was not perfect. But the green tank top and brown corduroy jacket, which George had found in a box behind the thrift shop on Grundy Street, fit much better. His leather boots, old and in need of repair, came from Mr Furlong's garden shed. Only the mice George had evicted from them would notice their absence.

Wren's long hair was also gone. George had cut it short. He didn't do a great job of it, but thanks to a comb and some of Mr Furlong's Brylcreem, it looked OK.

He now looked quite normal. So much so that George was starting to forget how he'd looked before. But he would always remember those eyes.

Even looking as normal as he did, Wren had to remain hidden within the confines of Patrick's Corner during the day. Most men were overseas fighting; a young man of fighting age, wandering around out of uniform, would attract unwanted attention. So, Wren only emerged in the dead of night and was always back before sunrise.

"I have to go to school now," said George, getting up from his chair reluctantly. "Tomorrow is Saturday. I'll go up to the woods first thing with Chip. Unless you find it tonight, of course." He turned to leave. "Oh, I almost forgot." He reached into his satchel and pulled out a book. "Another one from the library. This one's about history. Not *my* favourite subject, but I thought you might like it. It's got kings and queens in it."

George tried to get two books a week out for Wren, who would devour each one in a single sitting. He made no requests for the type of book, but they all seemed to hold his interest. But books were not Wren's only source of education. He had a way of learning that George could never properly understand. Wren would see something new and unknown to him, close his eyes for a few short seconds, and by the time he opened them again, he knew more about the thing than George did.

"Thank you, George," said Wren, receiving the book and holding it with both hands, as if it were a sacred object.

"You're welcome," George replied, smiling. "Finished this one?" From the floor next to the chair, he picked up *From Mine to Mill — The Story of British Steel*.

Wren nodded and George placed it in his satchel, then turned and left the shack.

He followed the river back to the small wooden bridge where he'd first seen Wren, then made his way through the thicket of trees to emerge onto Church Lane. He joined the narrow back lanes behind the cottages and ran to school as fast as he could. A bell rang in the distance. George was going to be late for school — again.

8

A POCKET FULL OF SPROUTS

Christmas Day 1944

"Yummy. Sprouts," said George, a little too enthusiastically.

"You don't like sprouts," said Mrs Furlong, eyeing him with suspicion.

"At Christmas I do." He smiled and held out his plate. "I love 'em," he said.

Mrs Furlong spooned two steaming sprouts onto his plate.

"Can I have more please?" he said, still smiling.

Mr Furlong now gave him a quizzical look. "You alright, George? Didn't bang your head on the ice this morning, did you?"

George smiled and adjusted his paper crown.

That morning he'd been out early and fought his way to the shack through waist-high snowdrifts to give Wren his present. He'd made him a model of Kelha out of wood and painted it black. Wren said it was perfect.

But it wasn't nearly as impressive as the gift George had received from his parents: a wooden spitfire, carved by his dad and painted by his mother. It was beautiful and was now the most precious thing George owned.

"Pass the carrots please, Mary," said Mr Furlong.

Mary had arrived the day before and would be staying until the day after Boxing Day. It had been several months since George had seen her, and he loved having her back. The place felt warmer and happier with her around.

"So lovely to have you back, dear," Mrs Furlong said for the hundredth time. She loaded Mary's plate with sprouts, and Mary quickly passed a few along to George when she wasn't looking.

Mr Furlong led them in prayer. He gave thanks for having Mary back and asked that George's parents be kept safe from harm. After that, they pulled homemade Christmas crackers and ate a modest Christmas dinner, followed by the most delicious Christmas pudding George had ever tasted. Then, feeling full and content, they listened to the King's speech on the wireless.

Carols filled the airwaves when Mary and George volunteered to wash the dishes, and Mr and Mrs Furlong retired to the sitting room for a game of cards and a small glass of sherry.

Mary washed, and George, standing on a small step next to her, dried.

"Who gets the sprouts?" she said, smiling while taking in the snowy scene outside the window.

"What?" said George, almost dropping a plate.

"The sprouts in your pocket?"

"Excuse me?" George tried to hide his panic. "I don't know what you—"

"Yes, you do, George Moss. I saw you sneakily stuffing them into your pockets." She gave him a sideways glance. "Besides," she said, screwing up her face, "you stink of sprouts."

"Ah," he said, "You saw that. You won't tell, will you?"

"I won't, if you tell me what you intend to do with them. Are you building a weapon to kill the Nazis? Because that might just work."

"Pigs," George blurted out, not catching Mary's joke.

"Pigs?" Mary blinked.

"Yes. Pigs," he said again, this time with more certainty.

"Go on..." she said, taking another plate from the pile of dishes and dunking it in hot water.

"Sorry?"

"Tell me about the pigs."

"Right, yes...of course.... Well, they're for the pigs...for Christmas."

"For the pigs...for Christmas," she repeated slowly.

"Yes. Well, they should have a good Christmas too, right?" he said. "Just because they're pigs doesn't mean they shouldn't have a nice Christmas, does it? It's for the ones in the field up by Windmill Hill. Miserable-looking things, they are."

"So you're giving them sprouts to cheer them up? Mum's sprouts?" She stared at George for what felt like an age. "Poor pigs," she said, laughing. "You're an odd one, George. But you don't fool me. I'll find out what you're *really* up to." She smiled playfully and blew soap bubbles from her hand into his face.

George wiped them away with the tea towel and smiled back innocently, wondering if he'd got away with it.

"Come with me," he said, pushing his luck. "They're really nice pigs. I've named them and everything."

"In this weather? No way." She shook her head. "You're quite mad, you know. Anyway, you won't make it to Windmill Hill and back in time for church."

George had forgotten about church.

Wrapped in their finest and warmest winter clothing, Mary and George walked through the snow-covered churchyard, behind Mr and Mrs Furlong.

The sky was darkening, but the snow-covered ground held on to its light like a sponge. Lights within the church filtered through the stained glass, painting the surrounding trees with blues, reds and yellows. Any other night, huge black curtains would have covered those windows, but a few months earlier, the *blackout* had been relaxed to a dim-out, and the mayor of Hurstwick had insisted that St Mary's would be a beacon of hope on Christmas night. If the tower still had bells, George was sure they would be ringing loud in defiance.

A large portion of the church building was now deemed safe; only the tower was still out of bounds. The area around it was cordoned with a rope perimeter, ineffective against the local children, who liked to play on the piles of rubble stacked high against the tower walls. George had seen them more than once being chased off by an angry-looking Patrick.

George looked up at Mary, who had not said a word since leaving the cottage. Her cheeks were red with the chill air, and she looked nervous.

"You OK?" he asked. "Don't you like church?"

"I do like church, George. Just not fond of all the gossip that happens before and after."

George didn't understand, but nodded as if he did.

They had reached the open door of the small, ornate porch where Mr and Mrs Furlong were stood talking to Father Elliott. He was a young man and new to the town, having arrived just a few months before the spire had left.

"Well, not to worry," he was saying to them both, his

head tilted, his hands clasped by his chest. "I'm sure young Mary will find an upstanding man after the war.... Ah, Mary, there you are. So nice to see you again."

"Father Elliott." She nodded politely, but George saw annoyance flicker across her brow.

"Well, let's not dawdle out here in the cold, get inside, you lot," he said, smiling and waving them in. He then craned his neck, looking past them to greet more members of his congregation as they advanced gingerly up the icy path.

Before following the others through, George glanced back towards the one-armed angel that marked the entrance to Patrick's Corner. He was desperate to see Wren, mostly so he could get rid of the sprouts. Their dampness was seeping through the lining of his pockets. Thankfully, he couldn't smell them anymore. But others could. He'd noticed heads turning in his direction, noses twitching with subtle expressions of disgust — some not subtle at all.

After three carols, which George mouthed more than he sang, he made for his escape.

Holding his stomach, he tapped on the arm of Mrs Furlong and pleaded to be excused. "Eaten too many of your lovely sprouts," he said. Mrs Furlong, having noticed the smell too, willingly let him go, telling him to head straight back to the cottage. Mary shook her head with a knowing smile.

Alone in the church porch, George held on to the ice-cold handle of the heavy door and pulled it open. He stepped outside and closed it quietly, just as the church organ sounded the opening chords of *O Come, All Ye Faithful*.

The glowing churchyard was empty and still. George ignored the paths, and dashed across undisturbed snow towards Patrick's Corner. In places, the snow reached his knees, so he slowed as he ploughed through, careful not to trip on buried tombstones.

Under the blank stare of the one-armed angel, George ducked beneath a snow-laden branch of a fir tree. As he did, he noticed the dark undergrowth ahead suddenly brighten. He looked behind in time to see Mary's silhouette at the porch door. When she turned to close it, George dropped to his knees, taking cover behind a snowy shrub.

He held his breath, watching her as she stood, scanning the churchyard. She was looking for him.

Not seeing him on the path leading back to Church Lane, she stepped forward and looked out towards Patrick's Corner. But with the door now closed, it was too dark to see anything. She opened her handbag and rummaged inside. A second later, she clicked on her blackout torch. Like all blackout torches, the light was feeble, and not nearly bright enough to reach George and his hiding place. But she wasn't looking that far ahead; she was looking down to the ground, to the virgin snow to the side of the path. Correction — the *once* virgin snow. It was now split by a deep and narrow trench that would lead her straight to George.

His heart sank as he watched her following the trail. His only option would be to go to her, and head back to the cottage together.

He sighed with defeat. But as he stood, a firm hand on his shoulder pushed him back down. It was Wren, crouching next to him. His dark eyes moved from George to Mary, who was still walking towards them.

George pointed to the tracks in front of them. "We have to go," he whispered, "she found my track, she'll find us."

Wren just stared ahead, watching as Mary got closer.

"Come on," urged George, starting to panic. But to George's annoyance, Wren continued to stare, looking as serene as ever. He then turned to George and smiled.

George felt dismayed. "Do you want her to find you? Because she will, you know. And when she does—"

Wren placed a finger on one side of George's chin. And with a gentle push he directed his head, and attention, back to Mary.

She was now halfway between the church and the angel, but she was no longer walking. Instead, she was looking around, confused, her warm breath suspended in the freezing air around her. "George!" she called out into the emptiness. Her voice sounded small and muffled, and George wanted to go to her.

Why had she stopped? he wondered. Then, movement on the ground caught his eye, and he understood.

The deep channel in the snow, the track that betrayed his position, was closing. It was as if the two sides were being sewn together from the bottom up, leaving the snow looking undisturbed and pure once more. George clapped a hand over his mouth, catching a short laugh of wonder before it could escape. Mary hadn't heard it. She continued to peer into the darkness and at the ground around her, no doubt questioning her sanity.

George felt sorry for her standing alone, with only the soft sounds of carols from the church for company. "She looks cold," he whispered. "Can you make her go back inside?"

Wren said nothing at first. He was looking at Mary; his eyes seemed to be smiling.

"Please?" said George.

Wren nodded, then looked up to the church roof, where a breeze arose from nowhere, lifting a thin layer of snow into the air that was lightly deposited as fluffy flakes around Mary below. She shivered but continued to peer into the gloom. Another dusting swirled about her, more this time, swept up from the ground. She laughed as she watched the flurry encircle her like stars, caught in the dim glow of her torch, while the rest of the churchyard remained still.

As the flurry faded, Mary glanced once more into the darkness, looked at the virgin snow ahead of her, then retreated into the warmth of the church.

"Thank you," whispered George, as he sank back from the bush and looked at Wren, who didn't seem to notice him at all. He was staring at the closed church door, smiling.

Eventually, Wren turned to him. "You smell...horrible," he said.

"Yeah. Sorry about that."

9

PARTY TIME

May 1945

It was a bright spring morning as George ran through a sea of bluebells, which broke against the old stone shack in Patrick's Corner. He had news for Wren. Not news of a found key, which George had lost hope of ever finding, and suspected Wren had, too, but good news nonetheless.

George burst through the door eagerly, but found the shack empty.

He glanced into the two rubble-strewn back rooms, but they were just as empty. He thought it strange; Wren was always back by morning; he searched for the key under cover of night, then hid out in the shack by day. That was the routine. So far, it had never changed.

George stood in the doorway and looked outside. His concern was starting to grow, but not yet outweighing his joy for last night's news. Maybe his friends had found him, taken him home. Or the man from the War Office had finally tracked him down, and was currently interrogating him in a darkened room, with one of those bright lamps shining in his eyes. He hoped he was wrong on both counts, especially the second one.

"Wren!" he called, careful not to be heard by anyone further afield, but there was no reply.

Deflated, he sat on the doorstep and gazed upon Patrick's Corner. It was teeming with life. Blackbirds, jays, and woodpigeons busied themselves collecting twigs from the sun-dappled ground, while woodpeckers drummed overhead. And for the first time, sounds from outside the corner could be heard; laughter and music leaked through the trees, making the town feel closer than ever before.

There was a sound high above him, a strange sort of bird call. At first, he paid it little attention, but its regularity piqued his interest. He stood and looked up into the canopy, which glowed as the May sunshine filtered through. Only the giant pine tree stubbornly refused to allow sunlight in, leaving the ground around it devoid of colour and life. The bird call continued. But now it was accompanied by movement. It was coming from the pine.

George walked to the tree, ducked under its low branches, and entered its cool, hall-like interior. He then walked across the springy pine-covered ground to the trunk and looked up. High above him, looking tiny, was Wren. He was smiling down at George and gesturing for him to follow.

George prided himself as an excellent climber and found the ascent easy. With each branch within easy grasp of the last, he made swift progress. But about halfway up, he made the mistake of looking down. He'd never been so far from the ground before in his life.

"This is fine," he called up to Wren. "I can see from here. Lovely view." But he couldn't see *anything* through the tree's thick crown.

"No. You must continue, George," replied Wren. "You will not fall. I will not allow it."

George remembered Wren saving him from the fall in the barn, and he found the courage to continue.

As he climbed, the sound of celebration grew louder, and it became brighter around him. Soon he felt a cool breeze on his skin. After a few more feet, he was at the top.

Wren was sat, looking very relaxed, on a branch that seemed too thin to hold him. He looked comfortable and at home — so much so that it made George feel uncomfortable; he hugged the tree for reassurance, then followed Wren's gaze.

Through the branches to the west, George could see Bramfield Park, its broad trees shimmering in the breeze. The music he could hear was coming from the bandstand, where a jubilant crowd were gathered, dancing and waving flags joyfully.

"We won," said George. "They surrendered."

"So I see."

George smiled, then looked south to High Street. It, too, was alive with activity. Packed full of people, it was busier than market day. A large lorry edged its way through the crowd, people sitting on its roof and clinging to its sides, cheering and waving. Bunting was being tied to every lamp-post and would soon cover the entire length of the street, ready for the biggest party the town had ever witnessed. Church bells carried on the wind from neighbouring villages. But no bells rang out in Hurstwick. Out past the edge of town, a train sent out celebratory whistles. Its grey-white steam beat rhythmically upwards as it thundered through the rolling countryside.

George took in the view, then turned his attention back to Wren and the tree in which they sat. There was cover, but not enough to hide them completely. "What if someone sees us?" George asked.

"If they see me, I will have nobody to blame but myself,"

he said, smiling across to George. "You have done so much for me. And you have done all you can."

George smiled back, then sighed. He wanted to get back down to where he felt less exposed. But Wren didn't look ready to leave. He was looking back out to the crowd in the park. For a moment, George thought he saw Wren sway with the music. But then he stopped, and shot George a brief look to see if he'd noticed. George hid his smile by looking away. "What are you doing up here, anyway?" asked George.

"I often come up here. I find it peaceful."

"But what do you *do* up here?"

"I watch."

"What do you watch?"

"Everything."

"Why?"

He looked at George, then seemed to lose focus, his stare drifting past him as he considered his answer. "It's what I do," he said finally, his eyes locking on his again. "It's what I am."

"I don't understand."

"I am a Watcher." He looked back towards the park.

Wren had never talked about himself before. In the past, he'd asked George many questions, and George did his best to answer. Yes, he'd told George about the key and Kelha, but that was because he'd needed his help; this was the first time Wren had talked about *himself*, and George wasn't going to let it stop there.

"Are you like a birdwatcher?"

"No, George. I Watch our borders."

"What for?"

"Normally, for protection."

"From?"

Wren opened his mouth to talk, but then closed it again and turned away.

George didn't push for more. Those tiny bits of information, which he didn't fully understand, felt like treasure. Maybe he would share more another day. But the sounds of celebration reminded George that his time with Wren was ending.

"I can't believe it's over," said George. "I thought the war would last forever."

"You will be with your parents soon?"

George nodded. He couldn't wait to be with them. At the same time, he didn't want to say goodbye to Wren. He hated the idea of leaving him alone, with no one to help him. "Will you be alright on your own? Without me?" A knot tightened in his throat as he spoke.

Wren shifted on his branch to face George. "Yes," he said. "Do not worry about me. I may not find the key, but Kelha will soon heal. I can feel her. She gets stronger every day." He smiled and reached across, placing a hand on George's shoulder.

Another question bubbled up, and George couldn't stop it. "Were you watching us from up there?" He nodded skywards.

Wren's smile dissolved, and he withdrew his hand. "Yes," he whispered.

"Why?"

"I watch what I am asked to watch."

"How long were you up there?"

Wren paused, then said, "For a long time."

"Are there more? Watching us now, I mean."

Wren looked to the band on his wrist and pulled his sleeve over it. Then he closed his eyes and shook his head.

George wasn't sure if that meant *no, there are no more*, or *no, I don't wish to talk about it*. Either way, George wished he'd never asked. He should have been satisfied with the nuggets of treasure Wren had happily provided, but he'd been greedy and asked for too much.

"You should go, George," said Wren softly.

"Sorry?"

"Please, George."

"But...I didn't mean to upset you. You don't have to tell me anything." George shrugged and tried to make light of the situation. "I was just curious, that's all."

Wren turned away.

"Wren?"

"Please go. Be with them." He nodded towards the town.

George stared at Wren's back, not knowing what to say. "I'm sorry," he whispered. "I'll leave you alone."

Wren said nothing, and George began the slow climb down, trying hard not to cry, afraid he'd never see his friend again.

"Wait!" Wren called from above.

George was almost at the bottom. He looked up as Wren climbed rapidly down until he was on the branch just above George. He was smiling broadly at George and looked at him for the longest time, then said, "I don't think I want to be alone, George. I've been alone for a long time. I want to go out there. I want to go to the party."

"Wha...to the party?" said George, convinced he'd misheard him.

"Yes, George — to the party."

Wren was determined to go into town, and there was nothing George could do or say to stop him. He followed warily behind as Wren walked through the churchyard gate and turned towards the high street and Station Road. But George's concerns about Wren being noticed, bundled into a van, and taken away for questioning, were unfounded. With celebrations in full swing, no-one paid him any attention. After all, he looked and sounded more like a local than ever. Only his stillness, in stark contrast to the excitement of those around him, set him apart. George relaxed a little and allowed himself to enjoy the moment.

As George watched him walk among the locals, he marvelled at their ignorance. These people were in the presence of the most interesting person to ever set foot in their little town, yet not one of them gave him a second look. They were a part of a historic event, that, in the grand scheme of things, dwarfed the one they were celebrating. If only they knew. But no one would ever know. For a moment, George felt sorry for them.

But they were joyous in their ignorance. There was an energy in the town as hope and relief crackled in the air like electricity. Music from gramophones placed by open windows flooded the streets as British reserve was cast aside and people hugged and danced and sang. The lorry full of revellers had returned. It tooted its horn, causing Wren to jump. He laughed at his own reaction, then turned to George, who smiled reassuringly.

Wren's curiosity pulled him in every direction. Each second brought something new to see, new to hear. They passed a pub where a group of singing men burst from the doors carrying a piano and its pianist into the street. The pub landlady followed, protesting at first, but was soon swept up in the revelry.

Down residential side streets, they saw tables set outside packed with people eating, drinking, and waving flags. Every street they passed was a barrage of colour and sound.

Eventually, they found themselves being herded along into Bramfield Park where they watched the joyous crowd assembled around the flag-covered bandstand. The band played as people, young and old, danced together. Those too old or too tired to dance sat on benches clapping in time to the music, while a long conga line weaved and ducked through the crowd. Children chased each other between the dancing couples, toy aeroplanes held high as they continued the battle for the skies. But for some, the celebrations seemed bittersweet. George could see them at the edges of the park, smiles not quite reaching their eyes as they looked upon the crowd, longing to see their loved ones among them.

Wren found a space standing in the shade of a large oak, while George sat on the grass under its smaller neighbour. With a calm fascination, Wren looked upon the crowd. And the longer Wren stood under that tree, watching, the more he seemed to loosen up. He stood a little less straight, a little less stiff. And his foot started to tap in rhythm to the music and his hand casually slipped into his jacket pocket. He was fitting in.

There was laughter coming from behind. George turned to see a group of young men and women, arms linked, stumbling across the road towards them. They passed under the oak, crashing into Wren, swallowing him up. Only one of the group noticed him. She slammed into him so hard she nearly knocked him over. She grabbed him by the arm, apologising while laughing, and tried to pull him along.

George froze. It was Mary.

"The party," said Mary, smiling widely at Wren, "is over there," she threw a thumb over her shoulder towards the bandstand. "No point just watching."

Wren didn't speak. Instead, he smiled and politely shook his head.

"*Come on*," she said, looking him right in the eyes. "Come dance with me. I mean us...."

Still, Wren didn't move.

George got to his feet, watching intently, his heart throbbing in his neck. This was the first time someone, other than himself, had taken any notice of Wren. Why, thought George, did it have to be Mary?

Mary's carefree manner dissolved, and she let go of Wren's arm, composing herself. Her smile was still there but was now different, smaller, unsure. She tilted her head, then pulled a stray lock of hair back behind her ear, and considered Wren more closely. George waited for her expression to change to one of shock or fear, but it didn't. She looked puzzled by his appearance but not horrified — and her smile was growing again. Wren held her gaze but said nothing.

"Come on, Mary!" called a woman from her group, who were now almost at the bandstand. "Bring your handsome friend."

Just then, another group emerged and engulfed the pair, whisking Mary away, but leaving Wren standing alone once more. From the midst of the jubilant group, and unable to escape their gravity, Mary looked back and smiled at Wren. She raised a hand in a slight wave and was then consumed by the joyous crowd.

George fell to the ground with relief while Wren's eyes remained fixed to the point where he'd last seen her.

After some time, Wren settled against the wide trunk of the oak. There he remained until the sun dipped behind the trees and the crowd thinned. Most moved on to the local pubs, aiming to keep the party going until sunrise. Those who remained lit a bonfire, and with arms interlocked they circled the spitting flames, singing, laughing, and falling.

Wren and George left the park to wander the streets and cobbled alleys, Wren still spellbound by the mood of the town.

"I'm tired," said George, fighting a yawn. He leaned

against a lamppost, and feeling a chill, placed his hands in his pockets. "I need to go to bed. I'm gonna head back. You should get back, too. You were lucky earlier. I mean, someone could have noticed you. *Mary* noticed something about you, if you ask me. She was looking at you all funny."

"Mary," said Wren.

George thought he saw a smile creep at the edge of his mouth as he said her name. "Yeah. *Mary,*" George said. "She works for the *War Office*; she could get you arrested, you know. Which reminds me; what would you have said if she'd asked for your name?"

"I would have told her and asked for hers?" He sounded unsure.

"Just as I thought," said George, more to himself. "And how do you think she would react to a strange name like Wren? It would have led to questions like, where are you from, Wren? What do you do, Wren?" He sighed. "Do you understand? It was dangerous. If you're gonna continue popping into town willy-nilly, we need to work on your story. OK?"

Wren smiled and nodded.

"Good," said George, fighting another yawn, this time unsuccessfully. "But not tonight. We can work on it tomorrow. I'm exhausted."

"Goodnight, George," said Wren. "And thank you. I am glad I got to see all of this from down here." He inhaled a lungful of night air. "It is more real...up close."

Wren walked out onto the street alone.

With the blackouts removed from the windows, pools of warm light settled on the cobbles. It was a street Wren had walked many times in the dead of night, but always in the shadows and away from the eyes of others. On those occasions, he had been searching, listening.

Wren's attention was drawn to the sound of breaking glass. He looked up to a window above the barbershop and the rooms occupied by Henry Crinklaw. His light was on.

He had watched the man closely and at the beginning, had even ventured into his room's unseen. But his search had turned up nothing of interest. They had nothing and knew nothing.

Wren looked through the wall at the man inside. He was slouching on a wooden chair, smoking while holding an empty glass in a limp hand. A smashed bottle lay by the foot of the wall he was staring at. The glass followed the bottle, and Wren looked away.

He continued walking. Drawn to the sound of music, he found himself outside The Plough, a large pub next to the police station. The piano was back inside, and the tune it now played was more mellow than before, accompanied by a multitude of voices singing as one. Silhouettes of the patrons swayed behind the latticed windows. He listened to their song. And then another song, and another. As he listened, a memory came to him; one from long ago. From a time when his watchtower was still within earshot of those he protected. He would listen to their songs. And sometimes he would turn his gaze towards them, and the warm glow of their fires.

The memory dissolved as a man and woman exited the pub, arm in arm. They didn't notice him, and Wren stood aside as they passed.

Further along the street, Wren stopped by the shop window of Waldron Antiques and gazed upon its contents. Inside was a large oval dining table, dressed with silver tableware. It was surrounded by lamps, coat stands, paintings and mirrors. A row of grandfather clocks of varying size lined the wall, their pendulums swinging lazily back and forth. And there was something else. A glow. A glow that was familiar to him. Was it the key?

As he moved closer to the window, he quickly realised the light was not coming from inside. It was a reflection. He raised his arm. It was the glow of his bracelet, pulsating at first like a heartbeat, then increasing in speed until it maintained a solid radiance that felt warm against his skin.

Kelha had healed.

By now she would have sent her call. They would be on their way. They would trace the bracelet, then take him home. Home.

After all this time, he expected to feel something, relief maybe. All he felt was guilt.

"Put that light out!" came a voice from behind. It was followed by a drunken laugh. Wren covered his wrist and turned to see three men in uniform stagger from a dark alley.

"Apologies for my friend," slurred one of them. "Too much to drink, methinks."

The drunkest of the three reached out and gave Wren a friendly pat on the shoulder, then ruffled his hair as they stumbled past. They mumbled some parting pleasantries and continued to meander up the street. Each sang their own version of the same song as they went.

Wren looked back to the window, then to his reflection. He raised a hand to straighten his hair. On the way down, his hand paused by his face. He ran a finger down the bridge of his nose, then stroked his jawline. It was a face that had once been so alien to him, but now it felt like his own. The thousands of human faces around him had once all looked the same, but now he could see the subtle differences between each one. As he inspected his face in the window, he could see clearly how much he looked like George.

He placed a finger over the glowing band and watched the light fade to nothing. Slowly, he walked to the top of High Street, where he stopped and stared at the band once more, mindful of protocol.

Evidence of your presence, both physical and in the memory of others, must be destroyed.

He let out a heavy breath. They would be here soon. He would go to the woods; he would wait for them there.

Laughter from across the road pulled him from his thoughts. In the darkness of Bramfield Park, a bonfire still popped and crackled, illuminating the faces assembled around it. One face caught his eye. It was Mary. She sat, hugging her knees, staring into the flaming glow with a subtle smile. While those around her huddled together, laughing and talking, she stared dreamily into the fire. A young man fed the flames with the branch of a tree, sending embers swirling into the black sky. Wren watched the fiery fragments climb, then dissolve, until all he could see was the blanket of stars above him.

He looked back to Mary, then towards Church Lane, shrouded in darkness. As he did, he felt the burden of the band upon his wrist and the duty he was expected to fulfil.

A sound reached him from far away. It was like distant thunder. He tilted his head to listen to the low rumble he could now feel through his feet. He turned and walked up a deserted Station Road. As the sound grew, his walk turned into a jog, then a run, until he was sprinting down the centre of Station Road, past pubs, where music and laughter could still be heard, past the dark alleys, the sleeping shops, the war memorial.

At the end of the road was the railway station: a red-brick building, silent and in shadow, its hefty wooden double doors closed for the night. At incredible speed, he leapt the small flower-filled roundabout set before it, heading straight for the doors. With a flick of his hand, they burst from their hinges, landing with a crash inside the ticket hall. He slowed to a walk as he passed the two ticket windows with their blinds pulled down, then made his way across the walkway that formed a bridge spanning the tracks below. Stairs on either side led down to the platforms, but he wouldn't need those. Instead, he remained on the bridge, illuminated by the weak electric lightbulb above him.

He looked south, listening intently as the rumble grew louder. The track below clicked and vibrated with a high-pitched ring.

Lights appeared in the distance.

This was much slower than the passenger train he'd seen earlier, but he'd seen this type many times before. It crawled towards him, its heavy load in no rush to arrive promptly. The dark lumbering mass of metal and wood passed under the bridge, shrouding Wren in a cloud of steam.

When the steam cleared, the bridge was empty. Wren was gone.

Crinklaw sat looking at the broken bottle and glass on the floor. He really should clean that up, he thought, and he regretted throwing the glass. He would need to replace that before the landlady noticed.

He stood, then almost fell, then walked to the drinks cabinet and fumbled around for another bottle. There was sherry, gin, and vodka. All excellent substitutes, but he wanted whisky; he was in a whisky mood.

"Pub!" he said out loud to the empty room. He disliked the idea of spending tonight with the locals, and would much prefer to be back in London with Philby, Perkins, McKinsey, and the rest of his lot. But his desire for whisky was strong. And it did sound like they were having a bloody good time out there.

He took his coat from the back of the door but struggled to put it on. His arm, or the sleeve of the coat, possibly both, was refusing to cooperate. When he directed his wandering gaze towards the area of difficulty, he noticed he was still holding a bottle of vodka. He staggered back to the cabinet and returned the bottle with a loud crash, allowing the coat to slip on with ease. Next, he scanned the room for his hat. This would be much easier if the room stood still, he thought. Eventually, he found his hat, and the door, and he stepped into the hallway. Before closing the door, he reached in and flicked the light switch, leaving the room in darkness.

Only, it wasn't dark.

Years of habit, of being careful and not wasting energy, brought him back into the room. It must be the desk lamp, he thought, and switched it off. But as the lamp was already off, he only succeeded in making the room even brighter. He turned it back off, quickly, then noticed his legs were glowing; the light was coming from *under* the desk.

He knelt and saw a blue-white glow pouring from the carry holes cut into the sides of a cardboard box. He dragged it out, tore off the lid and stared inside. It contained everything found at the crash site. It wasn't much, and all of it had been labelled as irrelevant. He was supposed to have thrown it away months ago. There was a man's belt, a broken portion of a walking cane, a buckle from a shoe, a shotgun cartridge, and an old boot. The item currently glowing, casting a shadow of Crinklaw across the ceiling, had been labelled *large ball bearing*. No one had looked twice at the thing.

Crinklaw cupped it in his hands, feeling suddenly elated. The case hadn't progressed for nine months and had been driving him slowly mad. On paper, his assignment was an exciting prospect: a Nazi secret weapon that could leave a vast area of destruction without explosion or fire damage and leave no trace of the weapon itself: quite a challenge, and one he was *initially* geared up for. And when the theory had gone from German secret weapon to something of an extra-terrestrial nature, the little boy in him had been awoken and his enthusiasm taken to a level he didn't think possible. But when reality set in, and the answers failed to reveal themselves, it dawned on him that he'd been side-lined in this war. While his colleagues were cracking codes and working behind enemy lines, lapping up medals and recognition, he was wandering the back lanes of a nowhere town, stagnant, forgotten; no progress, no leads, no glory. Until this.

The light then died.

"No." He shook it. "Come back." He shook it again and slapped it against the palm of his hand. It had been warm, but now he could feel it cooling. "No, no, no." he began to sob.

Then he fell back to the floor and looked up at the dark ceiling. He hiccupped and wiped his mouth with his sleeve.

Moments later, he was asleep.

10

THE KEY TO KELHA

With the war in Europe officially over, George expected a letter to arrive at any moment. It would tell him it was time to return home, which was something he desperately wanted; he longed to be with his parents again. But not yet. Wren still needed him.

That morning, George woke early and wrote a letter of his own. In it, he told his mother that he needed to stay for at least another month to help Mr Furlong down at the allotment. It was a lie, and he hated lying. But George convinced himself it was for good reason.

Deep down, though, George suspected Wren would be fine without him. Last night, he had proven that he could blend in well enough with the locals. But if Wren was ever to have a conversation with one, he would need to have a story — an identity, a background. One week to come up with something convincing, and another week to rehearse until it was *completely* believable, should do the trick, he thought.

With his letter in hand, George rounded the corner onto an almost deserted high street. There was a chill in the air, and the bright morning sun touched only the roofs and chimneys of the buildings, leaving the street dull in contrast to the brilliant blue sky. The road was littered with newspapers, paper hats and confetti. Most of the bunting was still up, flapping in the breeze, but much had come loose and was snaking across the grey cobblestones.

On a typical Wednesday the shops would be open by now. But not today. The few that were, lay empty. A lonely barber rested on his broom, looking out from his window. A woman swept the pavement in front of the empty tea room next door. She hummed a tune, smiling to herself.

Somewhere behind George a door slammed, the noise of it echoing down the quiet street. He spun in time to see Mr Crinklaw powering towards him, his stride long and full of purpose. *This was it. He'd somehow worked it all out, and now he knew everything.* George tensed his shoulders, waiting to be seized by the man who was now almost upon him.

"Out of the way, boy," Crinklaw snapped, as he charged past, almost tripping over him.

George sighed with relief, but it was short-lived. He had seen something in Crinklaw's face he didn't like. It was a look of triumph. He'd found something out, learned something of importance.

George turned and followed the man, alternating between running and walking to keep up. He wasn't worried about losing him, though; there was only one place he'd be going.

As the large red-brick building of the police station came into view, George slowed. Crinklaw dashed up the steps, clearing three at a time, and disappeared inside. George counted to twenty, then followed him in, walking as quietly as he could down a hallway lined with shiny white bricks.

The tall wood-panelled front desk in the waiting room

was unmanned and its flap, leading to the office behind, was left open. George heard the tapping of a typewriter, indistinct conversation, and music coming from the other side. He crept to the desk and peered over.

A small group of police officers were gathered by the wireless at the far wall. They seemed cheerful and were talking and laughing while they drank from enamel mugs. A woman sat a few desks away, typing, trying to work while keeping an ear on the light-hearted conversation.

But the conversation stopped when Crinklaw appeared from a side door holding a small box and a folder. The mood in the room changed instantly; the banter ceased, the music was switched off, and the officers disbanded, moving back to their desks to look busy.

Crinklaw paid them no attention. He made straight for his small wooden desk, home to a black typewriter, a lamp, and a telephone. He placed down the folder and the box, then hung his coat over the back of the chair before sitting. Then he took a sheet of paper from the folder, fed it into the typewriter, and started to type. He was not good at typing. He stabbed at the keys slowly and deliberately, clunk, clunk, clunk.

"Hetty could do that for you," said a large balding officer, walking to his desk with a cup of tea and a newspaper.

Crinklaw ignored the man and continued to stab. Key. By key. By key.

"Please yourself," grumbled the man, as he sat down.

The office gradually got busier, while George's side of the desk remained empty. He watched as more staff filed through the back door. One officer, a red-haired young man, entered with a look of urgency about him. He approached the older, balding officer, who was now comfortably engrossed in his newspaper, and stood by his desk.

"Sir," the young officer said to announce his presence.

"Ah, Ian," he said, placing the paper down. He leaned back in his chair, interlocking his fingers over his sizeable gut. "So. What's your take on it, then?"

"It's strange, sir. Never seen anyfink like it. The doors 'ave been completely taken off their 'inges."

"And what's strange about that?"

"Well. These are big heavy doors, sir. The force needed to do that would've been immense."

"A car?"

"Well, that's the strangest bit, sir. There's no sign of any impact on the doors themselves."

"Strange indeed." The large officer shot a glance to Mr Crinklaw, who had stopped attacking his typewriter, and was now listening. He then looked back to the young officer. "Anything stolen?" he asked.

"No, sir."

"Not much we can do, then. Write it up," he said and returned to his newspaper and cup of tea.

"Yes, sir," said the young officer, turning on his heels to write his report.

Crinklaw returned his focus to the typewriter. He continued to stab out the last few lines, then removed the paper and placed it into an envelope, which was sealed and placed into a brown folder containing a stack of documents.

He looked around to see if anybody was watching, then slid the small cardboard box closer and removed the lid. After a second glance around, he reached into his coat pocket and removed a small metal object. George's mouth fell open. He knew immediately what it was. The object, now being placed carefully into the small brown box, was the key to Kelha.

He watched on, unblinking, as Crinklaw retrieved a leather briefcase from under his desk, flicked open the brass buckles, and placed both the folder and box inside.

"Nigel!" he called.

The desk sergeant George had spoken to almost a year before came into view. "Sir?" he said, standing casually next to Crinklaw's desk, hands in pockets.

"This needs to get to the War Office immediately. Direct to Malcolm Haywood. *Only* Malcolm Haywood, understood?"

"Direct to Malcolm Haywood, only Malcolm Haywood," repeated Nigel almost mockingly. "Got it, sir."

Nigel took the case, went to his desk, picked up a car key, then left by the back door. Crinklaw watched him go, a subtle look of satisfaction fixed across his face. He stood and put on his hat and coat. That was George's cue to get low and out of sight. Seconds later, Crinklaw passed through the reception and off towards the exit. Outside, he turned right, back the way he came. George followed but turned left, running alongside the black iron railings towards the side road, leading to the car park. Somehow, he had to stop that car.

George jumped backwards, narrowly avoiding the large black car as it roared its way onto High Street, sending confetti spiralling in its wake. Within seconds, it had disappeared around the bend in the road. The sound of its engine faded to nothing, leaving only the sound of distant church bells.

The *key* was gone. He had been too slow.

He felt like shouting and stamping his feet. Instead, he sat down at the side of the road and buried his head into his arms.

Wait a minute. Church bells?

The church *had* no bells.

George stood quickly. They were the bells of the level crossing.

Hope returned to him as he ran as fast as he could towards the sound. Moments later, he rounded the bend and found the car. Its path to London blocked by the long white gates of the level crossing. There was still a chance.

George approached the car cautiously, looking around to see if he was being watched. But this was the quiet end of High Street. There were no shops here, just a car repair garage, the dry cleaners, and the entrance to the coal yard. All were closed. The guard, who had shut the gates, now stood by them looking up the track, waiting for the train to arrive. George was almost in touching distance of the car, but was acting faster than he could think. He had no idea what he was going to do; he just knew he had to do something.

The train appeared. Its deep rumble drummed against George's chest, and the screech of metal on metal split the air and scratched at his teeth. He was in luck; it was a freight train, and was long, noisy, and very, very slow. It would give him time to think. Nigel, also expecting a long wait, switched off his engine, lit a cigarette and opened a newspaper.

George folded the now crumpled letter to his mother into his pocket, and, with one final look around, dived behind the car. Then he slowly raised himself up and looked through the back window. Nigel's newspaper blocked the rear-view mirror, allowing George to remain unseen as he pressed his face against the glass. The case didn't seem to be on the backseat. When the guard returned to his gatehouse, George positioned himself under the car's rear side window, to get a better look into the back. No. It definitely wasn't there. It had to be in the front.

What would he do once he'd found the case? He

couldn't just snatch it and run; he'd be caught. Somehow he'd have to distract the driver, then take the box from the case without raising suspicion. But how?

The train continued to rumble on by, only slightly quicker than walking pace. But it *would* eventually pass, so George needed to think, and act, quickly.

He thought about letting a tyre down, then snatching the key as Nigel got out to inflate it. But he didn't know how to let a tyre down. In the desperate hope it was already deflated, he looked at the wheel. No such luck.

But looking at the wheel gave George another idea. Crouching next to it, he grabbed the shiny domed hubcap with both hands and pulled. It was firmly in place. Gritting his teeth and closing his eyes, he pulled again, this time using all his weight. It was working. Slowly, it was sliding off the rim. At last, it came free, and George rolled onto his back with the shiny disc in his hands.

With a deep breath, he stood and walked to the open passenger side window. "Excuse me, sir," he shouted over the thunder of the train, "I think this is yours." He held up the hubcap.

"Ah," nodded Nigel, rolling his eyes behind his thick spectacles as if it was a common problem. "Thanks, lad. Just put it down there, will you?" He gestured to the passenger seat next to him. "I'll deal with it later."

George looked down to the passenger seat, where he'd hoped to find the case, but found only Nigel's police hat. He glanced into the empty footwell. It was nowhere to be seen.

"Come on, son." Nigel waved his hand impatiently. "Give it here."

Reluctantly, he dropped the hubcap onto the passenger seat, next to the hat, and backed away. He was out of ideas. Soon, he'd be out of time. The sound from the train had subtly changed, and the rumble felt less intense. The guard was descending the stairs, ready to open the gates.

Backing away, an idea struck him. How could he have been so stupid? The boot. The car boot. It had to be in there. He kicked himself for not looking there first.

George glanced to the guard now leaning on the gate, watching the train rolling steadily by, then back to Nigel, who continued to read his newspaper. There was still time. He darted to the rear of the car once more and dropped to a crouch. Without pause, he turned the chrome handle of the boot hatch. It was unlocked. Slowly and carefully, he lowered it. There it was. Inside, sitting next to a grubby tool bag, was the leather case. He slid it closer, unclipped the buckles, then lifted the lid to reveal the brown paper folder and small cardboard box.

The box opened easily, and George quickly removed the key and placed it in his pocket. Out of curiosity, he opened the folder, looking for the letter Crinklaw had written. But something unexpected caught his attention. It was his drawing of Wren. The one he'd made the morning after the crash and had left at the police station, with Nigel. He'd forgotten all about it. He stuffed that into his pocket, too, then closed the case and slid it back.

With his hands under the boot hatch, ready to close it, he stopped. The train had passed. And the only sound now was the beating of his racing heart. If he were to close the boot, Nigel would hear it and catch George red-handed. If he left it open, the guard might notice and alert Nigel, who would then suspect the boy with the hubcap responsible.

Just then, there was a loud metal crash. The guard had swung open the first gate and was walking across the track towards the second. Nigel had cast aside the newspaper, and was looking ahead, ready to go. The guard then swung the second and final gate, which would allow Nigel clear passage across the tracks.

George watched the heavy gate swing slowly towards its post. It connected with a loud crashing clang, perfectly disguising the thud of the boot as George slammed it shut.

He held his breath and waited.

Then the car's engine sputtered to life, and the long black car drifted forward. George stayed motionless watching it cross the tracks. The guard delivered a friendly wave to the driver, then returned to his gatehouse, as George slipped away unseen. The key to Kelha safe in his pocket.

George left the high street at the first opportunity and kept to the narrow back lanes that criss-crossed the town.

Eventually, after many twists and turns, down paths still untouched by the low sun, he made it to Church Lane, his legs shaking, his hair clammy with sweat. He wanted to sit and recover, but the idea of presenting Wren with the key drove him onwards. What would he say? How would he react? He had never seen Wren express joy. Would he now? Maybe they would go straight to the woods and raise Kelha, together. Or did she have to heal first? He didn't know.

With the town so quiet, George thought it safe to enter the churchyard through the front gate. Once inside, he hurried towards the corner.

"I've got a surprise for him," he whispered to the one-armed angel as he passed. She was silent, as always.

George pushed his way through the undergrowth, then made a line through the bluebells straight to the shack. Like the day before, it was empty, but this time so was the large pine. George called out, but there was no reply.

The shack, and in fact the entire corner, felt different to

George. It was a feeling he had noticed as soon as he'd entered. He couldn't explain it, so he tried to forget about it. But the feeling was still there, at the back of his mind, as he sat at the table staring at the key.

The key looked dull — like a simple ball bearing only slightly murkier, less shiny. If someone told you it was the key to a spaceship, you would pat them on the head and say: *yes dear, that's lovely*. You would then credit them with having a wonderfully fertile imagination, send them on their merry way, and do your best to avoid them in the future. Even George had doubts as he looked upon it. He wondered how it worked. There were no buttons or dials. He had images of a circular hole in the side of Kelha, where maybe the ball rolled down a tube and hit a lever that opened the door. When he thought of the other items belonging to Wren, tubes and levers didn't quite fit.

How Crinklaw had come to find the key, and how he had recognised its importance, George didn't know. The answers were probably inside the brown folder. The folder he'd left behind. The folder he should have taken.

In the cool shack, under a shaft of light breaking through the small square window, he rolled the key back and forth across the table. With his head resting upon his forearm, he watched the sunlight bounce off it and on to the stone walls, his eyes growing heavy until he slept.

The sound of metal on stone woke him. He blinked slowly. The shack was much darker; he must have slept for hours. After feeling about on the floor, he found the key, picked it up, placed it in his pocket, then walked to the door.

As he stood in the doorway, a thought struck him. He turned and went to the corner next to the wood burner, where Wren concealed his bag of tricks. George had seen him reach into it and retrieve the bag from thin air countless times, but he'd never tried it himself.

He knelt and gazed at the wall. Slowly, he reached into the seemingly empty corner. He felt nothing, just the cold stone wall. Frowning, he tried again, this time from a different angle. Again, nothing. After a few more attempts, and feeling ridiculous for waving his hands about in an empty corner, he gave up. It either *was* empty, or he was doing it wrong.

He left the shack.

The door felt heavy as he closed it behind him. The bluebells, now monochrome as darkness settled into the corner, hung their heads, reflecting George's sadness. He now understood the odd feeling that he couldn't shake. It was the same one he had experienced on his first visit to the corner, before Wren had moved in. It was the feeling that this place was abandoned.

In the churchyard's diminishing light, he stared up to the ruin of the tower as he ambled towards the gate. It would soon be night, and for the first time since Wren had moved to the shack, a day had passed without George seeing his friend.

He wondered if he'd been rescued. No, he thought. They were friends, and friends always said goodbye when they went away.

As he opened the small front door of the Furlongs' cottage, he remembered the letter. He would post it tomorrow; one day wouldn't make much difference.

Mr Furlong was standing in the hallway.

"Hello, sir," George said.

He beamed at George with eyes that were wet, then walked to him, and embraced him.

"Is everything, OK, sir?" said George, concerned.

He placed his hands either side of George's face and smiled. "We've got a lovely surprise for you," he said. Then he led George, arm around his shoulders, through to the sitting room. On the sofa, next to Mrs Furlong, sat a woman with a photo album open on her lap. On seeing George, she put it aside and pushed herself up. She took a long look at George, her hand shaking as it covered her mouth. It was his mother.

She rushed forward and hugged him tightly. "It's so good to see you, George, my boy. I've missed you so much."

Chip, who had been sleeping by the stove, raised his head and whined sadly as he watched them. George cried; he hadn't realised until now how much he'd missed her.

As they remained locked together, Mrs Furlong rose and went to the kitchen. "I'll make another pot of tea," she said as she passed them. George caught a glimpse of her; she was also crying. Mr Furlong followed her.

"How long are you here?" asked George, wiping his eyes with the back of his hand as she led him to the sofa where they both sat.

"Just tonight," she said. "Then tomorrow, we *both* go back, the two of us, together. And dad will be home soon." She squeezed his knee and smiled a familiar smile that George thought he'd forgotten. She seemed smaller than he remembered, and thinner too, with darker, sadder eyes, but she smelt the same: perfume and hospital.

George couldn't talk. He felt as if his throat had shrunk. His mind was full of Wren, the key, and the Furlongs. He was glad to see his mother, but at the same time, he wished she wasn't there. That made him feel terrible, so he gave her another tearful hug.

That evening they sat drinking tea and talking until late. His mother kept thanking the Furlongs for keeping her baby safe. They said it had been their pleasure and spoke of how helpful George had been; how when he wasn't helping on the allotment, he was out having adventures with his friends and taking Chip for long walks. They had no idea.

133

They were to leave on the early-morning train, which meant no more time to look for Wren. Even with time, he didn't think he'd have much success.

Up in his room, George threw all his possessions into a small case that lay open on the bed. There wasn't much. Just a few items of clothing, a couple of books, a few toys, the spitfire, and a photo of his parents. He prised up a loose floorboard and lifted out the small wooden box where he now kept his notebook. He placed the key inside and removed the book. At first, he'd written almost every night, but more recently he'd had less to say.

At his small desk, he wrote the final entry, placed the drawing of Wren inside, returned it to the box and set it back under the floorboards. He'd come back for it, he told himself. He would leave it here for now, and somehow he'd find a reason to return. Maybe a visit in the summer holidays. If not, he'd come back when he was old enough to travel on his own.

"So you're leaving?" Mary stood in the doorway. George wondered how long she'd been there and how much she'd seen.

"Come here." She held her arms open, and George ran to her. "I will miss you, my little cockney sparrow. I can't believe you're leaving us. And where were you yesterday? I didn't see you. Did you enjoy the celebrations?"

"Yeah, I did. It was brilliant. You?"

"Wonderful. Possibly the best night of my life." She squeezed him, then backed out of the room, smiling. "Goodnight, George. Sleep tight."

But George couldn't sleep. Happiness, sadness, and worry kept him up most of the night.

"Keep an eye out for him," he whispered to Chip, lying next to him. "If he's still here, he'll be needing a friend."

11

THE BEAST

It was early morning.

Under a cloud of smog of its own making, Ravensford steel mill sat surrounded by a black desert of coal. Under the watch of crows, perched upon the dormant cranes, a long freight train meandered towards it.

The mill was a collection of soot-covered buildings, silos, and tall chimneys. Black smoke and white steam issued from it in equal measure as it produced steel from iron around the clock. It never slept.

The train left the coal dunes, passing an unmanned anti-aircraft gun and searchlight surrounded by a circle of sandbags. Moments later, it converged with other tracks as it entered the mill's yard, looking toy-like against a huge black brick building.

As it slowed, Wren, clothes dirty and face blackened, climbed from the train, jumped to the ground, then hid in a dark corner of the yard.

When the train passed, he took in his surroundings. Across from him, was a wooden hut. From its windows came a warm yellow light, the only colour in this black and grey world. As Wren stared at the hut, its walls melted away to reveal tables full of men, feverishly tucking into a cooked breakfast. They were dressed in overalls and wore caps, their faces blackened and shiny from the heat of the place.

Wren retreated further into shadow as two men emerged, bringing with them the smell of bacon, reminding Wren of his hunger.

One man spoke while referring to a clipboard; the other listened and donned a thick pair of gloves that reached his elbows. Together the two men followed a line of tracks which fanned out to enter a vast brick building a short distance from the hut. From within this massive structure, possibly a thousand feet long, came the echoing sounds of metal on metal. The men, tiny against the wide opening, entered and were swallowed by darkness.

Moments later, a steam whistle sounded and the rest of the men, now fed and watered, poured from the hut, taking the same route as the two before.

Wren followed from the shadows as the men disappeared inside, but had no intention of going in after them. What he needed stood beyond this massive brick building. So he slipped down the outside, using the metal fire escapes attached to the length of its sidewall. Several minutes later, as the end of the building approached, he saw it: the blast furnace.

The furnace was a large, black, barrel-shaped structure over two hundred feet high, with a tangle of platforms, steps, and supports clinging to its exterior. It towered above everything, like a menacing beast, clouds of steam escaping from nostrils unseen.

This gigantic monster of metal and stone was the reason Wren was here, and the life of his friend depended on him reaching the very top of it.

Inside the belly of the furnace was a heat so intense that

only it could destroy his bracelet. A bracelet that was more than a rescue beacon, much more. It had a memory. Everything Wren had experienced while trapped here was stored within it. Allowing his people, who were secretive to the extreme, to retrieve those memories would mean death for George.

Why such secrecy was so important was a mystery to Wren. He was only aware of a small piece of what felt like a much broader mission. His single objective was to observe Earth's rate of technological advancement. That is all. And he was not in a position to ask why.

From the back corner of the building, a narrow metal bridge, shrouded in steam, left the fire escape to join a stairwell that climbed to the very top of the furnace. He was almost there. As he neared, the air grew thicker, and the heat intensified.

Even with the heat, a chill ran down Wren's spine. He stopped. Something was wrong. He retreated into the shadows of pipes running down the wall of the building, then looked towards the bridge. Something was telling him there was danger there. It was partially obscured by steam, and looked rickety — but it was empty.

He crouched. Adrenaline pumped through his body and time slowed as his attention was pulled again towards the bridge. Still, he saw nothing to account for the feeling of danger.

He closed his eyes and reached out to find other minds. The closest was in the building behind him, but it was concerned with earthly matters and posed no risk. He could also feel the presence of people far below the bridge, at the base of the furnace, working hard to control channels of liquid metal flowing from the belly of the beast.

But then he felt another mind. This one was closed to him.

They were here.

He knew they would be. The accuracy of the bracelet this far from Kelha would not be pinpoint, but it was enough to find this place. And they would have guessed his intentions by now.

Wren opened his eyes.

White steam rose through the grated floor of the bridge ahead. As it ascended, swirling and unfolding, it did something unexpected. It was diverted by something unseen, something hanging high in the air, hidden from view. He watched as the steam gave shape to it. But Wren already knew its shape. It was a cube.

Then came movement on the other side of the bridge. Somebody was descending one of the many stairwells attached to the furnace. As Wren readied himself to fade, slowing his breath, he glimpsed an approaching figure through the steam. His heart suddenly quickened with fear.

He had always known help would be quick to arrive, and he had imagined being rescued by one of his own: a Watcher. But this figure, now leaving the stairwell and crossing the bridge, was *not* of his kind. He moved differently. His arms were thick, and hung low past his narrow waist. His strong rounded shoulders rolled as he walked — and he walked with purpose. He was hunting.

Wren's fear continued to grow. Hunters were vicious, cold, and cunning. But fear would only distract Wren from his task, so he fought to control it, using it instead to sharpen his focus.

He watched the Hunter, clothed entirely in black, lean over the bridge and look upon the men working below. The fiery glow of molten metal revealed a face almost featureless, like Wren's had once been. But this face was fierce, with small black shark-like eyes. Its default expression was anger. His red hair was tied into a long, thick braid. It hung down his back, then looped up to pass over his shoulder. At the end of the braid was a cruel-looking blade, fastened to a metallic plate on his chest.

Wren could not believe the boldness of the creature. There was no attempt at concealment or disguise; it was reckless. And that made him even more dangerous.

Why send a Hunter? Had they expected him to resist rescue?

The Hunter stepped away from the edge. Surrounded by steam, he sniffed the air briefly, then crouched. For a second, Wren feared he'd been discovered, but the Hunter then leapt, and disappeared into his hidden craft.

Wren waited in the shadows, considering his next move while watching the clouds of steam deflect from the unseen edges of the cube. It was bigger than Kelha. Big enough for two. A Hunter and its prey.

Twenty minutes passed as Wren waited. The heat from the pipes was almost unbearable. A door slammed in the distance, and footsteps approached from behind. Wren decided not to fade. Instead, he would preserve his energy and wedge himself further between the hot pipes. The footsteps grew louder until a tall man, with a long grey beard, marched past and crossed the bridge directly under the cube.

Knowing the occupant's attention would be focused on the man, Wren used the pipes to scramble down to the level below. Once there, he walked away from the bridge, back along the fire escape.

Set against a chimney protruding from the building, he found a ladder and climbed to the topmost level, and entered through a small door set into the slope of the roof. It was dark inside and noisy. He rested in the shadows upon a narrow gantry, suspended high above a room full of pipes and machines.

Far below in the gloom, a stout man, wearing dungarees and a pair of circular spectacles, stood next to a bank of brass dials and gauges. He tapped one with his finger, then turned a valve. Satisfied with his tapping and turning, the stout man moved on, writing in his little brown book as he went.

Wren moved on, following the gantry as it went through an archway of a dividing wall, where he looked down upon a vast space alive with industry. Giant cauldrons, suspended from thick rails, poured liquid steel into moulds. At the same time, immense machines violently beat fiery slabs of metal, while a long line of glowing steel bricks passed under cooling jets of water. The sound of each hardened brick falling into awaiting train cars echoed about the cathedral-like interior. The noise and heat here were intense. And Wren was amazed at the carefree manner of those working in a place so charged and volatile. They stood, unflinching, as sparks and shards of hot metal filled the air around them.

Soon he was outside again, this time on the other side of the building, at the top of a stairwell leading to the ground, overlooking a desolate, grey landscape.

With the bridge to the furnace now under the watchful eye of the Hunter, the next best option would be the conveyor. He could see the base of it below, about five hundred yards to the south.

The conveyor was a metal cage, three hundred feet long, climbing at a forty-five-degree angle to the top of the furnace. Inside the cage were two heavy wagons, taking raw material from the ground to the large black funnel at the top.

Wren looked down over the edge of the railing. Two trains carrying iron and limestone passed the foot of the stairwell, crawling towards the base of the conveyor.

After descending the stairwell, he approached the train

and climbed one of the slowly moving cars. He clambered over the pile of limestone it carried, then dropped down the other side, back to the ground. Then he did it a second time, so that both trains were between himself and the Hunter on the bridge. Hunters could not see through objects, as Watchers could, but they had other skills.

As he walked along with the rumbling train cars, he considered dropping the bracelet into one, with the hope it would eventually find its way into the furnace. But the presence of the Hunter meant he could take no risks; he had to be sure of its destruction.

With the bridge now hidden from view by the bulk of the furnace, he climbed back over the trains to get conveyor side. He landed silently and hid behind a small wooden hut at the edge of an open yard, where a handful of men were working. They could not be allowed to see him.

On the far side of the yard were the large hoppers raised on stilts that would fill the wagons with raw material. An empty wagon descended the conveyor. As it came to a stop under the hopper, a man standing nearby shouted, "Clear!" and pulled one of two levers. There was an ear-splitting screech followed by a deep rumble as rocks from the hopper filled the wagon, which shook violently under the assault, causing a dust cloud to spill over its edge and fill the yard.

Using the cloud as cover, he moved in closer, running to hide behind an old damaged train car and a pile of railway sleepers.

His next run would be across open ground, and with no more cover in sight, he faded.

He sprinted across the yard. When he reached the underside of the conveyor, he leapt and pulled himself into the innards of the structure. The eyes of the men saw it all, but their brains refused to process the images, dismissing them as anomalies. It was a skill that took centuries to perfect — and a neat trick if you could pull it off.

His ability to fade was finite, so, in the dark underbelly of the conveyor, he unfaded and remained still, allowing his strength to return before starting his climb.

The underside of the conveyor was dark and noisy, housing the mechanics and the thick chains that moved the wagons on the upper side. Both sides were encased within the soot-covered metal framework.

At first the climb was made easy by the availability of ladders and steps, there to allow maintenance of the massive gears. After that, the only way to progress was to use the supporting metalwork like a climbing frame. As he climbed in the darkness, he was flanked by two thick chains, which would momentarily stop as the attached wagons, unseen above, emptied their loads at the top or were refilled at the bottom.

After a few minutes of steady climbing, the metalwork around took on a red hue. He was now directly above a group of men working to control the fiery channels of liquid metal, pouring from the furnace. A few days ago, this metal would have been destined to create tanks, guns, and warships, but perhaps now would become less harmful things.

The climb continued. Most would have tired at this point, but even a weary and hungry Watcher could climb for hours before feeling the strain. His mind wandered as he ascended. He remembered climbs from his past, before being sent off-world. Watchtowers so high they would take many days to climb. As Watchers became more experienced and learned to see further, they sought taller towers. On finding one, they would first need to climb it. No equipment, no shortcuts. If you could not climb it, you could not claim it.

Wren finally reached the end of his climb and dropped to a metal platform near the top of the furnace.

For the last thirty feet, he used a stairwell and emerged on a platform similar to the one below, but narrow and with no railing. It felt exposed. He looked down into the funnel that the platform surrounded. Like an open mouth of a beast, its hot breath ebbed and flowed, bringing waves of unbearable heat. But the real intense temperatures were contained within the belly, which was blocked by a valve in the funnel's narrow throat. The valve would only open once the raw material was ready to be swallowed.

He would not discard the band yet; not until the wagon arrived with the rock and iron. The thought of it lying exposed in an empty funnel, with a Hunter around, was not comforting.

While waiting, he walked to one of the corners of the platform until the bridge far below came into view. With his keen eyes, he could see the distortions around the Hunter's cube. It was still there. He just hoped the Hunter was too.

He backed away, then eyed the funnel that would soon swallow his bracelet.

Just then, there was a loud clang, followed by a deep continuous ratcheting sound. It was the wagon approaching. A moment later, it appeared with its heavy load. It stopped sharply at the edge, tipping its contents down the sloped sides of the funnel with a thunderous racket.

There was a deep thud, and a wave of heat as the valve opened to take in the rock. Wren removed his band, but then hesitated as the enormity of his actions dawned on him. No one had left the Nim before, at least none he had heard of. But his thoughts quickly turned to George, and he tossed the band into the flow of falling rock.

There would be no going back now.

A ferocious roar exploded behind him, followed by a

sudden pain between his shoulders, and Wren was thrown backwards off the steel platform.

Wren landed hard on his back on the metal platform below.

Looking up, he saw his attacker, staring down, teeth bared, fury in his eyes. As the Hunter turned away to seek the bracelet, Wren faded.

He tried to stand but, dazed and disorientated, he fell. Warm blood ran down the back of his neck and darkness crept in at the edge of his vision; he shook his head to keep it at bay. He tried to stand again, using the railing for support. Now on steadier feet, he pulled himself towards the stairwell, and climbed until he was back at the funnel's edge.

Still hidden, Wren cautiously approached the Hunter, who was standing with his hand outstretched towards the mass of rock, his bracelet — thicker and more ornate than Wren's —glowing brightly. The rocks, which had been falling into the furnace like sand in an hourglass, were now rising into the air, swirling and undulating.

With quick gestures, the Hunter skilfully sifted through the rocks, dismissing large portions of them back into the neck of the funnel. As the cloud of rock diminished, Wren caught sight of his bracelet. It would not be long before the Hunter saw it, too.

He moved closer to the Hunter. Then, with everything he had, Wren launched himself forward, keeping low, his shoulder slamming into his side. It felt like running into a tree. For a moment, Wren thought it hadn't been enough. But it was. The Hunter lost his footing and fell back. His arms were like windmills as he tried to find his balance, but it was no use, he fell to the platform below. Wren almost followed, but managed to stand firm.

The body of rock, no longer under the Hunter's control, fell with a crash, back into the funnel. Wren watched as the bracelet slid from view — consumed, finally, by the beast.

Wren sank to his knees, grabbing the sides of the platform to steady himself. He looked down to the Hunter, who had landed safely on his feet, then watched as he leapt effortlessly into the air, landing silently next to him.

Concentrating on remaining hidden, Wren tried to back away towards the stairwell, but in his weakened state, he stumbled into the funnel. Reacting quickly, he caught the edge with both hands, narrowly avoiding a fiery death as the valve closed several feet below him.

He could not find the energy to pull himself up. He decided quickly and calmly, that if he had to, he would let go. He would not allow himself to be captured. There were other ways they could extract his memories, more painful ways he would rather avoid. He was ready to sacrifice himself — for George.

The Hunter looked down into the funnel with his small, black eyes, and hissed angrily at its apparent emptiness. The V-shaped slit that formed his nose quivered as a sharp tongue tasted the air.

"Tas, org sharrad stakhoom," he growled, causing Wren to shudder. It had been over a hundred years since he'd heard his own language spoken. Coming from this Hunter, it sounded cold and harsh. "Why destroy it?" he continued, still in his own tongue. "What do you not want me to see?"

Wren remained silent. There was a smell of burning as Wren's skin began to blister against the hot metal of the funnel. Hunters relied on smell more than sight, but luckily, Wren could block both.

"Why are you hiding?" His tone was less aggressive as he

tried to appease Wren. "What are you afraid of? I'm here to take you home. Let Jenta do his job. Show yourself."

Without pause, he unclipped his long red braid of hair. And with a flick of his head, he whipped it around in a wide circle, then dropped to his knees quickly as it whipped around a second time. When the bladed tip failed to connect with anyone, he secured it back into place, growling with frustration.

"I sense you are still here, Watcher," he said, his voice again full of malice. "You cannot stay hidden forever. I can wait."

Wren remained calm. This would all soon be over.

"Your bracelet," said the Hunter, as he began to pace casually up and down. "It matters not. *You* will tell me what *it* would have revealed. In fact, I prefer it this way."

He stopped pacing, an inch from Wren's fingers, and crouched. At this distance, Wren could see the intricate tattoos on the Hunter's neck and hands that identified his tribe. He was from the swamplands, a region famed for the prowess of its Hunters and for the formidable creatures they preyed upon. They had sent the best. Wren wondered, once again, why they had sent a Hunter at all.

Wren's ability to fade was weakening. He loosened his grip, ready to join his bracelet. The valve below him was closed, but the heat in the throat of the funnel would be enough to end him.

The Hunter stood and turned his head sharply. Wren, struggling to turn his, followed his gaze. The stairwell was rattling. Men were coming, no doubt drawn by the strange spectacle of flying rocks.

From nowhere, the Hunter drew a long, curved blade, but changed his mind quickly and it collapsed back into its hilt. He then ran along the steel platform, leapt, and vanished into his cube.

Wren's spirits lifted as a sliver of hope returned. His grip tightened. He might just make it out of here.

The men appeared, exhausted by their climb. With looks of confusion, they peered down into the funnel, shielding their faces from the heat. One man then climbed a small bridge passing over the end of the conveyor. He stood, hands on hips, looking down into the empty wagon, then shrugged to the others.

If he could just make it to that wagon, Wren thought.

He pulled himself up and out of the funnel, rolled over on to his back, and looked to the sky, to the spot where the Hunter had disappeared. The disturbances in the air were still there. The Hunter was not finished yet. He was simply waiting for the men to leave.

Wren got to his feet and shuffled along the narrow platform, his burnt hands curled close to his chest. At the steps of the small bridge, he stood aside as the man came down and passed him. Then Wren climbed, each step feeling like it might be his last. But he made it, and was soon standing directly over the empty wagon.

Having found nothing unusual, all but one of the men made their way back to the stairwell. That remaining man leant out over the edge, pulled a flag from his back pocket, and waved it in the air. In response, the conveyor snapped back to life, and the wagon jolted, moving slowly away from Wren. Wren let gravity do its work and leant forwards, toppling over the waist-high railing of the small bridge and falling into the wagon.

Bouncing around as it descended, he watched the sky in hope. But, above the steel frame of the conveyor, he saw the familiar distortion in the air. It stayed with him almost to the bottom. Then, satisfied the wagon was empty, or fearful that Wren was making his escape via another route, it returned to the top of the furnace at blistering speed.

Wren unfaded.

Exhausted, bloodied, and burnt, he struggled to his knees. When the wagon halted abruptly under a shadow, he was thrown forward and his head struck the floor. Blood and sweat poured into his eyes as he turned to face the sky, looking for the source of the shadow. For a moment, he thought the cube was back. But this was worse...well, it was different.

The wagon had come to stop under the chute of the hopper that would soon fill it with tonnes of rock. A short, desperate laugh escaped Wren. He might end up in the furnace after all.

He thought about calling to the men for help, but that would only endanger them. If he had more energy he would reach out and jam the lever or the mechanism of the hatch above, but he didn't.

With no options available, he acknowledged the battered-looking chute above him with a look of gracious defeat, and he readied himself for death. He knelt, placed his hands on his thighs, and closed his eyes. When he did, he saw the face of George, and he smiled. Then another face appeared to him, illuminated by the glow of a bonfire, a subtle smile upon her lips. He opened his eyes, surprised by the vision, then sighed and took in his final surroundings. The wagon was almost a perfect cube, he noted. It was about the size of Kelha, but with no roof, a heavily dented floor, walls scarred by a million rocks, and a...ladder? He wiped the sweat from his eyes. Next to him was a column of metal rungs, welded onto the wall. Presumably to allow people in and out for maintenance. He didn't know; he didn't care.

With renewed energy, he crawled towards it. Ignoring the pain of his burnt hands, he gripped a rung tightly, and pulled himself to his feet.

"Clear!" came a distant call. It was followed by a dull metallic clang from above that echoed around the wagon.

Wren looked up to the chute about to deliver his fate, and heard the ear-splitting sound of a metallic hatch slowly opening above him.

12

___

SHOW AND TELL

August 2018 (Week five of the summer holidays)

It was early morning. Max sat alone at the kitchen table, crunching his way through the remains of last night's prawn crackers. They'd lost some of their crispness, but he liked the way they felt on his tongue. When the last one was gone, and the little white bag contained nothing but crumbs, he cleared away the empty foil tubs, sniffed the one that had once held sweet and sour chicken (his favourite), then loaded the dishwasher. All the while he tried not to think about the notebook he'd found under the floorboards.

Last night he had read it cover to cover. Then, it had been intriguing — exciting, even. But now, with the sanity and clarity that comes with morning light, it all seemed a bit silly; surely just the product of a child with an overactive imagination. Whatever it was, it was *not* to be taken seriously, he thought.

So why couldn't he stop thinking about it?

Every time he tried to think of something else, his mind turned back to it. It was getting annoying.

He stood at the sink and looked out the window to the

long narrow garden. It now looked less like a jungle and almost resembled an *actual* garden. He thought about going out there. Maybe he would mow the lawn. Or what if he went to the woods and looked for the crash site? There was a map in the library that....

"Stop," he said aloud to a silent kitchen.

He took a deep calming breath and slotted two slices of bread into the toaster. With his elbows on the counter and his hands placed either side of his head — to stop more thoughts seeping in — he stared at the toaster's ticking timer as it slowly turned.

He imagined it to be a ticking bomb, then wondered if bombs still ticked. He then wondered why the bad guys in movies didn't make explosives using wires of all the same colour, to stop the good guys from defusing them. Also, why didn't George leave the key at Patrick's Corner? That way—

"Oh, for God's sake!" He slapped his hands on the kitchen worktop, ran up to his room, threw the notebook and metal ball — which was definitely *not* a key — into his rucksack, ran back down the stairs, then wheeled his bicycle out through the front door, and slammed it behind him. All before his toast popped up.

Max stepped into the reception of the library and paused under the, quietly, humming air-conditioning unit above the entrance. The icy air was a relief from the heat outside and well worth the visit alone. Then, remembering the actual reason for being there, and feeling ridiculous for it, he walked towards the main hall.

Ben was the only member of staff Max could see. He sat behind the front desk, reading. He looked up from his book and gave Max a friendly smile as he passed.

As was usual for the time of day, the library was mostly empty. He'd expected Old Man Bartley to be camped in his usual spot, but was relieved to find him absent.

Max went to the dusty forgotten display and stood before the twisted piece of metal in the glass cabinet. After reading the plaque next to it, for the second time, he walked to the faded map on the wall. There was a large circle labelled "Crash site", but it covered about a third of the woods. If he *was* going to look for the site, this map wouldn't be much help.

"You again?"

Max turned as Mr Bartley entered the room. Looking as beige as ever, he took a local paper from the rack, then sat at the table.

"Hello," said Max.

"Why are you so interested in that?" asked Bartley, nodding toward the display. He removed a pair of reading glasses from their case, then snapped the case shut.

"Don't know," shrugged Max.

"Well, don't waste your time learning about that lie. And don't bother trying to find the truth," said Bartley. He was in a very different mood from last time they'd spoken, and back to his old grumpy self. "Trust me. It's not worth it. Before you know it, you'll be as old as me and none the wiser. Anyway, shouldn't you be playing video games or vandalising bus shelters?" He gave Max a sour look before disappearing behind his paper.

There was sadness in Mr Bartley's voice, and for a second, he thought about showing him the notebook — but decided not to. Mr Bartley was right; it *was* a waste of time, and even though Max had nothing else to waste his time on, he decided to forget about the whole thing.

"Damn thing cost my father his job," said Bartley, still behind his paper. He was talking more to himself than Max.

Max's mouth opened, and before he knew it, the name *Nigel* escaped his lips.

The newspaper flinched. It was a small, almost undetectable movement, but Max saw it. The paper slowly came down and, over the top of his reading glasses, Mr Bartley's eyes met his. "What...did you say?"

Max's mind raced, trying to think of a reply. George had written about Nigel the desk sergeant, who had been tasked to deliver the key to the War Office. Max guessed that failing to do so would have surely *cost him his job*. And hadn't Bartley said his dad was a police officer? One who was there at the time?

Somehow, with just those tiny fragments, Max had made a link. And judging by the look he was receiving from Mr Bartley, it was spot on.

Mr Bartley placed the paper on the table, removed his glasses, then repeated the question. His brow furrowed when Max didn't answer. He leaned forward. "Who you been talking to?"

"Nobody," said Max, feeling his cheeks redden and the desperate need to be somewhere else. "I think...er...you told me his name when we first met?"

"Oh," he replied. "Did I?" He paused as he considered this. Then, "No, I don't think—"

"Anyway, Mr Bartley, I really have to go now," he said, edging from the room as Mr Bartley's expression hovered between confusion and suspicion.

Max made his way through the main hall, feeling the man's eyes burning into the back of his head. He passed through reception, pausing to avoid crashing through the sluggish automatic doors, and caught a fleeting glimpse of Mr Bartley, standing with a lost look upon his face. Overcome by panic, Max burst out into the bright sunshine, slamming straight into Isaac.

"Watch out, Max. No hugs, no hugs," Isaac said, smiling and giving him a friendly slap on the shoulder. "Miss me?"

"Hey," he said, glancing back to the closing door. "You're back."

"Sadly, yes," replied Isaac. "You OK? You seem a bit...manic."

Max grabbed Isaac and spun him back towards the bike racks. "Follow me. I need to show you something."

They stood in shade under the bandstand, two silhouettes facing each other against the bright sunny backdrop of Bramfield Park.

"So? What is it?" asked Isaac.

Max wasn't sure how to start. Five minutes ago he'd firmly decided to forget all about the notebook, but that was before his run-in with Mr Bartley. Knowing the book referred to someone who was actually there at the time somehow seemed to give it more credibility. If the bit about Nigel was true, what else was?

"Hello. Earth to Max. Come in, Max," said Isaac. "Are you going to tell me what's going on? Otherwise, I need to take my game back. It's overdue."

"OK," Max said, taking off his backpack and reaching inside. "Look, before I show you this. I want you to know... I'm not saying I believe any of it. I'm just showing you what I found, OK?"

"OK," said Isaac, "just show me, and dial down the dramatics."

That stung. Max was trying to play it cool, but apparently, he was failing miserably.

"I found this," he said, handing Isaac the notebook. "It was under the floorboards in my room."

Isaac looked unimpressed as he took the book and flicked through its pages. "Looks old," he said.

"Read it," said Max.

"I don't *read* in the summer holidays." Isaac laughed. Then, noticing Max was serious, he turned back to the first page and started to read.

After the first few lines, Isaac looked back to Max with a raised eyebrow. He pushed his glasses further up the bridge of his nose, then sat cross-legged on the floor and continued to read. Max assumed Isaac would read the first page, then fling the notebook back to him with a sarcastic comment. But he didn't. He sat there for half an hour in complete silence. Until finally, he closed it with care, as if handling a priceless artefact from a museum's archive.

Max, who had spent the last thirty minutes sitting at the edge of the bandstand, staring toward the church, got to his feet and placed his hands in his pockets. "Well?" he said sheepishly.

"Well..." said Isaac, still looking at the notebook.

"Come on...what do you think?" said Max, trying not to sound impatient.

"What do *you* think?" replied Isaac.

"I asked first."

"Well," Isaac said again. He stood and handed the diary back to Max. "The ending is a bit...abrupt. What happened to this Wren guy? Why didn't the kid tell someone about him? Didn't they have stranger danger back in those days?"

"You believe it?" asked Max.

"Believe it? Why would you *not* believe it?" asked Isaac, "Maybe not all of it's true. But yeah, sounds legit to me."

"Wha...what?" Max was shocked. He'd expected Isaac to reject it and maybe even mock him. "But this Wren guy...you did *read* it, right?"

"Yeah, I *read* it. It's far-fetched in places, but some of it could be true."

Max had to sit down again. He wasn't expecting this from Isaac. Part of him wanted him to dismiss it all as fantasy or a hoax, but Isaac didn't seem bothered by the more fantastical aspects.

"Shame this George kid didn't leave you the key," Isaac said, looking out towards the church. "That way, you'd know if any of this was real."

"He did," said Max after a pause.

Isaac turned to face him. His eyes narrowed with suspicion. "Show me."

Max put the diary back into the bag and pulled out the metal ball. He held it up between finger and thumb before passing it to Isaac, who held it in the cup of his hands and looked upon it with wide eyes. To Max, it was merely a metal ball, but Isaac seemed to see something different, something incredible. Then Max remembered Isaac's room: a shrine to space and science fiction. Of course, he was more likely to believe; he'd been reading, watching and probably dreaming about things like this for years.

"It's just a ball," said Max, starting to doubt his own words.

"Probably," replied Isaac, "but what if it's more?"

Max looked again, this time allowing himself to imagine the possibility that he was looking at something special.

"What are you two gawking at?" came a voice from behind.

It was Ellie.

It took more to convince Ellie. In fact, she wasn't convinced at all.

Max didn't want her finding out about the notebook; it

embarrassed him. It felt childish. But Isaac, who seemed to know Ellie well from school, excitedly blurted out the entire story.

As Isaac retold the story in his own words, Max felt his scepticism return, even stronger than before. When Isaac had finished, he held up the small metal ball, claiming it was, "quite possibly the most important object ever to be held by human hands."

Max cringed.

"So, let me get this straight," said Ellie, barely suppressing a laugh beneath her serious expression. "Alien crashes, destroying the church spire. Boy finds said alien in barn. Alien turns human. Boy befriends alien. Together they search for a missing spaceship key. Boy *finds* key, but loses alien?"

Isaac nodded. His smile faltered on hearing how absurd Ellie's version sounded.

"Look, guys," said Ellie as she took the ball from Isaac. "I'm not saying this is a load of old crap" — she tossed the ball casually from hand to hand — "I'm not. I'm really not. But it *so* is a load of old crap. Come on—" she began laughing. Max laughed, too, uncomfortably and forced.

"Hey, can you not throw it around like that?" said Isaac. "That thing could be...priceless."

"It's just a giant marble." She threw it back to Isaac, who clumsily caught it with both hands.

"Well, there's a simple way to find out if it's crap or not," said Isaac, regaining his composure. "We take this to the crash site." He held up the ball.

"What?" said Ellie. "OK, assuming this is all real, which it isn't, what do you expect to happen?"

"Well, it says in the book, that Kelha—"

"Excuse me, who now?" Ellie interrupted.

"The cube...the ship...Wren's ship," answered Isaac. "It's

activated by *this* key. And as the key has been under Max's bedroom floor for the past seventy-odd years, the ship is probably still out there, waiting to be activated."

"And I suppose you know how to *activate* it?"

"Well, no. It didn't come with instructions." Isaac looked to Max for confirmation. "Did it?"

Max shook his head.

"Shame," said Ellie. "So, I suppose one of us will, out of the blue, magically gain an understanding of how alien technology works and activate the spaceship," she said, air quoting the word *spaceship*.

There was a moment of silence where Max wished an asteroid would strike the bandstand and end it all.

"OK," said Ellie finally. "I'm bored as hell. How do we find the crash site? Oban Wood is huge. Is there a monument or something? Maybe a grave for the German pilot?"

"Nothing, as far as I know," said Isaac.

"Just...hold on a minute." Max stood in between them. "Can you both just listen to yourselves? This is mad. There's nothing to this; Ellie's right."

"Of course I'm right. But I'm also bored and have nothing else to do right now. And the thought of watching you two loons prance about in the woods trying to summon a spaceship from the ground sounds like a right laugh."

"You think it's buried?" said Isaac, ignoring the insult. "Interesting..."

"No, I think it's in a magical cave guarded by a troll," said Ellie flatly. "Isaac, I don't think it's buried. It doesn't exist, is what I think."

Isaac didn't seem to be listening. "There's a map in the library," he said, "we'll go there first and—"

"No!" said Max, raising his voice.

"What, why?" asked Isaac.

"Because..." Max didn't finish the sentence, hoping that

because was going to be enough of a reason.

"*Because?*" pushed Isaac.

Max sighed. "Old Man Bartley."

"What about him?"

Max was reluctant to continue, knowing it would only increase Isaac's excitement. But Isaac and Ellie were staring at him intently, waiting. His cheeks reddened again. "Nigel, the desk sergeant in the notebook. The one who was supposed to take the key to London?"

"Yeah, what about him?" said Isaac.

"He's...Old Man Bartley's...old man."

"His dad?" said Ellie. "How do you know?"

Max looked at Isaac, who seemed stunned by the news. "Old Man Bartley mentioned his dad today at the library. Something about him losing his job because of *The Incident*. I remembered; he'd mentioned him once before, said he was a policeman. I put two and two together, blurted out the name Nigel and...well, judging by his reaction—"

"And you still don't believe any of this?" Isaac said, almost bouncing with excitement. "Look, we'll go to the library. Ellie and I can go in first; if the coast is clear, we'll signal for you to follow."

Max shook his head. "There's no point. I looked at the map; it's useless. Not detailed enough."

"OK," said Isaac, handing Max the key and thinking of another plan. "Then...we pick up a local map from the shop and try our luck. One of the big fold-out types; I like those." Isaac jumped down from the bandstand and ran to his bike. "Coming?"

Ellie followed looking amused, then looked back at Max. "You know I'm in, just for the entertainment value. Come on, Max," she said, smiling at him. "Got anything better to do?"

He hadn't.

13

VISIONS

"Why buy a map when we could just use our phones?" Ellie said. She was standing on the extended bolts of Isaac's back wheel, gripping his shoulders as they rode across Bramfield Park.

"We need a *real* map," replied Isaac. "We might not get a signal in the woods. Plus, maps are cool."

"Maps are *cool?*" Ellie shook her head. "You are such a geek."

"And proud of it." Isaac smiled.

Max followed on his bike, deep in thought, his mind flipping between belief and doubt. If it were not for the Bartley connection, he'd be as sceptical as Ellie, who clearly thought the whole thing was nonsense.

At the shop on the corner of Station Road and High Street, they bought the map and as many snacks as they could carry, then set off toward Church Lane.

They passed Max's cottage and joined the small dirt track that led to the bridge. After crossing the bridge, they followed the sun-baked path that ran downhill between the hedgerow and the field. At first, the going was easy as they sped along, leaving clouds of yellow dust billowing behind.

But soon they were climbing, and Isaac, with the added weight of Ellie on the back, was starting to tire. They continued on foot, with Ellie pushing Isaac's bike alongside Max, while Isaac walked ahead studying the map.

The heat was oppressive, so when the hedgerow gave way to a large lonely oak tree offering shelter, they took it. Max and Ellie rested against the thick trunk, and together they watched Isaac struggle with the oversized map.

"We've got no chance of finding it, you know," Ellie said to Max.

"So, you think there is an *it*?"

"No, we won't find *it* because *it* doesn't exist, remember?"

"You don't buy any of this?" asked Max. He knew the answer.

"Do *you*?"

Max shrugged. "I don't know."

"I mean," continued Ellie, "it's intriguing, and if I'm honest, I kind of hope there's some truth to it...but...really? Aliens? Spaceships? Here? *Anywhere* for that matter?" She shrugged and shook her head. "It's silly."

"So why come along?" said Max.

"Told you. Nothing better to do." She made herself comfortable under the tree and pulled out her phone. "Anyway," she said, furiously tapping away, "What about you? You sound doubtful, yet here you are."

"Well, it's hard *not* to follow Indiana Jones over there, isn't it?"

She moved her phone out of the way to look at Isaac. "*That's* who he reminds me of."

"I heard that," said Isaac, not looking up from the map. They both laughed.

After a few moments of head-scratching and chin-stroking, Isaac stood and looked towards the town. "I've got it!" he said, looking pleased with himself.

"He's found the Temple of Doom," muttered Ellie.

Isaac brought the map over and placed it on the ground. "Look," he said, "to reach the woods after hitting the church, this thing would've been travelling at crazy speeds. We know both the old shack and the spire was destroyed. So if we draw a straight line from the church here" — he moved his finger across the map slowly — "and *through* the shack, here, then continue in a straight line across the fields, it leads us to the point where we need to enter the woods." He tapped his finger at the edge of Oban.

"Then what?" asked Ellie, paying more attention to her phone than the map. "We still need to find where this thing *supposedly* came down."

"Well, the diary said it split the ground, turning up all the trees. We should see evidence of that. Even if it's just a patch of younger trees."

"Come on then," said Ellie, standing and putting her phone away in her back pocket. "Let's go find your alien."

They hid the bikes in an overgrown ditch near the tree, then crossed the dry furrowed field towards the tree line of Oban. The pace was slow, but eventually they made it to the path that skirted the woods. Max had hoped for some shade, but apart from the odd large branch overhanging the path, there was none, and the afternoon sun continued to beat down on them from a cloudless sky.

They walked single file, with Isaac still taking the lead. When he wasn't looking at the map, he was using it folded to fan himself, or unfolded as a sunshade. "Can the map on your phone do this, Ellie?" he said with a broad smile.

Ellie showed him one of her fingers. "Just lead the way, *map boy*."

Eventually, Isaac stopped walking. "This is where we enter," he said. With one eye open, and an arm outstretched, he pointed to the church. Then he glanced back to the map and to the woods behind him. "Yup, this is definitely it. We're lined up perfectly between the church and the shack."

The division between field and wood was abrupt, with no gradual introduction; one moment they were in the dry heat of the field, the next in the cool embrace of Oban Wood. Its thick, bent old trees provided instant relief from the sun.

Isaac continued to lead, this time using a small compass attached to his house key. "We just need to keep heading north until we find...something."

"Or," said Ellie, "we emerge on the other side of the woods, having found nothing."

"Or that," said Isaac, unfazed by her pessimism.

They walked on, mostly in silence. Isaac, determined to stay in a straight line, climbed over logs, slashed his way through bushes, and ducked under low branches. Ellie and Max meandered more freely in his wake.

"What should we be looking for exactly?" asked Ellie, who seemed ready for another break. Max wanted one, too.

"I don't know, exactly," said Isaac. "Maybe a bare patch or a long dip in the ground, like a scar, perhaps. Or just a load of old dead trees. We'll know it when we see it."

When they did stop for a break, Isaac sat on a tree stump studying his map, eating a melted Mars Bar, while Ellie wandered around, trying to get reception on her phone.

Max reclined on the soft dry ground, using his rucksack as a pillow. He watched the sunlight dance through the canopy overhead and listened to the sounds of summer: the birdsong, the buzzing, the rustle of leaves, the distant sound of an aeroplane. He dug his fingers into the earth at his sides and inhaled. He was sure his lungs never filled this much in London. With another deep breath, he closed his eyes, feeling relaxed and content. He was enjoying the experience of just being outside with his friends. It was something he had never done before.

Were they his friends? he wondered. There had been no ritual to perform, or contract to sign. It was something that had always puzzled him. If they *were* his friends, they were his first....

"This is interesting."

Ellie's voice came from far away, causing Max's muddled thoughts to evaporate. He propped himself up on his elbows and looked around. Ellie was halfway up a tree, staring at her phone.

"What is it?" asked Isaac.

"It's a phone."

"Funny. What's *interesting*?"

"Well, according to the map on my phone, which is obviously not as cool as your paper one—"

"Damn straight," said Isaac under his breath.

"—we seem to be right next to a long strip of woodland, which looks...well...different." She climbed down the tree, skilfully, then jumped to the ground and walked towards them.

"Different, how?" asked Max.

"You be the judge."

Max noted the serious expression on Ellie's face. This time there was no hint of humour or sarcasm.

The three crowded around Ellie's phone. It showed a satellite image of the woods. To the east of the blinking blue dot showing their position was a long strip of trees. They were a brighter green than the surrounding woods — and looked just like a scar.

"Wow," whispered Isaac.

"It gets better." Ellie zoomed out until the north edge of the town came into view. Her finger traced the length of the scar and continued until it met the church. "A straight line to the church, ladies and geeks."

"Huh," said Max. "Sorry, Isaac, Ellie's map wins."

"Fair enough," said Isaac, stuffing his map into his bag. "Lead the way, phone girl."

Following Ellie, they moved east towards the strip. As they went, the undergrowth thickened until they met an impassable wall of brambles. It snagged at their clothes and clawed at their skin. Unable to breach the wall, they followed it north, hoping to find a gap near the tip of the scar.

"How far?" said Isaac, starting to look tired.

"We're about halfway," replied Ellie, checking her phone.

"What?" said Isaac. "Only halfway? We've been walking for...ages. Surely a plane would have been stopped by the first few trees?"

Max thought Isaac made a good point and remembered Old Man Bartley making a similar one.

"Come on," said Ellie, "let's keep moving."

Ten minutes later, Ellie stopped, looked at her phone again, then turned right. "This way," she called. "We're here."

They found no gap in the bramble wall, so, using sticks, the three slashed their way through it. It was tough going, and at times, Max got the feeling the brambles were somehow fighting back. But they did it.

It was lighter inside the wall. The birdsong, plentiful before, was amplified here, and a galaxy of bugs filled the air, warmed by sunlight pouring through a much thinner canopy. The large twisted and knotted trees were now gone, replaced by younger, straighter varieties. And the ground sloped down to form a dell covered in fern, where scattered between the trees were strange mounds covered in grass and sprinkled with summer flowers. On closer inspection, they were the remains of trees long dead.

"What now?" said Max, looking to Isaac.

"I don't know," he replied. "Look at the key, I suppose. Is it doing anything?"

Max removed it from his bag and held it in the palm of his hand. It was cold and heavy. The three looked on in anticipation.

"Does it feel *different*?" asked Isaac after a while.

"Same."

There was a pause.

"How about now?"

"No, Isaac. It's the same."

Isaac's face fell.

Max expected Ellie to look triumphant, but she didn't. She looked disappointed at first, but then hid the look quickly behind an expression of mild amusement.

Just then, there was a flutter in the air and a tiny bird appeared. It settled on a dead branch, reaching, like a zombie's arm, from a nearby grassy mound. The small bird considered the newcomers for a moment, then, with another flutter, was gone again.

There was a collective sigh.

"Well," said Ellie. "Wren turned up." She blew the hair from her clammy face and walked away.

"Maybe you need to walk around a bit," said Isaac to Max, refusing to give up. "Maybe you need to get directly over the right spot before it does...whatever it does?"

"Hah!" said Ellie unimpressed. "Look, it was a superb idea, Isaac. Well, OK, it wasn't...but it's been a pleasant trip to the woods; you know, exercise, fresh air, etcetera. But *really*? That," she pointed to the ball, "is just a metal ball. And this," she spread her arms wide, "is just another bit of the woods, albeit with slightly different trees." Sceptical Ellie had returned.

Isaac looked too tired to fight. He walked away, hitting random shrubs with his stick as he went.

Max felt his embarrassment return, as if this was somehow his fault. But all he had done was find the thing. Isaac had led them here with crazy ideas of finding space-ships. He himself wasn't expecting *anything* to happen. Still, deep down, buried beneath the embarrassment, was a splinter of disappointment.

He watched Ellie and Isaac wander off to occupy their own space, Isaac looking deflated, Ellie looking bored. Even though the day was almost over, no one seemed in a rush to return. The place was peaceful, like a secret garden. Max wondered how many others had fought their way through the bramble wall. He guessed not many; why would they bother?

He wandered between the mounds and the tall silver birch. There was a small hill. It was grassy, surrounded by ferns, and peppered with trees. He found himself drawn to it. He climbed to the top and looked around, taking in the sights of the dell. He liked it here. It was brighter and warmer than the rest of the woods and cooler than the exposed fields. It felt familiar.

The feeling of familiarity quickly passed and he sat on the grass and held up the ball; he watched the sunlight bounce off its milky surface. *Just a ball*, he thought. Then he had another thought; one that seemed to come from else-where. The thought said, *You should place this on the ground.* So he did. And Max's world went black.

Darkness enveloped him. It was uniformly black, lacking any afterglow of the bright summer's day he'd just inhabited. He blinked several times, but it made no difference. A distant rumble came from below him. Well, he guessed it was below, but he had no sense of up or down. The rumble made him think of London, and the underground trains he would sometimes feel under his feet near his estate. He could hear Ellie and Isaac talking, but they sounded distant, as if in another room. He tried to call out to them, but he could no longer speak.

Slowly, his vision returned, but all he could see was the ball in front of him. A light grew inside it. It was dull at first but grew stronger in pulses. The pulses became quicker, and the light brighter, until all around was a brilliant white. He tried to look away but couldn't; he had no head to turn, or eyes to close. Then someone was there with him. He felt his mind being interrogated. The someone, or something, was poking around in his thoughts. But as quickly as the presence was felt, it was gone again.

The white light was also gone, and he could now see Isaac and Ellie talking to each other. Only, he saw them not from his position on the hill; he was looking up at them from below the ground. At a guess, *thirty feet* below the ground. They were standing by a tree and were partly obscured by a network of roots twisting through the earth. His eyes — though he was sure they were not his eyes — went to where *he* was sitting. He could see himself cross-legged, slumped forward and unconscious. Next to his feet, he saw the ball, which he now recognised and accepted beyond any doubt as the key to Kelha.

Then darkness returned, and with it a sensation of travelling. Without bodily senses to rely on, Max couldn't explain how he knew he was travelling, but he was. He was going from one place to another, very quickly.

The black slowly took on a green hue, and soon it was bright around him. The colours became varied, as though he were looking at a bright sunny day through a frosted bathroom window. There were sounds around him, too, the buzzing of insects and strange bird-like sounds. Were they birds? He wasn't sure.

Gradually more details emerged — texture, light, and shadow. Long, thick blades of grass towered above him. Everything was in focus, crisp and sharp. He reached out his hands to part the grass as he moved forward. But the hands he saw were not his. They were large, muscular, and covered in tattoos. He tried to pull his hands back, but they were not his to control. Suddenly he understood; he was there only to observe.

The sights and sounds were rich in detail, far richer than he was used to. But his primary sense was something other than sight. Like smell, but not smell. Scent interwoven with light. The world was ablaze with aromas, but they did not overwhelm. There was one scent he was concerned with above all others, a scent he could filter from the thousands around him. This scent had a musky heat, like warm, damp straw. Somehow, he could also smell — no, taste and see? — wariness and caution. He softened his step as a result.

As he continued through the tall grass, the ground beneath his bare feet turned to mud and then to water that slowly rose around him as he advanced. Soon, the water had reached his neck and he stopped. The grass, which continued into the water, and still concealed him, was now coming to an end. Only a few more feet of it separated him from an open pool of dark water.

He looked up. Several feet above him, beyond the tips of the grass, he saw the musky scent. It was visible as a long, purple thread of smoke. Thin and fragile, it snaked through the air. He watched it for a while as it drifted in the wind, shuddering every few seconds like a heart monitor.

His eyes followed the thread across to the muddy bank on the far side of the pool. There, drinking from the water among black, shiny twisted tree roots, was a deer. No. Not a deer. It was the colour of one, the size of one, and seemed to have the head of one, but that's where the similarities ended. Its antlers were V-shaped and started as a thick ridge running along its snout. Its posture was that of a hyena: long front legs; strong, rounded shoulders and small, sturdy hind legs. The purple thread originated from the creature's nostrils, which opened wide and closed to thin slits just above the surface of the water. Another thread of scent came from under the creature's chest and weaved off into the trees behind it. This one seemed more solid and didn't waver in the wind.

He watched the animal intently as it drank, its eyes flicking around looking for danger. It brought its head up sharply as if hearing something, giving Max his first full view of the creature. Its mouth was long, like that of a lizard, and set under its chin were two sharp-looking tusks. The dark water dripped from the fur of its lower jaw into the pool as it tilted its head, bird-like, surveying the area for danger. Definitely not a deer.

Satisfied it was alone, the animal relaxed and dipped its head and continued to drink.

Max wasn't sure if it was his own heart or the heart of his host, but he felt it slow dramatically. His breathing also slowed. After one prolonged, deep intake of air, he submerged himself fully into the pool and swam. He cut slowly through the water, close to the bottom, careful not to disturb the silt. He rolled onto his back, looking up for the shadow of the animal. When it came into view, he turned over again and edged forward until it was in striking distance.

He felt his hand reach for a blade strapped to his leg. The animal had ceased drinking again. So he waited. The creature's mouth then entered the water, its thick purple tongue flicking in and out as it drank.

Now.

With an explosive push, he propelled himself upwards. First, he grabbed the long tongue and pulled the animal's head into the water, burying his blade into its throat. Next, gripping the knife while releasing the tongue, he reached for the antler and pulled the rest of its body into the water. It kicked and writhed. It was strong — stronger than him. Still holding tight, he swung around to the back of the animal to avoid its powerful legs. It thrashed under him as blood and mud clouded the water. He could no longer see his prey, but he could feel it. Still it thrashed, bucking and twisting, but he held on tightly until the thrashing stopped, and they both sank to the bottom. There was a final twitch from the beast, and he let go, allowing it to float to the surface. He followed, guiding it to the bank, then he dragged it through the mud, over the thick roots and into the dense, long grass. The kill wasn't over yet; he might have to defend it.

Finally, once the alarm calls of the surrounding wildlife subsided and normality returned, he allowed himself to relax. He turned to face the animal, placed a hand upon its head and closed its eyes. While removing the blade from its neck, he uttered words under his breath. Max didn't understand them, but the tone was one of respect.

He left the wet and bloodied animal, returning to the water's edge to clean his blade. The mud and blood fell away from his hands and face. And as he cleaned his arms, he noticed bright markings upon the surface of his bracelet: two lines, a triangle, and a circle. He swiped them away with his finger, and another, more complex set of markings replaced them. Until this point, Max had been unaware of any emotion coming from his host. But now he felt fear and hatred surge within. *He is alive.*

The vision dissolved, and Max was surrounded by darkness once more. With no time to process what he'd just seen, he was moving again, hurtling through space. Now something else was coming into view. It was a face.

He heard laughter — a familiar laugh. The face came into focus. It was his mother. She was smiling and looking directly at him. Then she was gone, and he was left looking at a desk. It was the reception desk of the library. A hand reached out and switched off the computer screen and picked up a cup.

Max knew he was behind the eyes of someone else now. But this was different. The colours were wrong. Beautiful, but wrong. Some colours he recognised, but others were new to him. *New colours?* The idea was ridiculous. But here they were. Reddish greens and blueish yellows. They were colours he could not name — or later even remember.

In the small kitchen, he opened a dishwasher and placed the cup next to some others. Then he turned and walked back out to the reception. As well as strange new colours to deal with, there was a vast amount of detail. Everything was in focus to a level of clarity he didn't think possible: the intricate spider web vibrating above the air-conditioning unit, the thread of the carpet, the scratches on the study benches. Everything was clear and full of texture. The writing on every book spine, no matter how far away, was sharp and readable. Max felt dizzy.

He rounded the reception desk and walked towards the automatic doors. As he looked around the library, the walls faded; he could still see them, but could also see through them, into side rooms, storerooms, and even the empty bathrooms. As he neared the doors, Max felt the keys in his hand and placed one into a box on the wall and turned it, then pressed a button and watched the steel shutters slowly fall.

When the shutter reached the ground, Max was alone in the dark once more, feeling the sensation of movement again. Max was returning.

In the darkness was a voice. Like a warm wind, it blew through him. It sounded close but felt distant.

"Help him. Save him."

"Max!"

"Max? Are you OK?"

"I think he's dead."

"Shut up, Isaac!"

The light of the world came back to him, along with the sounds and smells of Oban, and the faces of his friends.

"Snap out of it, Max!" said Ellie.

They were both kneeling before him, each with a hand on his shoulder.

"Wakey, wakey, Max," Isaac said and slapped his cheek.

"There we go," said Ellie, looking relieved. "He's fine. You're fine, Max."

Together, they pulled him to his feet. But it was too soon. He gripped his stomach, then a second later, vomited. Ellie and Isaac jumped back.

"Aw, man, you almost got us," said Isaac, holding his hand to his nose and mouth.

"Are you OK?" asked Ellie, concerned. "What happened to you?"

Max was *not* OK.

"...fine," he eventually said, "I'm fine...need some space,

173

please." Ellie stepped back even further; Isaac, not wanting to get caught by a second wave, was already several metres away.

Max sat back down and didn't talk for a while, trying to process everything he'd just experienced. He picked up the ball by his foot. It looked different now. Around its centre was a thin line of blue-white light. Isaac and Ellie moved in for a closer look.

"It's true," said Max. "It's all true."

14

THE NIGHT SHIFT

Colin the nightwatchman entered the portacabin to begin his shift. It had just gone five, and the bypass construction workers were leaving for the day.

"Alright, mate," said a stout man. He was wearing a hi-vis jacket from which protruded an impressively large gut, barely covered by a vest decorated with the remnants of a meat pie. "Any chance you can move that last excavator up to the woods before morning?" he asked. "It's just...I'm supposed to do it, but need to get home to bed. Not feeling great. Probably something I ate." He slapped his sizeable gut and made an unconvincing *sick* face.

Colin knew the man wanted to get to the pub in time for the game. But he didn't mind. Getting to move the machinery around, which didn't happen often, was *the* highlight of his job. "No problem," he said, trying not to look too pleased.

"Legend! Knew I could count on you." The man dug the key from his pocket and threw it to Colin. "Cheers, mate."

"Enjoy the game," said Colin as the man walked away.

"Will do," said the man, not realising his slip.

The last of the crew piled into a mini-van, which sped

off up the wide sandy trench that would soon be the Hurst-wick bypass. The men would be dropped at their temporary digs in the surrounding towns and villages, where most of them, Mr Meat Pie included, would head to a local pub, watch the game, and drink heavily, win or lose.

Colin watched the van disappear over the brow of the hill. He was now alone and ready for the long shift ahead. It was usually a quiet shift with not much to report. The night before, he'd watched four episodes of *Red Dwarf* while eating two microwave mini pizzas. After that, he reset an alarm (triggered by a fox), walked the perimeter (mostly to get some fresh air), read the paper, and completed an extra hard sudoku puzzle. Tonight, he planned to do exactly the same, but without the fox bit, and it would be pasties instead of pizzas.

The job was simple: don't let anyone steal anything. Theft of construction vehicles did happen, but it was rare. Stealing fuel, however, was much more common. The four fuel trucks and twenty-odd construction vehicles under his protection were all at the far end of the trench. He could just about see them from the cabin window but had a perfect view via a wall of TV monitors at his security desk.

It was a quiet and lonely way to make a living. Most of the time he was sat on his backside staring at the monitors. But he loved his job. He was perfect for it. Colin liked his own company and, because he prided himself on having a great imagination, he never really got bored. Most nights, while sitting at the security desk in the pitch dark, surrounded by monitors and blinking lights, he would imagine himself the pilot of a space freighter, protecting the fuel supply of the rebellion on the front line of a galactic war. He kept that to himself, of course; he was a profes-sional, after all.

So, as long as that fuel was still there, and all the

machinery was still in one piece when the crew turned up next morning, Colin would get to keep his job as space pilot.

That night, he did his regular checks. The fuel was secure, the gates locked, CCTV on, motion detectors on, photon cannons armed, and shields up. Everything was fully operational and in order.

Back at his desk, he propped up his tablet just below the bank of monitors, poured himself a coffee, then sat to watch another episode of *Red Dwarf*. He'd just watch one, he told himself. Then he'd move the excavator before it got too dark. Maybe after he'd have—

There was a *click*, and everything went off. The monitors, the microwave, everything. Colin looked out the window. Even the large floodlight at the end of the trench was off.

"Bloody generator," he said to himself as he stood and walked to the cabin door.

With his hand on the door handle, he stopped. Something was amiss. He looked back to his security desk. The tablet — why was that dead? He returned to the desk and picked it up. He pressed the power button, but nothing happened. He pulled out his phone — also dead. He looked at his digital watch — dead. This couldn't be right.

He opened the door and looked around.

He didn't know what he was looking for. His imagination half expected to see the sun going supernova. But the evening was beautiful, calm, and quiet, not at all an end-of-the-world type of evening. He scanned the sky, hoping to see an alien armada streaking across it — but there was nothing.

Then, without fanfare or drama, the TV monitors fuzzed back to life. The security lights clicked on, as did his watch, his tablet and everything else in the cabin. Normality returned.

Twenty minutes of listening to the local radio station for

an explanation left him none the wiser. Nobody else seemed to have shared his experience. It must have been just him.

Colin recorded the incident in the Incident Log Book, then watched more of his TV program. But his heart wasn't in it; he felt a sense of unease, that something was wrong. To snap himself out of it, he thought he'd get on and move the excavator.

The excavator was bright orange. It had large caterpillar tracks and a long articulated arm with a toothy bucket at the end. As the sky darkened, Colin climbed into its cab. He brushed the seat clean of crumbs and pie wrappers, sat down, inserted the key, and powered her up. It rumbled down the centre of the wide, flat trench flanked either side by embankments of brown earth obscuring the view of the green fields beyond. Up ahead he could see the fuel trucks, along with bulldozers, rollers, loaders and more excavators. All were neatly lined up under a towering floodlight.

At the end of the trench, just past the machinery, looking like a cross-section illustration, was a forty-foot-high bank of earth and roots, crowned with a line of trees awaiting execution. It was Oban Woods. As he got closer, Colin could see banners hanging from the trees, left by protesters the day before. They were twirling and flapping in the breeze.

In Colin's opinion, the protesters had been pretty half-arsed since their success with the "Save the Newt" campaign. The result of that victory meant the bypass had been diverted *through* the woods, instead of going around it. Most of the protesters had then started to worry that if they also won the Save Oban Wood campaign, the road could be diverted again, this time closer to their homes in the surrounding towns and villages. So when the bypass reached the woods, they didn't put up much of a fight; they simply drove off in their spotless Range Rovers and were never seen again.

Colin slowed the vehicle to a crawl as he passed the other excavators. Like a mechanical brontosaurus king, his excavator rolled by its bowing subjects with its toothy head held high. He looked at how neatly they had all been parked. If he could park his just as well, Mr Meat Pie might make a habit of leaving him the keys, making Colin's job even more exciting than it already was.

The most straightforward place to park looked to be at the far end of the row, closest to the woods. But once there, the temptation to have a little dig before parking was too strong for Colin. There was still some light, and he knew the CCTV cameras didn't quite cover the very end of the trench. So he rolled closer to the wall of earth and roots, gripped the two joysticks either side of his seat and imagined himself about to mine a deep-space asteroid.

He pushed the left lever forwards, extending the hydraulic arm. There was a jolt as it stopped just short of making contact with the bank. Colin pushed the joystick forward harder, but the arm didn't budge. He pulled back on the joystick, and the arm returned to its original position. He tried again. Again the arm refused to extend fully, and stopped just short of the earth. Annoyed, he pushed harder on the lever, causing vibrations to rock the cab. Colin, fearing he'd broken something, let go of the controls instantly.

The possibility of breaking a machine he shouldn't really be driving made him feel sick in the pit of his stomach. He jumped out of the cab and examined the arm's hydraulics for leaks or signs of damage, but everything seemed alright. He climbed back into the cab and took a long deep breath. *Maybe I better just park it,* he thought. He turned the machine away from the woods, to face its neatly arrayed counterparts. They seemed to judge him: *Can't even dig with a digger.* Ignoring their silent mockery, and concerned he might have broken the thing, he tried extending the arm again. This time, it reached out fully, without complaint. Relieved, and now with something to prove, he spun the machine back to face the foundations of Oban Wood.

Colin tried again. But to his frustration, it still refused to obey him. No matter how hard he pushed the lever forward, it just wouldn't connect with the bank.

Colin said bad words, words his mother wouldn't approve of. As his frustration turned into determination, an idea formed. If the arm refused to reach the bank, then he would drive the machine forward, forcing it to comply.

It was not one of Colin's best ideas.

He put the machine into gear and slammed his foot on the pedal. This should have moved the digger forward, but it didn't. Instead, the caterpillar tracks spun wildly on the spot, throwing dust into the air. He cried out in a frustrated rage that turned into an angry sob. The surrounding cab buckled under an unseen pressure. A crack formed across the window as the engine whined, and black smoke billowed from the vents behind him. Eventually, the windows shattered, and Colin screamed as he scrambled from the now violently shaking machine. After a mad dash, he took cover behind a nearby row of portable toilets.

While Colin had his head buried between his knees, the digger's mechanical arm bent itself backwards, sending hydraulic fluid spewing in all directions. The force of the movement set the arm's bucket free. It looped through the air, its cables trailing like tendons behind it, and slammed into the base of the towering floodlight.

The engine noise subsided. And when silence had

returned to the bypass, Colin cautiously poked his head around to survey the damage.

Even in the dull light, Colin looked green. He stared at the dead excavator. Its arm was twisted and bent backwards, hydraulic blood dripping on the sandy ground.

Colin swallowed. "Oh," he said.

There was a sharp twang as somewhere to his right a steel cable snapped. It was followed by the screech of twisting metal. He turned his head slowly to the source. It was the floodlight. He watched, slack-jawed, as it toppled, falling squarely across the four parked fuel trucks, sending a bright orange mushroom cloud into the early evening sky.

"Bollocks," he said.

15

___

FAKE NEWS

"Was that thunder?" said Ellie.

"Summer storm?" suggested Isaac with a shrug.

The three were almost out of the woods, and just in time, for it was becoming virtually impossible to see in the darkness.

"Nearly there, Max," Ellie said, placing a tender hand on his shoulder. "Feeling any better?"

Max nodded, but he wasn't.

Back at the crash site, he'd told them everything he'd seen in his vision, in as much detail as he could to ensure the memory didn't fade, like dreams often did. Even though it sounded absurd, he felt no embarrassment, and he was too sick and too tired to care if they believed him. The only thing he didn't mention was the voice. *"Help him. Save him."* He wasn't sure why. It didn't sound any crazier than the rest of it. Maybe it was because answering that call for help came with risks attached, and he had no desire to endanger himself or his friends.

On the walk back through the woods, Max had remained silent, while Ellie suggested explanations for his "episode" — as she called it. She and Isaac discussed what meaning, if any, the visions might have. Isaac spoke more than Ellie on the matter. He explored all avenues of his imagination, breathless with excitement, while she tried to keep the conversation grounded in reality.

They emerged from the wood. The lights of the distant town flickered as the fields slowly released the heat of the day. Max gazed at the church spire illuminated against the indigo sky, and, once again, struggled to imagine something smashing through it, hurtling over the fields, and sinking into the woods. It didn't seem possible.

As with most journeys with an unknown destination, the way back felt quicker. And soon they were approaching the lonely oak, now just a shadow against the distant clouds on the horizon. As they passed under the tree, Max tuned back into the conversation as it turned to the subject of what to do next.

"...then we'll come back tomorrow," Isaac was saying, "and try to raise it from the ground. I've got a few ideas—"

"No," said Max, a little louder than he intended. It was his first word for at least half an hour, and it caught them by surprise. "I'm never going near that place again," he continued in a calm voice. "And I don't think you should either. You two don't seem nearly as scared as you should be."

"You'll feel different in the morning," replied Isaac.

"I won't. I know what I saw back there was real. The man...that thing — whatever he is, is real. He's angry that Wren is alive, and he's coming for him. If we get in the way...."

"You don't know that," said Isaac. "He might just be—"

"Listen to you two," said Ellie. "I believe you saw...things, Max. But it was just a hallucination caused by some bug; you were really sick back there. Think about how absurd it would be if it was real. An alien crashes to earth during

World War Two. Seventy-odd years later, he's still here and working in the library. Really, Max? You believe that?"

"I know what I saw." Max shook his head. "I'm not going back there," he added, looking at Isaac. "The tattooed man is coming."

They recovered their bikes in silence and rode down the dirt track. A police helicopter passed overhead, heading east towards the bypass, while a warm breeze brought the sound of distant sirens.

Max woke late after a restless night, his sleep disturbed by echoes of his vision. The hunt, in particular, played over and over but different each time. Sometimes the tattooed hands would part the tall alien grass to reveal Isaac and Ellie, standing on the banks of the pool, unaware of the danger they were in. Other times those same hands would part foliage of a more earthly variety. Instead of the pool, he would see his house, defenceless in the dark, a thread of scent escaping his bedroom window.

He turned over, blinked the sleep from his eyes, and looked at the alarm clock. It was almost eleven-thirty.

His stomach grumbled, complaining it hadn't yet been filled since being emptied so violently the previous day. Downstairs in the kitchen, he replenished it with three bowls of cereal, and a slice of toast with jam.

There was a note on the table. *Tried to wake you but thought you were dead. Have a beautiful day. Love you xxx.*

He trudged off to the front room. With the curtains drawn and the lights off, he sat on the sofa and clicked on the TV. He quickly muted it; his head hurt and wasn't ready for sound just yet. He stared blankly at the screen. A man wearing a hard hat and hi-vis jacket was being interviewed on the local news. He was gesturing wildly, looking excited while his interviewer looked on, half amused, half concerned. Probably another item about the bypass protests, thought Max.

Thinking about the bypass took his mind to the woods, and then to the visions. In hope of finding distraction, he flicked through the channels. But distraction came in the form of a ringing doorbell. With a groan, he dragged himself to the window and pulled the curtain aside. Daylight punched him in the face. Then, recovering from the blow, he looked again, shielding his eyes. It was Isaac. He was on his bike, looking unnerved and impatient. Not noticing Max, he rang the bell a second time. Max walked down the dim hallway as the bell rang a third time. "Hi," he croaked as he opened the door.

"Hi?" replied Isaac. "Do you not check your phone?"

Max shook his head, wearily.

"I've been calling and sending messages all morning."

"Sorry. It's probably dead."

"I thought *you* were dead."

"Maybe I am," he yawned.

"Tell me you've been watching the news?"

Max shook his head again. "Just got up."

"Max, it's all happening, and you're missing it."

Ellie leant over the wall that separated their two front gardens. "Told you he wasn't dead. Did you see the news, Max?" She looked him up and down briefly, with a slightly amused look.

"No," he said, not noticing the look but feeling a powerful desire to close the door and go back to bed.

"Believe *now*?" Isaac asked Ellie with a triumphant smile. "No way this is all a coincidence."

"Ah, you think it's linked," she replied. "Of course you

do." She looked at Max then filled him in, "They found an old bomb from the war up at the bypass, and it went off."

"Don't believe that. It's fake—"

"No, no, no. Don't say fake news. I might have to hit you."

"Ok, well, then...it's not true. It's a good old-fashioned cover-up."

She rolled her eyes and looked back to Max, who sighed, then turned and walked back up the hallway into his living room. Isaac and Ellie exchanged looks, shrugged, then followed.

Max stood in front of the TV, holding the remote. He flicked back to the news and turned up the volume, as Isaac and Ellie arrived and stood beside him.

"...the explosion was seen for miles around. Emergency services are at the scene now, along with two military heli-copters. The only statement to be released so far confirms that one man, a night watchman for the site, is being treated for minor injuries. As we wait for an official statement from the authorities, a two-mile exclusion zone has been put in place, and the airspace surrounding the town is now closed to all civilian air traffic. We have yet to receive more information on earlier reports that the cause was a World War Two bomb. We'll bring you more news as we get it. Back to you, Samira."

Isaac huffed. "A bomb. What a load of sh—"

"It could be a bomb," Ellie interrupted.

Max turned to face Isaac. "If it's not a bomb, what is it?" he asked, starting to wake up and realising he was wearing his slightly-too-small Batman pyjamas in front of his new best friends.

"Unexploded bombs turn up all the time," said Isaac. "They found one a few years ago when they were extending the school playing field."

"I remember that," said Ellie.

"Yeah. And do you remember the helicopters flying in and the two-mile exclusion zone?"

Ellie shrugged.

"No. You don't," said Isaac. "Because they didn't do any of that. They just cordoned off the area with some police tape and put a policeman on guard. Then a couple of army types turned up in a Land Rover and blew it up. And that was it." He took off his backpack and placed it, gently, on the floor, then slumped down on the sofa. "I've seen two military helicopters today, guys! *Two*."

A shadow moved across the front room window, followed by a deep rumble as another passed overhead.

"Three," Isaac said, pointing up. "This has to be linked to that key," he continued. "We heard the explosion. Remember? We thought it was thunder. That must have been about half an hour after the key started glowing. What if the glowing key means Kelha is now awake? And if she is awake, I think she's defending her hiding place from the bypass. The ground works have already reached the edge of the wood. They were due to start ploughing through it today. In a week or so it would have reached the crash site. She's protecting herself."

Max looked at Ellie, waiting for her to laugh and bring the conversation back down to earth. But she didn't.

"What?" she said, returning his look. "I don't know what to believe anymore."

"I'm right, and you know it," said Isaac. "But there's only one way to find out what's happening over there. We need to take a look."

"You're forgetting about the two-mile exclusion zone," said Ellie.

"No, I'm not." Isaac smiled, opened his backpack, and pulled out his brother's drone.

"And Jacob is suddenly fine with you using that?" said Max.

"Hah. Good one." Isaac laughed. "Desperate times call for desperate measures, and I desperately want to find out what's going on over there."

"You're nuts, Isaac," Ellie said, smiling. "Let's go."

"You're both nuts," said Max. "Getting involved is... dangerous. For all we know, the tattooed man...thing...could be here now. He might be looking for the key. Now it's active he might be able to *trace* it. We should just give it to the police and let *them* deal with it."

"You could do that," said Isaac, "but what happens then? What about Wren? After everything that kid went through to keep him safe. He'd have the police on his back *and* this tattooed killing machine. I'm not Mr Hall's biggest fan, Max, but that seems harsh."

"You think the other person in the vision was Mr Hall?" said Ellie, surprised.

"Thought that was obvious," said Isaac, glancing at Max, who nodded in agreement. "I mean...I've suspected for a long time the guy wasn't human. This only confirms it."

"Oh," said Ellie, "yeah, I suppose...."

"I could get rid of the key; hide it," suggested Max.

"Wren wants to get home," said Isaac. "You should give him the key. If you don't want to, I'll do it."

"No," said Max. "I should do it."

Ellie placed a supportive hand on his shoulder, and with a straight face said, "It's what Batman would do."

Isaac held in a laugh.

The three of them rode down the centre of a deserted high street, rucksacks packed in preparation for what could be a long day. Isaac's was heavy with the drone, and hung low on his back.

"You didn't tell me you had a bike," Isaac said to Ellie. "It would have been useful information yesterday."

"You didn't ask. And besides," she said with a smile, "I didn't need it yesterday; I had you."

Isaac shook his head.

"This place is a ghost town," said Max, looking down the empty side streets.

Ellie nodded. "I've never seen it this quiet," she said. "Everyone must be at Windmill Hill."

"All trying to get on TV, no doubt," said Isaac.

"Windmill Hill?" Max asked.

"It's the only place outside the exclusion zone you can get a view of the bypass," said Isaac. "I was there this morning. You can't see much. Everything interesting is hidden behind a smaller hill, which, sadly, happens to be *inside* the zone."

The only vehicle on the road was a TV news van, parked outside the supermarket. Luckily for the owner, Hurstwick's usually omnipresent traffic wardens were nowhere in sight — probably at the bypass trying to put tickets on illegally parked helicopters.

A bearded man in sunglasses, shorts, and T-shirt left the supermarket hurriedly, carrying what looked like a week's worth of shopping. "Open up," he said, giving the rear door a kick with his sandalled foot.

The doors swung open, and a familiar-looking woman reached out to take the bags. "Really?" she said. "*Just a few supplies*, you said. Did you leave anything for the locals?"

"Just the healthy stuff." He smiled, and when the bags were in, he slammed the doors, jogged around to the driver's side, then climbed in.

"See!" said Isaac, looking back to Max as they passed the

van. "Sophia Jansson. She's *national* news. She wouldn't be up here for an *unexploded bomb* story. They know this is big, I'm telling you."

Moments later they were outside the library, locking up their bikes.

"Well," said Ellie, looking at Max. "Have you thought about how you're going to do this?"

"I think it's best if I just give him the key." He shrugged while he fiddled with the straps hanging from his backpack. "Say nothing, ask nothing, and...see what he says."

"No small talk. Like it." Isaac said. "It's what I would do. Play it cool — casual."

Max wasn't cool or casual; he was nervous and trying not to show it. He also felt disconnected, as if this was happening to someone else, not him. This time yesterday, he was full of scepticism about the key and the contents of the notebook. It was just an entertaining distraction from boredom. But now everything was different. Now he lived in a world were aliens worked in libraries and spaceships buried underground put visions in your head. He wondered if he was going mad.

As they walked through the automatic doors, they were met by an empty reception desk. Behind it, through the open door of the back room, they saw Max's mother and Mr Walsh, the caretaker. They had their backs to them, watching the news on the small wall-mounted TV above the fridge. The sound was off, being a library, and they stood reading the subtitles while speaking quietly.

The rest of the library was as empty as the streets outside. There was no sign of Mr Hall.

They split up. Max went along the centre of the main room, while Isaac went left, and Ellie went right. They met at the other end, looked at each other, and shook their heads. They parted again, drifting aimlessly around, picking up random books. Every so often they would cast a look towards the reception or the various doors marked Staff Only. Anyone watching would think they were casing the joint.

They regrouped outside the Local News and History room.

"Perhaps he's gone to Windmill Hill, with everyone else," Isaac said. He looked into the empty room. "Bet your life that's where Bartley is. Probably telling his crazy stories to the news crews as we speak."

"Only they don't sound crazy anymore, do they," said Max walking into the room and glancing at the display and the wreckage behind the glass.

"You know what the best thing to do now is?" Isaac said. Then, not waiting for an answer, "Go fly a drone. Come on, are you not just a little curious to see what's happening over there?"

"You two go," said Max. He could see Isaac was itching to leave. "I'll wait here for him. I'll call you. Let you know how it went." He craned his neck to eye the reception, then looked at his watch. "He's probably gone for lunch. They take it in turns."

"Or...he might have left town?" Ellie said.

Isaac nodded in agreement. "I'd skip if it was me. This place is probably already crawling with army and government types. Look, we'll wait with you, in case he's stupid enough to hang around. But I'll be in the games room next door." He smiled, tipped the brim of his cap, then left.

"I'll just be out here," said Ellie, thumbing over her shoulder. "I'll come running if I see him." She smiled and turned away.

Max faced the empty room, grabbed a book at random, then sat down at the table, placing his bag beside him. He opened the bag and removed the key. Holding it under the table, he eyed the thin ring of light around its centre. A blue light began to grow under his fingertip where he touched the surface. Quickly, he pulled his finger away, in case of accidentally causing something to happen that he might regret. With the fear that he might have already caused Kelha to self-destruct, he placed the key in his pocket.

From his position he had a good view of the library floor and the reception area beyond. If this room remained empty, it would be the most discreet place to give Mr Hall the key.

Ten minutes had passed when he saw Mr Walsh leave, and his mother take her seat behind the front desk. Max shifted his chair sideways until she was hidden from view, blocked by part of the wall.

He turned his attention to the book in front of him. As he absently flicked through its pages, he thought about all the ways this could pan out. Would Mr Hall thank him? Would he be pleased? He couldn't imagine Mr Hall expressing gratitude or pleasure, but he could easily imagine him being angry or defensive.

A thought started to form in Max's mind, but it wouldn't develop fully. It would begin to take shape, then fall apart. The harder he tried to grasp it, the less substantial it became. Soon, even the memory of a near-thought escaped him. He yawned and pushed the book away. Too tired to read, he crossed his arms and stared out into the library and waited. He would wait for as long as it took, and he would be vigilant. But maybe just close his eyes for a second...

SNAP! Went Old Man Bartley's glasses case, waking Max from his dreamless sleep with a jump. Max rubbed his eyes and looked around for his friends; they weren't there. Mr Bartley was sitting adjacent to Max, calmly turning the pages of his newspaper. "So, are you here to tell me what you know?" he said, not looking at Max as he spoke. "Or are you going to run off again?"

Max tried to stand, but Bartley reached over and placed a firm hand on his shoulder. "I would prefer it if you didn't go anywhere just yet," he said in a strong but library-quiet voice.

Too tired to resist, Max sat back down and glanced towards the exit in time to see his mother leaving for lunch. He wondered if that meant Mr Hall was back.

"You know something, don't you?" said Bartley, "about what's going on? I'm not stupid, you know. The only kids I've seen pay any attention to that" — he nodded towards the glass cabinet — "are school kids forced to pay attention by teachers. Teachers passing on the lie to a new generation of blinkered sheep. Get 'em early, and they won't question anything.

"And then *you* show up taking an interest, and things start to happen. So, young man, I want to know who you are and what you know."

Max no longer felt intimidated by the man; he felt sorry for him. He'd, apparently, been ridiculed for his theories for most of his life, but he'd been right all along.

"You're right," said Max, deciding he deserved to know the truth. "I do know something. Quite a lot, actually."

Bartley leaned back in his chair, ready to listen. "Maybe you can start by telling me how you knew my father's name. Because *I* didn't tell you."

"I read about him — in a diary."

Bartley tilted his head, waiting for more information, but Max didn't offer any. "And..." he prompted.

Max sighed. "I can't tell you everything. Not yet. But... you were right about that." He nodded to the display. "It is a lie."

"And the truth? If it wasn't a plane, what was it?" Bartley said, crossing his arms.

Max took a deep breath. "A spaceship." It sounded absurd out loud. Even after all he'd seen, he felt ridiculous for saying it. He should have said *spacecraft*, he thought. Somehow that sounded slightly less silly.

Mr Bartley's face dropped. His hands slapped the table, and he pushed himself to his feet, sending his chair crashing to the ground. "Are you making fun of me, boy?" he snapped.

"No," said Max, surprisingly calm. "I'm not. It's true." He kept his eyes locked on Bartley's. "I'm telling you the truth."

Bartley considered Max carefully. After a lengthy pause, he walked over and stood by the display cabinet. "What's your name?"

"Max."

"Well, Max. Wild theories don't help anyone," he said, staring at the twisted piece of metal. "They didn't do my old man any good."

The path was clear for Max to leave, but he stayed and turned in his chair to face him. "So your father had theories?" he asked.

"Just the one. Same as yours." Bartley took a breath and seemed to relax again. "Ok. So if you're not mocking me, where's your evidence? My dad had nothing, apart from what he heard; the drunken ramblings of some government man he drove about, day in, day out. *That* man, Henry something-or-other, was the first to be driven crazy by all this."

"Crinklaw," said Max. "Henry Crinklaw."

Bartley stared at him, his bushy grey eyebrows colliding above eyes that were quivering, as if retrieving a memory. Then he nodded. "Yes. That was him — Crinklaw. Whose diary did you read, Crinklaw's? No. Don't tell me," he said, "I'm done with all this. I...I don't want to know."

Mr Bartley suddenly looked small and fragile, like a man who'd spent his entire life looking for an answer, and now, within touching distance of the truth, seemed to fear it more than anything.

Just then, Isaac and Ellie burst into the room. "He's coming," whispered Ellie. "Hall's coming."

The two positioned themselves behind Max as the dark shape of Mr Hall appeared, framed by the white archway. His eyes moved from one face to the next, then he spied the fallen chair. "Are these three...*bothering* you, Mr Bartley?" he said in his precise monotonal way.

"No," he replied quickly. "This young man was giving me a...history lesson. Weren't you?"

Max nodded as Isaac and Ellie seemed to notice Bartley for the first time. Mr Hall picked up the chair, then looked at each face again. It was now or never. He'd prefer not to do this in front of Bartley, but he didn't have much choice. The tattooed man was coming, and Max didn't want to still have the key when he got here.

With his heart pounding in his chest, he reached into his pocket, feeling the warm key in his hand. But then, the thought from earlier, the one Max couldn't quite grasp, came back to him. This time it was clear and fully formed, and it filled him with relief; his body relaxed and his heart returned to normal. Calmly and without a word, he removed the key from his pocket and placed it on the table.

He watched Mr Hall's face intently.

Ellie and Isaac watched too as Mr Hall glanced at the key. "No toys in the library," he said flatly, regarding the object with little interest. Then he turned and left the room.

Isaac looked stunned. Ellie walked to the door, watching as Mr Hall glided towards the front desk.

"I don't get it," Isaac said, breaking the silence. "Did he not *recognise* it?"

"Maybe it's been too long and he's forgotten?" Ellie said.

"He didn't recognise it," said Max, "because he's never seen it before. It's not him. I knew it before I put it on the table, but I had to be sure."

"What do you mean?" asked Ellie. "How do you know it's not? It has to be. He's weird and scary."

"Exactly," said Max, "Not the type of person my mum would smile at. Not a smile like the one I saw. And not the type of person George would want as a friend."

Max was suddenly aware of Old Man Bartley. He was looking at the key, still on the table, with its ring of light.

"I've changed my mind," Bartley said, a slight tremble to his voice. "I want to know *everything* you know. Everything."

Max nodded. "Then you might want to sit down," he said. Isaac sighed and muttered something about a drone.

"This," said Max, holding up the key as Bartley took a seat, "was taken from the boot of your father's car by a boy called George Moss. He was trying to return it to its owner. His name was Wren."

Bartley remained silent while Max told him everything, including the visions. As the old man listened, he seemed to transform. His face lightened as the constant dark frown, which he carried everywhere, dissolved.

"Can I hold it?" Mr Bartley asked, pointing to the key with a shaking finger, once Max had finished.

As he held it, a single tear escaped the corner of the old man's eye and ran down his weathered cheek. "Nobody believed him," he said in a small voice. "Not even me in the end." He held up the key between his thumb and forefinger, turning it. "You mentioned the drawing? I don't suppose—"

Max removed it from his bag and laid it flat on the table.

Bartley shook his head and puffed out a laugh in disbelief. "The trouble he got into for losing these. It ruined his career...ruined him. He would always say that whatever came down in those woods was *out of this world*. Nobody took him seriously. I believed him when I was a kid; you believe everything your father says when you're a kid...but then I saw what it did to our family. It tore it apart. He turned to drink in the end.

"When I got older, and after he died, I looked into it more. I refused to waste time thinking about his flying saucer theories. But I was sure *that*" — he pointed to the exhibit — "was a lie. And if I could just prove it, then that would be something. But...you're telling me...he was right." Two more tears chased the first down the old man's face. His chin trembled as he tried to hold himself together while Isaac and Ellie glanced around the room uncomfortably.

Mr Bartley straightened up, wiped his eyes with the palm of his hand, and smiled at the three of them. "Silly old fool, eh?" He handed the key back to Max, then blew his nose on a handkerchief. "Thank you," he said. "Thank you for telling me the truth." He stood and picked up his hat from the table.

Max stood, too. "What are you going to do now you know all this?"

"I don't think I need to do anything. Things seem to be happening on their own, don't they?" He turned and walked away. Max knew he was referring to the goings-on at the bypass, and he was right. Things were happening, and Max felt time slipping away; he could almost feel it ticking inside his chest.

Bartley turned before leaving the room, "However, I suggest you go find..." he paused, "Ben? Is it?"

Max nodded.

Bartley smiled. "Well, you find him, and give him that." He nodded to the key. "Oh, and stay away from strange men with tattoos."

16

EYE SPY DRAGONFLY

From a distance, as they approached on their bikes, Windmill Hill looked like a dollop of mint ice cream topped with sprinkles. Those sprinkles were the people of Hurstwick, and probably many from other nearby towns and villages.

The hill had never seen such a gathering. On a typical day, you could expect to find a handful of dog walkers, launching their hairy missiles from the backs of Volvos. But today, it was buzzing with activity. The small car park was overflowing, and parked cars lined the roads, spilling down the sides of the hill. Two opportunistic ice cream vans had arrived. Both had lengthy queues of people looking hot and in need of refreshment. But most people were swarming around the TV news crews that delivered their reports to the nation. Kids and adults alike edged their way into shot for their fifteen seconds of fame.

"Wow, *everyone* is here," said Ellie, as they collapsed, breathless, on a grass verge next to their bikes and stared at the enormous crowd.

"He could be anywhere," said Max. "Why do you think he would be here, Isaac?"

"I —"

"He doesn't," interrupted Ellie. "He just wants to get closer to the bypass so he can launch his toy."

"It is not a toy," Isaac said. "Anyway, where else would he be? We waited long enough at the library, and he wasn't showing. He won't be at the crash site; without the key, what would be the point? This is where I would come."

"Can we talk about why you think it's this Ben guy?" said Ellie, retrieving a bottle of water from her bag then taking a swig.

"I'm not one hundred percent sure it is," said Max. "But I can't imagine who else it could be."

"What about the old caretaker?" said Isaac, exhausted and lying flat on the grass with his bag beside him. "You said you saw Wren closing the shutters. Doesn't Mr Walsh lock up?"

Max nodded. "He does. But when I think back to the vision. I — he — was looking down at my mother; Mr Walsh is short. I just have this feeling that it's him. I can't explain it." He slapped his bike pedal with his hand and watched it spin.

"I don't even remember another guy at the library," said Ellie after a pause. "What does he look like?"

Isaac opened his mouth to respond, but then closed it again. With a confused expression, he looked to Max for help. But Max was looking just as perplexed.

"I...don't know how to describe him," said Isaac, sitting upright. "He's just normal-looking. Max?"

Max shrugged. "Tall. White..."

"Well, that narrows it down," said Ellie. "We're looking for a tall white man. Great."

"If he's here, we'll find him," said Max. Though he wasn't sure of it.

"It makes sense," said Isaac, "if you think about it. He must have been living in this town for seventy-odd years.

Maybe he has a knack for hiding in plain sight. If he didn't, wouldn't the locals get suspicious of a man who didn't age? I might not be able to describe him or even picture him right now, but I'm sure he's not old. Thirty? Forty, tops?"

Max nodded in agreement.

"Why stay in Hurstwick?" said Ellie. "Why not travel the world? See the sights?"

"Maybe he did," said Isaac. "Maybe that's what he does. He goes off for a while, then comes back with a different identity. I don't know. Or maybe he stays because this is where the key is, and Kelha."

Max felt the ticking clock again, this time louder, thumping in his chest. They were wasting time. He stood and scanned the crowd. Sat at a picnic table under the shade of a tree was a small group of people. They were old — ancient, even — and they watched the crowd with concern. Max had seen them before but couldn't think where. As if sensing his gaze, one woman looked over. Tall and elegant, she smiled and gave a polite nod. Max smiled back, then turned away. "Come on," he said. "We need to find him."

They separated, and each pushed their bikes through the crowd looking for Ben. They regrouped on the other side, where they got a good view of the bypass, its vast sandy channel cutting through the rolling green countryside. A police car sped along it, a trail of dust in its wake, but soon disappeared from view behind a hill within the exclusion zone.

"See. Not much to see from here," said Isaac, nodding towards the hill.

"Any sign of Ben?" asked Max, ignoring the view.

Isaac shook his head, and Ellie, having no idea what Ben looked like, shrugged.

From nowhere, a helicopter roared overhead, causing a

dust-storm to rise around them. A portly man standing next to Max held on tight to his hat with one hand, while his other held a pair of binoculars to his eyes. "That one's carrying troops, Doris," he shouted over the noise. His disinterested-looking wife sat on a deckchair, shielding her rocket-shaped ice lolly from the swirling dust.

They watched the helicopter as it circled the bypass. It was large and black with two sets of rotors. It hovered for a while, then dropped behind the hill.

"OK, Isaac," said Ellie. "You might be right about this. This *is* something else. You don't bring troops in to defuse a bomb." She lowered her voice. "So how do we launch the drone without people noticing?"

"We have to get closer. The range on this thing means we need to be inside the exclusion zone," said Isaac.

"Right," said Ellie, frustrated, but not surprised. "You failed to mention that before."

"Oh, did I?" Isaac smiled. "Look, you don't have to come. It would be good to have someone on the lookout while I fly it. But I—"

"I'll come," she said, then turned to Max. "Max?"

Max was staring at the smaller hill, wondering if Wren was inside the exclusion zone, and wishing he'd brought his binoculars.

"Are you OK going in there?" asked Ellie.

Max, who would typically not be OK with something like this, nodded.

They locked their bikes to a fence post, climbed over a wooden stile, and joined a steep chalky path descending the hill. The din from the crowd behind grew quieter as they went. Max was relieved to leave it. He disliked crowds. He was never comfortable in them. Until a few weeks ago, he would have considered three to be a crowd.

At the bottom of Windmill Hill, the path levelled out and was lined with long grass and summer flowers, and a scattering of trees: hawthorn, sycamore, and ash. They walked on in silence, keeping an eye ahead, expecting a police barrier around every bend.

As they rounded a dense thicket of bush and tree, they saw a man and his dog approach.

"You can't go much further," he said when he'd reached them. "Police have blocked off the gate down there."

They thanked him and stepped aside, allowing the man to pass, then waited until they were alone before continuing.

"It might be fine," said Isaac. "Might just be a locked gate with some police tape. If it is, we'll just climb over."

They continued down the narrowing path that was slowly disappearing in a sea of grass. After a while, they saw the gate ahead, police tape tied around its gateposts flapping in the breeze. Behind it was a grassy field that merged with a narrow strip of woods skirting the foot of the hill.

They stopped and surveyed the area.

"We can hide in those trees and launch from the field," said Isaac.

"Just one problem," Ellie said, grabbing them both by the shoulders and pulling them into the grass. "Look!" she pointed. Not far from the gate, under the shade of a broad tree, was a policeman sitting against the trunk looking very bored.

"Damn it!" Isaac struck the ground with the palm of his hand. "I bet they have every path blocked."

"Then we won't take a path." Ellie pulled out her phone and brought up a map of the area, "Look. If we keep low and move west, we might find another way in. Ah," she said, sounding doubtful. "We'll be very close to Moore's Farm, though."

"Moore's Farm?" said Max. "Where George found Wren." He wondered if it was the same Farmer Moore that George had been so afraid of, or a less frightening descendant instead.

Isaac leaned in to look at the map. "Why not just go to the farm? It looks perfect. It's in the exclusion zone, so should be empty, and looks to be in range for the drone."

Ellie shrugged. "We could try," she said.

They both looked at Max, who said nothing but nodded in agreement.

They backed up until the policeman was no longer visible, then left the path. After twenty minutes of walking west across the meadow, they reached the boundary fence of the farm. They stood on its bottom rung, looking out across the open field of wheat, unmoving in the now still air. When they were certain they were not being watched, they climbed over and crossed the field. On the far side, they squeezed through a gap in the hedgerow, then clambered down a small bank to a dry tractor-gouged path that ran between the fields. They followed it north.

Moments later, they reached a closed metal gate, beyond which sat a collection of buildings, old and new. They were clustered together, contained within a stone wall on one side and a row of trees and hedges on the other.

"Well, we're in the exclusion zone," said Isaac, checking his phone, "and still too far out for the drone, but only just. If we can make it to those buildings, we'll be in range. We'll also have the cover we need."

They climbed the metal gate and followed the path. If Max felt any guilt or apprehension for trespassing, it had been drowned out by his now constant internal ticking clock.

"If we run into anyone," Ellie said as they neared the buildings, "we say we're looking for our dog. OK?"

"OK," said Isaac. "What's the dog's name?" he added.

"There is no dog, Isaac. It's a pretend dog."

"I know, but we need to decide on a name. In case someone asks, and we all say different names."

"Buster," said Ellie flatly.

"Too obvious. How about Norman?" said Isaac.

"Doesn't really sound like a dog's name," said Max.

Isaac shrugged. "Clive?"

"Again, not doggy enough," said Max. "How about Bruno?"

"Shut up, guys. It's Ginger. And before you ask, Isaac, she's a two-year-old red setter with a wheat intolerance, an irrational fear of squirrels and a flatulence problem."

"Where's Ginger's lead?"

Ellie gave Isaac a cold stare, then looked ahead. She was too hot and bothered to play his games.

Isaac looked to Max, raised his eyebrows and mock wiped sweat from his brow. And they went on in silence.

Now inside the yard, they passed an empty cowshed, and a long low brick building, that, by the smell of it, had recently been home to pigs.

"Wow," said Isaac. "They really cleared out everything."

"Yeah," said Ellie. "What happened over there to make them this cautious? Why empty out an entire farm, over a *mile* away?"

"*Something* scared them," said Max.

A large metal building dominated the yard, surrounded by smaller outbuildings. All of them were chained and padlocked, but one looked perfect. Set back behind an ancient-looking wall was an old black wooden barn. It sat alone, its double doors open, tempting them inside. They looked to each other, nodded, approached, then entered through its doors cautiously.

It was cool and dim inside the barn. The current owners were using the building to store broken bits of machinery, much of which looked as if it hadn't been touched in decades.

"This could be where George found Wren," Isaac whispered.

"It is," said Max. It had to be.

"First Contact," said Isaac, nodding. He reached out a hand and gently touched the inside wall. Then, responding to a look from Ellie: "Just saying, if this *is* where George met Wren, it's a place of historical significance — First Contact. It's special."

"You're special," Ellie mumbled picking up a piece of dusty machinery from a work bench, then returning it as it fell apart in her hands. "Anyway, didn't you say he saw him first on the bridge?"

"Yeah. Ah, but...that was just a close encounter."

Ellie smiled at his nerdiness, while brushing the dust from her hands.

"Are we in range?" asked Max, looking through a hole in the wooden wall of the barn.

Isaac pulled out his phone. "Perfect," he said. And then in his best American accent: "We are in range of target."

"OK, Captain America," Ellie said, "let's just do this before someone finds us."

"Captain America does not have a drone—"

"Whatever. Just get on with it."

They climbed the ladder leading to the dark, dusty loft, and found the hatch opening they had seen from outside. Looking out, beyond the yard below, out past the old wall, they saw a vast field of wheat stretching to the hill. The hill stopping them — and the nation — from seeing what was *really* going on at the bypass.

Isaac liberated the drone from his bag, unfolded its four limbs and flicked each propeller with his finger. Then he flicked a switch on the drone's underside before placing it gently on the floor. He locked his phone into a cradle attached to the remote control, and flicked another switch. An amber flashing light appeared on both the remote and the drone. They both blinked for a few seconds before turning a solid green. The phone screen came alive to show Ellie's trainers and a partial view of the hatchway, and the field beyond. Isaac extended the remote's aerial and stepped back, then nodded to Ellie and Max to do the same.

Max felt the ticking clock once more; this time in the pit of his stomach. It was urging him on, imploring him to keep moving, to find Wren and rid himself of the key, which now felt so heavy in his possession.

"Help him. Save him."

As the voice came to him, Max's legs gave way, and he stumbled.

Ellie caught him. "Woah! Are you OK?" She threw a concerned look to Isaac, as she helped Max steady himself.

"Yes, fine. Just tired. I'm fine, though." He nodded to Isaac. "Carry on. Let's just do this, quick."

"Roger that," said Isaac. "Ten, nine, eight—"

"*Isaac!*" Ellie and Max shouted in unison.

"OK, OK."

The four propellers snapped into life, blowing away dust and straw from the floorboards. The whine of the motors increased in pitch until the drone slowly rose and hovered before them.

Isaac pivoted the drone's camera to face them. "Selfie!" He smiled and tapped a button on the remote to take a photo. He was the only one smiling.

"Isaac. Please..." pleaded Max. "We're wasting time. Just launch it."

"Just testing it all works. Here we go. *Fly* my beauty — *fly!*"

Skilfully, he directed the drone through the hatch. It dipped low over the yard, passed through a gap in the old brick wall and moved across the field at pace. The pitch of its whining motors fell away as it went.

"I'm impressed," said Ellie, watching as it sped off. "Not the first time you've flown that thing, I take it?"

"Nope. Jacob went skiing with the school earlier in the year. I had an entire week with it."

Isaac made himself comfortable in the hatch opening, his legs dangling over the edge. Max and Ellie kneeled behind him. They watched the video feed showing the blur of wheat field passing, while the hill ahead slowly grew to fill the screen. Soon the field came to an end, and Isaac increased the drone's altitude, clearing the trees at the foot of the hill.

Max tried to spot the drone, but it was already lost in the distance, as was the whine of its motors.

"Finally, we get to see what all the fuss is about," said Isaac, as he took it over the hill.

Max and Ellie leaned in, watching the screen. They watched the hill fall away to reveal lush green fields. Isaac adjusted the camera, bringing the sandy strip of bypass into view, then locked the drone into position and turned his attention to the camera controls. As the camera panned along the track, they saw a group of temporary buildings. Further along, there was a makeshift roadblock guarded by two heavily armed police officers.

"Let's hope they don't shoot the drone down," said Ellie.

"No way," replied Isaac. "They wouldn't risk firing

bullets into the air." He turned to face them, a worried look on his face. "Would they?"

Ellie shrugged. "Doubt it. But can you imagine?"

"I'd rather not. Why would you say that?" Isaac turned back to the screen and took the drone a little higher, just in case, then continued to pan the camera. "Bingo!" he said, hitting the record button as a row of four military helicopters entered the frame. The rotors of the large Chinook, which was the latest to arrive, were still turning slowly as troops unloaded large crates from its gaping rear hatch.

As they continued to pan left, past the helicopters, they came to a large black patch on the ground. It was slightly out of focus at first but soon sharpened to reveal the mangled remains of what looked like three or four burnt-out trucks, smoke still rising from the ashes. A fire truck stood nearby.

Further along still was a row of construction vehicles. The first two looked fire-damaged but not completely destroyed. In front of these were three more objects of similar size, covered in large black sheets flapping in the wind.

Isaac zoomed out to take in the broader scene. A dark green tent, the size of a small house, came into view. Gathered outside were a group of about forty people, most wearing hard hats and hi-vis jackets over civilian clothes. A few were army types, high ranking judging by their uniforms. All of them stood behind a wall of sandbags, looking out towards the wide track.

"Wonder how often generals and dignitaries attend routine bomb detonations," Isaac said.

"My guess would be, never." Ellie replied. "What are they doing? Are they watching something?"

"Go left," said Max.

Isaac obliged, and the focus of the crowd's attention appeared on the phone's screen. They were watching a single excavator as it trundled towards the end of the dirt track. Several remote-controlled cameras, set up along its route on tripods, turned to follow the machine as it passed.

Those on the ground had gone to extraordinary lengths to ensure secrecy. Large canvas screens had been set up to block the view of anyone outside the bypass. And armed soldiers stood high on the bank, among the trees of Oban. Instead of looking down to the approaching digger, they observed the woods for uninvited spectators.

The digger stopped abruptly, and the driver, dressed in army fatigues, jumped from the cab and waited as another man approached. This second man, or it could have been a woman, looked *very* different from the first. He or she was covered from head to toe in thick armour. They waddled more than walked. Their large helmet, with Perspex visor, was surrounded by an armoured collar that offered protection to the back and sides of the head but dipped at the front to allow them to see.

"What is going on?" whispered Ellie.

"No idea," replied Isaac. "Whatever they're doing, they need to do it soon; my battery is down to sixty-two percent already. I have to bring it back before it reaches fifty if I want to see my next birthday."

They watched as the heavily armoured person was squeezed into the cab by the soldier. There was an exchange of upwardly pointed thumbs, then the soldier retreated to join the others behind the sandbags.

Moments later, the engines of the excavator grew louder, and with a jolt, it lurched forward, gradually speeding up, racing towards the high bank of earth below the trees of Oban. As it moved faster and faster, it became clear the intention was to crash the machine. But then, just metres from the bank, it stopped abruptly, as if hitting an invisible wall. The digger was no longer moving, but the caterpillar tracks continued to spin, throwing dry orange dirt into the air. Inside, the driver argued forcefully with the controls, trying everything to propel the machine forwards. But it was no good. A cloud of black smoke erupted from the machine's exhaust, and the tracks stopped turning.

Once the dust and smoke had cleared, the operator slowly drew the mechanical arm high in the air, like a hammer about to strike. Then, with full force, they drove the heavy bucket down towards the bank.

Max, Isaac and Ellie didn't see it connect; the screen went black.

When the image returned a second later, there was nothing to see but a green blur of countryside as the drone plummeted to the ground.

"No, no, no!" cried Isaac, as he struggled to regain control. He somehow managed to save it, and all three sighed in relief.

"Man, I'm good," said Isaac breathlessly, with a hand on his chest.

"And modest," said Ellie. "Get back up there. See what happened."

He was already on it, quickly returning the drone to its position high above the hill, just as a sound, like metallic thunder, echoed across the fields towards them.

After some searching, they found the digger. It was a long way from the bank — and the wrong way up. Its caterpillar tracks, motionless, were facing the clear blue sky. The cab had been crushed like a tin can, and the driver was climbing from the broken window. A second later, Isaac discovered the hefty mechanical arm. It was detached from its body, twisted and broken, lying just metres from the stunned crowd behind the sandbag wall. Paramedics, carrying a stretcher, pushed a line through the onlookers to get to the upturned digger.

"What just happened?" said Max.

"No," said Ellie, shaking her head. "No."

"I think," said Isaac, "we need to see that again."

He closed the live feed, and a list of video files appeared on his phone. He selected the latest one and scrubbed to near the end of the recording, just before the blackout, then backed up a few seconds before pressing play. Just as the mechanical arm of the digger was about to plunge towards the bank, he pressed pause, then nudged it forward, frame by frame.

"Oh, wow," said Ellie. She sat down and stared into space.

"Huh," replied Max, not quite believing his eyes.

It was only about a second of footage, maybe less. But before everything went black, the digger could clearly be seen leaving the ground, like a toy picked up by an unseen child.

POP! POP! POP!

"What's that sound?" Max said. It was coming from over the hill.

POP! POP!

"Oh, no!" Isaac said, panic in his voice. He returned to the live video feed. Flashes were coming from the ground. *POP! POP!* A soldier stood by the tent was shooting at the drone.

"Hell, *no* you don't!" shouted Isaac, his fingers moving like crazy as he tried everything to evade the gunfire. Skilfully, he flipped the drone over and zig-zagged back towards the farm.

"No. Don't bring it straight back!" said Ellie. "You'll lead them here."

"Excellent point!" He changed direction and flew over Oban. Anyone watching from the ground would think it was heading towards town, not Moore's Farm.

Hardly breathing, they watched the feed as the drone skimmed over the canopy.

"Right, that should do it," said Isaac, turning the drone around to bring it back. "That was *too* close." The tip of the aerial shook as Isaac concentrated on the screen.

The drone was now passing over a large clearing in the woods. They could almost make out the farm buildings in the distance. "Thirty percent battery," said Isaac, shakily. "We should just about make it—"

Crack!

The screen fizzed and went black.

Max and Ellie exchanged perplexed looks, while Isaac slapped the side of the remote and jumped to his feet.

"What the? Where's the...."

The image returned. It showed a tilted view of the clearing: long grass and a corner of sky. It was no longer airborne. The drone was down.

Isaac stared open-mouthed at the screen. Ellie placed a hand on his shoulder. "Oh, man..." she said.

Isaac sat back down, placed the controller to the side and slowly contracted into a ball. "I'm dead," he said. "He is *literally* going to kill me."

"Maybe it's OK. Maybe it had a soft landing," said Max, as he picked up the controller and began to move the levers, but it was clear the drone was dead. "The camera still works," he said, regretting it immediately.

Isaac shot him a look: "Well that's just *great*, then. Everything is great. Hey, Jacob, I killed your DragonFly, but don't kill me, the camera still works—"

"Shhh!" Ellie cut him off. "Listen."

"No, Ellie, I won't shhh, I've just—"

She slapped a hand over his mouth. "Shhh...."

A slow crunch of footsteps was approaching. The three moved away from the hatch and retreated further into the loft, hiding among the dusty rafters. They listened intently, trying to find the direction of the sound. In his imagination, Max saw a line of armed soldiers stealthily entering the barn door below.

"There." Ellie pointed to the remote control still in Max's hand. "It's coming from the phone."

They watched the screen intently, trying to catch a glimpse of movement. The footsteps stopped, and a shadow covered the grass. A boot appeared, black and hugging the foot tightly. *Not army,* thought Max. A black-clad knee and thigh came into view, as someone knelt beside the injured drone. Next, a hand reached into the long grass, retrieving a fragment of drone casing, which was then lifted out of shot. There was a prolonged inhalation of breath followed by shorter sniffing sounds before the flimsy piece of plastic was discarded. The knee raised, and the boot disappeared as the sound of footsteps departed.

They were stunned into silence, the glow of the phone illuminating their faces, fearful in the darkness. For the hand they all saw, was grey, large, and covered with tattoos.

17

RETURN TO PATRICK'S CORNER

Isaac took the remote control from Max's clenched hands, then turned off the phone's screen, leaving them in darkness. "So," he said, "it's been really nice knowing you guys."

Ellie threw back her head and groaned. It was a groan that said: *why the hell did I get involved in any of this.* Max just stared into the gloom, still seeing echoes of the bright screen.

They left the barn in a hurry, deciding to head back to the hill and the safety of the crowd. They strode across the yard, up the path to the gate, and along the track. When they reached the gap in the hedgerow, they climbed through and crossed the wheat field, feeling more exposed than the last time they crossed it.

Max walked ahead. He felt cold in the heat. He was afraid. It was the sniffing sound that had given Max a shiver he had yet to recover from. It chilled his blood.

At the edge of the field, they climbed the fence and crossed the meadow. When a police helicopter flew overhead, they took cover under a tree. It circled above for a while, then moved on in the direction of the town.

It was cool under the tree, but there was no temptation

to stay. The idea of the tattooed man being out there somewhere pushed them onwards. Even Max found himself yearning to be back among the crowds upon the hill. They moved on.

After reaching the thicket of trees, they began to climb the steep, chalky path of Windmill Hill.

"I'm out," said Isaac near the top. He was leading the way. The stile was just a few yards ahead, and they could see the edge of the crowd.

"Out?" said Ellie, at the rear. "Out of what?"

"There's stuff going on we don't understand," he said, continuing with his climb. "Stuff that's none of our business. Why should we put ourselves in danger trying to help Wren? We don't know him. He might not be happy about us knowing who he really is. What if we find him and he kills us for knowing too much?"

"I don't think so," said Max breathlessly.

"But you don't *know* so, do you?" said Isaac, stopping and turning to face Max.

"You don't have to help," said Max, walking past him. "Neither of you do. It's alright. It really is. I'll find him on my own if I have to."

"Why do you *have* to, though?" asked Isaac.

"I just do. Someone..." Max stopped himself.

"What is it, Max?" said Ellie. "Someone what?"

Max sighed and stopped. He had one hand on the stile, ready to climb over. "Someone asked me to."

Isaac's brow creased as he stared up at Max through his thick glasses. "What do you mean?"

"I mean just that," said Max. "Someone asked me. I don't know who. It's just a voice I heard. I heard it at the crash site, and again just now in the barn."

"Why didn't you tell us?" Ellie shook her head and shrugged. "What did they say?"

He looked to the two of them. Ellie was no longer the sceptic; after what she'd seen at the bypass, how could she be? And Isaac, once eager for adventure, was probably regretting ever running into Max. He couldn't blame him. "She — I think it's a woman — just asks me to help him, to save him."

"You know, you really shouldn't do things because a voice in your head tells you to," Isaac said.

Max allowed himself a slight smile. "I know."

"Where shall we look next?" asked Ellie, looking up to him sympathetically.

"You don't have to, Ellie."

"I know. I want to." She turned to Isaac. "You know this Ben, right? Do you really think you're in any danger from him? Would he kill you for knowing too much? And if he does...well, we've already established that your brother's going to kill you. Wouldn't you rather be killed by an alien librarian? Oh," she said with mock excitement, "you could be the first person killed by an alien. You'd be famous." She smiled and threw an arm around Isaac's shoulder. "Anyway, we should be more concerned about the tattoo guy. Did you see his hands? His fingers had biceps—"

Isaac slipped out from under her arm, took off his glasses and rubbed the sweat from his eyes. "This isn't funny, Ellie. Look, you're right, I don't think Ben would hurt us. He's a friendly guy. But don't you see? If *we* are looking for Ben, and *tattoo guy* is looking for Ben, then it's likely that we'll cross paths at some point. And that thought doesn't fill me with joy."

Ellie swallowed and looked to Max for help.

"Tattoo guy...might be looking for us too," Max said reluctantly.

"OK," said Isaac. "Something else you're not telling us?"

"He found your drone."

"So? There is nothing on that drone to tie it back to us. I made sure of it." He pointed his finger at Max as he spoke.

"Your smell."

"Excuse me?" Isaac almost laughed. "Wasn't expecting you to say that."

Max didn't want to scare them, but they needed to be aware of the risks.

"Go on," prompted Ellie.

"He can smell. Incredibly well," Max continued. "He uses smell more than sight, and his eyes are better than ours. In my vision, when I was him, it was like I could *see* the smells, thousands of them. Each one was a string stretched out, connecting with others like a web. When I was hunting — when *he* was hunting, I felt that if he wanted to, he could follow a scent in any direction. One way would lead him to his prey, while the other would lead him to every place that poor creature had been. The smells, they're not fragile or temporary like we experience smell. They leave permanent marks in the air, and he can read them like a book."

"So when he sniffed the drone..." Ellie trailed off and took a deep breath.

"So what if he could smell *us* on the drone," said Isaac. "Why would that be significant to him?"

"On its own, it wouldn't be," replied Max. "But if we assume he picked up the same scent at the crash site—"

Isaac held up a hand to stop Max, then turned away. He was looking back down the hill, absent-mindedly kicking a clump of grass. "Well," he said eventually, putting his glasses back on and facing Max and Ellie. "Let's go find Wren. Maybe *he* can save *us*."

218

The crowd on Windmill Hill had grown in their absence. More cars, more TV crews, and now a hot dog van had arrived, too. The locals seemed to be having a marvellous time, and a few barbecues had been lit around the edges. It was like a bank holiday, but on a Wednesday.

Max noticed more police, too, and he started to worry about the drone's remote control in Isaac's backpack.

After retrieving their bikes, the three made it back through the crowd, keeping an eye out for Ben, just in case. A large portion of the crowd were gathered around Sophia Jansson as she delivered her report. Max didn't watch the news much, but even he recognised her. She would usually be in some far-off war zone, sporting an armoured vest and helmet while tanks rumbled past behind her. Max hoped this would be one of her more sedate, less eventful stories. But even if she didn't know it right now, she was covering the biggest story of her life.

She stood addressing the camera, her back to the bypass: "— the official statement, declaring that last night's explosion was caused by an unexploded bomb, is now coming under scrutiny from members of the local community, and some members of the media too," she said, in the way reporters often talk, with their voices going up and down in melodic patterns, which would sound ridiculous around the breakfast table, but perfectly fine on TV.

"As we saw," she continued, "a military helicopter, believed to be carrying troops, has arrived on the scene, which is not standard procedure for an incident of this kind." She put a hand to her ear, presumably to listen to a question from the studio. "Indeed," she replied to the unheard question, "we have now heard from *multiple* sources that a drone was observed hovering above the site for several minutes, in a clear breach of the no-fly-zone. Reports say it retreated towards the town of Hurstwick, just a few miles from here, after being *shot* at from the ground. We heard those shots from here, David, but cannot confirm that the drone was the target; authorities have declined to comment on the situation." She smiled to camera and tilted her head. "Back to you in the studio."

"We need to go," said Max. He'd noticed the police starting to take a keener interest in the crowd, and felt it was a good time to leave.

"Where to?" asked Ellie.

"The only other place I can think of — Patrick's Corner."

Max, Ellie and Isaac rode under the covered gate, then fanned out, taking different paths through the still church-yard. They stood high on their pedals, combing the area for others who might be present. The place was deserted. The clicking of their rolling bicycles and birdsong were the only sounds.

"Not a soul in sight," said Ellie, as she joined Max and Isaac under the one-armed angel.

They dropped their bikes into the undergrowth, walked along the wild path, and passed through the thick tangle of nettles and prickly bushes.

"You really think he's in here?" Ellie whispered, unpicking a thorny vine from her T-shirt.

Max shrugged.

They emerged into the wooded corner with a few extra scratches to add to their growing collection. Max hadn't been back here since the day he'd moved to Hurstwick. He now viewed the place in a very different light. Then, it had been merely an abandoned shack, home to pigeons and spiders. But now, after reading George's notebook, it had a history that felt real to him. He could see Wren and George together here; George visiting daily, bringing food and books. And Wren, sitting among the flowers, eyes closed, taking in the sounds of the corner by day, and by night, creeping out to search for his lost key. The key now safe in Max's backpack.

The sun was getting lower in the sky, some of its rays making their way through the trees to dance across the grey stone walls of the shack.

"Hear that?" whispered Ellie.

"I don't hear anything," Isaac said.

"Exactly."

The corner seemed to be silently watching them. No bird song, no buzzing. Just a heavy silence as they approached the tiny house.

Max stood by the door while Ellie went to the small square window beside it. She cupped her hands against the cracked glass and peered through. She looked back to the boys and shook her head. Then she nodded towards the rusty door handle before moving to stand behind Isaac, who stood behind Max.

Max took a deep breath and reached for the handle. But before his hand could touch it, the door was yanked open from the inside. He snapped his hand away in terror and fell back, causing all three to fall to the ground like dominoes. They looked into the now open doorway, where Max sensed a pair of eyes in the darkness watching them.

"Wren?" Max whispered. "Is that you?"

A man resembling Ben, but much older, ducked through the doorway into the light. He wore a cream-coloured suit and held a white hat in one hand and a black walking stick in the other. He studied the three sprawled on the ground, a look of bemusement across his face. "Why are you down there?" he said.

The three looked up, unable to speak.

The man put on his hat and dipped the rim towards them. "George Moss," he said with a friendly smile. "And if you're looking for Wren, then I'm guessing one of you found my journal."

Outside, George sat on a part of broken wall at the collapsed end of the shack. He leant forward, resting his gnarled hands on his walking stick, while Max, standing before him, told him everything, from finding the box under the floorboards, the visions, the strange happenings at the bypass, and finally, what they'd seen after the drone crash.

When Max finished, George removed his hat and fanned himself. His breathing was laboured and raspy.

"So he didn't leave," he said quietly to himself. "He was here all along. He must have thought I'd abandoned him."

"You thought he left?" asked Ellie. She was sitting next to Isaac on a vine-covered boulder, behind Max.

"Yes," he replied with a sigh. "It's all there in my journal. I found the key on the same day I lost him. I returned to London the day after that. If I'd thought he was still here, I would have left the key for him to find. But I assumed his friends rescued him." There was a long pause as he looked upon the corner with a sad smile. "This place is much smaller than I remember," he said eventually. "I was twelve when I was last here. I always wanted to return and see the place again, but...life happens and takes you in other directions. Then the memories fade, they merge with dreams, until you question what's real and what's imagination. But watching that news report this morning — hearing the names Hurstwick *and* Oban Woods.... Well, it brought it all flooding back. And here I am, over seventy years later and it all feels like yesterday."

"You look just like him, you know," said Isaac. "I couldn't picture him before, until I saw your face."

Max nodded in agreement.

"To be expected, I suppose," he replied. "Did I write about it? About what happened in the barn?"

Max nodded.

"It was quite amazing," said George shaking his head as more memories came back to him. "And as for not remembering what he looks like, well that's not a surprise. He had a way of slipping from people's minds. Probably how he stayed here undiscovered for so long."

"Will you help us find him?" Ellie asked. "We need to give him the key, and we need to warn him."

"Yes, yes, of course," said George. "But...something doesn't add up." He pinched the top of his nose and screwed his eyes shut, trying to remember something important. "I still don't get why he's here. He wore a bracelet. Like all the objects he possessed, it was beautiful. He told me that when Kelha healed, she would send a message to his home, and his rescuers would find him by using the bracelet. Now it sounds to me like Kelha is fully healed, judging by her exploits at the bypass. So why can't they find him? I don't understand."

"I don't think he wants to be found," said Max. "Not by this tattooed man, anyway. He believed Wren was dead. When he discovered he wasn't, he felt anger, and also.... I felt fear in him, too. I think he came for him before, years ago. Maybe the first time was to take him home, but this time I think he wants to...." He stopped, remembering he was talking to someone who cared deeply for Wren.

"Then we better find him and warn him." George pushed down on his walking stick with both hands and stood with a grunt. "I think I might know where he is. And it's not far."

They walked with him and left the corner. George paused when he reached the one-armed angel. "One of Wren's many gifts," he said, "was concealment. Not only could he make himself slip from your mind and memory, but he could also make a place disappear. Not from view, but from concern. I used to perceive it like a bubble. I could feel it as I stood at its edge." He placed a hand on the statue's foot. "I used to feel it standing here. I think to others, it would have felt like danger...a creepy feeling, perhaps. But to me, because I was welcome, it felt safe and warm."

"This place has always creeped me out, if I'm honest," said Isaac. "In fact, it creeps everyone out. No one goes in there. Oh, apart from the new guy, of course." He nodded sideways to Max.

George smiled. "I think that's because the bubble is still here." He patted the angel's foot and the three picked up their bikes, then moved out into the churchyard.

When they reached the main path, George turned to face the trees of Patrick's Corner. "I think he liked it here because of that." He pointed to the tall lone pine tree with his walking stick. "At the time it was the highest point in town. From its very top he would watch for hours. It was a comfort to him. And I think it was the centre of the bubble." He looked at each of them. Then he smiled. "Amazing. Even now, your minds will not turn to it."

There was a look of confusion between the three, then a smile slowly travelled from Ellie's eyes to her mouth. "I know where he is, too." She turned and looked up to the church tower.

Max looked, too. It was now in shadow, the sun low behind it. He had seen it many times before, but somehow it felt as if he were seeing it for the first time. He was suddenly aware of its immense size.

"He's up there?" said Isaac, now looking up with the others.

"One way to be sure, I think. Don't you?" George said. "I can't make it up there, I'm afraid, but I'm sure your young legs will make short work of it."

"What?" said Isaac. "You want us to break into a church?"

"Of course not," said George. "The door is probably open." He walked to one of the nearby benches and planted himself down, then coughed several times into a handkerchief. "Run along," he said, composing himself. "Tell him I said hello. You never know; he might even be waiting for you."

They left George on the bench and lined their bikes against the stone wall of the church, then made their way to the porch.

Max took hold of the iron ring set on the large wooden door. He turned it to raise the latch, then pushed; it opened with a low creak.

He looked back to see George watching from the bench. The old man gave them an encouraging nod, then raised his head to admire the tower.

"Really not sure about this," Isaac said, looking into the church over Max's shoulder. "Maybe we should just call him down?"

"No. Someone else might hear," Ellie said, moving past and stepping inside.

Isaac and Max followed and closed the door.

The porch was white-walled, with a flagstone floor, worn down its centre by two centuries of worshippers coming and going.

They gazed upon the grand interior of the church, with its rows of dark pews interspersed by thick stone pillars supporting an intricately decorated ceiling. The space was bathed in multi-coloured light bursting through the stained glass windows. As they edged further in, they stayed out of the light, keeping to the shadows along the back wall, looking for a way up.

They found it in the corner: a wooden spiral staircase that took them to a mezzanine smelling of polish, candle wax, and incense. A large window, shaped like a bishop's hat, illuminated a long table set against a wood-panelled wall. There were two doors, one on each side of the table. One was ornate and grand and set deep within the wood. The other, far less grand, shabby even, was set flush against bare stone. The table itself was covered in a white sheet. Laid upon it were several long silver candlesticks. Next to those, Max spied an uncapped bottle of polish and a rag. Someone was still here. He looked around for a clue as to where they might be.

The answer came quickly, as Max heard another door closing somewhere in the distance. It was followed moments later by muffled voices and a shadow that broke the strip of light beneath the oak door. Grabbing the arms of his partners in crime, he dragged them towards the shabby door. He hoped it would be unlocked and prayed it might lead them to the spire. Thankfully, it opened easily, but led nowhere. It was a large storage cupboard, large enough for the three of them to pile inside.

Once in, they closed the door immediately and pressed their ears against it to listen. They heard the other door open, then close. Footsteps and voices drew nearer.

"Well, thank you, Peter. I don't know how you do it. The clock seems to be keeping perfect time once more," said a man's voice.

"Ain't no bother, father," said a second voice that Max instantly recognised as Mr Walsh the caretaker. "I'll just finish the last of these, and I'll be off. Need to get back to close up at the library."

"Of course. Well, thank you again, kind sir. Twenty years your junior and I find it awfully tiresome climbing up there. You must tell me your secret."

"If I gone an' told you all my secrets, they'd not be very secret now would they, father. All I'll say is, my good health is all because of him upstairs."

"Amen to that, Peter, amen. Well, I'll see you tomorrow."

"Right you are."

They heard footsteps retreat down the spiral staircase as Mr Walsh began a tuneful whistle; then the occasional clang of metal on metal as he polished the candlesticks.

The three waited silently in the darkness. Five minutes passed, then ten, then fifteen. After twenty minutes, the whistling finally stopped, and they heard Mr Walsh clear away his things. Isaac drew away from the door and turned on his phone to check the time. In doing so, he illuminated the cupboard. Around them, Max saw shelves full of cleaning products, paint, varnish, white spirit, and various types of...polish. Ellie saw the look of defeat on Max's face and followed his gaze.

"Well, this was a *great* place to hide," she whispered.

They heard footsteps and jingling keys approaching. Ellie grabbed the door handle and leant back with all her weight. But it was no good. Mr Walsh, it seems, was surprisingly strong, and pulled the door open with ease.

Ellie flew out of the cupboard and landed at the man's feet.

"What the..." Mr Walsh stepped back in surprise. His bushy white eyebrows climbed his forehead like two miniature ferrets trying to escape his face. "What are you doing in here?" he asked, the ferrets returning to their original positions as a look of recognition replaced surprise.

"Mr Walsh," said Max, "I know this must look bad, but, we need —"

"—to find our dog," interrupted Isaac. "Yes, our dog...erm, came in, and we, erm, followed it."

"Yes," added Ellie, nodding at Isaac to continue.

"Ginger. Yeah. That's her name. We thought she might have come in here, " he gestured to the cupboard interior. "But she...didn't." Isaac stepped out, kicking over a bucket, then awkwardly placed it back inside. He stepped over Ellie and squeezed past Mr Walsh. "Ginger!" he called, half-heartedly with a side glance to Mr Walsh. "Here, girl," he said. "Nasty squirrel's gone now."

Ellie snorted out a laugh, then quickly disguised it as a sneeze. "Erm, yeah, she's frightened of squirrels," she said, rubbing the tip of her nose to hide her growing smile.

They watched Mr Walsh intently, hoping he would buy the dog story, but it wasn't looking promising. His eyes disappeared under his eyebrows as he frowned. "Follow me," he said sternly, then turned and walked away.

To Max's surprise, he didn't walk to the staircase. Instead, he went to the ornate wooden door and opened it.

"This way," he said.

Max couldn't read the tone in his voice. It wasn't anger, but it was firm. He looked at his friends, who seemed reluctant to follow. Ellie nodded to the stairs, showing her desire to leave.

"You coming?" Mr Walsh asked, waiting by the open door.

Mr Walsh was not kicking them out. He was leading them somewhere; Max didn't know where, but he knew if he left now, that would be it. He wouldn't find Wren in time, and the ticking clock in his stomach would consume him. The only way was forwards — and hopefully, upwards.

"We're coming," said Max, and walked towards him. He didn't look back to his friends but felt their disapproving stares. But, to his relief, he heard them follow.

They followed him through a small carpeted hallway to another door. Mr Walsh opened it, and they entered in silence. It was a sizeable room, well lit by another bishop's-hat-shaped window. A circle of bell ropes dropped from holes in the high ceiling.

Mr Walsh closed the door and walked to the centre of the room. "Tell me what you see," he said, turning to face them.

"Excuse me?" said Ellie, crossing her arms, in her best impression of a girl serving detention.

"In this room. Tell me what you see."

"Ropes?" said Isaac.

"Well done. What else?" His eyes narrowed as he watched them carefully.

"What do you *want* us to see?" said Ellie. "There is a lot of stuff in here."

"Look, and tell me," he said, starting to sound impatient.

"It's a room," said Isaac, "where people ring the bells."

The old man sighed. "And what is *in* this room?"

Ellie groaned impatiently, then stabbed a finger towards each item as she called it out: "Ropes, dusty old books, a cupboard, a notice board, a shelf with handbells, a window, a coat stand, a clock, a door, a stack of chairs, a—"

"Stop, stop, stop." Mr Walsh held up both hands. He looked at Max and Isaac. "You see it too? You see the door?"

"Well...yes." Max pointed to the door. "Just there, behind you."

Isaac shrugged and also pointed to the door. "Are you

OK, Mr Walsh? Has that furniture polish affected you somehow?"

He dismissed the comment with a wave of his hand. "You'll be surprised just how many people never notice that door. And if they do, how few feel a desire to go through it."

Max studied the door. It was small and painted black against a brilliant white wall. He had noticed it as soon as he'd entered the room; before he'd seen the bell ropes, or anything else for that matter.

"Now, go to it," said Mr Walsh. He stayed in the centre of the room and watched them, first as they hesitated and exchanged looks of concern, and then as they walked towards it with apprehension.

"Open it, Max," he said in a soft encouraging voice.

Max grabbed the handle, pushed his thumb down on the metal paddle to raise the latch, then pulled the door open. Inside it was dark, but they could see the first few steps of a winding staircase climbing steeply into the gloom.

"Do you feel it?" asked Mr Walsh.

Max did. It was a feeling of comfort or contentment. Like the feeling he used to get on his balcony in the high-rise. The feeling of home. He looked to his friends; they smiled back, presumably feeling something similar.

They all nodded to Mr Walsh.

"That means you're in the club," said Mr Walsh with a relieved smile. "If you weren't, you'd have felt something else, and dare go no further." He laughed.

"So you know?" said Max. "Do others?"

The old man nodded. "Oh, yes...but only a few of us are left now. We seem to last longer than most, but I get the feeling *he'll* just keep on going." He smiled again. "But now, there's you three." He waved them towards the stairs. "Go on. He's waiting."

With a deep breath blowing out his cheeks, Max stepped through the small door onto the creaky steps. Ellie went next, closely followed by Isaac.

"Hope you find your dog," said Mr Walsh to Isaac as he entered.

"There was no dog," Isaac said, turning to Mr Walsh.

"No? Really?" he said, sarcastically, then chuckled to himself as he closed the door on them.

They climbed the stairs, ducking under beams and supports as they went. Rickety walkways led off to dark and dusty spaces, but they continued upwards. They heard the slow monotonous clunk of the church clock, and caught glimpses of cogs and springs in the dim light. It became lighter as they climbed higher, and soon they emerged into a space where rope met bell.

All the bells had been thoroughly decorated by the local wildlife, leaving a pungent smell in the air. Through horizontal slits in the stone walls, they looked out to the churchyard, and the town and countryside beyond. They were now higher than most of the surrounding trees, but still not as high as the towering pine.

"Wait, look," Isaac said. "It's Ben."

With the light on his phone, Isaac was inspecting an old black-and-white photo in a frame on the wall. Dated 1957, it showed a group of merry-looking men wearing overalls and flat caps. Behind them stood St Mary's Church, with its newly rebuilt spire, barely visible through the scaffolding. One man in the photo — taller than the rest, with jet-black hair and a broad smile — stood with his hand resting across the handle of a mallet. There was no doubt about it — it was Ben.

"It's him," said Max, leaning in to get a better view. "And

he hasn't changed a bit." He looked around the bell chamber, noticing the two types of stonework. They were now standing at the point where the old tower ended and the new began.

"He looks sad," said Ellie.

"He's smiling," replied Isaac.

"Not his eyes," she said.

They left the belfry using a well-hidden ladder fixed to a wall in the darkest corner. As he climbed, Max caught sight of the tiny figure of Mr Walsh through one of the slits in the wall. He was heading across the churchyard towards the gate. Max looked out towards his house, then looked away quickly, trying not to think about how this day might end.

The ladder took them to a small dark space criss-crossed with rafters. The ceiling was low; too low to stand. They flicked on their phone lights and moved, crouching, in the only direction clear of cobwebs, their lights catching movements of bats in the shadows.

"This must be it," Max whispered. They had come to a set of wooden steps leading up to a hatch. Its edges glowed with a warm light.

"Can I hear music?" asked Ellie.

"I hear it too," said Max.

Max climbed the steps and pushed the hatch up and over. It slammed to the floor, throwing dust into the air.

They entered and stood beside the opening.

The room was tall and octagonal and lit by a single naked bulb. Against the wall furthest from them was a single bed just inches from the ground, with several neat piles of books stacked next to it. In the centre of the room, a ladder climbed and disappeared through a small dark hole in the high ceiling. Soft music floated down from above. It crackled as if played on a very old record player.

"Sounds like the stuff my grandad used to play," whispered Ellie with a smile. "You think Ben is up there?"

"He could be right in front of us," said Isaac, even quieter, "and we wouldn't even know it."

"True," came Ben's familiar voice from above, "but I'm not. So make yourself comfortable. I'm on my way down."

18

HIM UPSTAIRS

Not sure how they could make themselves comfortable in a room with no furniture, they shuffled closer together and waited in silence.

Max was calm. For a moment, he ignored his internal ticking clock, which he'd hoped would stop once Wren had the key. And he looked to his friends. Isaac was breathing erratically, staring at the ladder, unblinking. He was not calm. Ellie was far from her usual confident self, too, and didn't seem to know what to do with her arms. But she gave Max a warm look of encouragement, then dusted a cobweb from his shoulder.

The music above stopped mid-track. And all three looked up as Ben descended from darkness into the room. He stepped off the ladder, turned to face them, and smiled.

As Max looked at Ben, a sliver of doubt entered his mind. This couldn't be Wren. It was just Ben. He looked closer, trying to see something he hadn't before; a hint of something alien. He was taller than he remembered, black hair, medium length; he wore jeans and a black sweater and was slightly unshaven. He looked more dishevelled than usual, but...it was just Ben. He looked closer at his eyes. They were dark and intense, but — human.

Ben tilted his head and eyed Max's bag. "I see you have brought me a gift," he said.

"Oh, yes, of course," said Max, suddenly feeling flustered. He slid the bag from his shoulders, retrieved the key, and held it out in his open hand. Ben studied it briefly before looking back to Max.

"As I feared," said Ben. "She has been awakened."

"Sorry," Ellie said, looking sheepish. "I think that might have been us."

Ben shook his head as if to say: *no matter*. He took the key and ran a finger across its surface, causing the blue ring of light to fade. Then, casually, he placed it into his pocket, as if it were merely a house key. After more than seventy years of separation, Max expected him to seem more emotional; happy, even.

Max closed his eyes and took a deep breath, expecting to be released from the maddening ticking clock within. But it continued relentlessly; if anything, it was now louder. It felt like a train powering towards them.

He was about to say something, but Isaac spoke first. "So...you can go back home now?" he asked.

Wren's expression became sombre. "I am home," he said. "How did you come by the key?" he asked Max.

"George found it."

Ben's eyes narrowed as Max said the name. Then he smiled and said, "Oh, he did, did he?"

"Well," continued Max, "he took it from the back of a police car that was taking it to London. I don't know where *they* found it. He tried to give it to you, but couldn't find you. So he hid it under his floorboards the night before he left for London."

Wren crossed his arms. "You know an awful lot about this."

Max pulled the notebook from the bag. "He wrote about it. Everything's in here. I found it with the key." He handed it to Ben, who smiled as he flicked through the pages. The smile faltered as he examined the illustration of his former self. He folded it away, then handed the book back to Max.

"You found it under the floorboards?" said Ben.

"Yes."

"You live in the Furlongs' old cottage?"

Max nodded.

Ben said nothing at first, just stared at Max. Max thought he saw a flicker of sadness in his eyes. Then he said, "And that's George on the bench down there?"

"Yes," said Max, sliding the book back into his bag.

Wren turned away and walked over to an empty space on the wall. He reached up. There was a *fizzing* sound. When he drew his hand back, it was holding a bag. *His bag of tricks*, thought Max; he *is* Wren. Wren opened the bag and placed the key inside before returning it to its impossible hiding place. Max could feel Isaac geeking out beside him.

"By the way," said Ellie as Wren turned to face them. "You should probably know that Mr Bartley knows about all this." She glanced at Max, unsure if she should continue, but Max wasn't listening; he was rubbing his temple, trying once again to quieten the ticking clock. "He was there when we tried to give the key to Mr Hall," Ellie continued. "You see, we thought Mr Hall was...you."

Wren sighed and nodded. "Mr Hall, you say?" He smiled. "Not a terrible guess. He's a Nebraxion from Nebra 57, in the outer rim."

"Really?" said Isaac. "I knew it. I just *knew* it." He looked at Ellie with a *see I told you so* look.

"Sorry," said Wren quickly with a smile. "I couldn't resist. I think he's from Swindon originally."

Ellie laughed while Isaac — with a tight-lipped smile — shook his head, disappointed to have fallen for it. Then he laughed too. "Well played," he mumbled.

"Someone has come for you," blurted Max, unable to contain it any longer. The laughing stopped. "He wants to...I don't know what he wants. But he's here now. He's looking for you."

Wren's eyes narrowed and he stepped forward. "What do you know of him?"

"He saw him in his vision," said Isaac before Max could answer. "Then we all saw him on video from...we had a drone, but it crashed—"

"Vision?" Wren said, now looking only at Max.

Max nodded. "I think Kelha showed me things."

"Improbable," said Wren.

Max felt his face redden under Wren's gaze. "Well, I saw things," he continued. "Two things. I saw you...well, I saw what you saw. I could see through your eyes as you were closing up at the library."

"And the other thing?" said Wren, studying Max carefully.

"Someone hunting. Stalking a beast...thing. I — I don't know what it was. It wasn't here, though. It wasn't Earth. And I only saw his hands. They were covered in tattoos." He looked to his friends for support.

"Jenta," Wren said, almost too quiet to hear.

"Is that his name?" Ellie asked. "We think he's here. We saw him about—"

Max's legs gave way. It was happening again. The smell of rich earth filled his senses as the world around him disappeared. He heard the voices of his friends, distant and muffled as before. They were panicking, but he was not. He waited for another vision to appear.

Seven chimes of a bell rang out as a green and gold light grew around him.

Soon, the world came into focus, and he was walking among trees. He stopped, then knelt. His hand hovered over a broken twig, and he felt a warm, prickly sensation in his fingers. He turned his head and saw a familiar-looking stone shack. He was in Patrick's Corner.

Countless tendrils of wispy air criss-crossed the corner. Thin like cotton, they hung swooping from tree to tree. Others formed small bounding arches on the ground. As he took a deep breath, all but four of the threads dissolved, three purple, one of dark blue. These four were thicker and together went from the shack, across the ground, and passed through a dense thicket. He followed them to the statue of the angel, where he noticed a fading blue patch of light upon her foot. Three of the strands moved off across the dim churchyard and met three bikes set against the wall, before disappearing through the large wooden door of the church. The other thread, dark blue, went its own way, rounding a bush off to the right. He lowered himself into the undergrowth and moved slowly and silently through it. When he heard the sound of laboured breathing ahead, he stopped and parted the bushes. There, before him, was....

"George!" Max shouted.

Isaac, Ellie, and Wren were looking down at him. He was

238

on the floor back in the tower, sweat pouring from his forehead.

"It's OK," Ellie said, trying to calm him. "George is down in the churchyard—"

"He's in danger. George is in danger." Max struggled to his feet and rubbed his eyes to clear the fog. He looked to Wren in desperation. "He's being hunted. It's Jenta. You have to help him," he pleaded.

Wren's puzzled expression turned quickly to one of realisation. He ran to the edge of the room and stared down to the base of the wall. Max knew he was looking through it.

"Follow me," Wren said. In one smooth movement, he grabbed his bag and flung it over his shoulder as two straps appeared and coiled together like vines, securing it to his back.

"If he's out *there*," said Isaac, "shouldn't we stay in *here*?" He looked at Ellie for support, but she was already following Wren through the hatch.

"He knows where we are," said Max, beginning his descent. "Want to be trapped up *here*?"

"I should have stayed at home," Isaac said. He glanced around the room, then scrambled to follow.

They made short work of the descent, scrambling down through the dark innards of the tower, and quickly found themselves back within the white walls of the porch.

Wren was waiting for them. "Listen carefully," he said. "I do not mean to scare you. But the only way you get out of here alive is for me to leave and for him to follow. Get away from here. As soon as I go through this door, make your way to the chapel at the far end of the church. There is a door there. Leave fast and don't look back. Find a crowded place and stay there."

"I'm sorry I brought him here," said Max. "It's my fault."

Wren gripped Max's arm. "No," he said firmly. "It's me who should apologise. I shouldn't even be here. I've put so many in danger."

"George," Max said, suddenly remembering. "Will he be OK?"

"I will make sure of it. As soon as I leave — go." He turned and walked to the door; before reaching it, he disappeared and the door opened — without the creak it had made earlier — then closed again just as silently. If there was any doubt in anyone's mind that Ben was Wren, and that Wren was not of this world, it evaporated at that moment.

Isaac opened his mouth to say something, but was dragged away by Max before he could speak.

They ran down the centre aisle towards the chapel and the other exit.

"Wait!" Ellie stopped, causing a squeak from her trainers to bounce around the building. "Our bikes," she said.

"I really don't care about our bikes," Isaac said, jogging on the spot, eager to get as far away as possible.

She looked at Max. "Does he know we're here?" she asked.

Max nodded.

"You don't know that for sure," Isaac said.

"He does. Trust me."

"Just wait." Ellie ran to a nearby stack of chairs. Taking one off, she placed it under a window, climbed on to it, and looked out.

"What do you see?" said Isaac.

She turned away from the window, then sunk slowly into the chair. Her face was devoid of colour as she looked at

Max and shook her head, clutching the back of her neck with both hands.

Max ran to join her and pulled off another chair.

She tried to stop him. "No, Max. We need to go. Please."

"I need to see."

Distorted through the ancient glass, he saw the dark menacing figure standing between the bright white headstones. He was dressed in black from head to toe, long red hair tied into a plait, a curved blade in his hand.

At his feet, his cream suit jacket darkened with blood, was the body of George.

Wren's blood was boiling. The hairs on the back of his neck bristled as he looked upon Jenta.

Jenta laughed, sensing Wren's anger, then knelt over the bloodied figure of George. He placed a hand just inches from his chest. "He still lives, Rahiir!" he called out into the deserted and darkening graveyard, then stood and held his arms wide. "And he can be saved. You have the means to save him, do you not?" He walked away from George as an invitation. "Just show yourself and tend to him. Nobody needs to die tonight."

Wren moved between the headstones, ignoring the invite and instead drawing closer to Jenta. This Hunter could not be trusted. If he was to save George, if he was indeed saveable, he would have to take out Jenta first.

He could not win in a fair fight with a Hunter; they were too strong. But Wren had no intention of fighting fair. Unlike the last time they met, at the top of Ravensford furnace, Wren was now prepared. He had his *bag of tricks*, as George called it. And from it, he pulled a small white object and held it tightly. It was armed. He just needed to get close enough to use it.

"You are mad at me," Jenta said with a wicked grin. "Come on...heal him. His light is fading fast, but it still flickers." He sniffed the air and his focus turned to the church window and then to the three bikes leaning against the stone wall. "If you do not save the *old* one, perhaps you'll save the young ones? Their scent is still fresh. Shouldn't be too hard to find."

Wren moved closer still, ignoring the threat. Just a few more steps and he would be close enough.

"Come with me, Rahiir. You left the Pillars of Kartaan for this? The Tree of Nakrite? You were High Nim, and you chose to live here with...vermin. There is no balance here. There has been no balance here for thousands of years." Jenta growled, his stance shifting from relaxed to a state of readiness as he drew his blade. "You are close," he said. "What is it you have? A disruptor? A binder? I sense you are about to attack, but do not be foolish, Rahiir. We know why you are here. You found him."

Those words threw him, almost causing him to lose his focus. *Found who?*

Just then, the church door burst open. "What have you done!" shouted Max, clearing the steps in a single bound and sprinting towards George.

Ellie and Isaac emerged after him, calling him back.

As Jenta turned to face Max, Wren launched himself forward and struck Jenta between the shoulder blades with the disruptor. It exploded on contact, taking Jenta to the ground, and Wren too. Knocked backwards by the blast, he unfaded as he hit the ground.

As well as the ringing now in his ears, he could hear Max frantically calling to George. Then there was a hand on his shoulder. It was Ellie. She knelt beside him.

"Are you OK, Ben?" she said. "Are you hurt?"

He ignored the question and pulled his bag around to his chest and removed a small white disc.

"It's not too late to save him," he said, handing her the disc. "Pass this over his wounds, slowly, until its light fades." He gently pushed her away. "Go."

Ellie ran to George.

Max's fury carried him forward. As he ran, he didn't think about the ominous figure standing just yards from George. Only as he got closer did he become aware of the danger he was in. There was a shift in Jenta's stance and Max braced himself, still running. Then there was a flash and Max was knocked to the ground, but not by Jenta.

A bright light, accompanied by a silent pulse of energy, had swept his legs from under him. He hit the ground with a thud, just inches from a headstone spliced in two by the blast. Disoriented, and with the smell of blood in his nose, he climbed to his feet and searched for George.

He found him and knelt beside him.

"George." The word scraped his throat as it came out. "Wake up, George. Wake up!"

Isaac arrived at his side, and they both tried to rouse the man.

Seconds later, Ellie joined them. "Show me the wound," she said urgently.

Isaac pointed to George's collarbone, and Max watched as Ellie ran a small white disc over the bloody shoulder and neck. It glowed a bright orange as she moved it slowly around.

"Wren said this will help," she said, breathless and shaking.

Max undid the top buttons of George's shirt, exposing more of the wound to the disc. He felt warm blood on his hands and immediately felt queasy. *It's too much blood*, he thought. *It's too deep.*

He looked over to Wren and was relieved to see him standing, hunched over the prone figure of Jenta. Wren bent down to retrieve the sword by his side, then gave the body a light kick, then another. Satisfied he was unconscious, he examined the sword, then somehow caused the blade to retract into its long handle. Max, feared Jenta would leap to his feet and continue the fight. When he didn't, he returned his attention to George and the disc. Its glow was lessening. Eventually, it shone no more, and Ellie stopped, falling back on the grass, her eyes moistening with tears.

There was no movement from George, his face like a statue. But as Max's hope disappeared, George's chest rose, his back arching as he took a sharp intake of breath. Max let out a short, involuntary laugh as George took another breath. They looked on, stunned. The old man's eyes remained closed, and he was still a terrible mess, but he was now a terrible *breathing* mess.

Wren fell to his knees next to them. "Well done," he said to Ellie, while taking George's hand, tenderly. "I'm sorry, old friend," he whispered to him. "So sorry."

"Will he be alright?" asked Isaac, shaken.

Wren blinked. It was a slow, deliberate blink. When his eyes reopened, they were black oily pools, which passed over the body of George. "The wound has healed," he said. "But he needs rest." He turned his black eyes towards the church and then Patrick's Corner. "We need to move both of them now. We'll not be alone for long."

After hiding Jenta between two large tombs, Wren carefully lifted George over his shoulder and took him to

Patrick's Corner. Ellie followed while Max and Isaac kept a wary eye on the still unconscious Jenta.

"And you thought this would be a dull place to live," said Isaac, sitting on a low gravestone, bouncing his knee nervously while looking at the sleeping Hunter. "Look at him. Who wears a blade in their hair?" he continued. "Think he uses it? Or is it just for show? Also...no attempt to disguise himself. What if someone..."

Max wasn't listening. He was standing, watching the trees, waiting for Wren to return. Moments later, he did, looking tired but determined.

Moving Jenta took all three of them, and in the end, he was dragged more than carried. Max held his ankles while Isaac and Wren were at the *scary end*, as Isaac put it. Jenta's massive and terrifying head, which looked both cat-like and snake-like, lolloped as they walked. Isaac had to turn his head away to avoid being cheek to cheek with it. "He's not a looker, is he?" he said. Then glanced over to Wren. "Sorry. No offence."

"None taken, Isaac," replied Wren breathlessly. "He'd be considered *very* ugly where I'm from." He smiled. "Me? I *was* much more of a looker, if I say so myself."

They dumped Jenta unceremoniously in the corner of the shack. Then Wren secured his wrists and ankles with a silver rope that seemed to tie itself.

Ellie was sat next to George, who was asleep on the cold floor, his head resting on her rolled-up jumper. Wren knelt beside her and examined George's wound.

"When will he wake?" she asked him.

"Soon, I hope." He smiled at Ellie.

Isaac retreated and stood in the doorway, staring at Jenta

uneasily. "I'll go hide the bikes," he said. Max, who had collapsed exhausted against the wall, made a move to help. But Isaac stopped him. "Stay there. You look like you need the rest."

Max nodded his thanks, then closed his eyes, trying not to think of how close to death they'd all just been. He breathed slowly, trying to tame the internal ticking clock. If he focused on it, he found he could quieten it.

A stillness settled over the shack, and for a while, nobody spoke. When Max counted eight chimes of the church clock, Isaac returned. The room darkened as he stood in the open doorway. "I need to go," he said, "I'm late for dinner." He looked at his phone. "Six missed calls."

"How are you going to explain the lost drone?" asked Ellie.

Isaac shrugged. "I'll think of something. To be honest," he looked at Jenta, barely visible in the shadows, "I'm not that bothered anymore."

Wren turned to Isaac, "Thank you," he said. "Thank you all. You should all get back. Your parents will be wondering where you are."

Max got to his feet. "What will you do next?" he asked.

"I'll wait for George to wake," he replied. "Then return with my...rescuer."

"How?" asked Max.

"He'll lead me to his ship."

Ellie got to her feet and joined Isaac in the doorway. Max remained still. He was desperate to extinguish the ticking of the clock, which now felt like a countdown — a countdown to what, he didn't know — but he knew leaving now would not stop it. "Is there anything I can do to help?" he asked.

Wren shook his head.

"I could come back with some food," Max suggested.

"No," Wren said firmly. "I cannot ask you to help me."

"You don't have to ask," he said, equally firm. "I'm helping you."

Wren turned to Max, studying him. Then he looked, first to George, then back to Jenta. He sighed. "OK." His tone was soft once more. "I would be most grateful for your help." He looked up as the sound of a helicopter passed overhead. "I think I will need it."

"I'm not sure I can go back," Isaac said, looking over his shoulder to Patrick's Corner, now in shadow. "And I don't mind telling you, I'm scared. If you two had any sense, you would be too."

Ellie sighed. "If you weren't scared, there'd be something wrong with you."

Max nodded in agreement. "I'm more scared of what happens if Ben fails to return home with that...thing. What happens if he breaks free? What happens to George and Ben? What happens to us, our families?"

Pushing their bikes, they emerged onto Church Lane with all its chocolate-box beauty. Behind the pretty white-framed windows of its cottages sat a world of tea and biscuits, jam and scones, Radio 4, and knitted toilet roll covers. A cosy world blissfully unaware of the dormant threat a brief walk away. To Max, the whole scene suddenly felt fragile, at risk.

The three of them stopped under the weeping willow. Ellie and Max sat on the wall, Isaac on the pavement, his feet on the cobbled road; he was peeling the bark from a small twig while he stared into space.

They remained silent, each deep in their own thoughts. Max listened to the sound of the distant police helicopter, which seemed to have been permanently circling the town since they returned from the hill.

Ellie eventually broke the silence. "What next?" she asked.

Max shrugged. "I'll go home, have my dinner, wait for my mum to fall asleep, then sneak back out with some food."

"OK," said Ellie. "Knock for me before you go. I'll tell my dad I'm staying over at a friend's house."

"Good idea," said Max. "Isaac, you mind if I tell my mum I'm staying at yours?"

"Do what you want," he replied. He stood and mounted his bike, looked at them both briefly, nodded his farewell, then rode off.

"It's strange, isn't it," said Ellie quietly, as they watched Isaac ride away. "Our world has now changed — at least our view of it has. Aliens are real. We've met two of them. But everything still feels...the same," she sighed. "Strange...."

19

CONVOY TO OBAN

Dinners were eaten, stories of sleepovers were told, bags were packed, and parents were hugged. Hugs that lingered slightly longer than the usual hug of an early teen, but not so long as to raise suspicions of any sort.

It was dark when Max and Ellie made it back to the churchyard. They circled the church to make sure they were alone. Then, to make completely sure, they circled a few more times. Each time they looked to the gate, hoping to see Isaac.

"Just us," said Max as they stopped by the one-armed angel.

"Just us," repeated Ellie.

"Yeah, right." Isaac stepped out from the shadows, rucksack on his back, sleeping bag hanging by his legs. "You really think I would let you two have all the glory."

Ellie smiled, dropped her bike and hugged him. "I knew you'd come."

"OK, OK," he said, embarrassed by her enthusiasm. He rolled his eyes at Max, who smiled in return. Then Ellie punched him lightly on the arm to offset the hug.

"Why the change of heart?" Max asked, suddenly feeling more positive about their chances. He felt like hugging him too, but refrained.

Isaac shrugged. "You were right," he said, raising his bike from a bed of fern. "We need to make sure Ben gets that thing as far away as possible. If we can help, we should. Not knowing how you two were getting on would have driven me nuts. So here I am. Also, I didn't want to be around when my brother finds that his beloved drone is missing. Tomorrow I can tell him it was sacrificed for a good cause."

"Like he'll believe you," said Ellie.

"You never know. Maybe Jenta will let me get a selfie with him as proof."

The shack was barely visible in the darkness. If it wasn't for the dimmest of lights escaping the small square window, they would have missed it. They lowered their bikes silently to the ground, and Max pushed open the door, hoping to find the balance of power still in Wren's favour.

Inside, George was in the same position as before. He was still sleeping. In the corner opposite, untouched by light, was the dark mass of Jenta, his state of consciousness unknown. The source of the dim but warm light was suspended in mid-air, a foot from the ceiling. It was an orb, undulating slowly as if caught in a breeze and humming quietly. The light had a strange quality that seemed to almost avoid the edges of the room, keeping them in shadow.

They stepped inside and closed the door quietly.

Wren didn't acknowledge them. He was sat cross-legged on the floor, deep in thought, studying an array of objects laid out before him. Next to the items were two bags of the same design. One was Wren's, one Jenta's. As Max got closer, he could see most of the items had the same soft white metallic look as the key, while others had a grey-green finish, and were more ornate in their appearance. There was the white disc that had healed George, and the dark handle of the blade that had almost killed him. There was also the blade from Jenta's braid, several inches of red hair still attached. In the centre of it all, sat together side by side, were two spherical keys. They were identical. He wondered which one was Kelha's.

Max opened his own bag and placed two Tupperware boxes down next to Wren. "I wasn't sure what you like," he said quietly. "So I brought a bit of everything. There're biscuits, bread, some sausage rolls, fruit, and a bar of chocolate."

"Thank you," Wren said. "But I'm not hungry. George will wake soon, and I'm sure he'll be famished."

Wren seemed less amiable than before, making Max feel as if he'd walked into a room after a heated argument.

"Is George any better?" Ellie asked, as Max retrieved the food and placed it next to George.

"He just needs rest," said Wren. "When he wakes, he'll feel better than ever. You did well."

Ellie smiled and made herself comfortable at George's side. "I've brought him a change of clothes. He's about the same size as my dad, I reckon." She looked him up and down. "Probably different tastes, though," she added.

Isaac stepped into the light, attracted by the alien objects arranged on the floor. "Are they his?"

"Some are," said Wren. "Some are mine."

"Aren't you worried you'll get those mixed up?" Isaac said, pointing at the two keys.

"No. I have linked them. Both will now work with any *willing* ship." He picked up a small block of solid glass about the size of a matchbox and held it to the light. "This, however, worries me — deeply."

"What is it?" Isaac leaned in to take a closer look.

"A detonator," said Wren.

"Whoa." Isaac stepped back "Where's the bomb?"

"I couldn't get him to say," he replied, placing the item back down with the others. "There might not be one," he added, noticing the concern on Isaac's face.

Isaac regarded the blade with the hair still attached. "Bet that pissed him off."

"Just a little."

Max moved closer to the dark shape of Jenta, hoping he was still unconscious. But then he noticed two bright points of reflected light. They disappeared momentarily as Jenta blinked. He was awake.

As Max's eyes adjusted to the gloom, he could see that Jenta looked less refined than before. His neat plait was now loose. Strands of his thick hair stuck out untidily and covered his face; a face that was wet with sweat, or blood, Max couldn't tell.

Even with his feet and hands bound, Jenta felt like a threat. Given a choice, he'd rather be locked in a room with a tiger.

Max's gaze was snatched away by movement from the other corner, followed by a low groan.

"George," said Ellie. "Are you OK?"

Max and Isaac rushed to his side, then helped Ellie prop him up against their backpacks. He tried to talk but his throat was too dry. After several mouthfuls of water, he tried again.

"What happened?" he said, his voice like gravel. "Did you find him? Was he there?"

Max smiled and nodded, then moved aside, allowing him a clear view of his old friend.

George seemed to search for words, but none came. So he gave up and just smiled. The smile pushed his cheeks into his eyes, forcing a tear to escape. "My Wren," he said.

Both stood, George with some help, and hugged fiercely. George then held Wren at arm's length to get a better look. "Incredible. Just incredible," he said, shaking his head. "You haven't aged a day. And you look like a thirty-year-old me — only not quite as handsome, of course."

"I have good genes to thank," Wren laughed and brought him in for another hug. "It's good to see you, old friend."

"Such a beautiful reunion," growled Jenta from his darkened corner. The bass of his voice sent a shudder through Max's chest.

George looked over Wren's shoulder and peered into the darkness. Jenta leaned into the light and grinned, revealing his sharp white teeth. "Feeling better?" he said. He looked at each of them with his small black eyes, and sunk backwards. "Don't ...get...used to it," he whispered from the shadows.

"My rescuer," Wren said, to answer George's unspoken question.

"He speaks English?" Isaac said in disbelief.

"Badly, but yes," said Wren.

There was a brief silence as everyone absorbed this news. Then Ellie tried to lighten the mood. "So, how do you feel, George?" Her eyes flicked to the corner, uneasily.

George looked away from the corner and turned his attention to those around him. He rolled his shoulders and pushed his arms back and his chest out. "You know, now you ask," he said, opening and closing his fists, bending his knees, and rotating his hips. "Never better. But I don't understand..." He spotted his blood-stained jacket on the floor, and noticed the blood down his shirt. "Did I miss something?"

"We can fill you in later," said Wren. "Right now, we need to talk about something else." He turned, then packed away all the items on the ground into the two bags — all apart from a small dark cylinder, the size of a permanent marker. This he handed to Isaac. "Hold this," he said. "If he moves, point it at him." He motioned for the others to head towards the door.

"Excuse me?" Isaac replied, "and where are you lot going?"

"To get some fresh air." Wren slapped Isaac reassuringly on the back, smiled, then walked to the door.

"*I* like fresh air," said Isaac, glancing towards the dark corner.

"You'll get plenty tonight, Isaac."

"But...how do I use this thing? What does it do?" he asked, turning the object over in his hands. "There're no buttons. What end do I point at him? Both look the same." He looked afraid. "Are there instructions?"

"If he tries anything, just point either end at him. *It* will know what to do, and you'll be just fine." He opened the door and gestured to the others to leave.

"We won't be long," Max said, hesitant to leave his friend in the company of an alien psychopath. "Right?" He looked at Wren.

Wren nodded and gave Isaac a thumbs up.

Once outside, Wren closed the door, then led them up the steep bank behind the shack. "Do not worry about Isaac," he said to Max and Ellie as they followed. "I have complete faith in him."

Max nodded but still didn't like it. As they climbed, he looked behind to see if George needed help. He didn't.

George now moved like a much younger man and scaled the bank with ease. Max could see the broad smile on his face in the torchlight.

Ellie nudged Max as they clambered up the bank. "I think I know why so many of the locals live to such an old age," she whispered. "They must all be friends of Wren."

They soon reached the top and scrambled down the other side, using the tree roots as steps. The sound of the stream grew louder, and Max saw splinters of moonlight caught on its lively surface.

At the water's edge, Wren turned to face them. "We need to talk privately," he said. "Away from Jenta. He will not hear us here."

Max glanced in the direction of the shack, still concerned for his friend.

"I have to take Jenta back," Wren said, looking at George.

"I thought you were going to say that," said George. "Did he come for you before?" he asked, with a puzzled look.

Wren nodded.

"But you chose not to go with him."

"I couldn't, not then."

"Why?"

Wren hesitated. "I was starting to like it here. I had reasons to stay. One of those was your safety. Allowing Jenta to find me and take me back would have put you in danger. No one could know of my existence. And you knew too much."

"Sorry," said Ellie, raising a hand. "But we know quite a bit, too. Are we in danger if you go back?"

"No," said Wren. "Not anymore. I managed to get information from Jenta, just fragments. But it seems things are happening on my world. Things that mean this situation of ours will barely register as a concern for them. Jenta is now acting alone, with no authority. When he came for me before, he was supposed to find me and take me home. When he failed to do so, he lied to them. His ego would not allow him to admit failure, so he told them I had died. But he never believed that himself. He suspected I was still alive. And he left a device to alert him if Kelha was ever awakened. Now he's back, to cover his tracks; to make the lie a truth.

"But he has broken many of our laws to get here. His punishment will be severe. Once we return, it'll be in his interest to remain quiet."

"What'll happen to you when you return?" asked Max. "What's your punishment?"

"Watchers are rare, and valued," he replied. "I will be reassigned, sent elsewhere. That will be my punishment."

Max got the feeling Wren was underplaying the risks to himself, that he was making a great sacrifice by returning. "I should have left that key under the floorboards," he said.

"I shouldn't have put it there in the first place," said George.

"I'm the one at fault here," Wren said, quietly.

"But you didn't know that maniac would come for you," George said.

There was a long silence. Max's mind once again went back to Isaac in the shack and then to his internal ticking clock. He wondered if he should mention it. It might be important.

"He is very different from you," George said, after a while. "I mean...different from the you I found in the barn. Are you even the same...species?"

"Yes," said Wren. "We are born the same, but when we come of age our physiology changes drastically. Some of us become highly specialised. We become Watchers, Healers,

Makers. There are many kinds. I am a Watcher; Jenta is a Hunter."

"Is it normal for a Hunter to be sent on a rescue mission?" asked George.

"No, it's not," said Wren. "It's one of two things I do not understand about all this. It makes no sense to send a Hunter; they are reckless, dangerous. They should have sent a Watcher."

"Why won't he let you stay?" asked Ellie. "If you being here is now of *little concern*, why is he bothering?"

"Like I said: ego. It's an obsession for him. I am a loose end."

"Aren't we loose ends, too?" asked Ellie. "The rest of your people might have other things to worry about. But if he's as obsessed as you say he is, won't he find a way to get back here?"

"To be sure of your safety, I will keep Jenta in hibernation for a very long time. Long enough for you all to live out your lives, without fear of him returning."

Ellie sighed, looking relieved but sad. Perhaps she also sensed the sacrifice Wren was making. "What's the second thing?" she asked. "You said there were two things you didn't understand?"

Wren looked at Max. "The second thing is, why are you getting these visions? That's the biggest mystery of all."

Max said nothing. He didn't know the answer, so he shrugged.

"What can we do to help?" asked George.

"Jenta's ship, Velkha," Wren said. "I need to find her. Kelha can only support one life. Velkha will support more. I've tried to summon her using his key, but I am too far, or she will not answer to me."

"It — I mean she," Ellie said, "could be in the clearing, in the woods. That's where we lost the drone, and where we first saw Jenta."

"Then we go to the woods," Wren said. "Once we are close, I can use the key to locate her. But we can't risk being seen by others. So, if you are all still willing to help, I'll need you to go ahead, to be my eyes. I won't have the energy to fade, restrain Jenta, *and* see all I need to see."

The three nodded.

"And Kelha?" George asked. "What happens to her when you go?"

"Before I leave, I will need to bring her to the surface. Then —"

He didn't get to finish. From the direction of the shack came a thunderous crash of splitting wood and falling stone. At the same time, the trees around them sprang to life with the flap of startled birds.

"Isaac!" Max shouted as he turned to look up the bank.

Wren was already running. The others followed as fast as they could.

Moments later, Max rounded the shack, stumbling over the remains of the wooden front door, now in splinters on the ground. He shielded his eyes from the flickering blue light erupting from the doorway, causing shadows of trees to dance around the corner, and he called for his friend. The air was thick with dust and light. There was no reply. He called again.

"Max?" Isaac replied, coughing. "Check this out. I need to get me one of these."

As Max's eyes adjusted, Isaac came into view. He was illuminated by a stream of light that cracked and snapped as it poured from the device in his hand. It was a light that pinned Jenta against broken rafters in the corner of the ceiling — with an expression of agony and anger twitching across his snake-like features.

With care, Wren took the device from Isaac's shaking hand, and the light vanished. There was the sound of falling timber in the darkness, and a heavy thud as Jenta fell to the ground.

Max stood alone at the churchyard gate, illuminated by a small light from under its crooked roof. He wore dark jeans, a hoodie, and a backpack. A single wire descended from his left ear, connecting to the phone in his pocket. His appearance reminded him of older kids he would watch from the high-rise; the ones that would hang out down on the corner by the phone box after dark. He doubted if they were part of a convoy escorting a homicidal alien back to his ship. But then, who knew?

Behind him, in the blackness of the churchyard, he could just make out the three figures in the shadows. Two straight and tall, one robust and hunched. They were waiting for Max's signal. Before that signal could be given, Max would need the all-clear from Isaac and Ellie, who had left the churchyard first, heading up Church Lane towards the copse at the end. Max checked his watch; it was two-thirty-five.

Somewhere in the darkness, an owl hooted.

A few hours earlier, after securing Jenta — and hearing Isaac's account of his failed escape — they had gathered in the shack around the glowing orb. It descended from the ceiling to hover just above the ground. Like a campfire, it gave off a cosy heat, and it wasn't long before Max, Ellie, and Isaac started to drift off. Max had dipped in and out of sleep, listening to Wren and George as they talked in hushed tones, like old friends.

Jenta made no further attempt to escape. Instead, he sat

silently in the corner, his eyes closed, delivering no more threats or menacing grins. Max hoped he'd now accepted his captivity, but suspected otherwise.

Wren woke them at two, an hour after the last helicopter had been heard. George had eaten while they'd slept, and changed out of his blood-stained clothes; he was looking eager to get going.

After forming a basic plan on how to proceed, they packed their things and left the shack together. Jenta was at Wren's side, his stride restricted by the thin silver rope that linked his ankles and bound his hands in front of him.

As they left the corner, Wren stopped and stared into the black veil of the western edge of the graveyard. After checking Jenta's bindings, he handed Isaac the cylinder, which Isaac had renamed "the wand", and instructed them to wait. Then he left them, walking off between the graves, until he was absorbed by the night. While they waited, the moon emerged from behind a cloud, only to return quickly behind another. They saw Wren in that moment. He was standing by a grave, his head bowed, a hand gently resting upon the headstone. A few minutes passed, and he rejoined the group, without explanation, and took the wand back from Isaac.

They continued to the gate with one more false start. This time it was Ellie who dashed off. They waited patiently while she "made a quick call to mother nature". Only when she had returned, looking sheepish, did the convoy to Oban Woods truly begin.

As per the plan, Isaac and Ellie went ahead, Ellie using her phone to navigate to the clearing, Isaac using his to talk to Max, who would be at the back of the convoy. George and Wren would be in the middle, flanking Jenta. But for now, they continued to wait for the all-clear.

Max looked at his watch again: two thirty-nine.

"*Church Lane, all clear. Over,*" came the voice of Isaac over Max's earpiece a few minutes later.

"OK," whispered Max, resisting the urge to say *Roger*. He stepped out into Church Lane. Looking left, he saw a single streetlight throwing its golden glow over the lane's cobbles, partially lighting the nearest cottage. All else was dark. In the opposite direction, on Station Road, a lone fox casually cantered across from the park, disappearing between a silent kebab shop and equally still pub.

"Station Road all clear," said Max, turning to face the dark churchyard. He gave the thumbs up. Seconds later, three shadowy figures passed under the roof of the gate, turning left toward the cottages. Max held back as they passed him, then followed.

The single streetlight that marked the halfway point of Church Lane died as Wren, Jenta, and George approached. When it flickered back to life moments later, they had already passed beyond its glow. When Max reached the same spot, it refused to illuminate him too.

"*Keep coming,*" came the voice of Isaac. "*We can just about see you now. We're heading to the bridge. Over.*"

"*You know, Isaac,*" Max heard Ellie's voice now. "*You don't need to say 'over'. It's a phone, not a radio.*"

"*I know — Over.*"

Max slowed his pace as he heard a scuffle ahead. In the pale moonlight, once again free of cloud, he could see Jenta refusing to move. He appeared to be waiting for Max to get closer. When he did, he glared at him wickedly, and flicked his small black eyes towards a cottage shrouded in darkness. It was Max's cottage. Wren moved him on with a violent shove. Max waited, then continued to follow, trying to remain calm, but his heart was racing, and his legs were beginning to shake. In Max's mind, the cottage seemed to watch him as he passed, pleading with him to enter and let others face the dangers. But he couldn't. He had to see this through.

"Path to the bridge is clear," said Isaac. *"Unless you count the giant dog turd Ellie just stepped in."* Isaac laughed. *"Over and — ouch... Ellie!"*

The convoy crossed the wooden bridge. Instead of taking the path north, like the day before, they took the path that followed the stream east. It would eventually lead to the east side of Oban and the clearing where they'd lost the drone.

Soon, the sounds of the stream faded as the path curved away from it, its gentle gurgling replaced by an orchestra of crickets from the dark hedgerows. With a moon almost full, and a sky almost cloudless, Max could see well enough without his torch. He could see Wren, George, and Jenta about twenty metres ahead. Isaac and Ellie, too far to be seen, continually checked in with an *all clear* at every bend in the path, while Max reported from the rear. The path behind was ghostly clear.

So far so good.

The black shadow of Oban Wood was getting closer all the time, back-lit by the floodlights at the bypass. Where the floodlights failed to reach, stars peppered the sky. Max was admiring the sight when Isaac's panicked voice crackled in his ear, *"—on the field. Repeat — there — field."* The reception was sketchy, but Max got the gist.

In the distance, moving across the field, away from the woods and towards the town, was a single light.

Max stepped off the path and hid amid the long grass. "Hide!" he called to Wren. But Wren was standing tall, watching the light as its beam caught the tips of the wheat.

Max got back on the path and ran to him. "Ben, they'll see you."

"I need him to," he replied. "Signal him with your light, Max."

"But who is it?"

"It's Mr Bartley. I think he's found something of interest."

There was a shift in Jenta's posture, and he turned his head slowly to watch the man crossing the field.

Max flashed his light. Almost instantly, Bartley's torch flicked off in response. They could still see him, though; a dark shape among the bluish wheat. But he was no longer moving.

"Call him, Max," Wren said calmly. "Tell him it's you."

"Mr Bartley!" Max shouted as he waved his light in the air. "It's me. It's Max."

No response.

Then, slowly, Bartley began to wade towards them. When he was close enough to see that Max had companions, he stopped in the waist-high crop, and shone his torch onto each of the awaiting faces; first Max, then George, then Wren. Finally, he turned the beam onto Jenta, who grimaced and turned away from the bright beam. Mr Bartley gasped and lowered the light to the bound and heavily tattooed hands. "Oh," he said, looking at Max, concerned. "It's him."

"It's OK," Max said, not quite believing it himself. "Ben's taking him back." He said this slowly, unsure if he was sharing too much of the plan.

Then came the sound of running on the path, and Isaac and Ellie emerged from the darkness.

"Oh...hey, Mr...Bartley," said Isaac between breaths, bending over with his hands on his thighs.

Bartley ignored him and turned his attention back to Ben.

"Mr Bartley." Wren greeted him with a nod. "Midnight stroll?"

263

"Ben," replied Mr Bartley, returning the nod. "Trouble sleeping after my chat with young Max earlier," he said, his face stern but not unfriendly. "Boy, do I have things to say to you. But it looks like you've more pressing matters right now." He glanced again at Jenta.

"Even more pressing, now I see what you've found."

Bartley raised his eyebrows in surprise. "This?" he asked, lifting an orange carrier bag from the sea of wheat. "You know what this is?"

"I do. You found it at the crash site."

Jenta straightened himself and looked to Wren, then back to Mr Bartley.

"Yes, I did. There were more of them. But I only took one."

"I would like to take a closer look," said Wren. "If I may?"

"Of course." Mr Bartley stepped closer.

Wren shoved his knee into the back of Jenta's leg, causing him to fall to the ground with a grunt. He then tasked Isaac to watch over him, handing him the wand once more.

Bartley retrieved a long triangular prism from the bag. It reminded Max of a large Toblerone chocolate bar, of the size only seen at Christmas or in airport shops. It was dark in colour, but unlike a Toblerone was split into two halves. In the middle, linking the two halves, was a glass cylinder about four inches long. Inside the cylinder was a dark oily substance, smoky at the edges, which slowly swirled within a glowing purple liquid.

Wren half-turned to look at Jenta and said something softly in his own tongue. Jenta looked away, uninterested. Wren turned back to Bartley. "How many?" he asked.

"There was a whole cluster of them. Six, I think. What are they?"

"Explosives," Wren said flatly.

Mr Bartley stiffened.

"They are used for mining asteroids," continued Wren. "One is enough to obliterate Oban entirely," he said. "Link *six* together, and the surrounding towns would be destroyed too."

Bartley offered the device to Wren, who reached out to take it. But Wren paused when he noticed a shift in Jenta's body language, and he quickly withdrew his hands. "I can't touch it, can I?" he said, turning to face Jenta. The Hunter responded with something that almost looked like an innocent shrug, followed by one of his wicked grins.

"Why?" said Bartley. "I don't want it." He looked at the others, desperate for help.

Wren placed a reassuring hand on his shoulder and eyed the device. "It's OK, Mr Bartley. You just keep hold of it for a moment. If I touch it, it will go off. All of them will."

"W...what...do I do with it?"

"We need to disarm it," Wren said calmly, still staring at the object. He wrung his hands through his hair, then rubbed at the stubble on his chin. "Max, could you please take it from Mr Bartley?"

Max wasn't keen on going near an object capable of flattening an entire wood, but he pushed his fear aside and stepped forward. Maybe *this* was the source of his ticking clock. "What do I need to do?" he asked.

Max took the item in his hands and forced himself to not think of it as a bomb. This was made easy by the fact it looked nothing like one. But still, his hands felt sweaty, and his breathing became shallow and fast as he held it.

Under instruction from Wren, he held the two ends of the prism and simultaneously twisted them in opposite directions. They turned with resistance, but then clicked into place. As a result, the dark oil-like substance and the purple liquid merged, then lightened until it became clear like water. Once it was clear, Max was able to push the two ends together, enclosing the glass cylinder within the prism. It sealed with a satisfying *clunk*. As soon as he'd closed it, the intensity of his internal ticking lessened. Max now knew how to stop it completely.

"Good," Wren said. "One down. Five to go." He smiled at him. "Can you do that?"

Max nodded. He wanted to do it. Anything to finally end the monotonous thud that was driving him mad.

"Thank you, Max," Wren said, taking hold of the device. "This changes our plan, though. I'll take our handsome friend here to the clearing alone. It's now more important that the rest of these are disarmed. Disable them in exactly the same way. Once I've secured him aboard Velkha, I'll meet you all at the crash site. Wait for me there. Stay close to Kelha. If you have this—" he handed Max the key "—she'll keep you safe. Don't lose it, will you?" He smiled.

Wren walked to Isaac, who'd been gripping the wand firmly with both hands, never taking his eyes off Jenta. But when the time came to hand the device back to Wren, Isaac's hands spasmed from gripping it so tightly, and it fell into the long grass beside the path.

Max watched the events unfold as if in slow motion. Jenta flipped to his feet, shoulder barging George to the ground as he launched himself at Wren. He slammed his head into his chest, taking him down, causing the bomb to fly from Wren's grip. At the same time, Isaac had dropped to the ground to retrieve his weapon. He quickly found it and aimed it at Jenta, who was now on top of Wren, beating him fiercely with his bound fists. A crackle of blue light jumped from the wand. It deflected off Jenta's thick bracelet and shot across the dark field into the woods. Ellie screamed at Jenta to get off, and bravely kicked the hulk of his back repeatedly, but with no effect.

It was now Max's turn to act. He rushed to where the bomb had fallen in the grass and picked it up. His intention was to strike Jenta with it, but he hesitated. *What if it exploded on impact?*

Ellie didn't hesitate. "That'll do," she said, taking it from Max. She ran at Jenta and swung it like a baseball bat, planting it squarely at the back of Jenta's head with a dull, sickening thud.

Jenta released a primal cry that silenced the crickets. He stood, turning, ready to strike his attacker. Instead, his legs gave way, and he fell to the ground, rolling into the long grass where he lay motionless, face down.

Mr Bartley, who was probably now wishing he had stayed in bed, pulled George to his feet, while Isaac, Ellie and Max watched Jenta, waiting for him to get back up. Ellie prepared for another swing, shifting her weight from foot to foot. But he didn't move.

The crickets resumed their tuneless song as Wren stirred and groaned on the ground behind them.

They crowded around him, helping him to a sitting position. Apart from a few scrapes, he looked mostly unharmed.

"Are you OK?" Ellie said, still wielding the deadly Toblerone. She had the look of someone who had just woken from a terrible nightmare.

Wren nodded and gingerly got to his feet.

"Good swing, Ellie," George said, "Lucky it didn't blow—"

"Yeah, are you crazy?" Isaac interrupted. "You could have killed us all."

She spun to face him. "Well, I didn't, did I?" she replied sharply. "Anyway, it's disarmed."

"Oh. So now you're an alien explosives expert, are you?"

Max could see Isaac was terrified and just venting. Ellie must have seen it, too; she took a calming breath and bit her lip. Without another word, she picked up the shopping bag and placed the bomb inside. Isaac tried to compose himself, but was visibly shaken. He turned away and pointed the wand to where Jenta had come to rest.

"Er...where is he?"

All of them aimed their lights to the spot where a thin piece of silver rope now lay upon a flattened patch of grass.

Jenta was gone.

20

KELHA RISING

They huddled together, feeling exposed, sending beams of light towards every sound or hint of movement in the darkness.

"Anyone see him?" Max asked. His immediate fear was for his mother. Jenta knew where they lived. "Wren?" he asked, trying not to sound panicked. "Do you see him?"

Wren was standing in the field. His eyes were black as he scanned the horizon. His head stopped. "Yes," he said. "He's heading to the clearing. To Velkha."

Max followed his gaze but saw nothing.

Wren returned to the path, removing both his and Jenta's bags from his back and placing them on the ground. "Max," he said, kneeling while sifting through their contents. "You have the key. I want you to take this too." He handed him the detonator. "I cannot risk him getting hold of it. I'm going after him, but once he's had time to lick his wounds, he'll be after me."

Max took it, eyeing it with concern.

"Don't worry, Max. It cannot be triggered accidentally. You have to take it; we can't destroy it or risk hiding it. So keep it safe and disarm those bombs. And do it quickly; there is a chance, and it's a small chance, that if he gets to Velkha, he could trigger them another way." He reached into the bag and pulled out the healing disc and handed it to Ellie. "You have a knack with this. Take it. Hopefully, you won't need it." He stood and placed both bags across his back, a strap of each crossing his chest. He looked towards the woods, then turned to face his worried-looking companions. "I'm sorry for the danger I've put you all in. Stay near Kelha; she will keep you safe and will help you where she can. Once I have Jenta, I will meet you there."

Isaac held out the wand for Wren.

Wren shook his head. "You need the practice, Isaac." He looked to George and smiled, then turned and sprinted into the darkness, towards the woods.

They watched in silence until they could no longer see him.

"He'll be alright," said George.

Max nodded but wasn't sure. "If anyone's coming with me," he said, placing the detonator into his rucksack, "we need to go now."

"And you must go quickly, too," said George, "but I don't remember the way." He looked disappointed and gestured for them to hurry along.

"I'll show you the way," said Old Man Bartley, stepping forward with his hand outstretched. "James Bartley," he introduced himself. "We can follow at our own pace."

"George Moss," he replied, shaking the younger man's hand. "Very good to meet you." He turned and looked at Max. "Go. We'll be right behind."

Max, Isaac and Ellie hurried across the field. At the edge of the wood, they encountered police tape tied to metal spikes in the ground, but with no sign of anyone to stop them, they simply ducked underneath.

"We'll need to move quietly," said Max. "There might be army or police in there."

"Could be," said Isaac. "But I doubt it. It's really late, and we're still a long way from the bypass."

"Let's just be careful," said Ellie as they entered the woods.

Exhausted, but too afraid to stop and rest, they stumbled through the darkness until they reached the bramble wall. They searched for the gap they had beaten through previously, but it was hopeless. And Max wasn't sure he had the energy to fight his way through again.

Just then, a tearing, rustling sound met their ears. For a split second, Max imagined Jenta ploughing towards them through the bushes. But it wasn't him; it was the bramble wall opening before them, tendrils unwinding and snapping apart to present a path, just for them. Kelha *was* helping. As soon as the gap was wide enough, they rushed through.

"Of course, the brambles parted for us," muttered Ellie. "Why wouldn't they. It's all perfectly normal."

"We saw it too, Ellie," said Isaac. "If you're crazy, we all are."

On the other side, they made their way down into the mist-filled hollow. They weaved between the mounds of the old dead trees, which at night felt even more grave-like. Then they climbed the small hill where Max had experienced his first vision. From the top, they sent their bright torch beams out in search of the explosives. They found nothing.

"How are we supposed to find them?" said Isaac. "Where do we start? We should have asked Bartley—"

Just then, all three of their lights flickered, then died.

Isaac and Ellie panicked and started whacking the torches against the palms of their hands.

"Stop," said Max calmly. "This is Kelha again... just like with the bramble wall. She's helping us."

"Not very helpful if you ask me," said Ellie, unconvinced.

They looked around in the pitch black.

"It's too dark," said Isaac. "I'm not even sure my eyes are open."

But slowly, as their eyes adjusted to the darkness, a faint purple glow emerged. It was down the slope to their right.

"There!" cried Ellie. "I see it."

They scrambled down the hill towards it, grabbing tree trunks for support.

At the base of the hill, hidden under a large fern, were five identical objects. They seemed to burst from the earth like precious dark crystals, each one glowing at the midpoint from the purple liquid within. Max noticed the gap and the shallow hole where Mr Bartley had removed the first.

"Right," he said, "I suppose I better get started." He took a deep breath and the torches flicked back to life, startling Isaac and Ellie.

Torch in one hand, wand in the other, Isaac turned away, watching the dark woods for a sign of Jenta. Ellie stood just behind Max, providing him with enough light to work.

Max removed earth from around the base of the closest device, then pulled it free and held it carefully in both hands. He twisted both ends. When the black oily substance had merged with the purple glowing liquid and became clear, he pushed the two halves together. He felt that same satisfying *clunk* as before. He let out a long breath and passed it over his shoulder to Ellie.

"Don't hit anyone with that," said Isaac, now watching them.

Ellie was about to respond angrily, but Isaac interrupted. "Look, I'm sorry," he said with a sheepish smile. "You saved our lives. I was just...anyway...I'm sorry."

She returned the smile, then hit Isaac playfully with the bomb, making an explosion sound as she did so.

"Are you kidding me!" Isaac said in disbelief. "Seriously, Ellie, what the—"

"Feel free to help, people?" said Max. "There *are* enough of these to go around."

"No, no, no," replied Ellie. "You are doing a brilliant job. Plus, I'm holding the torch. Important...."

"Yeah, and I'm on the lookout for what's-his-face," said Isaac.

"Then do it quietly, please."

They remained silent while Max repeated the task three more times. After each successful deactivation, his internal countdown diminished in volume but seemed to quicken in pace.

One more.

Max stood and stretched, circling the final device while Isaac and Ellie stood nervously by. Max could feel their eyes on him.

His hands were damp with sweat and shaking. It didn't matter that he'd deactivated the other devices perfectly; if he messed this last one up, they were dead.

Max knelt and removed it from the ground. Holding its two ends as before, he twisted. Only this time, his sweaty hands failed him, and it slipped from his grip, falling to the ground with a thud.

"Can you boys stop dropping things?" Ellie shouted in despair as Isaac lurched back, tripping and falling into a large fern.

The glow of the device had brightened on impact. The oily black substance in the cylinder began to swirl faster, getting ever smaller until it resembled a tiny shiny black marble. Max rubbed his hands vigorously on his jeans to dry them, then retrieved the device from the ground. It was vibrating, and a low hum started that quickly increased in frequency as the black marble shrunk to the size of a pinprick.

"Close it, Max!" shouted Ellie over the noise. She stepped back, taking the light with her.

He twisted both ends of the prism. They turned, but with more resistance than before. Eventually, they locked into position, but the hum continued to increase in frequency and was now shrill in their ears. He tried pushing both ends to close it, but it refused to give.

"What now?" shouted Ellie. She had dropped her torch and was holding both hands over her ears.

"Well, this is great!" shouted Isaac, climbing out of the fern "I always knew I'd die watching someone play a deadly game of Bop It." He closed his eyes and screwed up his face in anticipation of the imminent explosion. "At least I won't have to face my brother tomorrow."

Max was out of ideas. There was no point running. Wren had said that just one of these would wipe out the entire woods. He placed the device on the ground and stepped back. The purple glow was so intense they could not look at it directly. The three friends turned away, huddled together. They hugged. Max tried not to cry.

"Well, we saved the town!" shouted Ellie. "That's something, right?"

Max nodded. He looked at the surrounding woods, now purple with stark black shadows. He hoped Jenta was nearby; if the blast took him out too, his mother would be safe.

Then, quite suddenly, the sound ceased, and the light faded. Slowly, they turned to face it. The black marble was growing again, until it was a swirling black cloud of oil, just like before. The dark cloud then merged with the liquid; soon the cylinder was clear, appearing to contain nothing but water.

Before it could change its mind, Max dropped to the ground and pushed at both ends. This time it slammed shut.

There was a moment of stunned silence and an exchange of cautious looks. When it was clear it would not pop back open and kill them all, Isaac and Ellie jumped around like lottery winners, Isaac punching the air and kicking a nearby clump of grass. They had done it, and apart from the poor clump of grass, no one had come to any harm.

With armfuls of alien explosives, Isaac and Ellie returned to the top of the hill, while Max walked to the gap in the bramble wall to wait for George and Mr Bartley.

He sat alone on a moss-covered rock and stared into the darkness, grateful for the first silence he'd experienced in two days. The ticking clock ticked no more. The silence was bliss.

Through the gaps in the trees, he looked at the stars in the night sky, and thought about what Ellie had said earlier; about everything being different yet feeling the same. The stars looked the same to Max, but they did feel different. They felt closer than ever before — like suns. One of them, he knew, was a sun to Jenta and Wren.

He heard George and Mr Bartley before he saw them. When he saw their lights he signalled them with his, to show them the way.

"You did it?" George asked as he approached, a look of worry across his face.

"Well, we're all still alive, so I guess so," said Max with a broad smile.

"Are you sure it was all of them?" asked Bartley. "There might be more somewhere else."

"It's all of them," said Max, choosing not to tell them about the now absent ticking clock.

George slapped him hard on the back. "Excellent news, young man. I am enjoying my newfound mobility and would have hated for it to come to a premature end."

Max led them down into the hollow, then up the hill to join the others.

"What do we do now?" asked Mr Bartley, looking at the pile of bombs with a frown.

"Well," said Max, slipping off his bag and placing it on the ground. "Wren said we should stay here and wait for —"

And it happened again. Max collapsed.

What now? he thought, as the familiar smell of rich earth washed over him. Couldn't Kelha just send him a text?

An explosion of scent filled the night as he ran, anger and hatred surging through every cell in his body, branches breaking against him as he forced a path through the woods. He wanted to kill. He *needed* to kill. He slowed to a silent jog as a barrage of new scents came to him. He dismissed all but one. It was the scent that fuelled his rage; the scent that had poisoned his mind for more than seventy years.

Kill. Kill. KILL.

No. Not yet. First, he would get him to talk; he needed answers. He needed to know the location of the Maker. Only then would he kill him. And he would enjoy it.

He saw the thin colourful thread of scent weave between

276

the trees before descending into a gully, where it stopped. His prey had faded. He knew he would. But he could not hide.

Without slowing, he reached down and clawed up a handful of dry earth. He threw it with force while leaping to where the scent trail ended. The dirt spread into a fine cloud, betraying Wren's position. He saw his shape, and came down on him with all his weight, feeling his feet connect with something substantial. Wren appeared, flying through the air, long arms and legs flailing; there was a loud crack of ribs as he landed across a sturdy tree trunk.

As he walked to his injured prey, a wave of satisfaction washed over him. Soon he would have what he wanted. Soon he could leave this hell.

Darkness returned, as did the smell of moist earth. Then Max found himself sitting alone on a smooth grey floor.

Well, this is different, he thought. He was having another vision, but looking through his own eyes. Apart from the grey floor, everything else was black. Despite the enveloping blackness, he could see his own body perfectly well, lit by an unseen source.

Ta Kaah.

The voice of Kelha?

Ta Kaah.

This time there was a direction to the voice, and he turned and walked towards it.

Ta Kaah.

As he walked, a black cube emerged, darker than the blackness around it. He stopped, waiting for something to happen, but nothing did. He was sure he was looking at Kelha, or at least a representation of her. He stepped closer.

Ta Kaah.

The voice was loud and definitely coming from the cube.

A deep penetrating hum grew around him as he felt a warm sensation in his feet. He looked down. He was standing in a puddle of blue-white light. Instinctively, he stepped back, and the light faded, as did the warmth. The light reappeared as he stepped forward again. This is where Kelha wanted him to stand, so he stayed.

The light swirled around his feet, some leaving the surface and dancing over the top of his trainers. Soon his entire body felt warm, and the hairs on the back of his neck tingled. He shook the feeling away.

As he watched with wonder, a thin sliver of light, like a glowing tadpole, left the pool and meandered towards the cube. When it reached Kelha, it climbed her surface in a perfectly straight line, until eye level with Max. It then grew and split into three patches of light, one large in the centre, two small on either side. They flashed brightly, then disappeared. Left behind in their place were two hand-shaped indentations, and another of a face — *his* face.

The light under his feet was gone, as was the low hum. The next move, Max suspected, was his. This was an invitation. He knew it.

Kelha did not try to hurry Max, but the memory of what he'd seen through the eyes of Jenta drove him to act. He stepped forward, inspecting the impressions in the seemingly solid wall of Kelha. One at a time, he placed his hands into the waiting moulds. Closing his eyes and taking a deep breath, he sunk his face into...well...his face.

At first, nothing happened, and he wondered if he was doing it wrong. Was this the way to open Kelha?

Nothing continued to happen, until he opened his eyes. That's when the light show began.

The lights felt familiar, like the ones you see when you

stand up too quickly. When that happened, Max would usually just push his palms into his eyes and shake his head, maybe sit down again. But this time, he could not move or close his eyes. So he watched them.

The lights flashed, faster and faster. Then the sounds started. No — they were voices. *Lots* of voices. They came with images. Kelha was showing him objects. They flashed past his eyes at speed; some he'd seen before, others he had not. There were objects that opened, twisted, came apart, slotted together. Thousands of them filled his mind. He focused on the voices. At first, they had sounded like an unbroken stream of sound, almost like a song. But then he started to hear gaps, distinct words. He could recognise where one word ended, and the next began. But more than that, he could *feel* their meaning.

The images soon died away, and the words stopped. The blackness returned. All Max could hear now was the wind; and he felt it on his face. Then, as if someone had flicked a switch, a forest appeared. He was above it, flying over it, trees passing quickly below, spreading in all directions. In the distance, against a beautiful blue sky, he could make out grey mountains, with unusually steep inclines; their summits were covered in snow. No mountains like this existed on Earth. This was Wren's world.

He looked back down to the endless forest passing beneath him. It was dense and vibrant. He caught glimpses of a purple river shining under its canopy.

He was following it.

Looking forward, he saw what must be his destination — a giant tree. Ancient and proud, it stood a hundred times larger than those around it. Its massive twisting trunk disappeared into a vast green crown that seemed to emit clouds of vapour. The trunk continued through the thick foliage and emerged to reach skyward. At the very top was a platform, intricately carved. On the platform was a woman.

As he got closer, he saw she wore a long light blue dress, the same colour as the sky behind her. Her face was beautiful, sad, and alien to Max. Her hair was long and black. He stopped before her.

"*Ta Kaah*," she said, in a familiar voice.

She repeated it over and over. It was *her* voice Max had been hearing. The woman could not see him. Instead, she looked through him, out towards the horizon. "*Ta Kaah*," she repeated. Max understood her clearly: *Save him.*

She closed her large, dark sad eyes and turned away. The connection was lost.

He stepped back from Kelha, watching the cavities of his face and hands slowly fill with a grey foam until the surface of the cube was perfectly flat and smooth once more.

The cube faded, and Max's friends appeared around him.

George and Bartley leaned in close while Ellie and Isaac hung back, waiting for him to vomit. But he didn't. He stood, with help, and brushed himself down. "Change of plan," he said. "Jenta has Wren. And I'm going to get him back."

Max didn't have time to explain what he'd just experienced. He wasn't sure he *could* even with all the time in the world. There was one thing he was sure of, though: he *knew* things; things he hadn't known before. Things about Kelha, and about Wren, about his technology and his culture. He was also pretty sure he knew some, if not all, of his language. For a second, Max imagined a world where knowledge and language could simply be downloaded to people's minds — a world without French teachers.

With a sense of urgency, he picked up his bag and scrambled down the small hill. Max had a plan. It was a simple one, given to him by Kelha. But the knowledge he'd been given to execute it felt fragile. If he didn't act fast, it would fade.

"Are you OK, Max?" Ellie called after him.

"What?" He turned to face them. "Erm...yes, sorry. I'm fine. But I'll need you to follow me. We need to move away from this hill."

"What are you doing?" Ellie asked, picking up her bag.

"Wren wanted Kelha above ground," said Max, "Only he's not coming back here, so—"

"You're going to raise Kelha?" Isaac asked doubtfully.

"Yes," he replied, his confidence surprising himself as much as the others.

Isaac and Ellie stood motionless, not knowing how to respond.

"Come on," said George, starting to follow Max, along with Mr Bartley. "I think we'd better listen to the boy."

Isaac and Ellie carried the explosives and followed.

When they got to the bramble wall, Max turned to face the hill, now invisible in the darkness. "We should be safe here," he said, removing the key from his bag. "You might want to get behind me, though," he added.

They took cover behind Max, exchanging uncertain looks.

Max stepped forward to give himself more space. He looked at the key in his right hand, then placed his left forefinger gently on its milky white surface. In his mind, he simply asked for control. When a tiny pinprick of light grew within its core, diffused like a bright star behind a thin sheet of cloud, he knew it had been granted. The sphere then shrunk to better fit the hand of its new owner. The internal glow disappeared, replaced by a blue light that roamed upon its surface. He knew what to do, as if he'd done it a thousand times before. He flicked the light with his finger. It leapt free of the sphere and formed a bright disc, the size of a dinner plate, that surrounded the ball and the hand that held it. The disc was composed of many distinct rings, like the rings of Saturn. Max knew that each one corresponded to a specific attribute of Kelha: position, orientation, speed, visibility, and many more. Selecting between the rings was a simple case of tightening or loosening his grip.

His friends behind him, bathed in the blue light, looked on dumbfounded.

With a deep breath, Max reached towards the hill with the key. Then, as if gripping a stiff doorknob, he turned his hand slowly, causing a rumble deep beneath their feet, followed by a dull cracking sound of roots rupturing. A rustle from the invisible canopy accompanied each crack, sending leaves raining down around the hill, illuminated by the blue glow and the four beams of torchlight. Max's hand continued to turn, and soon the trees upon the hill began to rise and lean. Eventually, some fell, caught by the surrounding wood. The shape of the hill was changing: parts were sinking while other parts bulged. Birds and creatures, unseen, took flight.

With a deep thud, a massive portion of the hill collapsed, leaving a large root-covered mass of earth that continued to rise until it was clear of the ground. It rose higher. Ten feet, fifteen, twenty. Max flicked his wrist, causing huge clumps of dirt and clay to fall from it, revealing a sharp corner of the cube within.

"Hello, Kelha," George whispered from behind Max.

Isaac laughed, flicking his torch to Max then back to the floating boulder of earth as it slowly climbed.

Max loosened his grip, selecting a different ring, and turned his hand back the other way. In response, Kelha rotated, causing the remaining bulk of earth and root to fall away. There she was, clean and sharp, a perfect cube — blacker than night.

Max brought the key close into his chest, summoning Kelha. She glided silently towards him, landing gently among the ferns as Max's hand fell to his side, and the disc of light around the key disappeared.

There was a hushed silence and a warm smell of freshly turned earth in the air. Applause and laughter erupted from his friends as they slapped him on the back, complimenting his epic driving skills.

They approached the cube. Isaac and George were the first to reach it, running their hands over its surface.

"I never thought I'd see her," George whispered.

"Is she how you imagined?" asked Isaac, a look of wonder across his face.

"No. She's beautiful. I'm not sure how a cube could be beautiful, but look at her." He shook his head in amazement. "Just — beautiful."

Mr Bartley silently studied the cube, then reached out a hand to touch it, to see if it was really there. Max couldn't read minds, but he knew Bartley was thinking about his father.

Max took in the sight. George was right: she was beautiful.

Wren had talked about Kelha as if she were alive. But Kelha had told Max otherwise. She was intelligent, yes, and also organic, but she wasn't alive. Neither was Velkha. Which was good, because Kelha had shown Max a plan that, if successful, would result in the destruction of at least one but possibly both craft.

The plan. The sense of urgency suddenly returned to Max. He was about to make the next move when he became aware that not everyone was looking at the black cube; Ellie was looking at him. She was staring at him with a puzzled expression. He shot her a small, uncomfortable smile.

"Why are you here, Max?" she said, almost to herself, in a daze.

"Sorry?" he replied, confused by the question.

Ellie suddenly seemed to realise she'd spoken out loud. She looked at the others, who were now looking at her. She composed herself and asked again. "Why are you here, Max? I mean...why did you move here, to Hurstwick? When I asked you before, when we first met, you just shrugged. But you didn't answer."

Max felt his cheeks redden. "Why do you want to know?"

Ellie ignored his question and asked another. "Also, no offence, but how does a librarian afford a cottage on Church Lane? Apart from a few who have lived there forever, everyone else is a banker, or a hedge-fund manager, whatever they are."

"Are you OK, Ellie?" Isaac said with a look of concern. "None of that is important. Did you *not* see what just happened here? Man, I thought *I* was socially awkward," he added under his breath, then went back to admiring the cube.

Ellie let the comment slide. "It's important *because* of what just happened here."

George placed a hand on Max's shoulder. "It's OK, Max," he said softly. "I think I know where she's going with this. And it's OK." George nodded to Ellie to continue.

"I'm sorry, Max, if I'm making you feel uncomfortable," she said, stepping forward. "but you must see why I'm asking?" She glanced at the cube. "Why did you move to Hurstwick? And why to that cottage?"

There was a silence as everyone waited for Max's response.

Max sighed. He knew where she was going with it too. But it was a dead end. It had to be.

"Just before Christmas," he said, staring at the cube to avoid Ellie's gaze, "we got a letter. Apparently, my grandfather died. We never even knew he existed. See, it was on my dad's side. My mum never knew much about my dad's family. She wasn't with him long enough, and he died before I was born. She told me that a few distant relatives turned up to the funeral, cousins and a great aunt, but they never kept in touch. And she never heard from them again. But then this letter arrived, saying my grandfather had left us the cottage on Church Lane. That it was ours to sell or move into. My mum visited, saw a job advertised for a librarian; that's what she did in London, and we moved."

"So you're a Furlong," George said. It wasn't a question.

"Yeah, I suppose, but my mum gave me her name. She never got a chance to marry my dad."

Ellie took a deep breath. "Before we left the graveyard," she said, fidgeting with her fingers, "I ran back to see the grave. The one Wren visited. I couldn't help it. You all must have been curious, too. Anyway, it was a woman: Mary Furlong."

"Who's that?" asked Isaac, his interest recaptured.

"Mary," said George, "was the only child of Jenny and Don Furlong. She was like a big sister to me. She wrote to me for a while, after I returned to London, but eventually we lost touch. In her last letter she mentioned a man. Love of her life, apparently. I never once imagined it could be..." George didn't finish. Instead, he studied Max intently, making him feel even more uncomfortable.

"Aha!" blurted Isaac, now seeing the relevance of the conversation. "So if Mary was an only child and your dad was a Furlong, then Mary could be your...what? Grand...no, *great*-grandmother?" Isaac's smile fell away as the final

285

possibility revealed itself to him. "And if Mary and Wren were.... Oh my!"

"Can we *not* have this conversation now, please?" Max said abruptly, brushing George's hand from his shoulder and turning away.

"Sorry," Ellie said.

She started to follow him, but George held up a hand. She stopped and nodded.

A silence fell over the group as Max walked away.

His heart was racing, and his blood was pumping in his ears. Time was running out, but he couldn't move on without processing the thoughts now rushing through his mind. He needed to stop and think, or he might explode.

The torchlight from the group faded as he moved further into the darkness. Glancing over his shoulder, he could see them standing by the cube, talking. Probably about him. He wanted to shout at them, tell them to shut up and to leave him alone. But he didn't. He stood watching them for a while, then, when he could watch no more, he turned away.

There was a sudden noise to his right. It was just a hedgehog. It emerged from under a bush and was chewing on a fat slimy slug, its wet nose twitching as it munched. He watched it devour the last of it, then continued to watch as it wandered off to find another.

Something slowly dawned on Max. How had he seen the hedgehog? He held no torch, and the key was no longer glowing, but somehow he could see quite clearly in the dark. He looked around for a source of light but found nothing. He closed his eyes tight, then reopened them. It should have been pitch black, but each tree, bush, vine, and plant, seemed to emit a soft dim light. His chest tightened as the truth took hold of him. A truth that had always been there but out of reach, out of focus.

For as long as he could remember, Max had known he was different. He was an outsider, disconnected from the world around him. He used to think he'd missed a lesson at school, one that taught kids how to behave around each other, how to fit in, be normal. Isaac probably felt the same, maybe even Ellie. That didn't make *them* part alien.

This wasn't helping. Max stopped himself spiralling into oblivion. There was no time to think. He would have to process this later, if there was a later. If anything, now he had another reason to rescue Wren. He was family.

He turned and walked back to his friends, feeling more like an outsider than ever before, but oddly, somehow, more comfortable in his own skin.

"I'm sorry," Max said to Ellie. "You're right, but I can't deal with this now. I just need to save him."

"OK," said Ellie. She walked to him and took his hand in hers. Isaac hung back, looking awkward. "What do you need us to do?" she asked.

Max instructed them to stand away from the cube. Under his control, Kelha silently rose to the height of the remaining trees, where she disappeared.

"Awesome," said Isaac, while the others shook their heads in amazement.

"You look like a Furlong," said George to Max. "But I think you have your great-grandfather's eyes."

Max smiled. "Let's go find him," he said.

21

THE CLEARING

With his newly gained knowledge, Max used the key to show him the way to Velkha. A thin needle-like light protruded from its surface, about an inch long, and pointed the way like a compass. Impressively, instead of a simple straight line, it steered them via the *quickest* route. It took them around ditches and impassable thickets, and then at last out onto a narrow track, barely a path, that led south-east towards the clearing. Here the group split once more. Max, Ellie, and Isaac ran along the path, while George and Bartley followed at their own pace, carrying the explosives between them.

"Why...couldn't...we take the...bloody spaceship," Isaac said to Ellie between breaths as they ran. "It would have been a lot quicker, don't you think?"

"Only room for one," replied Ellie.

"Maybe we could have sat...on top...while Max drove."

Max was about twenty feet in front, going over the plan in his head. It was a simple plan, but it relied heavily on Jenta making the right choice and on Max getting to Velkha before he did. He glanced at the key to make sure he was still heading in the right direction, then quickened his pace.

To Max's disappointment, his ability to see in the dark was proving unreliable. Like mobile phone reception, it seemed to come and go, and change in strength, jumping from four bars to one and back again. Right now, it was no-service, so he relied on his torch to light the way.

From behind him came a scream of pain followed by a thud.

Max spun, aiming his torch towards the source. He found Isaac on the floor, holding his ankle and shielding his eyes from Max's bright beam.

"Are you OK?" Max asked.

"I will be when you get that light out of my face." Isaac winced in pain and threw his head back. "Ahh. I think I've just twisted it, that's all." He tried to stand, but then slumped back down to the ground and grimaced.

"Don't move," said Ellie at his side. "You'll make it worse." She examined his ankle, then looked at Max and pursed her lips. "It doesn't look broken, but he won't make it."

"I'm dying?" Isaac squeaked.

"I *mean* you won't make it to the clearing. Not in time, anyway." She shook her head. "I can't leave him here alone, Max. Sorry."

"It's fine," said Max. "I'll be alright. Use the healing disc, then follow. George and Bartley will be close behind."

Ellie nodded. "Go," she said. "No. Wait." She stood and pulled Max in for a hug, then pushed him away again. "Don't get killed. Or...I'll kill you."

"I'll try not to," Max said, forcing a smile.

A part of Max wanted to stay with them, but he couldn't. He wasn't doing this just to save Wren; every one of them was at risk. Jenta wouldn't just kill Wren and be done with it. He had a lot of mess to clear up. After Wren, he would kill

Max, then his friends, and quite likely destroy the town too. Why not?

He looked at them both — the only friends he'd ever known — and hoped it wouldn't be the last time he saw them. He turned and ran along the path, strangely relieved he was doing *this* part alone.

"Good luck!" shouted Isaac. "We'll be there soon. Don't do anything cool without us."

The narrow track came to an end, and Max emerged into the moonlit clearing.

Exhausted from his run, he dropped to his knees amid the long, gently hissing grass and clicked off his torch.

He waited and listened; the crickets were once again in full voice, and he heard a distant cry that could have been a fox.

Once he'd regained control of his breathing, he stood and surveyed the area.

The clearing, made up mostly of long grass with a few large bushes dotted around, was about the size of two football fields, and was surrounded entirely by the dark trees of Oban. The key was pointing to the centre. Max saw no sign of Velkha, but he wasn't expecting to; she'd be hidden from view.

There was a movement to his left. A ghostly barn owl had entered the clearing and was hovering above the grass. Its dish-like face aimed towards the ground, it moved from point to point, then found a spot that held its interest. After making several slight adjustments to its position, it dropped into the tall grass. A few seconds later, it rose noiselessly and departed with its kill. Max watched the owl as it left, hoping its flight path would give a clue to Velkha's position, but it didn't.

Thoughts of another hunter drove him on, and Max moved away from the relative safety of the edge. In a crouching walk, he made his way towards the centre, feeling exposed like the young gazelle he'd watched a few weeks earlier on TV. He could almost hear the voice of Sir David Attenborough....

Here, in the grasslands of England, a foolish juvenile human is about to stumble into a deadly trap....

He switched the channel back to reality and kept a close eye on the key as he went. The glow of its needle was brighter now and attracting small flying bugs. Velkha was close.

He'd almost made it to the centre of the clearing when something on the ground caught his eye; lying in the grass, like a wounded animal, was the fallen drone. It didn't look that bad; definitely repairable, thought Max. If Isaac survives tonight, maybe his brother won't kill him after all.

If the drone *had* collided with Velkha, then she must be near. He continued to walk, this time with his arm stretched out, expecting to connect with her at any moment. When he didn't, he looked back to the key and found the light had flipped from one side to the other. He'd passed it. He turned and walked back, even slower this time, keeping a close eye on the needle of light. He watched as with each step it gradually rose until it was pointing to a space above him. He stopped and looked up, seeing nothing but the star-studded sky and streaks of wispy-thin cloud.

Max carefully stood to his full height, then reached his hand high above his head. Nothing. He jumped, hoping to touch it, but all he felt was the cool night air. He picked up a rock and threw it straight up. It hit something hidden above, then fell to the ground behind him with the sound of smashing plastic; the drone. *Maybe it's still OK,* he thought.

Not taking his eyes from the spot in the sky where he knew Velkha to be, he walked backwards to allow her some room.

Wren had talked about pairing the keys, so both would work with any willing ship. It was now time to see if Velkha was willing. If she wasn't, the game was over.

As before, he fired up the control rings about the key and held it out in front of him. He selected the ring that controlled Velkha's visibility and rotated his fist. As he did, a rectangular section of stars vanished from the night sky. Velkha was willing.

As she materialised, Max felt afraid, relieved, and excited all at the same time. With a nervous glance to the edges of the clearing, he brought the key towards his chest. Velkha descended silently, but then landed with a crunch upon the luckless drone.

Sorry, Isaac.

Max took a few steps back to admire Velkha. She was more imposing than Wren's Kelha, and not a perfect cube. She was rectangular, and larger. He stepped closer and noticed another difference; intricate patterns were carved into her surface, similar in style to the tattoos worn by Jenta. He reached out and ran his fingers over them, and knew, that if he wanted to, he could read them. But now was not the time.

With no obvious way of entry, Max wondered how to get inside. And no sooner had he wondered, the answer came to him. He could get used to this, he thought. Very handy come exam time. But only if "alien tech and its uses" was an exam topic.

Accessing his newly acquired knowledge felt weird but wonderful and impossible to describe. He'd always imagined that his mind existed a few inches behind his eyes. But this *new* information seemed to live elsewhere. His chest, maybe? He didn't know.

Max rushed to one of the two smaller faces of the cuboid. He placed the key against it. Immediately, the patterns on the surface of the ship where the key made contact twisted, warped, and rippled. The sphere was pulled from his hands as it sunk into the surface of the ship, embedding itself until only half of it remained visible.

To his right, a tall thin opening appeared, spilling a dull light onto the long grass. He stepped to the side and peered in. After looking back to the edge of the woods once more, he entered.

Inside, it smelled like Jenta: woody and musty. Nervously adjusting the bag on his back, he crept further in and found himself in a narrow walkway. Halfway along the corridor were two openings opposite each other. The room on his left was mostly empty, dark, with only a small square mat on the floor and three fierce-looking blades displayed on the wall. There was an empty slot for a fourth.

The room to his right smelled like meat. Inside, set against the wall, was a low, dark, wooden table. It was about a foot from the floor and had a black metal-looking dome set in its centre. Pots and cooking implements were secured to the wall; they looked very un-alien, surprisingly familiar. Max realised this was not just a ship for the Hunter; it was his home.

He continued along the walkway and emerged into a circular space with a large grey chair in its centre. Rooted to the floor with vine-like tendrils, the chair looked organic, as if it had been grown, not built.

Beyond the chair was another walkway, identical to the one he'd just emerged from, presumably leading to more rooms. But he didn't need to explore further.

A ring of white light on the floor surrounded the chair. As Max stepped into it, he gasped; the dark walls of Velkha had dissolved to reveal the clearing outside. Above him was a starry sky, only each point of light was brighter and clearer than any he had seen before. The musty, woody aroma of Velkha was also gone, replaced with the smells of the glade. It was as if he and the chair were now outside. Disorientated and confused, he quickly stepped back outside the circle, and the clearing was replaced by the dull interior of Velkha. Cautiously, he stepped towards the chair once more, and was once again surrounded by the long grass. As a quick experiment, he stretched his arm beyond the circle. He laughed as his hand and forearm disappeared from view. Isaac would *love* this, he thought.

He turned his focus back to the chair. This, he knew, was the heart of Velkha, artfully crafted (or grown) and shaped to fit Jenta's body perfectly. Its beauty struck Max, and he felt guilty for what he was about to do. He wanted the ship to feel mechanical, cold. But it didn't. He wanted it to feel menacing, like Jenta. But it didn't. He sighed as doubt crept into his mind. Kelha had told him that Velkha, like herself, was not a living thing. But could she lie? *Would* she lie to save Wren?

Something moved at the edge of Max's vision, and he turned to see Wren emerging from the woods. As Max's eyes strained to see more clearly, the image zoomed until Wren was standing eleven feet tall before him. Was it the ship doing the zoom thing? Or his eyes? He didn't know, but it was unnerving and made his stomach turn.

All he knew was that Wren was here. His face was bloody, his clothes were torn, but he looked strong and walked upright and proud. Most importantly, he was alone. Perhaps he'd defeated Jenta. Maybe his vision had ended too soon, and he'd missed the bit where Wren had fought back. But hope fell as swiftly as it had risen: Wren's hands were bound with the silver rope. Then Jenta emerged from the shadows behind, wearing both bags across his chest. He was looking unharmed and in complete control.

Seeing Jenta's cruel face again reignited Max's resolve. He turned back to the chair. It was time to execute the plan, or die trying.

Quickly, he slipped his bag from his shoulders and removed a single explosive. He pulled apart its two ends and twisted. Then he wedged it between the roots at the base of the chair.

"I'm sorry, Velkha," he said. "I hope this doesn't hurt."

He turned back to check on Wren and Jenta. They had both stopped. Wren looked puzzled, while Jenta's expression was one of dismay quickly turning to fury.

Jenta started running towards Velkha, Wren dived into his path, and they both tumbled into the tall grass and began to fight.

Quickly, Max removed the small detonator from the bag and slid it into his pocket. He picked up his bag and sprinted from the circle. But he was too fast; he slipped on the smooth floor and slammed into the wall. He got to his feet, then made a mad dash down the corridor to the exit. Only there was no exit, just a wall. In his panic, he'd run the wrong way. He turned and raced back through the chair room, cutting across the circle of light, catching a split-second glimpse of Wren and Jenta fighting at the edge of the clearing. He sped along the corridor, this time seeing the grass and the night sky, framed by the tall thin exit.

Once outside, Max desperately clawed at the key, trying to prise it from the grip of Velkha, but it merely spun in its housing; the harder he tried to grip it, the more it spun. The sounds of fighting behind him stopped, and he sensed Jenta bearing down on him. Max knew how to do this. He just needed to stay calm and think; instructions would come.

And they did. Instead of trying to claw the key out, he cupped his hand just below it, ready to receive it, and without fuss, out it popped.

The doorway sealed silently just as a pair of powerful hands gripped Max's shoulders and threw him backwards through the air. He landed painfully on the sun-hardened ground; the wind knocked out of him.

Ignoring the pain, he quickly got to his knees to peer over the long grass. Jenta turned to face him and took a long, deep breath. His slit-like nostrils quivered as the sides of his muscular neck expanded. Max knew what Jenta was doing. Using the smells that hung in the air, he was building an intricate picture of the surrounding scene.

Jenta half turned his head back to the ship and then to Max. His top lip twitched, and for a second Max glimpsed his shark-like teeth.

Without taking his eyes off Max, Jenta swung one bag around to his front and retrieved the other key. He turned it over in his fingers, examining the small sphere. His already narrow eyes narrowed further as he looked back to Max. He tilted his head and emitted a low rumbling growl, which Max felt more than heard.

Jenta turned to face Velkha and held the key against her. There was a dull clunk as it knocked against the surface. Nothing happened. He tried again. *Clunk.* And again. *Clunk.* Velkha was refusing to open, or Kelha was interfering from afar — Max didn't know or care.

What he did know was that it was time for him to act. But he couldn't. Not only had he lost the key when Jenta had thrown him through the air, but he'd also lost his ability to move.

As Max was scanning the ground nearby for the key, he

became aware that Jenta was approaching. He locked eyes on Jenta as he padded through the grass with the purpose of a leopard. Within seconds, the grey bulk of his alien face was just inches from his own.

"Where is it?" he barked, hot saliva spraying Max. "The *other* key, give it to me."

"Leave him here," Max replied, his voice weak. Every muscle in his body was going into spasm as he stared into Jenta's dead eyes. "Let him stay," he pleaded once more, close to tears but with a look of determination.

Jenta covered Max's face with his massive, tattooed hand. This time he whispered, "He does not belong here. Give...me...the key. I will not ask again."

"I don't have it," said Max, praying Jenta wouldn't search him and find the detonator instead.

Smelling the truth, Jenta violently pushed Max to the ground and turned to seek the key for himself.

Max's limbs were now responsive, and he tried to crawl away. But Jenta returned swiftly, sweeping away his legs.

"You are not going anywhere," he hissed, pressing his black-clad foot firmly onto Max's back, pinning him down. He then turned away to continue his search.

Max rolled over but stayed put. "Why won't you let him stay? He doesn't want to go with you," he said desperately. His ribs burned as he spoke, and he was dizzy with the pain.

"He's not taking me back." It was Wren. He was on his feet again and walking towards him. There was blood down the side of his head, his hair matted. He was lopsided as he walked, holding an elbow into his side covering a bloody wound. His still-bound hands were bruised from beating Jenta.

Jenta paid no attention to his arrival.

"His plan is to kill me," Wren continued, as Max tried to

get to his feet. "Once he has, he will destroy all evidence of my existence here. Why he doesn't end me now, and be done with it, I do not know."

Jenta continued to ignore the conversation, walking to and fro, parting the long grass as he combed the area methodically.

"I know why he won't kill you," said Max, hoping to distract Jenta.

Jenta stopped briefly, and gave Max a look he couldn't read.

"He wants something from you," Max said. "Information he can take back. Information that someone values *so* much they'll forgive all his crimes."

Jenta glared at Max. Max slid his hand into his pocket and closed it around the detonator.

"What information?" asked Wren.

"I don't know."

Jenta returned to his search.

"But it's something important. Something to do with why they sent you here in the first place...a location..." Max said, his head spinning as he sifted through the muddled fragments of his earlier vision. "A location of someone...I don't know — it's gone. No. I remember. A Maker. He wants to know the location of a Maker. He thinks you found him."

Wren didn't reply; he just looked confused. The look on Jenta's face told Max he was right. The Hunter bristled with contained rage.

Max had said enough. He now had to be careful. The only thing keeping him alive was Jenta not having control of Velkha, and it needed to stay that way. He looked around, hoping to catch sight of the key. If his super sight would ever return, now would be a marvellous time.

Surely Wren could see it, he thought, and he looked to him. Wren was bruised and battered, swaying from exhaustion, but some of it was an act — he shot Max a subtle smile and flicked his eyes down to the ground. Max looked and saw it; a dim glow was drifting through the grass towards Wren. Not wanting to draw Jenta's attention to it, he snapped his eyes away, looking in the opposite direction.

This was good, thought Max. Wren had found the key and somehow summoned it. Was he also masking its scent? Why else could Jenta not sniff it out? It didn't matter. Wren would soon have the key. The problem was, Wren didn't know the plan.

Agitated by Max's words, Jenta moved more erratically, striking the long grass, eyes to the ground, moving ever closer to Wren.

Suddenly, Jenta stopped.

Max felt the heavy weight of the detonator in his hand. For the sake of his friends and loved ones and the entire town, he was prepared to set it off. Three lives to save thousands. He hoped that Isaac and Ellie were still where he'd left them.

"What were you doing in there?" Jenta asked, turning to Max, before slowly walking towards him.

Max stepped back and looked to Wren, who was now staring intently at the ship, his eyes black once more. Max spotted his eyebrow flick with surprise. Wren then turned his attention to Max's closed hand, then to the key, now by his feet. Finally, he looked back to Max — and nodded.

Wren understood the plan.

"Tell me what you were doing in there," Jenta demanded, stopping just a few feet from Max. He sniffed the air.

Max didn't answer.

"Tell me," said Jenta, his eyes narrowing, his nostrils flaring. "Or I end you now." His eyes flicked down to Max's hand, and he sniffed again.

Torchlight suddenly illuminated Jenta's face. He grimaced, and looked past Max, who turned to see Isaac, Ellie, George and Mr Bartley exit the woods.

Jenta hissed angrily at the interruption, pushing Max away. "I'll deal with you next, boy," he growled, and extended his ugly curved blade. Then, with a terrifying roar, he sprinted towards the newcomers.

"Now!" shouted Max, starting to back away from Velkha.

The key sprang from the grass into Wren's bound hands. In less than a second, Wren had ignited its blue disc of light, then thrust the key high in the air, causing Velkha to hurtle from the clearing. Her exit was accompanied by a powerful shock-wave, throwing Jenta, Max, and Wren clean off their feet. Max somehow held on to the detonator. As he flew through the air, he triggered it with a single thought, then landed hard on the ground, rolling several times before coming to a stop.

For a second or two, daylight returned to the clearing — and most of Europe. It was the blinding light that signalled the destruction of Velkha.

Once it faded, Max tried to stand, but his body felt broken, his limbs refusing to follow orders. With the air now thick with dust from the shock-wave, he was unable to see a thing. He tried to call for his friends, but no words would leave his burning throat. He tried to take a deep breath, but the pain in his ribs wouldn't allow it. He coughed and tasted blood.

As the dust began to settle, he noticed the long grass was now gone, stripped bare by the shock-wave and there was a shallow crater where Velkha had once been. The entire world seemed to glow orange. Max saw the shadowy form of Jenta looking skyward to the source of the glow; thousands upon thousands of shooting stars lighting up the night sky as fragments of Jenta's home re-entered the atmosphere.

Max took in the beautiful sight, forgetting for a moment that this was far from over.

He could see Wren trying to get back to his feet, and he heard his friends calling from the edge of the clearing. From a distance, the flight of Velkha must have looked like an explosion. Ellie was screaming Max's name, but he couldn't make a sound in return.

Wren finally stood, but only for a second before falling back to the ground. Max dragged himself over to him, knelt by his side, then loosened his bindings and cast the silver rope aside. A shadow fell over them. It was Jenta. He was a silhouette against a background of raining fire. He stood silent over them, tall and firm, unharmed by the night's events.

Wren attempted to stand again, but Jenta viciously kicked him back to the ground. Wren tried again, and this time flickered like a broken hologram as he got to his knees, disappearing for a split second, then reappearing. Jenta kicked him to the ground once more.

"No," sobbed Max, throwing himself between them. "Leave him alone."

Jenta snarled, kneeling on Wren's throat while grabbing Max's and squeezing.

The edges of Max's world closed in around him. Desperately, he struck Jenta in the head and face. It was futile, like striking steel with straw. Jenta smiled coldly as the two of them continued to hit him feebly. Wren went limp first, and dropped the key he'd been holding. Jenta watched it roll away, then released Max's throat to retrieve it. Max coughed painfully, holding his neck with both hands, and drawing in deep, burning, but blissful breaths.

As Jenta stood to study the key, Max shuffled closer to Wren, whose chest was rising and falling slowly with each laboured breath.

Jenta glanced down at them both. "One moment..." he said, sounding almost civil, before turning and walking away.

With his back to them, Jenta was looking upon the dying light show in the sky. It dawned on Max that he was, in complete denial of reality, trying to summon Velkha. But the key was devoid of light — just a cold metal sphere.

Bartley, Ellie, and Isaac appeared through the dust. They crowded around Max and Wren, eyeing Jenta warily. Ellie gave Max a covert nod as George appeared, his jacket rolled up under his arm.

"Everyone OK?" George whispered with concern.

Max tried to say he'd been better, but all he could manage was a groan.

On seeing the state of Wren, George gently placed his rolled-up jacket on the ground, then knelt beside him and held his bloodied hand. "It's OK, Wren," he whispered. "Everything will be OK. Stay with us, old pal. We've got this."

Wren squeezed George's hand weakly but said nothing, his dark eyes opening barely a crack.

"What have you done?" came Jenta's voice. It was flat and lacked any hint of threat or emotion. Max sensed defeat in his tone. He had lost all hope of returning and was now at his most dangerous. It was now that Max would offer him his escape. Well, that was the plan, but Max's throat would not allow the words to come.

Jenta dropped the dead key to the ground and turned to face them. He walked calmly towards the group, his eyes cold, his intent clear.

Max would have to force the words out, or they would all die. "It's...time...for you to leave now," said Max, the sounds finally leaving his torn throat. "Kelha," he continued, "will... take you...but she will take only one."

Jenta stopped. "She will not take me."

"Look." Max nodded towards the key on the ground.

It was no longer dead; it was alive and pointing the way to Kelha.

"I see," said Jenta, his voice calm. "She is above ground?"

Max nodded.

"How?"

"Just leave," said Max, every word painful.

Jenta looked back to the key, and then to Max. "So...you leave me a ship that will take only one. And I leave Rahiir, to stay with you on this filthy rock of yours." He was talking to Max, but never took his eyes off Wren. "Yes. I leave him here. I leave his *body* here," he said, smiling and taking a step forward.

"That...won't work for you," said Max. The words were coming more easily. "If he dies, Kelha leaves without you. You'll be...trapped here."

"*On this filthy rock*," Ellie added, exchanging a small high five with Isaac.

It was Max's turn to smile.

Jenta threw his head back and forced a laugh. "Why would she do that? I have both keys. I control her." He tilted his head, waiting for an answer.

Max answered. And when he did, the menacing grin fell from Jenta's face.

"Say...that...again." Jenta's small black eyes flicked from Wren to Max, anger rippling just below the surface of his skin.

Wren slowly turned his head to look at Max. It was dark, and Wren's face was caked in blood and dirt, but Max thought he saw him smile.

"I said," said Max, gingerly climbing to his feet. "She will leave...because I told her to."

Only Wren and Jenta understood his words. The others

heard a language that sounded, to the untrained ear, a bit Swedish and a bit Japanese. Whatever it was, it wasn't English.

"She's watching all of this right now from her hiding place," Max continued in English. "She is awake and ready to go. If Wren *dies*, she *flies*."

"Nice," said Isaac to Max. "You just think of that?"

"Yeah." Max coughed, then gripped his side in pain.

Jenta stepped back; Max could see his mind racing as he considered his next move.

There was a long silence before Jenta finally spoke. "Very well. I leave him here," he said. He looked at the key on the ground but made no attempt to retrieve it. Instead, he began to slowly circle the group. "I will even leave him here alive," he said, a menacing smile returning to his thin grey lips. He then bent down to retrieve the blade he had dropped during Velkha's departure. "I will leave him here alive — but alone. Without his friends for company." He flourished his blade skilfully in the air, then examined its razor-sharp edge for theatrics. "I doubt Kelha will mind if I kill the rest of you. Surely she wouldn't leave Wren alone with me now, would she?"

Max nodded to George.

"No," said George. "She wouldn't. But we thought you might say that." He unravelled his jacket on the ground to reveal the *armed* explosive inside. "So we brought some insurance. Just in case."

Max held up the detonator, giving Jenta his best stern look. Inside, he was terrified.

"Wait! You know what insurance is right?" Isaac said to Jenta. He turned to George. "We just need to be clear; they might not have insurance where he's from. That's all I'm saying. If—"

"I think he gets it, Isaac," said Ellie, nudging him in the side.

"OK, OK, just checking we're all on the same page," said Isaac. "But just to be one hundred percent clear," he called to Jenta, "Come any closer, and my friend here blows this thing up. Insurance."

Jenta ignored Isaac's ramblings as he stared at the device and sniffed the air, tasting Max's resolve.

Max was prepared to go through with it. They all were. Better to go in an explosion than at the hands of this cruel and twisted creature. It would be a quick death, and the town and all those in it would be safe from this monster.

Jenta, about fifteen feet from the group, stared at the detonator in Max's hand. He seemed to be considering the distance, and his chances of reaching Max before he could trigger it. Mr Bartley also seemed to sense this, for he stood and walked forward, placing himself between Jenta and the group. Ellie, Isaac and George then joined him, forming a defensive wall in front of Wren and Max. They couldn't stop him, but they didn't need to. They just needed to slow him down.

Wren remained quiet. But his breathing was becoming more and more laboured. He looked weak and at the edge of consciousness. This needed to end soon, thought Max.

"You won't make it in time," said Bartley, nervously, to Jenta, who had begun circling the group once more, illuminated by the beams of their torches. "You might as well take that ride home. There's no shame in it."

Jenta ignored him, his thick legs bent as he stepped sideways, holding his blade towards them. As Jenta circled, so did the wall, always keeping themselves between the Hunter and the detonator.

When Jenta had gone full circle, he bared his teeth in frustration and hissed. Max closed his eyes, preparing to detonate. But he opened them again as he heard the blade collapse into its hilt. Jenta straightened from his predatory crouch. "I will return, Rahiir," he said, squinting into the bright torchlight. "And if I don't, do you think this will have gone unnoticed? You are a fool. A disgrace—"

"Look, are you going or what?" interrupted Ellie.

Jenta snarled.

"Yeah," said Isaac. "Go home."

"Please go," Max said, from behind them. His voice was weak. He was worried for Wren, his condition worsening by the second.

Jenta sniffed the air once more. Then he turned and ran, picking up the key as he went, heading towards Kelha.

They kept their lights trained on him, his long dishevelled red hair trailing behind as he ran through the clearing at an impressive speed. Within seconds he had melted into Oban Wood.

The defensive wall didn't relax just yet. Instead, they surrounded Max and Wren, scanning the woods with their lights in readiness for a surprise attack. When it looked as though the attack would not come, Max disarmed the explosive, and the group closed in around Wren.

George gently lifted Wren's head and placed his rolled-up jacket underneath. "He's gone, Wren," George said. "Everything will be OK. He's gone. You can stay now."

Wren's eyes opened a crack, and he smiled up at his rescuers. His breathing was slow. "Thank you," he said, his words barely audible, "for everything. Thank you."

Ellie held out the healing disc. "Where does it hurt?" she asked.

Wren raised a bloodied hand and closed it around hers, moving it and the disc away. "I'm lucky," he said, looking at them all. "Lucky you are all here...with...me—"

"Let us help," pleaded Max.

Wren shook his head. "Watchers...we...normally die alone." Wren continued, looking at Max. "I am glad I got to meet you, Max. You look...like a Furlong." He smiled, closing his eyes, his chest rising and falling, each breath weaker than the last.

"But...I've got your eyes," whispered Max.

As the words came, so did the colour, and a level of detail Max could never have imagined. His range of perception deepened and widened as new layers of reality unfolded, revealing themselves. He really did have Wren's eyes.

"Don't listen to him, Ellie," Max said. "Start with his chest and work your way to his side...here." He pointed to Wren's left side, above his hip.

"How...how do you know?" she said, unsure.

"I can see it." And he could. Two black clouds were growing within Wren, one starting in his chest and one down his side. They were growing quickly, and the darkness would soon consume him.

As Ellie worked the disc over Wren's body, Max could see the battle raging within. Where the bright disc passed, the dark clouds recoiled, but soon they grew in other places; in his neck, his temple, his stomach. But Ellie continued, moving the disc, driving the clouds away. When the disc could heal no more and lost its glow, Ellie moved it away.

No one made a sound as Max examined Wren again. The darkness was now all but gone. That which remained didn't grow and would only fade with time and rest. "I think you did it, Ellie," said Max.

Ellie smiled, letting out a long-held breath. "*We* did it," she said.

Relief washed over the group. There were grins all round, but no cheering or celebrating, just quiet relief.

George clutched Max's shoulder and squeezed, quickly

releasing his grip when he saw the pain in his face. "Sorry, Max. But well done," he said, giving him an awkward thumbs up instead.

"Yes," hissed a low voice from behind them in the darkness. "Well done, Max."

Torch beams converged, illuminating Jenta standing just feet from them. "You know," he continued, "I don't think I *will* go back just yet." With a bone-chilling roar, he sprung into the air, his blade held high, pointing down, ready to drive it into Max.

But Jenta never came down; held by a claw of blue-white light, which cracked and fizzed, he hung above them, his roar now just a pitiful cry.

They all followed the light. It led to Isaac.

"I forgot I had this thing," he said, a look of surprise on his face.

22

THE NEW GUARD

They paused and looked upon the town as they left the woods. Only the church steeple caught the sun's first rays; it glowed like a crimson spike against the cloudless sky. It was going to be a beautiful day in Hurstwick.

George and Mr Bartley took turns to support Wren, who struggled to walk unaided. It was a miracle he was walking at all. The disc had helped, but Kelha, who Max summoned to the clearing, also played a part in his recovery.

Before stowing Jenta aboard Kelha, Wren had entered alone. When he emerged sometime later, he looked stronger than before. His eyes were brighter; he stood taller.

He asked for Max's help to get Jenta inside. The others, in a better physical state than Max, offered their assistance, but Wren insisted it could only be Max.

Stepping into Kelha felt like entering a giant organism. She was unlike Velkha in every way. The air inside was warm and moist, and a thick blanket of mist hung at their feet. While the interior walls of Velkha were smooth like black marble, Kelha's were textured like tree bark. The most obvious difference was that, instead of a chair, Kelha had a man-sized cocoon. It was suspended in the centre of the cube, held in place by thick twisting vines from above and below. Running from the walls to the cocoon were thin luminescent threads. They looked fragile. Max wondered if it were these that had been damaged in the crash and taken so long to heal.

The cocoon was semi-transparent, and a soft orange light pulsated deep within, revealing a network of veins just under its waxy surface. Max knew it had once contained Wren and was probably his home for many years.

As they approached, the cocoon unfurled, sending out long tentacles that roughly enveloped Jenta, snatching him away. "Gentle, Kelha," Wren said in his own tongue. She ignored him, and if anything, was even more brutal as she took the Hunter and sealed him inside. Wren, amused by her loyalty, smiled as a tentacle slipped back out and caressed his cheek, before retreating into the cocoon once more.

With Jenta contained, and the remaining explosives collected from the edge of the clearing and placed onboard, it was time for Kelha to leave. Only the brightest stars were visible as she rose elegantly into the early-morning sky, jet black against dark blue and indigo. She faded, then Max felt a breeze on his face as she sped away unseen.

After crossing the small wooden bridge, where George and Wren had first met all those years ago, they followed the river path and took the back way into Patrick's Corner, climbing up and over the bank. They didn't stay long. After collecting some belongings, they took the bikes and made their way to Mr Bartley's house.

The sky began to lighten above as they walked the deserted streets of Hurstwick. The only sign of life was a lonely street sweeper, spinning its brushes as it trundled up Station Road, its single revolving yellow light throwing shadows across Bramfield Park as it went. They followed at a distance, then ducked into Cotton Street where Mr Bartley lived.

His home was modest but cosy. In the kitchen they sat slumped around the wooden table while Bartley, with the help of George, made a fry-up. Max wasn't hungry until he smelled the bacon, then he devoured the breakfast as if he'd never seen food before.

They ate in silence, then Bartley cleared the table and made a pot of tea.

Conversation was difficult. It was unclear what topics were appropriate after such a night. Max and Wren would no doubt have a lot to talk about, but now didn't seem like the right time. Wren said a few words of thanks and reassured them that Kelha would keep Jenta in hibernation for a very long time and that he was someone they no longer needed to fear.

Prompted by questions from Ellie, George talked about his life after leaving Hurstwick, about his kids and his grandkids. Wren smiled as he listened. It was a conversation that brought to Max thoughts of his own family — about how little he knew of his father's side.

The police helicopter was once again circling above. After several more cups of tea, Bartley turned on the small kitchen radio in time for the news. Apart from last night's *unexpected meteor shower*, which apparently was the *largest and brightest since records began*, the ongoing activity at the bypass was still the major story of the day. The newsreader didn't make a link between the two events. Why would she?

They took turns to clean themselves up in the small bathroom upstairs, and Ellie used the healing disc to remove the bruising from Max's neck and shoulders.

When the sun had risen to fill the small, well-kept garden with light, George and Mr Bartley went outside, where they sat on white plastic chairs and talked. Isaac and

Ellie slouched in the living room, the curtains pulled closed and the lack of sleep finally catching up with them.

Max was tired, too, but he had questions for Wren. As they sat at opposite ends of the table, cradling their mugs of tea in the quiet kitchen, he asked his first. "Did you know?" he said. "About me, I mean?"

"No," said Wren. "Not before you came to my tower with stories of visions. It was then I noticed your resemblance to the Furlongs, and the young George."

"George?" Max was confused for a moment, then remembered how Wren got *his* looks. "Of course," he added quietly. "Daytime TV would go nuts over this story," he said.

Wren chuckled, then smiled sadly at Max. "I never knew Mary had a child," he said. "We were very much in love. She knew all about me, accepted me. But one day she changed. She went cold, wouldn't speak to me, then left England to stay with her cousin in Canada. I was heartbroken. But after two years of silence, she wrote to me out of the blue, telling me she was coming back and that she was sorry that she had left. She said she wanted to see me again. But she never made it back here. There was a storm...." He trailed off, then drank some tea.

"I now see why she ran," he continued after some time. "She was pregnant, and she was scared. She knew who I was, but she must have feared what that meant for our child."

"And after she died," said Max, "the Furlongs said nothing to you?"

"They didn't know about us. Our love was a secret." He took another sip of tea. "She was close to her cousin. I suspect she knew."

"My grandfather," said Max, "who left us the cottage. Your son. Did you ever see him around?"

"After Jenny and Donald Furlong passed, the cottage

remained empty for many years. I believe the family in Canada used it from time to time, but I paid little attention to any comings or goings. So it's possible I could have seen him, I suppose." He stood and walked to the window and looked out into the garden. "And your father?" Wren asked, his back to Max.

"Died before I was born," Max said.

Max had more questions, but they could wait. Wren had mourned the loss of Mary for many years. In the last few hours, he'd lost a son and a grandson, too.

Just then, Isaac entered the kitchen, followed by Ellie. "Time for me to face the music," he said. "I never did get the selfie."

"I need to go, too," said Ellie, yawning.

It was the afternoon when they all gathered in Mr Bartley's dim hallway. Max looked upon the unlikely group of people with the uneasy feeling that everything would be very different from now on.

The three friends left together, pushing their bikes to the end of the street, then down Station Road towards Church Lane. Max closed his eyes, feeling the warm sun on his face, and filled his lungs with fresh air. It felt good.

It had been a summer like no other — the longest six weeks of Max's life. For the last few days of it, Max, Ellie, and Isaac spent their time under the bandstand surrounded by trees already trying out their autumn colours.

They stayed away from Windmill Hill. Once the crater in the clearing had been discovered, more press had arrived, and the skies above Hurstwick were a constant buzz of helicopters. But then, after two weeks of no more strange happenings, the military moved out and construction of the bypass resumed without further weirdness.

Isaac's parents grounded him for five days for destroying the drone and forced him to pay for a replacement from his savings. He accepted the punishment with grace and even offered to pay extra, allowing Jacob to buy an even better one. His parents, impressed by his mature outlook, shortened his sentence by two days. He confided in Max a regret for not finding this maturity earlier in life; *"Think of all the stuff I could've got away with."*

When Max started his new school, he was relieved to find himself in the same class as Isaac. Ellie was a year above, but the three hung out at break and walked home together every day.

He was relieved to find that, just like his old school, the other kids paid him zero attention; his curse of anonymity was still intact. He would just blend into the background, disappear, be a nobody. It was the way he liked it. He used to think it was because he was Mr Average, bland and uninteresting. Now he wondered if it was the opposite. Perhaps it wasn't a curse. Maybe it was a skill — one he'd been born with.

Ellie and Isaac still noticed him, though. When out of earshot from others, Isaac would bombard him with questions. *Could he still speak alien? Had he had any more visions? Was his super sight back? Could he see into the sixth form girls' changing room?* — Ellie overheard that one and delivered one of her trademark dead arms — *Did he feel any different? What about his smell and other senses, had they improved?*

Ellie asked only two questions; the same two questions that kept Max awake on some nights: *Who was the Maker? And would anyone else come looking for him?* Eventually, though, the questions abated, and conversations returned to more earthly subjects.

Max still had questions that only Wren could answer, but he wasn't ready to ask. He knew Wren was patient, infinitely so, and knew he would be there when he *was* ready.

There was also a conversation Max needed to have with his mother. He had no idea where to start with that. *Hey, mum, did you know dad was part alien? Oh, and the guy you work with, the one that looks about the same age as you? Yeah, he's my great-grandfather....*

Maybe he'd park that conversation for now; come back to it in a hundred years.

Max thought about his father every day. He wondered how much he'd known. He also thought about the child of Wren and Mary; the grandfather who'd left them the cottage. When he was ready, he would try to find out as much about them as he could.

When Max slept, he dreamt. The dreams felt different now. They lingered longer, flashes of them returning during his waking hours. Some dreams were recurring, like the one where he would see a woman in a blue dress looking out from a platform set high upon a giant tree. That dream, he knew, was from a memory of a vision. But there were others. Dreams of things he hadn't seen before but felt just as real: a woman walking through a garden surrounded by oversized plants; a room full of tools and machines with a man hunched over a table crafting wooden toys. Another man, wearing army fatigues, was crouching by the open doorway of a helicopter as it flew low over a desert. And finally, a woman, writing equations on a blackboard while a grey cat with yellow eyes snaked around her ankles.

He kept these dreams to himself. They were only dreams.

George remained in town for a while as a guest of Mr Bartley. He spent long days walking and talking with Wren. More than once, Max saw them both sitting in Market Square eating ice cream. Anyone would think they were grandfather and grandson.

Eventually, George returned to London. Goodbyes, hugs, and promises to keep in touch were exchanged at the train station. They watched as he passed through the barrier. Out of habit, he pushed the button to call the lift, then, remembering his improved mobility, decided to take the stairs instead. He turned and smiled broadly before descending to the platform. It was the goodbye he'd always wanted.

Later, Wren formally introduced them to the members of The Old Guard. Mr Walsh they already knew, but the others Max recognised from around town. More recently he had seen them on top of Windmill Hill. They seemed happy to meet what they called The New Guard, and were eager to share their stories.

They were the last of a generation that knew Ben for who he really was. They were his friends. People who, over the years, had each earned his trust, learnt of his true identity and protected his secret.

Together, they sat around a large table in Mr Walsh's garden, which backed onto the churchyard. They talked for hours. Max found it funny how the conversation flipped from the mundane to the extraordinary very naturally. One minute they'd be talking about an impossible thing that Wren had once done, the next, lamenting the lack of quality cakes at last weekend's charity bake-off.

Isaac and Mr Bartley sat either side of Father Elliot, the oldest-looking member of the club. He had a mop of white hair and earlobes that reached his shoulders. Isaac was telling him about Jenta. The old vicar, who at this point had consumed far too much sherry, gesticulated wildly, declaring his disappointment at having missed the excitement, claiming he would have *made short work of the red-headed beast, and given him a good thrashing.* Isaac laughed, then quickly caught himself so as to not offend.

Ellie was sitting with Mrs Waldron. A tall, elegant woman, she owned Hurstwick Antiques and was probably far older than most things in her shop. The two were deep in conversation, poring over a photo album spread on the table. She was pointing out past members of the club and showing old photos of Ben, who over the years had gone by many names. He would normally masquerade as a nephew or a cousin of one of the group.

Isaac's drink exploded from his nose when Ellie showed him a photo of Wren with a mullet and handle-bar moustache. Wren just smiled and stroked his top lip as if considering a return of the tash.

As they laughed and talked, Max sat on a comfortable, high-backed garden chair, watching them. He felt relaxed around them, and not at all awkward for not joining in. He was just happy to be in their company.

He rested his eyes and took a deep breath, listening to the voices of his friends. He heard the creak of the thick pages of the photo album as they were turned, and the ice clinking in Mrs Waldron's glass of Pimm's.

After a while, he shifted his focus to listen to the trickle of water from the pump in Mr Walsh's pond. Then a bird singing in a nearby tree. He continued to breathe and listen. Breathe and listen. Breathe...and...listen. He heard a radio from the vicarage next door, a ping from a microwave oven, the tyres of a car rolling over the cobbles of Church Lane. He heard the metallic squeak from the weathervane upon the church steeple as it turned to point north, the grinding cogs of the church clock locking into place, the rapid heart-beats of bats as they woke to prepare for evening flight —

He snapped open his eyes and the surrounding conversations continued uninterrupted.

He was about to close them again when he realised Wren's chair was empty. He turned and spotted the open gate leading directly to the darkening churchyard.

With no one noticing, Max stood and left the garden. He peered into the stillness towards the one-armed angel, stark white against the dark green of the trees. He walked towards her, then passed under her stony gaze and entered Patrick's Corner for the first time since the night of the convoy. It was silent, but not deserted.

He continued to walk, but not to the shack. Instead, he went to the base of the enormous pine tree, ducking under the low branches to reach its thick trunk.

He ascended without fear. The climb felt natural to him.

"Hey, Wren," he said at the very top.

Wren smiled warmly at Max, then shifted over to make room. They looked up at the darkening sky where the first early evening stars flickered.

"Now," said Wren, adjusting his position to face the town, "let me show you how to use those eyes of yours."

The end...

THE BIT WHERE I BEG FOR A REVIEW

Thank you for making it all the way to the end. I hope you liked it. If you did, it would be great if you could write a short review on Amazon. Self-published authors, like myself, don't have large marketing budgets. Instead, we rely on good-looking people like yourself to get the word out. If you don't have time for a review, a simple rating would also be very much appreciated.

ACKNOWLEDGMENTS

My biggest thank you goes to Sarah, my wife. Without her support and understanding, this book wouldn't exist. Also, thanks to my boys, whose brutal honesty stopped me creating a town called Hitchworth; a melding of our town and the town next door, which they said it was "lame". They approved of Hurstwick. So that's good. Also, a huge thank you to my editor Nick Hodgson for her keen eye and guidance. And lastly, thank you to my beta readers, who caught some extra bits and encouraged me with their kind words.

Thank you,

Rob Winters, October 2020.

rawinters@me.com